Count Lev Nikolayevich Tolstoy (9 September [O.S. 28 August] 1828 – 20 November [O.S. 7 November] 1910), usually referred to in English as Leo Tolstoy, was a Russian writer who is regarded as one of the greatest authors of all time. He received multiple nominations for Nobel Prize in Literature every year from 1902 to 1906, and nominations for Nobel Peace Prize in 1901, 1902 and 1910, and his miss of the prize is a major Nobel prize controversy. Born to an aristocratic Russian family in 1828, he is best known for the novels War and Peace (1869) and Anna Karenina (1877), often cited as pinnacles of realist fiction. He first achieved literary acclaim in his twenties with his semi-autobiographical trilogy, Childhood, Boyhood, and Youth (1852–1856), and Sevastopol Sketches (1855), based upon his experiences in the Crimean War. Tolstoy's fiction includes dozens of short stories and several novellas such as The Death of Ivan Ilyich (1886), Family Happiness (1859), and Hadji Murad (1912). He also wrote plays and numerous philosophical essays. (Source: Wikipedia)

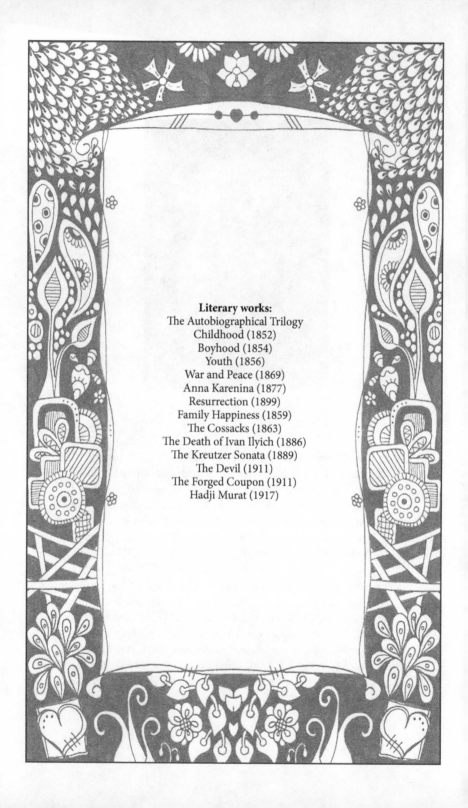

Literary works:
The Autobiographical Trilogy
Childhood (1852)
Boyhood (1854)
Youth (1856)
War and Peace (1869)
Anna Karenina (1877)
Resurrection (1899)
Family Happiness (1859)
The Cossacks (1863)
The Death of Ivan Ilyich (1886)
The Kreutzer Sonata (1889)
The Devil (1911)
The Forged Coupon (1911)
Hadji Murat (1917)

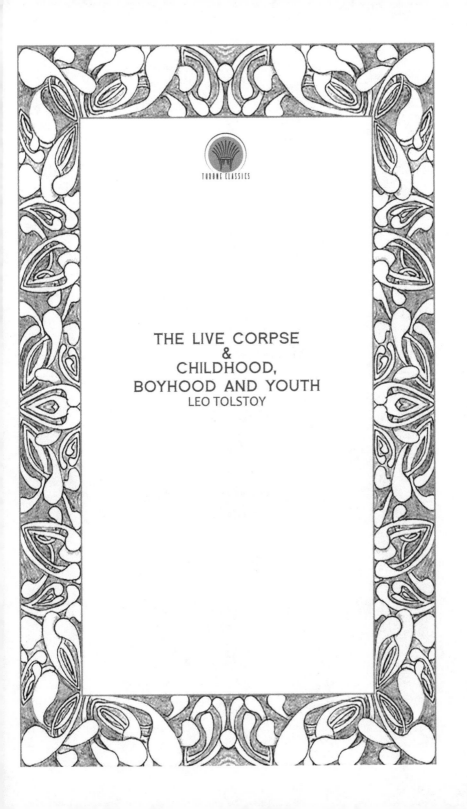

THRONE CLASSICS

THE LIVE CORPSE
&
CHILDHOOD,
BOYHOOD AND YOUTH
LEO TOLSTOY

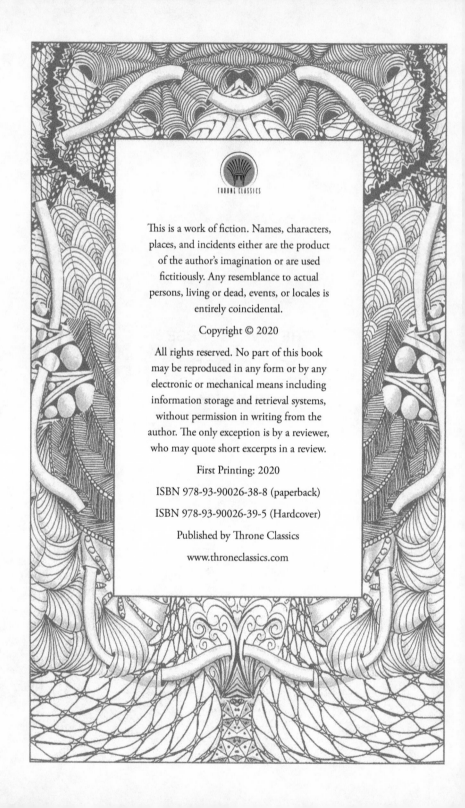

First Printing: 2020

ISBN 978-93-90026-38-8 (paperback)

ISBN 978-93-90026-39-5 (Hardcover)

Published by Throne Classics

www.throneclassics.com

Contents

THE LIVE CORPSE
&
CHILDHOOD,
BOYHOOD AND YOUTH

THE LIVE CORPSE

CHARACTERS

THEODORE VASÍLYEVICH PROTÁSOV (FÉDYA).

ELISABETH ANDRÉYEVNA PROTÁSOVA (LISA). His wife.

MÍSHA. Their son.

ANNA PÁVLOVNA. Lisa's mother.

SÁSHA. Lisa's younger, unmarried sister.

VICTOR MIHÁYLOVICH KARÉNIN.

ANNA DMÍTRIEVNA KARÉNINA.

PRINCE SERGIUS DMÍTRIEVICH ABRÉZKOV.

MÁSHA. A gipsy girl.

Másha's parents.

> IVÁN MAKÁROVICH. An old gipsy man.

> NASTÁSIA IVÁNOVNA. An old gipsy woman.

OFFICER.

MUSICIAN.

FIRST GIPSY MAN.

SECOND GIPSY MAN.

GIPSY WOMAN.

GIPSY CHOIR.

DOCTOR.

MICHAEL ALEXÁNDROVICH AFRÉMOV.

Fédya's boon companions.

  STÁKHOV.

  BUTKÉVICH.

  KOROTKÓV.

IVÁN PETRÓVICH ALEXÁNDROV.

VOZNESÉNSKY. Karénin's secretary.

PETUSHKÓV. An artist.

ARTÉMYEV.

WAITER IN THE PRIVATE ROOM AT THE RESTAURANT.

WAITER IN A LOW-CLASS RESTAURANT.

MANAGER OF THE SAME.

POLICEMAN.

INVESTIGATING MAGISTRATE.

MÉLNIKOV.

CLERK.

USHER.

YOUNG LAWYER.

PETRÚSHIN. A lawyer.

LADY.

ANOTHER OFFICER.

ATTENDANT AT LAW COURTS.

THE PROTÁSOVS' NURSE.

THE PROTÁSOVS' MAID.

AFRÉMOV'S FOOTMAN.

KARÉNIN'S FOOTMAN.

ACT I

Scene 1

Protásov's[1] flat in Moscow. The scene represents a small dining-room.

Anna Pávlovna, a stout grey-haired lady, tightly laced, is sitting alone at the tea-table on which is a samovár. Enter nurse, carrying a teapot.

NURSE. May I have a little hot water, ma'am?

ANNA PÁVLOVNA. Yes. How's Baby?

NURSE. He's restless.... There's nothing worse than for a lady to nurse her baby herself! She has her troubles, and the child must suffer. What can her milk be like, when she lies awake crying all night?

ANNA PÁVLOVNA. But she seems quieter now.

NURSE. Quiet, indeed! It makes one ill to see her. She's been writing something, and crying.

Enter Sásha.

SÁSHA [to Nurse] Lisa is looking for you.

NURSE. I'm coming, I'm coming. [Exit].

ANNA PÁVLOVNA. Nurse says she keeps on crying.... Why can't she control herself?

SÁSHA. Well really, mother, you are amazing!... A woman has left her husband, her child's father, and you expect her to be calm!

ANNA PÁVLOVNA. Well, not calm ... But what's done is done! If I, her mother, not only allowed my daughter to leave her husband, but am even glad she has done it, that shows he deserved it. One ought to rejoice, not to grieve, at the chance of freeing oneself from such a bad man!

SÁSHA. Mother, why say such things? You know it's not true! He's not bad—but on the contrary, he's a wonderful man, in spite of his weaknesses.

ANNA PÁVLOVNA. Yes indeed, a "wonderful" man—as soon as he has money in his pocket—his own or other people's....

SÁSHA. Mother! He has never taken other people's!

ANNA PÁVLOVNA. Yes he has—his wife's! Where's the difference?

SÁSHA. But he gave all his property to his wife!

ANNA PÁVLOVNA. Of course, when he knew that otherwise he was sure to squander it all!

SÁSHA. Squander or not, I only know that a wife must not separate from her husband, especially from such a one as Fédya.

ANNA PÁVLOVNA. Then, in your opinion she ought to wait till he has squandered everything, and brought his gipsy mistresses into the house?

SÁSHA. He has no mistresses!

ANNA PÁVLOVNA. That's the misfortune—he seems to have bewitched you all! But not me—no! He won't come over me! I see through him, and he knows it. Had I been in Lisa's place I should have left him a year ago.

SÁSHA. How lightly you say it!

ANNA PÁVLOVNA. Not lightly at all. It's not a light thing for me, as a mother, to see my daughter divorced. Believe me it's not! But yet it is better than ruining a young life.... No, I'm thankful to God that she has at last made up her mind, and that it is all over.

SÁSHA. Perhaps it's not all over!

ANNA PÁVLOVNA. Oh! If he only consents to a divorce....

SÁSHA. What good will that do?

ANNA PÁVLOVNA. This good; that she is young, and may again be happy.

SÁSHA. Oh mother! It's dreadful to hear you speak so! Lisa can't love another.

ANNA PÁVLOVNA. Why not, when she's free? Many a man a thousand times better than your Fédya might turn up who would be only too happy to marry Lisa.

SÁSHA. Mother, it's not right! I know you're thinking of Victor Karénin....

ANNA PÁVLOVNA. And why shouldn't I? He has loved her these ten years, and she loves him.

SÁSHA. Yes, but not as a husband! They have been friends from childhood.

ANNA PÁVLOVNA. We know those friendships! If only the obstacles were out of the way!

Enter Maid.

ANNA PÁVLOVNA. What is it?

MAID. The mistress has sent the porter with a note for Mr. Karénin.

ANNA PÁVLOVNA. What mistress?

MAID. Our mistress—Mrs. Protásova.

ANNA PÁVLOVNA. Well?

MAID. Mr. Karénin has sent back word that he will come round at once.

ANNA PÁVLOVNA [surprised] We were just speaking of him! Only I can't think why ... [to Sásha] Do you know?

SÁSHA. Perhaps I do, and perhaps I don't!

ANNA PÁVLOVNA. You always have secrets!

SÁSHA. Lisa will tell you herself when she comes.

ANNA PÁVLOVNA [shakes her head. To Maid] The samovár must be made to boil again. Take it, Dounyásha.

Maid takes samovár, and exit.

ANNA PÁVLOVNA [to Sásha who has risen and is going out] It turns out just as I told you! She sent for him at once....

SÁSHA. She may have sent for him for quite a different reason.

ANNA PÁVLOVNA. What for, then?

SÁSHA. Now, at this moment, Karénin is the same to her as old Nurse Trífonovna.

ANNA PÁVLOVNA. Well, you'll see.... Don't I know her? She has sent for him to comfort her.

SÁSHA. Oh mother, how little you know her, to be able to suppose ...!

ANNA PÁVLOVNA. Well, we'll see!... And I am very, very glad.

SÁSHA. We shall see! [Exit, humming a tune].

ANNA PÁVLOVNA [alone, shakes her head and mutters] It's all right, it's all right!

Enter Maid.

MAID. Mr. Karénin has come.

ANNA PÁVLOVNA. Well then, show him in, and tell your mistress.

Maid exit by inner door. Enter Karénin, who bows to Anna Pávlovna.

KARÉNIN. Your daughter wrote to me to come. I meant to come and see you to-night, anyhow. So I was very pleased ... Is Elisabeth Andréyevna[2] well?

ANNA PÁVLOVNA. Yes, she is well, but Baby is a bit restless. She will be here directly. [In a melancholy voice] Ah yes! It is a sad time.... But you know all about it, don't you?

KARÉNIN. I do. I was here, you know, the day before yesterday, when his letter came. But is it possible that everything is irrevocably settled?

ANNA PÁVLOVNA. Why of course! Naturally! To go through it all again would be intolerable.

KARÉNIN. This is a case where the proverb applies: "Measure ten times before you cut once." … It is very painful to cut into the quick.

ANNA PÁVLOVNA. Of course it is; but then their marriage has long had a rift in it, so that the tearing asunder was easier than one would have thought. He himself sees that, after what has occurred, it is impossible for him to return.

KARÉNIN. Why so?

ANNA PÁVLOVNA. How can you expect it, after all his horrid goings-on—after he swore it should not happen again, and that if it did he would renounce all rights as a husband and set her perfectly free?

KARÉNIN. Yes, but how can a woman be free when she is bound by marriage?

ANNA PÁVLOVNA. By divorce. He promised her a divorce, and we shall insist on it.

KARÉNIN. Yes, but Elisabeth Andréyevna loved him so.…

ANNA PÁVLOVNA. Ah, but her love has suffered such trials that there can hardly be anything left of it! Drunkenness, deception, and infidelity … Can one love such a husband?

KARÉNIN. Nothing is impossible to love.

ANNA PÁVLOVNA. You talk of love! But how can one love such a man—a broken reed, whom one can never depend on? Don't you know what it came to …? [Looks round at the door, and continues hurriedly] All his affairs in a muddle, everything pawned, nothing to pay with! Then their uncle sends 2,000 roubles to pay the interest on their mortgaged estates, and he takes the money and disappears. His wife is left at home, with a sick baby, waiting for him—and at last gets a note asking her to send him his clothes and things!

KARÉNIN. Yes, yes; I know.

Enter Lisa and Sásha.

ANNA PÁVLOVNA. Well, here is Victor Miháylovich,[3] obedient to your summons.

KARÉNIN. Yes, but I am sorry I was delayed for a few minutes.

LISA. Thank you. I have a great favour to ask of you, and I have no one to turn to but you.

KARÉNIN. Anything in my power ...

LISA. You know all about ...?

KARÉNIN. I do.

ANNA PÁVLOVNA. Well then, I shall leave you [To Sásha] Come, we'll leave them alone. [Exit with Sásha].

LISA. Yes, he wrote to me saying that he considers everything at an end ... [struggling with her tears] ... and I was hurt!... and so ... In a word, I consented to break—I answered, accepting his renunciation.

KARÉNIN. And now you repent?

LISA. Yes. I feel that I was wrong, and that I cannot do it. Anything is better than to be separated from him. In short—I want you to give him this letter.... Please, Victor, give him the letter, and tell him ... and bring him back!

KARÉNIN [surprised] Yes, but how?

LISA. Tell him I ask him to forget everything, and to return. I might simply send the letter, but I know him: his first impulse, as always, will be the right one—but then someone will influence him, and he'll change his mind and not do what he really wants to....

KARÉNIN. I will do what I can.

LISA. You're surprised at my asking you?

KARÉNIN. No.... Yet, to tell you the truth—yes, I am surprised.

LISA. But you are not angry?

KARÉNIN. As if I could be angry with you!

LISA. I asked you because I know you care for him.

KARÉNIN. Him, and you too! You know that. I am thinking not of myself, but of you. Thank you for trusting me! I will do what I can.

LISA. I know.... I will tell you everything. To-day I went to Afrémov's to find out where he was. I was told he had gone to the gipsies—which is what I feared most of all. I know he will get carried away if he is not stopped in time—and that's what has to be done.... So you'll go?

KARÉNIN. Of course, and at once.

LISA. Go!... Find him, and tell him all is forgotten and I am waiting for him.

KARÉNIN. But where am I to look for him?

LISA. He is with the gipsies. I went there myself.... I went as far as the porch, and wished to send in the letter, but changed my mind and decided to ask you. Here is the address.... Well, then, tell him to return: tell him nothing has happened ... all is forgotten. Do it for love of him, and for the sake of our friendship!

KARÉNIN. I will do all in my power! [Bows, and exit].

LISA. I can't, I can't! Anything rather than ... I can't!

Enter Sásha.

SÁSHA. Well, have you sent?

Lisa nods affirmatively.

SÁSHA. And he agreed?

LISA. Of course.

SÁSHA. But why just him? I don't understand.

LISA. But who else?

SÁSHA. Don't you know he is in love with you?

LISA. That's dead and gone. Whom would you have had me send?... Do you think he will come back?

SÁSHA. I am sure of it, because ...

Enter Anna Pávlovna. Sásha is silent.

ANNA PÁVLOVNA. And where is Victor Miháylovich?

LISA. He's gone.

ANNA PÁVLOVNA. Gone! How's that?

LISA. I asked him to do something for me.

ANNA PÁVLOVNA. "Do something?" Another secret!

LISA. It's not a secret. I simply asked him to give a letter into Fédya's own hands.

ANNA PÁVLOVNA. Fédya? What—to Theodore Vasílyevich?

LISA. Yes, to Fédya.

ANNA PÁVLOVNA. I thought all relations between you were over!

LISA. I can't part from him.

ANNA PÁVLOVNA. What? Are you going to begin all over again?

LISA. I wanted to, and tried ... but I can't! Anything you like—only I can't part from him!

ANNA PÁVLOVNA. Then do you want to have him back again?

LISA. Yes.

ANNA PÁVLOVNA. To let that skunk into the house again?

LISA. Mother, I beg you not to speak so of my husband!

ANNA PÁVLOVNA. He was your husband.

LISA. No, he is my husband still.

ANNA PÁVLOVNA. A spendthrift, a drunkard, a rake ... and you can't part from him?

LISA. Why do you torment me! You seem to want to do it.... It's hard enough for me without that.

ANNA PÁVLOVNA. I torment you! Well then, I'll go. I can't stand by and see it....

Lisa is silent.

ANNA PÁVLOVNA. I see! That's just what you want—I'm in your way.... I can't live so. I can't make you out at all! It's all so new-fangled—first you make up your mind to separate, then you suddenly send for a man who is in love with you ...

LISA. Nothing of the kind.

ANNA PÁVLOVNA. Karénin proposed to you ... and you send him to fetch your husband! Why? To arouse jealousy?

LISA. Mother, what you are saying is terrible! Leave me alone!

ANNA PÁVLOVNA. Very well! Turn your mother out of the house, and let in your rake of a husband!... Yes, I will not remain here! Good-bye, then—I leave you to your fate; you can do as you please! [Exit slamming door].

LISA [drops into a chair] That's the last straw!

SÁSHA. Never mind.... It will be all right; we'll soon pacify Mother.

ANNA PÁVLOVNA [passing through] Dounyásha! My trunk!

SÁSHA. Mother, listen!... [follows her out with a significant glance to Lisa].

Curtain.

Scene 2

A room in the gipsies' house. The choir is singing "Kanavela." Fédya in his shirt-sleeves is lying prone on the sofa. Afrémov sits astride a chair in front of the leader of the choir. An officer sits at a table, on which are bottles of champagne and glasses. A musician is taking notes.

AFRÉMOV. Fédya, are you asleep?

FÉDYA [rising] Don't talk.... Now let's have "Not at Eve."

GIPSY LEADER. That won't do, Theodore Vasílyevich! Let Másha sing a solo now.

FÉDYA. All right! And then, "Not at Eve." [Lies down again].

OFFICER. Sing "Fateful Hour."

GIPSY. All agreed?

AFRÉMOV. Go on!

OFFICER [to musician] Have you taken it down?

MUSICIAN. Quite impossible! It's different every time.... And the scale is somehow different. Look here! [Beckons to a gipsy woman who is looking on] Is this right? [Hums].

GIPSY. That's it, that's splendid!

FÉDYA. He'll never get it; and if he does take it down and shoves it into an opera, he'll only spoil it!... Now, Másha, start off! Let's have "Fateful Hour"—take your guitar. [Rises, sits down opposite her, and gazes into her eyes].

Másha sings.

FÉDYA. That's good too! Másha, you're a brick!... Now then, "Not at Eve"!

AFRÉMOV. No, wait! First, my burial song....

OFFICER. Why burial?

AFRÉMOV. Because, when I'm dead ... you know, dead and laid in my coffin, the gipsies will come (you know I shall leave instructions with my wife) and they will begin to sing "I Walked a Mile" ... and then I'll jump out of my coffin!... Do you understand? [To the musician] You just write this down. [To the gipsies] Well, rattle along!

Gipsies sing.

AFRÉMOV. What do you think of that?... Now then, "My Brave Lads"!

Gipsies sing.

Afrémov gesticulates and dances. The gipsies smile and continue singing, clapping their hands. Afrémov sits down and the song ends.

GIPSIES. Bravo! Michael Andréyevich![4] He's a real gipsy!

FÉDYA. Well, now "Not at Eve"!

Gipsies sing.

FÉDYA. That's it! It's wonderful ... And where does it all happen—all that this music expresses? Ah, it's fine!... And how is it man can reach such ecstasy, and cannot keep it?

MUSICIAN [taking notes] Yes, it's most original.

FÉDYA. Not original—but the real thing!

AFRÉMOV [to gipsies] Well, have a rest now. [Takes the guitar and sits down beside Kátya, one of the gipsies].

MUSICIAN. It's really simple, except the rhythm....

FÉDYA [waves his hand, goes to Másha, and sits down on sofa beside her] Oh, Másha, Másha! How you do turn me inside-out!

MÁSHA. And how about what I asked you for?

FÉDYA. What? Money?... [Takes some out of his trouser-pocket] Here, take it!

Másha laughs, takes it, and hides it in her bosom.

FÉDYA [to the gipsies] Who can make it out? She opens heaven for me, and then asks for money to buy scents with! [To Másha] Why, you don't in the least understand what you're doing!

MÁSHA. Not understand indeed! I understand that when I am in love, I try to please my man, and sing all the better.

FÉDYA. Do you love me?

MÁSHA. Looks like it!

FÉDYA. Wonderful! [Kisses her].

Exeunt most of the gipsies. Some couples remain: Fédya with Másha, Afrémov with Kátya, and the officer with Gásha. The musician writes. A gipsy man strums a valse tune on the guitar.

FÉDYA. But I'm married, and your choir won't allow it....

MÁSHA. The choir is one thing, one's heart's another! I love those I love, and hate those I hate.

FÉDYA. Ah! This is good! Isn't it?

MÁSHA. Of course it's good—we've jolly visitors, and are all merry.

Enter gipsy man.

GIPSY [to Fédya] A gentleman is asking for you.

FÉDYA. What gentleman?

GIPSY. I don't know.... Well dressed, wears a sable overcoat—

FÉDYA. A swell? Well, ask him in. [Exit Gipsy].

AFRÉMOV. Who has come to see you here?

FÉDYA. The devil knows! Who can want me?

Enter Karénin. Looks round.

FÉDYA. Ah, Victor! I never expected you!... Take off your coat!...

What wind has blown you here? Come, sit down and listen to "Not at Eve."

KARÉNIN. Je voudrais vous parler sans témoins.[5]

FÉDYA. What about?

KARÉNIN. Je viens de chez vous. Votre femme m'a chargé de cette lettre et puis ...[6]

FÉDYA [takes letter, reads, frowns, then smiles affectionately] I say, Karénin, of course you know what is in this letter?

KARÉNIN. I know ... and I want to say ...

FÉDYA. Wait, wait a bit! Please don't imagine that I am drunk and my words irresponsible.... I mean, that I am irresponsible! I am drunk, but in this matter I see quite clearly.... Well, what were you commissioned to say?

KARÉNIN. I was commissioned to find you, and to tell you ... that ... she ... is waiting for you. She asks you to forget everything and come back.

FÉDYA [listens in silence, gazing into Karénin's eyes] Still, I don't understand why you ...

KARÉNIN. Elisabeth Andréyevna sent for me, and asked me ...

FÉDYA. So ...

KARÉNIN. But I ask you, not so much in your wife's name as from myself.... Come home!

FÉDYA. You are a better man than I. (What nonsense! It is easy enough to be better than I) ... I am a scoundrel, and you are a good—yes, a good man.... And that is the very reason why I won't alter my decision.... No! Not on that account either—but simply because I can't and won't.... How could I return?

KARÉNIN. Let us go to my rooms now, and I'll tell her that you will return to-morrow.

FÉDYA. And to-morrow, what?... I shall still be I, and she—she. [Goes

29

to the table and drinks] It's best to have the tooth out at one go.... Didn't I say that if I broke my word she was to throw me over? Well, I have broken it, and that's the end of it.

KARÉNIN. For you, but not for her!

FÉDYA. It is extraordinary that you should take pains to prevent our marriage being broken up!

KARÉNIN [is about to speak, but Másha comes up] ...

FÉDYA [interrupting him] Just hear her sing "The Flax"!... Másha!

The gipsies re-enter.

MÁSHA [whispers] An ovation, eh?

FÉDYA [laughs] An ovation!... "Victor, my Lord! Son of Michael!" ...

Gipsies sing a song of greeting and laudation.

KARÉNIN [listens in confusion then asks] How much shall I give them?

FÉDYA. Well, give them twenty-five roubles.[7]

Karénin gives the money.

FÉDYA. Splendid! And now, "The Flax!"

Gipsies sing.

FÉDYA [looks round] Karénin's bunked!... Well, devil take him!

Gipsy group breaks up.

FÉDYA [sits down by Másha] Do you know who that was?

MÁSHA. I heard his name.

FÉDYA. He's an excellent fellow! He came to take me home to my wife. She loves a fool like me, and see what I am doing here ...!

MÁSHA. Well, and it's wrong! You ought to go back to her.... You ought to pity her.

FÉDYA. You think I ought to? Well, I think I ought not.

MÁSHA. Of course, if you don't love her you need not. Only love counts.

FÉDYA. And how do you know that?

MÁSHA. Seems I do!

FÉDYA. Well, kiss me then!... Now, let's have "The Flax" once more, and then finish up.

Gipsies sing.

FÉDYA. Ah, how good it is! If only one hadn't to wake up!... If one could die so!

Curtain.

ACT II

Scene 1

Two weeks have passed since Act I. Anna Pávlovna and Karénin are discovered sitting in Lisa's dining-room. Enter Sásha.

KARÉNIN. Well, what news?

SÁSHA. The doctor says there is no danger at present, as long as he does not catch cold.

ANNA PÁVLOVNA. Yes, but Lisa is quite worn out.

SÁSHA. He says it's false croup, and a very mild attack. [Points to a basket]. What's that?

ANNA PÁVLOVNA. Grapes. Victor brought them.

KARÉNIN. Won't you have some?

SÁSHA. Yes, she likes grapes. She has become terribly nervous.

KARÉNIN. Naturally—after not sleeping for two nights, and not eating.

SÁSHA. And how about you.

KARÉNIN. That's quite another matter.

Enter doctor and Lisa.

DOCTOR [impressively] Yes, that's it. Change it every half-hour if he's awake, but if he's asleep don't disturb him. You need not paint the throat. The room must be kept at its present temperature ...

LISA. But if he again begins to choke?

DOCTOR. He probably won't, but if he should, use the spray. And give him the powders: one in the morning and the other at night. I will give you the prescription now.

ANNA PÁVLOVNA. Have a cup of tea, doctor?

DOCTOR. No thanks.... My patients are expecting me.

Sits down to the table. Sásha brings him paper and ink.

LISA. So you're sure it is not croup?

DOCTOR [smiling] Perfectly certain!

KARÉNIN [to Lisa] And now have some tea, or, better still, go and lie down!... Just see what you look like....

LISA. Oh, now I am alive again. Thank you, you are a true friend! [Presses his hand. Sásha moves away angrily] I am so grateful to you, dear friend! At such times one recog ...

KARÉNIN. What have I done? There's really no cause at all to thank me.

LISA. And who stopped up all night? Who fetched the very best doctor?

KARÉNIN. I am already fully rewarded by the fact that Mísha is out of danger; and above all by your kindness.

LISA [presses his hand again and laughs, showing him some money in her hand] That's for the doctor; but I never know how to give it....

KARÉNIN. Neither do I.

ANNA PÁVLOVNA. Don't know what?

LISA. How to give money to a doctor.... He has saved more than my life, and I give him money! It seems so unpleasant.

ANNA PÁVLOVNA. Let me give it. I know how. It's quite simple.

DOCTOR [rises and hands the prescription to Lisa] These powders are to be well mixed in a tablespoonful of boiled water ... [goes on talking].

Karénin sits at the table drinking tea; Sásha and Anna Pávlovna come forward.

SÁSHA. I can't bear the way they go on! It's just as if she were in love with him.

ANNA PÁVLOVNA. Well, can it be wondered at?

SÁSHA. It's disgusting!

Doctor takes leave of everybody, and exit. Anna Pávlovna goes with him.

LISA [to Karénin] He's so sweet now! As soon as even he was a little better he at once began to smile and crow. I must go to him, but I don't like leaving you.

KARÉNIN. You had better have a cup of tea, and eat something.

LISA. I don't want anything now. I am so happy after all that anxiety!... [Sobs].

KARÉNIN. There! You see how worn out you are!

LISA. I'm so happy!... Would you like to have a look at him?

KARÉNIN. Of course.

LISA. Then come with me. [Exeunt].

ANNA PÁVLOVNA [returning to Sásha] What are you looking so glum about?... I gave him the money quite well, and he took it.

SÁSHA. It's disgusting! She has taken him with her to the nursery. It's just as if he were her fiancé or her husband....

ANNA PÁVLOVNA. Whatever does it matter to you? Why need you get excited about it? Did you mean to marry him yourself?

SÁSHA. I? Marry that pikestaff? I'd rather marry I don't know whom, than him! Such a thing never entered my head.... I am only disgusted that, after Fédya, Lisa can be so attracted by a stranger.

ANNA PÁVLOVNA. Not a stranger, but an old playfellow!

SÁSHA. Don't I see by their smiles and looks that they are in love?

ANNA PÁVLOVNA. Well, what is there to be surprised at in that? He shares her anxiety about her baby, shows sympathy and helps her ... and she feels grateful. Besides, why should she not love and marry Victor?

SÁSHA. That would be disgusting—disgusting....

Enter Karénin and Lisa. Karénin silently takes leave. Sásha goes of angrily.

LISA [to Anna Pávlovna] What's the matter with her?

ANNA PÁVLOVNA. I really don't know.

Lisa sighs, and is silent.

Curtain.

Scene 2

Afrémov's sitting-room. Glasses of wine on the table. Afrémov, Fédya, Stákhov (shaggy), Butkévich (close-shaven), and Korotkóv (a tuft-hunter).

KOROTKÓV. And I tell you that he'll be out of the running! La Belle Bois is the best horse in Europe.... Will you bet?

STÁKHOV. Don't, my dear fellow.... You know very well that nobody believes you, or will bet with you.

KOROTKÓV. I tell you your Cartouche won't be in it!

AFRÉMOV. Stop quarrelling! Let me settle it ... ask Fédya—he'll give you the right tip.

FÉDYA. Both horses are good. All depends on the jockey.

STÁKHOV. Gúsev is a rascal, and needs a firm hand on him.

KOROTKÓV [shouts] No!

FÉDYA. Wait a bit—I'll settle your differences.... Who won the Moscow Derby?

KOROTKÓV. He did—but what of that? It was only chance. If Crakus had not fallen ill.... [Enter footman].

AFRÉMOV. What is it?

FOOTMAN. A lady has come, and is asking for Mr. Protásov.

AFRÉMOV. What is she like? A real lady?

FOOTMAN. I don't know her name, but she's a real lady.

AFRÉMOV. Fédya! a lady to see you!

FÉDYA [startled] Who is it?

AFRÉMOV. He doesn't know.

FOOTMAN. Shall I ask her into the dining-room?

FÉDYA. No, wait.... I'll go myself and see.

Exeunt Fédya and footman.

KOROTKÓV. Who can it be? It must be Másha.

STÁKHOV. Which Másha?

KOROTKÓV. The gipsy. She's in love with him, like a cat.

STÁKHOV. What a darling she is …! And how she sings!

AFRÉMOV. Charming! Tanyúsha and she! They sang with Peter yesterday.

STÁKHOV. What a lucky fellow that is!

AFRÉMOV. Why? Because the girls are all sweet on him? Not much luck in that!

KOROTKÓV. I can't bear gipsies—nothing refined about them.

BUTKÉVICH. No, you can't say that!

KOROTKÓV. I'd give the whole lot for one French woman!

AFRÉMOV. Yes, we know you—and your æsthetics!… I'll go and see who it is. [Exit].

STÁKHOV. If it's Másha, bring her in here! We'll make her sing.... No, the gipsies aren't what they used to be. Tanyúsha, now—by Gad!

BUTKÉVICH. And I believe they're just the same.

STÁKHOV. Just the same? When instead of their own pieces they sing empty drawing-room songs?

BUTKÉVICH. Some drawing-room songs are very good.

KOROTKÓV. Will you bet I don't get them to sing a drawing-room song so that you won't know it from one of their own?

STÁKHOV. Korotkóv always wants to bet!

Enter Afrémov.

AFRÉMOV. I say, you fellows, it's not Másha—and there's no room he can ask her into but this. Let us clear out to the billiard room. [Exeunt].

Enter Fédya and Sásha.

SÁSHA [confused] Fédya, forgive me if it's unpleasant—but for God's sake hear me!… [Her voice trembles].

Fédya walks up and down the room. Sásha sits down, and follows him with her eyes.

SÁSHA. Fédya! Come home!

FÉDYA. Just listen to me, Sásha … I quite understand you, Sásha dear, and in your place I should do the same—I should try to find some way to bring back the old state of affairs. But if you were me, if—strange as it sounds—you, dear sensitive girl, were in my place … you would certainly have done as I did, and have gone away and ceased to spoil someone else's life.

SÁSHA. Spoil? How? As if Lisa could live without you!

FÉDYA. Oh, Sásha dear! Dear heart!… She can, she can! And she will yet be happy—far happier than with me.

SÁSHA. Never!

FÉDYA. It seems so to you [Takes her hand] … But that's not the point. The chief thing is, that I can't!… You know, one folds a piece of thick paper this way and that a hundred times and still it holds together; but fold it once more, and it comes in half…. So it was with Lisa and me. It hurts me too much to look into her eyes—and she feels the same, believe me!

SÁSHA. No, no!

FÉDYA. You say "No," but you yourself know that it is "Yes"!

SÁSHA. I can only judge by myself. If I were in her place, and you answered as you are doing, it would be dreadful!

FÉDYA. Yes, for you … [Pause; both are agitated].

SÁSHA [rises] Must things really remain so?

FÉDYA. I suppose ...

SÁSHA. Fédya come back!

FÉDYA. Thank you, Sásha dear! You will always remain a precious memory to me.... But good-bye, dear heart!... Let me kiss you. [Kisses her forehead].

SÁSHA [agitated] No, I don't say good-bye, and I don't believe, and won't believe ... Fédya!

FÉDYA. Well then, listen! But give me your word that what I tell you, you won't repeat to anybody—do you promise?

SÁSHA. Of course!

FÉDYA. Well then, listen, Sásha.... It's true that I am her husband and the father of her child, but I am—superfluous! Wait, wait—don't reply.... You think I'm jealous? Not at all! In the first place, I have no right; secondly, I have no cause. Victor Karénin is her old friend and mine too. He loves her, and she him.

SÁSHA. No!

FÉDYA. She does—as an honest, moral woman can, who does not allow herself to love anyone but her husband. But she loves, and will love him when this obstacle [points to himself] is removed; and I will remove it, and they shall be happy! [His voice trembles].

SÁSHA. Fédya, don't talk like that!

FÉDYA. Why, you know very well that it's true! And I shall be glad of their happiness, and it's the best I can do. I shall not return, but shall give them their freedom.... Tell them so.... Don't answer—and good-bye!

Kisses her on the forehead, and opens the door for her.

SÁSHA. Fédya—you are wonderful!

FÉDYA. Good-bye, good-bye!... [Exit Sásha].

FÉDYA. Yes, yes.... That's the thing ... that's the thing!... [Rings].

Enter footman.

FÉDYA. Call your master.... [Exit footman].... And it's true—it's true.

Enter Afrémov.

FÉDYA. Come along!

AFRÉMOV. Have you settled matters?

FÉDYA. Splendidly! [Sings]

"And she swore by ev'ry power ..."

Splendidly!... Where are they all?

AFRÉMOV. They're playing billiards.

FÉDYA. That's right—we will too [Sings]

"Rest here, just an hour ..."

Come along!

Curtain.

ACT III

Scene 1

Prince Abrézkov, a sixty-year-old bachelor with moustaches, a retired army man, elegant, very dignified and melancholy-looking. Anna Dmítrievna Karénina (Victor's mother), a fifty-year-old "grande dame" who tries to appear younger, and intersperses her remarks with French expressions.

Anna Dmítrievna's sitting-room, furnished with expensive simplicity, and filled with souvenirs.

Anna Dmítrievna is writing. Footman enters.

FOOTMAN. Prince Abrézkov …

ANNA DMÍTRIEVNA. Yes, certainly … [Turns round and touches herself up before the looking-glass].

Enter Abrézkov.

PRINCE ABRÉZKOV. J'espère que je ne force pas la consigne.…[8] [Kisses her hand].

ANNA DMÍTRIEVNA. You know that vous êtes toujours le bienvenu[9]—and to-day especially! You got my note?

PRINCE ABRÉZKOV. I did, and this is my answer.

ANNA DMÍTRIEVNA. Ah, my friend! I begin quite to despair. Il est positivement ensorcelé![10] I never before knew him so insistent, so obstinate, so pitiless, and so indifferent to me. He has quite changed since that woman dismissed her husband!

PRINCE ABRÉZKOV. What are the facts? How do matters actually stand?

ANNA DMÍTRIEVNA. He wants to marry her come what may.

PRINCE ABRÉZKOV. And how about the husband?

ANNA DMÍTRIEVNA. He agrees to a divorce.

PRINCE ABRÉZKOV. Dear me!

ANNA DMÍTRIEVNA. And he, Victor, lends himself to it, with all the abominations—lawyers, proofs of guilt—tout ça est dégoutant![11] And it doesn't seem to repel him. I don't understand him—he was always so sensitive, so reserved …

PRINCE ABRÉZKOV. He is in love! Ah, when a man really loves …

ANNA DMÍTRIEVNA. Yes, but how is it that in our day love could be pure—could be a loving friendship, lasting through life? That kind of love I understand and value.

PRINCE ABRÉZKOV. Nowadays the young generation no longer contents itself with those ideal relations. La possession de l'âme ne leur suffit plus.[12] It can't be helped!… What can one do with him?

ANNA DMÍTRIEVNA. You must not say that of him—but it's as if he were under a spell. It's just as if he were someone else.… You know, I called on her. He begged me so. I went there, did not find her in, and left my card. Elle m'a fait demander si je ne pourrais la recevoir;[13] and to-day [looks at the clock] at two o'clock, that is in a few minutes' time, she will be here. I promised Victor I would receive her, but you understand how I am placed! I am not myself at all; and so, from old habit, I sent for you. I need your help!

PRINCE ABRÉZKOV. Thank you.

ANNA DMÍTRIEVNA. This visit of hers, you understand, will decide the whole matter—Victor's fate! I must either refuse my consent—but how can I?

PRINCE ABRÉZKOV. Don't you know her at all?

ANNA DMÍTRIEVNA. I have never seen her. But I'm afraid of her. A good woman could not consent to leave her husband, and he a good man, too! As a fellow-student of Victor's he used to visit us, you know, and was very nice. But whatever he may be, quels que soient les torts qu'il a eu vis-à-vis d'elle,[14] one must not leave one's husband. She ought to bear her cross. What I don't understand is how Victor, with the convictions he holds, can think of marrying a divorced woman! How often—quite lately—he has argued warmly with Spítsin in my presence, that divorce was incompatible with true Christianity; and now he himself is going in for it! Si elle a pu le charmer à un tel point[15] ... I am afraid of her! But I sent for you to know what you have to say to it all, and instead of that I have been doing all the talking myself! What do you think of it? Tell me your opinion. What ought I to do? You have spoken with Victor?

PRINCE ABRÉZKOV. I have: and I think he loves her. He has grown used to loving her; and love has got a great hold on him. He is a man who takes things slowly but firmly. What has once entered his heart will never leave it again; and he will never love anyone but her; and he can never be happy without her, or with anyone else.

ANNA DMÍTRIEVNA. And how willingly Várya Kazántseva would have married him! What a girl she is, and how she loves him!

PRINCE ABRÉZKOV [smiling]. C'est compter sans son hôte![16] That is quite out of the question now. I think it's best to submit, and help him to get married.

ANNA DMÍTRIEVNA. To a divorced woman—and have him meet his wife's husband?... I can't think how you can speak of it so calmly. Is she a woman a mother could wish to see as the wife of her only son—and such a son?

PRINCE ABRÉZKOV. But what is to be done, my dear friend? Of course it would be better if he married a girl whom you knew and liked; but since that's impossible ... Besides it's not as if he were going to marry a gipsy, or goodness knows who ...! Lisa Protásova is a very nice good woman. I know her, through my niece Nelly, and know her to be a modest, kind-hearted, affectionate and moral woman.

ANNA DMÍTRIEVNA. A moral woman—who makes up her mind to leave her husband!

PRINCE ABRÉZKOV. This is not like you! You're unkind and harsh! Her husband is the kind of man of whom one says that they are their own worst enemies; but he is an even greater enemy to his wife. He is a weak, fallen, drunken fellow. He has squandered all his property and hers too. She has a child…. How can you condemn her for leaving such a man? Nor has she left him: he left her.

ANNA DMÍTRIEVNA. Oh, what mud! What mud! And I have to soil my hands with it!

PRINCE ABRÉZKOV. And how about your religion?

ANNA DMÍTRIEVNA. Of course, of course! To forgive, "As we forgive them that trespass against us." Mais, c'est plus fort que moi![17]

PRINCE ABRÉZKOV. How could she live with such a man? If she had not loved anyone else she would have had to leave him. She would have had to, for her child's sake. The husband himself—an intelligent kind-hearted man when he is in his senses—advises her to do it….

Enter Victor, who kisses his mother's hand and greets Prince Abrézkov.

VICTOR. Mother, I have come to say this: Elisabeth Andréyevna will be here in a minute, and I beg, I implore you—if you still refuse your consent to my marriage …

ANNA DMÍTRIEVNA [interrupting him] Of course I still refuse my consent …

VICTOR [continues his speech and frowns] In that case I beg, I implore you, not to speak to her of your refusal! Don't settle matters negatively …

ANNA DMÍTRIEVNA. I don't expect we shall mention the subject. For my part, I certainly won't begin.

VICTOR. And she is even less likely to. I only want you to make her acquaintance.

ANNA DMÍTRIEVNA. The one thing I can't understand is how you reconcile your desire to marry Mrs. Protásova, who has a husband living, with your religious conviction that divorce is contrary to Christianity.

VICTOR. Mother, this is cruel of you! Are we really so immaculate that we must always be perfectly consistent when life is so complex? Mother, why are you so cruel to me?

ANNA DMÍTRIEVNA. I love you. I desire your happiness.

VICTOR [to Prince Abrézkov] Prince!

PRINCE ABRÉZKOV. Of course you desire his happiness. But it is not easy for you and me, with our grey hairs, to understand the young; and it is particularly difficult for a mother grown accustomed to her own idea of how her son is to be happy. Women are all like that.

ANNA DMÍTRIEVNA. Yes, yes indeed! You are all against me! You may do it, of course. Vous êtes majeur.[18] … But you will kill me!

VICTOR. You are not yourself. This is worse than cruelty!

PRINCE ABRÉZKOV [to Victor] Be quiet, Victor. Your mother's words are always worse than her deeds.

ANNA DMÍTRIEVNA. I shall tell her how I think and feel, but I will do it without offending her.

PRINCE ABRÉZKOV. Of that I am sure.

Enter footman.

PRINCE ABRÉZKOV. Here she is.

VICTOR. I'll go.

FOOTMAN. Elisabeth Andréyevna Protásova.

VICTOR. I am going. Please, Mother! [Exit.]

Prince Abrézkov also rises.

ANNA DMÍTRIEVNA. Ask her in. [To Prince Abrézkov] No, you

must please stay here!

PRINCE ABRÉZKOV. I thought you'd find a tête-à-tête easier.

ANNA DMÍTRIEVNA. No, I'm afraid … [Is restless] If I want to be left tête-à-tête with her, I will nod to you. Cela dépendra.[19] … To be left alone with her may make it difficult for me. But I'll do like that if … [Makes a sign].

PRINCE ABRÉZKOV. I shall understand. I feel sure you will like her. Only be just.

ANNA DMÍTRIEVNA. How you are all against me!

Enter Lisa, in visiting dress and hat.

ANNA DMÍTRIEVNA [rising] I was sorry not to find you in, and it is kind of you to call.

LISA. I never dreamed that you'd be so good as to call.… I am so grateful to you for wishing to see me.

ANNA DMÍTRIEVNA [pointing to Prince Abrézkov] You are acquainted?

PRINCE ABRÉZKOV. Yes, certainly. I have had the pleasure of being introduced. [They shake hands and sit down] My niece Nelly has often mentioned you to me.

LISA. Yes, she and I were great friends [glancing timidly at Anna Dmítrievna], and we are still friendly. [To Anna Dmítrievna] I never expected that you would wish to see me.

ANNA DMÍTRIEVNA. I knew your husband well. He was friendly with Victor, and used to come to our house before he left for Tambóv. I think it was there you married?

LISA. Yes, it was there we married.

ANNA DMÍTRIEVNA. But after his return to Moscow he never visited us.

46

LISA. Yes, he hardly went out anywhere.

ANNA DMÍTRIEVNA. And he never introduced you to me.

Awkward silence.

PRINCE ABRÉZKOV. The last time I met you was at the theatricals at the Denísovs'. They went off very well; and you were acting.

LISA. No … Yes … Of course … I did act. [Silence again]. Anna Dmítrievna, forgive me if what I am going to say displeases you, but I can't and don't know how to dissemble! I have come because Victor Miháylovich said … because he—I mean, because you wished to see me…. But it is best to speak out [with a catch in her voice] … It is very hard for me…. But you are kind.

PRINCE ABRÉZKOV. I'd better go.

ANNA DMÍTRIEVNA. Yes, do.

Prince Abrézkov takes leave of both women, and exit.

ANNA DMÍTRIEVNA. Listen, Lisa … I am very sorry for you, and I like you. But I love Victor. He is the one being I love in the world. I know his soul as I know my own. It is a proud soul. He was proud as a boy of seven…. Not proud of his name or wealth, but proud of his character and innocence, which he has guarded. He is as pure as a maiden.

LISA. I know.

ANNA DMÍTRIEVNA. He has never loved any woman. You are the first. I do not say I am not jealous. I am jealous. But we mothers—your son is still a baby, and it is too soon for you—we are prepared for that. I was prepared to give him up to his wife and not to be jealous—but to a wife as pure as himself …

LISA. I … have I …

ANNA DMÍTRIEVNA. Forgive me! I know it was not your fault, but you are unfortunate. And I know him. Now he is ready to bear—and will bear—anything, and he would never mention it, but he would suffer. His wounded pride would suffer, and he would not be happy.

LISA. I have thought of that.

ANNA DMÍTRIEVNA. Lisa, my dear, you are a wise and good woman. If you love him you must desire his happiness more than your own. And if that is so, you will not wish to bind him and give him cause to repent—though he would never say a word.

LISA. I know he wouldn't! I have thought about it, and have asked myself that question. I have thought of it, and have spoken of it to him. But what can I do, when he says he does not wish to live without me? I said to him: "Let us be friends, but do not spoil your life; do not bind your pure life to my unfortunate one!" But he does not wish for that.

ANNA DMÍTRIEVNA. No, not at present....

LISA. Persuade him to leave me, and I will agree. I love him for his own happiness and not for mine. Only help me! Do not hate me! Let us lovingly work together for his happiness!

ANNA DMÍTRIEVNA. Yes, yes! I have grown fond of you. [Kisses her. Lisa cries] And yet, and yet it is dreadful! If only he had loved you before you married …

LISA. He says he did love me then, but did not wish to prevent a friend's happiness.

ANNA DMÍTRIEVNA. Ah, how hard it all is! Still, we will love one another, and God will help us to find what we want.

VICTOR [entering] Mother, dear! I have heard everything! I expected this: you are fond of her, and all will be well!

LISA. I am sorry you heard. I should not have said it if …

ANNA DMÍTRIEVNA. Still, nothing is settled. All I can say is, that if it were not for all these unfortunate circumstances, I should have been glad. [Kisses her].

VICTOR. Only, please don't change!

Curtain.

Scene 2

A plainly furnished room; bed, table, sofa. Fédya alone.

A knock at the door. A woman's voice outside. Why have you locked yourself in, Theodore Vasílyevich? Fédya! Open …!

FÉDYA [gets up and unlocks door] That's right! Thank you for coming. It's dull, terribly dull!

MÁSHA. Why didn't you come to us? Been drinking again? Eh, eh! And after you'd promised!

FÉDYA. D'you know, I've no money!

MÁSHA. And why have I taken it into my head to care for you!

FÉDYA. Másha!

MÁSHA. Well, what about "Másha, Másha"? If you were really in love, you'd have got a divorce long ago. They themselves asked you to. You say you don't love her, but all the same you keep to her! I see you don't wish …

FÉDYA. But you know why I don't wish!

MÁSHA. That's all rubbish. People say quite truly that you're an empty fellow.

FÉDYA. What can I say to you? That your words hurt me, you know without being told!

MÁSHA. Nothing hurts you!

FÉDYA. You know that the one joy I have in life is your love.

MÁSHA. My love—yes; but yours doesn't exist.

FÉDYA. All right. I'm not going to assure you. Besides, what's the good? You know!

MÁSHA. Fédya; why torment me?

FÉDYA. Which of us torments?

MÁSHA [cries] You are unkind!

FÉDYA [goes up and embraces her] Másha! What's it all about? Stop that. One must live, and not whine. It doesn't suit you at all, my lovely one!

MÁSHA. You do love me?

FÉDYA. Whom else could I love?

MÁSHA. Only me? Well then, read what you have been writing.

FÉDYA. It will bore you.

MÁSHA. It's you who wrote it, so it's sure to be good.

FÉDYA. Well then listen. [Reads] "One day, late in autumn, my friend and I agreed to meet on the Murýgin fields, where there was a close thicket with many young birds in it. The day was dull, warm, and quiet. The mist ..."

Enter two old gipsies, Másha's parents, Iván Makárovich and Nastásia Ivánovna.

NASTÁSIA [stepping up to her daughter] Here you are then, you damned runaway sheep! [To Fédya] My respects to you, sir! [To Másha] Is that how you treat us, eh?

IVÁN [to Fédya] It's wrong, sir, what you're doing! You're ruining the wench! Oh, but it's wrong ... You're doing a dirty deed.

NASTÁSIA. Put on your shawl! March at once!... Running away like this! What can I say to the choir? Gallivanting with a beggar—what can you get out of him?

MÁSHA. I don't gallivant! I love this gentleman, that's all. I've not left the choir. I'll go on singing, and what ...

IVÁN. Say another word, and I'll pull the hair off your head!... Slut!... Who behaves like that? Not your father, nor your mother, nor your aunt!... It's bad, sir! We were fond of you—often and often we sang to you without pay. We pitied you, and what have you done?

NASTÁSIA. You've ruined our daughter for nothing ... our own, our only daughter, the light of our eyes, our priceless jewel—you've trodden her into the mire, that's what you've done! You've no conscience.

FÉDYA. Nastásia Ivánovna, you suspect me falsely. Your daughter is like a sister to me. I care for her honour. You must think no evil ... but I love her! What is one to do?

IVÁN. But you didn't love her when you had money! If you'd then subscribed ten thousand roubles or so to the choir, you might have had her honourably. But now you've squandered everything, and carry her off by stealth! It's a shame, sir, a shame!

MÁSHA. He has not carried me off! I came to him myself, and if you take me away now, I shall come back again. I love him, and there's an end of it! My love is stronger than all your locks ... I won't!

NASTÁSIA. Come, Másha dearest! Come, my own! Don't sulk. You've done wrong, and now come along.

IVÁN. Now then, you've talked enough! March! [Seizes her hand] Excuse us, sir! [Exit the three gipsies].

Enter Prince Abrézkov.

PRINCE ABRÉZKOV. Excuse me. I have been an unwilling witness of an unpleasant scene....

FÉDYA. Whom have I the honour?... [Recognises the Prince] Ah, Prince Abrézkov! [They shake hands].

PRINCE ABRÉZKOV. An unwilling witness of an unpleasant scene. I should have been glad not to hear, but having overheard it, I consider it my duty to tell you so. I was directed here, and had to wait at the door for those people to come out—more particularly as their very loud voices rendered my knocking inaudible.

FÉDYA. Yes, yes—please take a seat. Thank you for telling me: it gives me the right to explain that scene to you. I don't mind what you may think of me, but I should like to tell you that the reproaches you heard addressed to that girl, that gipsy singer, were unjust. That girl is as morally pure as a dove; and my relations with her are those of a friend. There may be a tinge of romance in them, but it does not destroy the purity—the honour—of the girl. That is what I wished to tell you; but what is it you want of me? In what way can I be of service?

PRINCE ABRÉZKOV. In the first place, I …

FÉDYA. Forgive me, Prince. My present social standing is such, that my former slight acquaintance with you does not entitle me to a visit from you, unless you have some business with me. What is it?

PRINCE ABRÉZKOV. I won't deny it. You have guessed right. I have business with you; but I beg you to believe that the alteration in your position in no wise affects my attitude towards you.

FÉDYA. I am sure of it.

PRINCE ABRÉZKOV. My business is this. The son of my old friend, Anna Dmítrievna Karénina, and she herself, have asked me to ascertain directly from you what are your relations … May I speak out?… your relations with your wife, Elisabeth Andréyevna Protásova.

FÉDYA. My relations with my wife, or rather with her who was my wife, are entirely at an end.

PRINCE ABRÉZKOV. So I understood, and that is why I accepted this difficult mission.

FÉDYA. At an end, and, I hasten to add, not by her fault, but by mine—by my innumerable faults. She is, as she always was, quite irreproachable.

PRINCE ABRÉZKOV. Well then, Victor Karénin, or rather his mother, asked me to find out what your intentions are.

FÉDYA [growing excited] What intentions? I have none. I set her quite free! Moreover, I will never disturb her peace. I know she loves Victor Karénin. Well, let her! I consider him a very dull, but very good and honourable man, and I think that she will, as the phrase goes, be happy with him; and—que le bon Dieu les bénisse![20] That's all ...

PRINCE ABRÉZKOV. Yes, but we ...

FÉDYA [interrupting] And don't suppose that I feel the least bit jealous. If I said that Victor is dull, I withdraw the remark. He is an excellent, honourable, moral man: almost the direct opposite of myself. And he has loved her from childhood. Perhaps she too may have loved him when she married me—that happens sometimes! The very best love is unconscious love. I believe she always did love him; but as an honest woman she did not confess it even to herself. But ... a shadow of some kind always lay across our family life—but why am I confessing to you?

PRINCE ABRÉZKOV. Please do! Believe me, my chief reason for coming to you was my desire to understand the situation fully.... I understand you. I understand that the shadow, as you so well express it, may have been ...

FÉDYA. Yes, it was; and that perhaps is why I could not find satisfaction in the family life she provided for me, but was always seeking something, and being carried away. However, that sounds like excusing myself. I don't want to, and can't, excuse myself. I was (I say with assurance, was) a bad husband. I say was, because in my consciousness I am not, and have long not been, her husband. I consider her perfectly free. So there you have my answer to your question.

PRINCE ABRÉZKOV. Yes, but you know Victor's family, and himself too. His relation to Elisabeth Andréyevna is, and has been all through, most respectful and distant. He assisted her when she was in trouble ...

FÉDYA. Yes, I by my dissipation helped to draw them together. What's to be done? It had to be so!

PRINCE ABRÉZKOV. You know the strictly Orthodox convictions of that family. Having myself a broader outlook on things, I do not share them; but I respect and understand them. I understand that for him, and especially for his mother, union with a woman without a Church marriage is unthinkable.

FÉDYA. Yes, I know his stu ... his strictness, his conservatism in these matters. But what do they want? A divorce? I told them long ago that I am quite willing; but the business of taking the blame on myself, and all the lies connected with it, are very trying.... [21]

PRINCE ABRÉZKOV. I quite understand you, and sympathise. But how can it be avoided? I think it might be arranged that way—but you are right. It is dreadful, and I quite understand you.

FÉDYA [pressing the Prince's hand] Thank you, dear Prince! I always knew you were a kind and honourable man. Tell me what to do. How am I to act? Put yourself in my place. I am not trying to improve. I am a good-for-nothing; but there are things I cannot do quietly. I cannot quietly tell lies.

PRINCE ABRÉZKOV. I don't understand you! You, a capable, intelligent man, so sensitive to what is good—how can you let yourself be so carried away—so forget what you expect of yourself? How have you ruined your life and come to this?

FÉDYA [forcing back tears of emotion] I have led this disorderly life for ten years, and this is the first time a man like you has pitied me! I have been pitied by my boon-companions, by rakes and by women; but a reasonable, good man like you ... Thank you! How did I come to my ruin? First, through drink. It is not that drink tastes nice; but do what I will, I always feel I am not doing the right thing, and I feel ashamed. I talk to you now, and feel ashamed. As for being a Maréchal de la noblesse, or a Bank Director—I should feel ashamed, so ashamed! It is only when I drink that I do not feel this shame. And music: not operas or Beethoven, but gipsies!... That is life! Energy flows into one's veins! And then those dear black eyes, and those smiles! And the more delicious it is, the more ashamed one feels afterwards.

PRINCE ABRÉZKOV. How about work?

FÉDYA. I have tried it, but it's no good. I am always dissatisfied with it—but what's the use of talking about myself! I thank you.

PRINCE ABRÉZKOV. Then what am I to say?

FÉDYA. Tell them I will do what they wish. They want to get married,

54

and that there should be no obstacle to their marriage?

PRINCE ABRÉZKOV. Of course.

FÉDYA. I'll do it! Tell them I will certainly do it.

PRINCE ABRÉZKOV. But when?

FÉDYA. Wait a bit. Well, say in a fortnight. Will that do?

PRINCE ABRÉZKOV. Then I may tell them so?

FÉDYA. You may. Good-bye, Prince! Thank you once again!

[Exit Prince].

FÉDYA [sits for a long time and smiles silently] That's the way, that's the way! It must be so, must be, must be! Splendid!

Curtain.

ACT IV

Scene 1

A private room in a restaurant. A waiter shows in Fédya and Iván Petróvich Alexándrov.

WAITER. Here, please. No one will disturb you here. I'll bring some paper directly.

IVÁN PETRÓVICH. Protásov, I'll come in too.

FÉDYA [seriously] If you like, but I'm busy and ... All right, come in.

IVÁN PETRÓVICH. You wish to reply to their demands? I'll tell you what to say. I should not do it that way—always speak straight out, and act with decision.

FÉDYA [to waiter] A bottle of champagne!

Exit waiter.

FÉDYA [taking out a revolver and putting it on the table] Wait a bit!

IVÁN PETRÓVICH. What's that? Do you want to shoot yourself? You can if you like. I understand you! They wish to humiliate you, and you will show them the sort of man you are! You will kill yourself with a revolver, and them with magnanimity. I understand you. I understand everything, because I am a genius.

FÉDYA. Of course—of course. Only ... [Enter waiter with paper and ink].

FÉDYA [covers the revolver with a napkin] Uncork it—let's have a drink. [They drink. Fédya writes] Wait a bit!

IVÁN PETRÓVICH. Here's to your ... great journey! You know I'm above all this. I'm not going to restrain you! Life and death are alike to Genius. I die in life, and live in death. You will kill yourself that two people should pity you; and I—I shall kill myself that the whole world may understand what it has lost. I won't hesitate, or think about it! I seize it [snatches revolver]—now! And all is over. But it is too soon yet. [Lays down revolver] Nor shall I write anything; they must understand it themselves.... Oh, you ...

FÉDYA [writing] Wait a bit.

IVÁN PETRÓVICH. Pitiful people! They fuss, they bustle, and don't understand—don't understand anything at all.... I'm not talking to you, I am only expressing my thoughts. And, after all, what does humanity need? Very little—only to value its geniuses. But they always are executed, persecuted, tortured.... No! I'm not going to be your toy! I will drag you out into the open! No-o-o! Hypocrites!

FÉDYA [having finished writing, drinks and reads over his letter] Go away, please!

IVÁN PETRÓVICH. Go away? Well, good-bye then! I am not going to restrain you. I shall do the same. But not yet. I only want to tell you ...

FÉDYA. All right! You'll tell me afterwards. And now, dear chap, just one thing: give this to the manager [gives him money] and ask if a parcel and a letter have come for me.... Please do!

IVÁN PETRÓVICH. All right—then you'll wait for me? I have still something important to tell you—something that you will not hear in this world nor in the next, at any rate not till I come there.... Am I to let him have all of this?

FÉDYA. As much as is necessary. [Exit Iván Petróvich.]

Fédya sighs with relief; locks the door behind Iván Petróvich; takes up the revolver, cocks it, puts it to his temple; shudders, and carefully lowers it again. Groans.

FÉDYA. No; I can't! I can't! I can't! [Knock at the door] Who's there?

[Másha's voice from outside] It's me!

FÉDYA. Who's "me"? Oh, Másha … [opens door].

MÁSHA. I've been to your place, to Popóv's, to Afrémov's, and guessed that you must be here. [Sees revolver] That's a nice thing! There's a fool! A regular fool! Is it possible you really meant to?

FÉDYA. No, I couldn't.

MÁSHA. Do I count for nothing at all? You heathen! You had no pity for me? Oh, Theodore Vasílyevich, it's a sin, a sin! In return for my love …

FÉDYA. I wished to release them. I promised to, and I can't lie.

MÁSHA. And what about me?

FÉDYA. What about you? It would have set you free too. Is it better for you to be tormented by me?

MÁSHA. Seems it's better. I can't live without you.

FÉDYA. What sort of life could you have with me? You'd have cried a bit, and then gone on living your own life.

MÁSHA. I shouldn't have cried at all! Go to the devil, if you don't pity me! [Cries].

FÉDYA. Másha, dearest! I meant to do it for the best.

MÁSHA. Best for yourself!

FÉDYA [smiles] How's that, when I meant to kill myself?

MÁSHA. Of course, best for yourself! But what is it you want? Tell me.

FÉDYA. What I want? I want a great deal.

MÁSHA. Well, what? What?

FÉDYA. First of all, to keep my promise. That is the first thing, and quite sufficient. To lie, and do all the dirty work necessary to get a divorce … I can't!

MÁSHA. Granted that it's horrid—I myself …

FÉDYA. Next, they must really be free—my wife and he. After all, they are good people; and why should they suffer? That's the second thing.

MÁSHA. Well, there isn't much good in her, if she's thrown you over.

FÉDYA. She didn't—I threw her over.

MÁSHA. All right, all right! It's always you. She is an angel! What else!

FÉDYA. This—that you are a good, dear girlie—and that I love you, and if I live I shall ruin you.

MÁSHA. That's not your business. I know quite well what will ruin me.

FÉDYA [sighs] But above all, above all … What use is my life? Don't I know that I am a lost good-for-nothing? I am a burden to myself and to everybody—as your father said. I'm worthless.…

MÁSHA. What rubbish! I shall stick to you. I've stuck to you already, and there's an end of it! As to your leading a bad life, drinking and going on the spree—well, you're a living soul! Give it up, and have done with it!

FÉDYA. That's easily said.

MÁSHA. Well, then, do it.

FÉDYA. Yes, when I look at you I feel as if I could really do anything.

MÁSHA. And so you shall! Yes, you'll do it! [Sees the letter] What's that? You've written to them? What have you written?

FÉDYA. What have I written?… [Takes the letter and is about to tear it up] It's no longer wanted now.

MÁSHA [snatches the letter] You've said you would kill yourself? Yes? You did not mention the revolver—only said that you'd kill yourself?

FÉDYA. Yes, that I should be no more.

MÁSHA. Give it me—give it, give it!… Have you read What to Do?

FÉDYA. I think I have.

MÁSHA. It's a tiresome novel, but there's one very, very good thing in it. That what's his name?—Rakhmánov—goes and pretends he has drowned himself. And you—can you swim?

FÉDYA. No.

MÁSHA. That's all right. Let me have your clothes—everything, and your pocket-book too.

FÉDYA. How can I?

MÁSHA. Wait a bit, wait, wait! Let's go home; then you'll change your clothes.

FÉDYA. But it will be a fraud.

MÁSHA. All right! You go to bathe, your clothes remain on the bank, in the pocket is your pocket-book and this letter.

FÉDYA. Yes, and then?

MÁSHA. And then? Why, then we'll go off together and live gloriously.

Enter Iván Petróvich.

IVÁN PETRÓVICH. There now! And the revolver? I'll take it.

MÁSHA. Take it; take it! We're off.

Curtain.

Scene 2

The Protásovs' drawing-room.

KARÉNIN. He promised so definitely, that I am sure he will keep his word.

LISA. I am ashamed to say it, but I must confess that what I heard about that gipsy girl makes me feel quite free. Don't think it is jealousy; it isn't, but you know—it sets me free. I hardly know how to tell you....

KARÉNIN. You don't know how to tell me ... Why?

LISA [smiling] Never mind! Only let me explain what I feel. The chief thing that tormented me was, that I felt I loved two men; and that meant that I was an immoral woman.

KARÉNIN. You immoral?

LISA. But since I knew that he had got someone else, and that he therefore did not need me, I felt free, and felt that I might truthfully say that I love you. Now things are clear within me, and only my position torments me. This divorce! It is such torture—and then this waiting!

KARÉNIN. It will soon, very soon, be settled. Besides his promise, I sent my secretary to him with the petition ready for signature, and told him not to leave till it is signed. If I did not know him so well, I should think he was purposely behaving as he does.

LISA. He? No, it is the result both of his weakness and his honesty. He doesn't want to say what is not true. Only you were wrong to send him money.

KARÉNIN. I had to. The want of it might be the cause of the delay.

LISA. No, there is something bad about money.

KARÉNIN. Well, anyhow, he need not have been so punctilious ...

LISA. How selfish we are becoming!

KARÉNIN. Yes, I confess it. It's your own fault. After all that waiting, that hopelessness, I am now so happy! And happiness makes one selfish. It's your fault!

LISA. Do you think it's you only? I too—I feel full of happiness, bathed in bliss! I have everything—Mísha has recovered, your mother likes me, and you—and above all, I, I love!

KARÉNIN. Yes? And no repenting? No turning back?

LISA. Since that day everything has changed in me.

KARÉNIN. And will not change again?

LISA. Never! I only wish you to have done with it all as completely as I have.

Enter nurse, with baby. Lisa takes the baby on her lap.

KARÉNIN. What wretched people we are!

LISA [kissing baby] Why?

KARÉNIN. When you married, and I heard of it on my return from abroad, and was wretched because I felt that I had lost you, it was a relief to me to find that you still remembered me. I was content even with that. Then when our friendship was established and I felt your kindness to me, and even a little gleam of something in our friendship that was more than friendship, I was almost happy. I was only tormented by a fear that I was not being honest towards Fédya. But no! I was always so firmly conscious that any other relation than one of purest friendship with my friend's wife was impossible—besides which, I knew you—that I was not really troubled about that. Afterwards, when Fédya began to cause you anxiety, and I felt that I was of some use to you, and that my friendship was beginning to alarm you—I was quite happy, and a sort of vague hope awoke in me. Still later, when he became altogether impossible and you decided to leave him, and I spoke to you plainly for the first time, and you did not say "No," but went away in tears—then I was perfectly happy; and had I then been asked what more I wanted, I should have answered "Nothing"! But later on, when there came the possibility of uniting our lives: when my mother grew fond of you and the possibility began to be realised; when you told me that you loved and had loved me, and then (as you did just now) that he no longer existed for you and that you love only me—what more, one would think, could I wish for? But no! Now the past torments me! I wish that past had not existed, and that there were nothing to remind me of it.

LISA [reproachfully] Victor!

KARÉNIN. Lisa, forgive me! If I tell you this, it is only because I don't want a single thought of mine about you to be hidden from you. I have purposely told you, to show how bad I am, and how well I know that I must struggle with and conquer myself…. And now I've done it! I love him.

LISA. That's as it should be. I did all I could, but it was not I that did what you desired: it happened in my heart, from which everything but you has vanished.

KARÉNIN. Everything?

LISA. Everything, everything—or I would not say so.

Enter footman.

FOOTMAN. Mr. Voznesénsky.

KARÉNIN. He's come with Fédya's answer.

LISA [to Karénin] Ask him in here.

KARÉNIN [rising and going to the door] Well, here is the answer!

LISA [gives baby to nurse; exit nurse] Is it possible, Victor, that everything will now be decided? [Kisses Karénin].

Enter Voznesénsky.

KARÉNIN. Well?

VOZNESÉNSKY. He has gone.

KARÉNIN. Gone! And without signing the petition?

VOZNESÉNSKY. The petition is not signed, but a letter was left for you and Elisabeth Andréyevna [Takes letter out of his pocket and gives it to Karénin] I went to his lodgings, and was told he was at the restaurant. I went there, and Mr. Protásov told me to return in an hour and I should then have his answer. I went back, and then …

KARÉNIN. Is it possible that this means another delay? More excuses! No, that would be downright wicked. How he has fallen!

LISA. But do read the letter! [Karénin opens letter].

VOZNESÉNSKY. You do not require me any longer?

KARÉNIN. Well, no. Good-bye! Thank you … [Pauses in astonishment as he reads].

Exit Voznesénsky.

LISA. What—what is it?

KARÉNIN. This is awful!

LISA [takes hold of letter] Read!

KARÉNIN [reads] "Lisa and Victor, I address myself to you both. I won't lie and call you 'dear' or anything else. I cannot master the feeling of bitterness and reproach (I reproach myself, but all the same it is painful) when I think of you and of your love and happiness. I know everything. I know that though I was the husband, I have—by a series of accidents—been in your way. C'est moi qui suis l'intrus.[22] But all the same, I cannot restrain a feeling of bitterness and coldness towards you. I love you both in theory, especially Lisa, Lisette! But actually I am more than cold towards you. I know I am wrong, but cannot change."

LISA. How can he …

KARÉNIN [continues reading] "But to business! This very feeling of discord within me forces me to fulfil your desire not in the way you wish. Lying, acting so disgusting a comedy, bribing the Consistorium, and all those horrors, are intolerably repulsive to me. Vile as I may be, I am vile in a different way, and cannot take part in those abominations—simply cannot! The solution at which I have arrived is the simplest: to be happy, you must marry. I am in the way; consequently I must destroy myself...."

LISA [seizes Victor's hand] Victor!

KARÉNIN [reads] "... must destroy myself. And I will do it. When you get this letter, I shall be no more.

"P.S. What a pity you sent me money to pay for the divorce proceedings! It is unpleasant, and unlike you! But it can't be helped. I have so often made mistakes, why shouldn't you make one? I return the money. My way of escape is shorter, cheaper, and surer. All I ask is, don't be angry with me, and think kindly of me. And, one thing more—there is a clockmaker, Evgényev, here. Can't you help him, and set him on his feet? He's a good man, though weak.—Good-bye,

"Fédya."

LISA. He has taken his life! Yes ...

KARÉNIN [rings, and runs out to the hall] Call Mr. Voznesénsky back!

LISA. I knew it! I knew it! Fédya, dear Fédya!

KARÉNIN. Lisa!

LISA. It's not true, not true that I didn't love him and don't love him! I love only him! I love him! And I've killed him. Leave me!

Enter Voznesénsky.

KARÉNIN. Where is Mr. Protásov? What did they tell you?

VOZNESÉNSKY. They told me he went out this morning, left this letter, and had not returned.

KARÉNIN. We shall have to find out about it, Lisa. I must leave you.

LISA. Forgive me, but I too can't lie! Go now—go, and find out ...

Curtain.

ACT V

Scene 1

A dirty room in a low-class restaurant. A table, at which people sit drinking tea and vódka. In the foreground a small table, at which sits Fédya, tattered, and much come down in the world. With him is Petushkóv, a gentle, mild man with long hair, of clerical appearance. Both are slightly drunk.

PETUSHKÓV. I understand, I understand. That is true love! Yes? Go on.

FÉDYA. Well, you know, if a woman of our class showed such feeling and sacrificed everything for the man she loved.... But she was a gipsy, brought up to money-hunting, and yet she had this self-sacrificing love! Gave everything, and wanted nothing herself! The contrast was so wonderful!

PETUSHKÓV. Yes, in art we call it "value." You can only get quite bright red by putting green round it. But that's not to the point. I understand, quite understand.

FÉDYA. Yes, and I believe the one good action of my life is that I never took advantage of her love. And do you know why?

PETUSHKÓV. Pity.

FÉDYA. Oh no! I never felt pity for her. What I felt for her was always rapturous admiration—and when she sang! Ah, how she sang—and perhaps still sings! I always regarded her as far above me. I did not ruin her, simply because I loved her; loved her truly. And now she's a good, happy memory! [Drinks].

PETUSHKÓV. Yes, I understand, I understand. It's ideal.

FÉDYA. I'll tell you something. I have had my passions, and once I was in love with a lady—very handsome—and I loved her nastily, like a dog. She gave me a rendezvous. And I did not go, because I thought it was treating the husband shabbily. And it is strange that, even now, when I remember it I want to feel pleased and to approve of myself for having acted honourably, but I always repent as if I had committed a sin! But in the case of Másha, on the contrary, I am always pleased—pleased that I did not pollute that feeling of mine.... I may fall lower still, sell all I have on me, be covered with lice and sores—but this jewel ... no, not jewel, but ray of sunshine, is still with me and in me.

PETUSHKÓV. I understand, I understand! And where is she now?

FÉDYA. I don't know! And I'd rather not know. All that belonged to a different life; and I don't want to mix it up with this....

A woman is heard screaming at a table behind. The manager and a policeman come in and take her out. Fédya and Petushkóv listen, and look on in silence. When all is quiet again,

PETUSHKÓV. Yes, your life is astonishing.

FÉDYA. No, it's most simple! You know, in the society in which I was born there are only three careers open to a man—only three. The first is to enter the civil or military service, to earn money and increase the abominations amid which we live. That was repulsive to me. Perhaps I had not the capacity for it; but above all it repelled me. Then the second is to destroy those abominations. To do that you must be a hero; and I am not a hero. And the third is to forget it all by going on the spree, drinking and singing. That is what I did. And this is what my singing has brought me to! [Drinks].

PETUSHKÓV. And what about family life? I should be happy if I had a wife. My wife ruined me.

FÉDYA. Family life? Yes, my wife was an ideal woman. She is still living. But how shall I tell you? There was no yeast in it—you know, the yeast that makes the beer froth! Well, there was nothing of that in our life: it was flat, and I wanted something to help me to forget—and one can't forget when

67

there's no sparkle in life. Then I began to do all sorts of nasty things. And you know, we love people for the good we do them, and dislike them for the harm we do them; and I did her much harm. She seemed to love me …

PETUSHKÓV. Why do you say "seemed"?

FÉDYA. I say it because there was never anything about her that made her creep into my soul as Másha did. But that's not what I meant to say. When she was pregnant, or nursing her baby, I used to vanish, and come home drunk; and of course, just because of that, I loved her less and less. Yes, yes! [in ecstasy] I have it! The reason I love Másha is that I did her good and not harm. That's why I love her. The other one I tormented, and therefore I don't like her.… No, after all, I simply don't like her! Was I jealous? Yes, but that too is past.…

Enter Artémyev, with a cockade on his cap, dyed moustaches, and old renovated clothes.

ARTÉMYEV. Wish you a good appetite! [Bows to Fédya] I see you've made acquaintance with our painter, our artist.

FÉDYA [coldly] Yes, we are acquainted.

ARTÉMYEV [to Petushkóv] And have you finished the portrait?

PETUSHKÓV. No, I lost the order.

ARTÉMYEV [Sits down] I'm not in your way?

Fédya and Petushkóv do not answer.

PETUSHKÓV. Theodore Vasílyevich was telling me about his life.

ARTÉMYEV. Secrets? Then I won't disturb you—go on? I'm sure I don't want you. Swine! [Goes to next table and calls for beer. He listens all the time to Fédya's conversation with Petushkóv, and leans towards them without their noticing it.]

FÉDYA. I don't like that gentleman.

PETUSHKÓV. He was offended.

FÉDYA. Well, let him be! I can't stand him. He is such a fellow, my words won't come when he is there. Now with you I feel at ease, and comfortable. Well, what was I saying?

PETUSHKÓV. You were speaking about your jealousy. And how was it you parted from your wife?

FÉDYA. Ah! [Pauses and considers] It's a curious story. My wife is married …

PETUSHKÓV. How's that? Are you divorced?

FÉDYA [smiles] No, I left her a widow.

PETUSHKÓV. What do you mean?

FÉDYA. I mean that she's a widow! I don't exist.

PETUSHKÓV. Don't exist?

FÉDYA. No, I'm a corpse! Yes … [Artémyev leans over, listening] Well, you see—I can tell you about it; and besides, it happened long ago; and you don't know my real name. It was this way. When I had tired out my wife and had squandered everything I could lay my hands on, and had become unbearable, a protector turned up for her. Don't imagine that there was anything dirty or bad about it—no, he was my friend and a very good fellow—only in everything my exact opposite! And as there is far more evil than good in me, it follows that he was a good—a very good man: honourable, firm, self-restrained and, in a word, virtuous. He had known my wife from her childhood, and loved her. When she married me he resigned himself to his fate. But later, when I became horrid and tormented her, he began to come oftener to our house. I myself wished it. They fell in love with one another, and meanwhile I went altogether to the bad, and abandoned my wife of my own accord. And besides, there was Másha. I myself advised them to marry. They did not want to, but I became more and more impossible, and it ended in …

PETUSHKÓV. The usual thing?

FÉDYA. No. I am sure; I know for certain that they remained pure. He

69

is a religious man, and considers marriage without the Church's blessing a sin. So they began asking me to agree to a divorce. I should have had to take the blame on myself. It would have been necessary to tell all sorts of lies ... and I couldn't! Believe me, it would have been easier for me to take my life than to tell such lies—and I wished to do so. But then a kind friend came and said, "Why do it?" and arranged it all for me. I wrote a farewell letter, and next day my clothes, pocket-book and letters were found on the river bank. I can't swim.

PETUSHKÓV. Yes, but how about the body? They did not find that!

FÉDYA. They did! Fancy! A week later somebody's body was found. My wife was called to identify the decomposing body. She just glanced at it. "Is it he?" "It is." And so it was left. I was buried, and they married and are living in this town, happily. And I—here I am, living and drinking! Yesterday I passed their house. The windows were lit up, and someone's shadow crossed the blind. Sometimes it's horrid, and sometimes not. It's horrid when I've no money ... [Drinks].

ARTÉMYEV [approaches] Excuse me, but I heard your story. It's a very good story, and more than that—a very useful one! You say it's horrid when one has no money? There's nothing more horrid. But you, in your position, should always have money. Aren't you a corpse? Well then ...

FÉDYA. Excuse me! I did not speak to you and don't want your advice.

ARTÉMYEV. But I want to give it! You are a corpse; but suppose you come to life again? Then they, your wife and that gentleman, who are so happy—they would be bigamists, and at best would be sent to the less distant parts of Siberia. So why should you lack money?

FÉDYA. I beg you to leave me alone.

ARTÉMYEV. Simply write a letter. I'll write it for you if you like; only give me their address, and you'll be grateful to me.

FÉDYA. Be off, I tell you! I have told you nothing!

ARTÉMYEV. Yes, you have! Here's my witness. The waiter heard you say you were a corpse.

WAITER. I know nothing about it.

FÉDYA. You scoundrel!

ARTÉMYEV. Am I a scoundrel? Eh, police! I'll give him in charge!

Fédya rises to go, but Artémyev holds him. Enter policeman.

Curtain.

Scene 2

The ivy-covered verandah of a bungalow in the country. Anna Dmítrievna Karénina. Lisa (pregnant), nurse, and boy.

LISA. Now he's on his way from the station.

BOY. Who is?

LISA. Papa.

BOY. Papa's coming from the station?

LISA. C'est étonnant comme il l'aime, tout-à-fait comme son père.[23]

ANNA DMÍTRIEVNA. Tant mieux! Se souvient-il de son père véritable?[24]

LISA [sighs] I never speak to him about it. I say to myself, "Why confuse him?" Sometimes I think I ought to tell him. What is your opinion, Maman?

ANNA DMÍTRIEVNA. I think it is a matter of feeling, Lisa, and if you obey your feelings your heart will tell you what to say and when to say it. What a wonderful conciliator death is! I confess there was a time when Fédya—whom I had known from a child—was repulsive to me; but now I only remember him as that nice lad, Victor's friend, and as the passionate man who sacrificed himself—illegally and irreligiously, but still sacrificed himself—for those he loved. On aura beau dire, l'action est belle.[25]... I hope Victor will not forget to bring the wool: I've hardly any left. [Knits].

LISA. I hear him coming.

The sound of wheels and bells is heard. Lisa rises, and goes to the edge of the veranda.

LISA. There's someone with him, a lady in a bonnet—It's Mother! I have not seen her for an age. [Goes to the door].

Enter Karénin and Anna Pávlovna.

ANNA PÁVLOVNA [kisses Lisa and Anna Dmítrievna] Victor met me, and has brought me here.

ANNA DMÍTRIEVNA. He has done well.

ANNA PÁVLOVNA. Yes, certainly. I thought to myself, "When shall I see her again?" and kept putting it off. But now I've come, and if you don't turn me out I will stay till the last train.

KARÉNIN [kisses his wife, mother, and the boy] D'you know what a piece of luck! Congratulate me—I have two days' holiday. They'll be able to get on without me to-morrow.

LISA. Splendid! Two days! It's long since we had that! We'll drive to the Hermitage, shall we?

ANNA PÁVLOVNA. What a likeness! Isn't he a strapping fellow? If only he has not inherited everything—his father's heart …

ANNA DMÍTRIEVNA. But not his weakness.

LISA. No, everything! Victor agrees with me that if only he had been rightly guided in childhood …

ANNA PÁVLOVNA. Well, I don't know about that; but I simply can't think of him without tears.

LISA. No more can we. How much higher he stands now in our recollection!

ANNA PÁVLOVNA. Yes, I am sure of it.

LISA. How it all seemed insoluble at one time—and then everything suddenly came right.

ANNA DMÍTRIEVNA. Well, Victor, did you get the wool?

KARÉNIN. Yes, I did. [Brings a bag, and takes out parcels]. Here is the wool, and this is the eau-de-Cologne; and here are letters—one "On Government Service" for you, Lisa [hands her a letter]. Well Anna Pávlovna, if you want to wash your hands I will show you your room. I must make myself tidy too; it is almost dinner time. Lisa, Anna Pávlovna's room is the corner one downstairs, isn't it?

Lisa is pale; holds the letter in trembling hands, and reads it.

KARÉNIN. What's the matter? Lisa, what is it?

LISA. He is alive!... Oh God! When will he release me! Victor, what does this mean? [Sobs].

KARÉNIN [Takes letter and reads] This is dreadful!

ANNA DMÍTRIEVNA. What is it? Why don't you tell me?

KARÉNIN. It is dreadful! He's alive, she's a bigamist, and I a criminal! It's a notice from the Examining Magistrate—a summons for Lisa to appear before him.

ANNA DMÍTRIEVNA. What a dreadful man! Why has he done this?

KARÉNIN. All lies, lies!

LISA. Oh, how I hate him! I don't know what I am saying ... [Exit in tears. Karénin follows her].

ANNA PÁVLOVNA. How is it he's alive?

ANNA DMÍTRIEVNA. All I know is, that as soon as Victor came in contact with this world of mud—they were sure to draw him in too! And so they have. It's all fraud—all lies!

Curtain.

ACT VI

Scene 1

The room of an Examining Magistrate, who sits at a table talking to Mélnikov. At a side table a clerk is sorting papers.

EXAMINING MAGISTRATE. But I never said anything of the kind to her. She invented it, and now reproaches me.

MÉLNIKOV. She does not reproach you, but is grieved.

EXAMINING MAGISTRATE. All right, I'll come to dinner. But now I have a very interesting case on. [To Clerk] Ask her in.

CLERK. Shall I ask them both?

EXAMINING MAGISTRATE [finishes his cigarette and hides it] No, only Mrs. Karénina, or rather—by her first husband—Protásova.

MÉLNIKOV [going out] Ah, Karénina!

EXAMINING MAGISTRATE. Yes, it's a nasty affair. It's true I am only beginning to look into it, but it's a bad business. Well, good-bye! [Exit Mélnikov].

Enter Lisa, in black and veiled.

EXAMINING MAGISTRATE. Take a seat, please. [Points to a chair] Believe me, I much regret to have to question you, but we are under the necessity ... Please be calm, and remember that you need not answer my questions. Only, in my opinion, for your own sake—and in fact for everybody's sake—the truth is best. It is always best, even practically.

LISA. I have nothing to conceal.

EXAMINING MAGISTRATE. Well then [looks at paper]—your

name, position, religion—all that I have put down. Is it correct?

LISA. Yes.

EXAMINING MAGISTRATE. You are accused of contracting a marriage with another man, knowing your husband to be alive.

LISA. I did not know it.

EXAMINING MAGISTRATE. And also of having persuaded your husband, and bribed him with money, to commit a fraud—a pretended suicide—in order to free yourself of him.

LISA. That is all untrue.

EXAMINING MAGISTRATE. Well then, allow me to put a few questions. Did you send him 1,200 roubles in July of last year?

LISA. It was his own money, the proceeds of the sale of some things of his. At the time I parted from him, and when I was expecting a divorce, I sent him the money.

EXAMINING MAGISTRATE. Just so! Very well. That money was sent to him on the 17th of July, two days before his disappearance?

LISA. I think it was on the 17th, but I don't remember.

EXAMINING MAGISTRATE. And why was the application to the Consistorium for a divorce withdrawn, just at that time—and the lawyer told not to proceed with the case?

LISA. I don't know.

EXAMINING MAGISTRATE. Well, and when the police asked you to identify the body, how was it you recognised it as your husband's?

LISA. I was so excited that I did not look at the body, and I felt so sure it was he, that when they asked me I answered, "I think it is he."

EXAMINING MAGISTRATE. Yes, you did not see well, in consequence of a very natural excitement. And now may I ask why you have sent a monthly remittance to Sarátov, the very town where your first husband was living?

LISA. My husband sent that money, and I cannot say what it was for, as that is not my secret. But it was not sent to Theodore Vasílyevich, for we were firmly convinced of his death. That I can say for certain.[26]

EXAMINING MAGISTRATE. Very well. Only allow me to remark, madam, that the fact of our being servants of the law does not prevent our being men; and believe me I quite understand your position and sympathise with you! You were tied to a man who squandered your property, was unfaithful—in short, brought misfortune....

LISA. I loved him.

EXAMINING MAGISTRATE. Yes; but still the desire to free yourself was natural, and you chose this simpler way, without realising that it would lead you into what is considered a crime—bigamy! I quite understand it. The judges will understand too; and therefore I advise you to confess everything.

LISA. I have nothing to confess. I have never lied. [Cries] Do you want me any longer?

EXAMINING MAGISTRATE. I must ask you to remain here. I will not trouble you with any more questions. Only kindly read this over and sign it. It is your deposition. See whether your answers have been correctly taken down. Please take that seat. [Points to an armchair by the window. To Clerk] Ask Mr. Karénin to come in.

Enter Karénin, stern and solemn.

EXAMINING MAGISTRATE. Please take a seat.

KARÉNIN. Thank you! [Remains standing] What do you want of me?

EXAMINING MAGISTRATE. I have to take your deposition.

KARÉNIN. In what capacity?

EXAMINING MAGISTRATE [smiling] I, in the capacity of Examining Magistrate, am obliged to question you in the capacity of an accused person.

KARÉNIN. Indeed! Accused of what?

EXAMINING MAGISTRATE. Of marrying a woman whose husband was alive. However, allow me to question you properly. Kindly sit down.

KARÉNIN. Thank you.

EXAMINING MAGISTRATE. Your name?

KARÉNIN. Victor Karénin.

EXAMINING MAGISTRATE. Your calling?

KARÉNIN. Chamberlain and Member of Council.

EXAMINING MAGISTRATE. Age?

KARÉNIN. Thirty-eight.

EXAMINING MAGISTRATE. Religion?

KARÉNIN. Orthodox; and I have never before been tried or questioned! Well?

EXAMINING MAGISTRATE. Did you know that Theodore Vasílyevich Protásov was alive when you married his wife?

KARÉNIN. I did not know it. We were both convinced that he was drowned.

EXAMINING MAGISTRATE. After Protásov's alleged death, to whom in Sarátov did you send a monthly remittance?

KARÉNIN. I do not wish to reply to that question.

EXAMINING MAGISTRATE. Very well. Why did you send money—1,200 roubles—to Mr. Protásov just before his pretended death on 17th July?

KARÉNIN. That money was given to me by my wife ...

EXAMINING MAGISTRATE. By Mrs. Protásova?

KARÉNIN. ... by my wife, to send to her husband. She considered that money to be his, and having severed all connection with him, considered it unfair to keep it.

EXAMINING MAGISTRATE. One more question—why did you withdraw the application for divorce?

KARÉNIN. Because Theodore Vasílyevich undertook to apply for a divorce, and wrote me about it.

EXAMINING MAGISTRATE. Have you got his letter?

KARÉNIN. It has been lost.[27]

EXAMINING MAGISTRATE. It is strange that everything which might convince the Court of the truth of your evidence should either be lost or non-existent.

KARÉNIN. Do you want anything more?

EXAMINING MAGISTRATE. I want nothing, except to do my duty; but you'll have to exonerate yourselves, and I have just advised Mrs. Protásova, and I advise you also, not to try to hide what everyone can see, but to say what really happened. Especially as Mr. Protásov is in such a condition that he has already told everything just as it happened, and will probably do the same in Court, I should advise ...

KARÉNIN. I request you to keep within the limits of your duty, and not to give me your advice! May we go? [Approaches Lisa, who rises and takes his arm].

EXAMINING MAGISTRATE. I am very sorry to be obliged to detain you ... [Karénin looks round in astonishment] Oh, I don't mean that I arrest you. Though that would make it easier to get at the truth, I shall not resort to such a measure. I only want to take Protásov's deposition in your presence, and to confront him with you—which will make it easier for you to detect any falsehood in what he says. Please take a seat. Call in Mr. Protásov!

Enter Fédya, dirty and shabby.

FÉDYA [addresses Lisa and Karénin] Lisa! Elisabeth Andréyevna!

Victor! I am not guilty! I wished to act for the best. But if I am guilty ... forgive me, forgive me! [Bows low to them].

EXAMINING MAGISTRATE. Please to answer my questions.

FÉDYA. Ask, then.

EXAMINING MAGISTRATE. Your name?

FÉDYA. Why, you know it!

EXAMINING MAGISTRATE. Please answer.

FÉDYA. Well then, Theodore Protásov.

EXAMINING MAGISTRATE. Your calling, age and religion?

FÉDYA [after a pause] Aren't you ashamed to ask such nonsense? Ask what you want to know, and not such rubbish!

EXAMINING MAGISTRATE. I beg you to be more careful in your expressions, and to answer my questions!

FÉDYA. Well, if you're not ashamed of it, here you are: Calling, graduate; age, forty; religion, Orthodox. What next!

EXAMINING MAGISTRATE. Did Mr. Karénin and your wife know that you were alive when you left your clothes on the river bank and disappeared?

FÉDYA. Certainly not! I wished really to commit suicide, but afterwards—but there's no need to go into that. The thing is, that they knew nothing about it.

EXAMINING MAGISTRATE. How is it that you gave a different account to the police officer?

FÉDYA. What police officer? Oh, when he came to see me at the dosshouse? I was drunk, and was romancing. I don't remember what I said. All that was rubbish. Now I am not drunk, and am telling the whole truth! They knew nothing. They believed that I was no longer alive, and I was glad of it. And everything would have gone on as it was, but for that rascal, Artémyev! If anyone is guilty, it is I alone.

EXAMINING MAGISTRATE. I understand your wish to be magnanimous, but the law demands the truth. Why was money sent to you?

Fédya is silent.

You received through Semyónov the money sent to you in Sarátov?

Fédya is silent.

Why don't you answer? It will be put down in the depositions that the accused did not answer these questions, and this may harm you and them very much. Well then, how was it?

FÉDYA [after a pause] Oh, Mr. Magistrate, how is it you are not ashamed! Why do you pry into other people's lives? You are glad to have power, and to show it, you torment not physically but morally—torment people a thousand times better than yourself!

EXAMINING MAGISTRATE. I beg …

FÉDYA. You've nothing to beg! I shall say what I think, and you [to Clerk] write it down! At least for once there will be sensible human words in a police report! [Raises his voice] There are three people: I, he, and she. Our relations to one another are complex—a spiritual struggle such as you know nothing of, a struggle between good and evil goes on. That struggle ends in a manner which sets them free. They were all at peace. They were happy, and remembered me with affection. I, fallen as I was, was glad that I had acted as I ought, and that I, a good-for-nothing, had gone out of their lives, so as not to stand in the way of people who were good and who had life before them. And so we were all living, when suddenly a blackmailing scoundrel appears who wants me to take part in his rascality, and I send him about his business. Then he comes to you, to the champion of Justice! The guardian of Morality! And you, who receive each month a few pounds for doing your dirty work, put on your uniform, and calmly bully these people—bully people whose little finger is worth more than your whole body and soul! People who would not admit you to their anteroom! But you have got so far, and are pleased …

EXAMINING MAGISTRATE. I shall have you turned out!

FÉDYA. I'm not afraid of anyone, because I'm a corpse and you can't do me any harm. No position could be worse than mine! So turn me out!

KARÉNIN. May we go?

EXAMINING MAGISTRATE. Immediately, but first sign your deposition.

FÉDYA. You'd be quite comic, if you weren't so vile!

EXAMINING MAGISTRATE. Take him away! I arrest you.

FÉDYA [to Lisa and Karénin] Forgive me!

KARÉNIN [approaches and holds out his hand] It had to happen!

Lisa passes by. Fédya bows low to her.

Curtain.

Scene 2

A corridor of the Law Courts. In the background a door with glass panels, beside which stands an usher. Further to the right another door through which the accused are led.

Iván Petróvich Alexándrov comes to the first door and wishes to enter.

USHER. Where are you going? You mustn't! Shoving in like that!

IVÁN PETRÓVICH. Why mustn't I? The law says the proceedings are public. [Applause is heard from inside the Court].

USHER. Anyhow, you mustn't, and that's all about it.

IVÁN PETRÓVICH. Ignorant fellow! You don't know whom you are speaking to!

A Young Lawyer in a dress-suit enters from the Court.

YOUNG LAWYER. Are you concerned in this case?

IVÁN PETRÓVICH. No, I am the public, and this ignoramus—this Cerberus—won't let me in!

YOUNG LAWYER. But this door is not for the public.

IVÁN PETRÓVICH. I know, but I am a man who should be admitted.

YOUNG LAWYER. Wait a bit—they'll adjourn in a minute. [Is just going, when he meets Prince Abrézkov].

PRINCE ABRÉZKOV. May I ask how the case stands?

YOUNG LAWYER. The Counsel are speaking—Petrúshin is addressing the Court.

Applause from within.

PRINCE ABRÉZKOV. And how do the defendants bear their position?

YOUNG LAWYER. With great dignity, especially Karénin and

Elisabeth Andréyevna. It is as if not they were being indicted, but they were indicting society! That's what is felt, and on that Petrúshin is working.

PRINCE ABRÉZKOV. Well, and Protásov?

YOUNG LAWYER. He is terribly excited. He trembles all over; but that is natural, considering the life he leads. He is particularly irritable, and interrupted the Public Prosecutor and Counsel several times ...

PRINCE ABRÉZKOV. What do you think the result will be?

YOUNG LAWYER. It is hard to say. In any case they won't be found guilty of premeditation; but still ... [A gentleman comes out, and Prince Abrézkov moves towards the door] You wish to go in?

PRINCE ABRÉZKOV. I should like to.

YOUNG LAWYER. You are Prince Abrézkov?

PRINCE ABRÉZKOV. I am.

YOUNG LAWYER [to Usher] Let this gentleman pass. There is an empty chair just to the left.

Usher lets Prince Abrézkov pass. As the door opens, Counsel is seen speaking.

IVÁN PETRÓVICH. Aristocrats! I am an aristocrat of the soul, and that is higher!

YOUNG LAWYER. Well, excuse me ... [Exit].

Petushkóv enters hurriedly, and approaches Iván Petróvich.

PETUSHKÓV. Ah, how are you, Iván Petróvich? How are things going?

IVÁN PETRÓVICH. Counsel are still speaking, but this fellow won't let me in.

USHER. Don't make a noise here! This is not a public-house!

Applause. The doors open. Lawyers, and the public—men and women—come out.

A LADY. Splendid! He really moved me to tears.

OFFICER. It's better than any novel. Only I don't understand how she could love him so. Dreadful object!

The other door opens. The accused come out: first Lisa, then Karénin. They pass along the corridor. Fédya follows alone.

LADY. Hush—here he is! Look how excited he seems!

Lady and Officer pass on.

FÉDYA [approaches Iván Petróvich] Have you brought it?

IVÁN PETRÓVICH. Here it is. [Hands Fédya something].

FÉDYA [Hides it in his pocket, and wishes to pass out, but sees Petushkóv] Stupid! Vile! Dreary, dreary! Senseless. [Wishes to pass].

Enter Counsel Petrúshin; stout, red, and animated. He approaches Fédya.

PETRÚSHIN. Well, friend! Our affairs are going well—only don't you go and spoil things for me in your last speech!

FÉDYA. I won't speak. What is the use? I shan't do it.

PETRÚSHIN. Yes, you must speak. But don't be excited. The whole matter is now in a nutshell! Only tell them what you told me—that if you are being tried, it is only for not having committed suicide: that is, for not doing what is considered a crime both by civil and ecclesiastical law.

FÉDYA. I shan't say anything!

PETRÚSHIN. Why not?

FÉDYA. I don't want to, and shan't. Tell me only, at the worst, what will it be?

PETRÚSHIN. I have already told you—at worst, exile to Siberia.

FÉDYA. Who will be exiled?

PETRÚSHIN. You and your wife.

FÉDYA. And at best?

PETRÚSHIN. Church penance, and of course annulment of the second marriage.

FÉDYA. Then they will again tie me to her—or rather, her to me?

PETRÚSHIN. Yes, that must be so. But don't excite yourself, and please say what I told you, and above all, don't say anything superfluous. However [noticing that a circle of listeners has formed round them] I am tired, and will go and sit down; and you'd better take a rest. The chief thing is, not to lose courage!

FÉDYA. No other sentence is possible?

PETRÚSHIN [going] No other.

Enter Attendant.

ATTENDANT. Pass on! Pass on! No loitering in the corridor!

FÉDYA. Directly! [Takes out revolver and shoots himself in the heart. Falls. All rush on him] All right, I think it is done.... Lisa!...

The audience, judges, accused, and witnesses rush out from all the doors.

In front of all is Lisa. Behind her Másha, Karénin, Iván Petróvich and Prince Abrézkov.

LISA. Fédya, what have you done! Why?

FÉDYA. Forgive me that I could not ... free you any other way.... It's not for you ... it's best for me. I have long ... been ready ...

LISA. You will live!

A Doctor bends over Fédya and listens.

FÉDYA. I need no doctor to tell me ... Good-bye, Victor ... Ah, Másha!... it's too late this time ... [Weeps] How good ... how good! [Dies].

Curtain.

Footnotes

[1] Protásov is his family name, but the name by which he is usually addressed is Fédya, an abbreviation of his Christian name—Theodore. The ceremonious form of address would be Theodore Vasílyevich.

[2] Elisabeth Andréyevna is the polite way of speaking of Mrs. Protásova, otherwise Lisa.

[3] The polite way of naming Mr. Karénin.

[4] The polite way of addressing Mr. Afrémov.

[5] I wanted to speak to you alone.

[6] I have come from your home. Your wife has entrusted me with this letter and besides ...

[7] About £2, 10s.

[8] I hope I am not forcing myself on you.

[9] You are always welcome.

[10] He is positively bewitched!

[11] It is all disgusting!

[12] For them, to possess the soul is no longer enough.

[13] She inquired whether I would receive her.

[14] However he may have wronged her.

[15] If she has been able to charm him to such a degree ...

[16] That's reckoning without your host!

[17] But it's beyond me!

[18] You are of age.

[19] It will depend.

[20] May God bless them!

[21] Under the Russian law divorce was only obtainable if ocular evidence of adultery was forthcoming, and a great deal of perjury was usually involved in such cases.

[22] It is I who am the intruder.

[23] It is surprising how he loves him—just as if he were his father.

[24] So much the better! Does he remember his real father?

[25] Say what one likes—it is a fine action.

[26] Had Tolstoy lived to give a final revision to this play, he would probably have made it clearer that Karénin sent a monthly payment to the clockmaker Evgényev, in response to the request contained in the last letter Fédya addressed to Lisa and himself; and that this money found its way to Fédya.

[27] Karénin does not produce Fédya's letter because it would have proved connivance in the divorce proceedings.

CHILDHOOD

I – THE TUTOR, KARL IVANITCH

On the 12th of August, 18— (just three days after my tenth birthday, when I had been given such wonderful presents), I was awakened at seven o'clock in the morning by Karl Ivanitch slapping the wall close to my head with a fly-flap made of sugar paper and a stick. He did this so roughly that he hit the image of my patron saint suspended to the oaken back of my bed, and the dead fly fell down on my curls. I peeped out from under the coverlet, steadied the still shaking image with my hand, flicked the dead fly on to the floor, and gazed at Karl Ivanitch with sleepy, wrathful eyes. He, in a parti-coloured wadded dressing-gown fastened about the waist with a wide belt of the same material, a red knitted cap adorned with a tassel, and soft slippers of goat skin, went on walking round the walls and taking aim at, and slapping, flies.

"Suppose," I thought to myself, "that I am only a small boy, yet why should he disturb me? Why does he not go killing flies around Woloda's bed? No; Woloda is older than I, and I am the youngest of the family, so he torments me. That is what he thinks of all day long—how to tease me. He knows very well that he has woken me up and frightened me, but he pretends not to notice it. Disgusting brute! And his dressing-gown and cap and tassel too—they are all of them disgusting."

While I was thus inwardly venting my wrath upon Karl Ivanitch, he had passed to his own bedstead, looked at his watch (which hung suspended in a little shoe sewn with bugles), and deposited the fly-flap on a nail, then, evidently in the most cheerful mood possible, he turned round to us.

"Get up, children! It is quite time, and your mother is already in the drawing-room," he exclaimed in his strong German accent. Then he crossed over to me, sat down at my feet, and took his snuff-box out of his pocket. I pretended to be asleep. Karl Ivanitch sneezed, wiped his nose, flicked his fingers, and began amusing himself by teasing me and tickling my toes as he said with a smile, "Well, well, little lazy one!"

For all my dread of being tickled, I determined not to get out of bed or to answer him, but hid my head deeper in the pillow, kicked out with all my strength, and strained every nerve to keep from laughing.

"How kind he is, and how fond of us!" I thought to myself. "Yet to think that I could be hating him so just now!"

I felt angry, both with myself and with Karl Ivanitch, I wanted to laugh and to cry at the same time, for my nerves were all on edge.

"Leave me alone, Karl!" I exclaimed at length, with tears in my eyes, as I raised my head from beneath the bed-clothes.

Karl Ivanitch was taken aback. He left off tickling my feet, and asked me kindly what the matter was. Had I had a disagreeable dream? His good German face and the sympathy with which he sought to know the cause of my tears made them flow the faster. I felt conscience-stricken, and could not understand how, only a minute ago, I had been hating Karl, and thinking his dressing-gown and cap and tassel disgusting. On the contrary, they looked eminently lovable now. Even the tassel seemed another token of his goodness. I replied that I was crying because I had had a bad dream, and had seen Mamma dead and being buried. Of course it was a mere invention, since I did not remember having dreamt anything at all that night, but the truth was that Karl's sympathy as he tried to comfort and reassure me had gradually made me believe that I HAD dreamt such a horrible dream, and so weep the more—though from a different cause to the one he imagined.

When Karl Ivanitch had left me, I sat up in bed and proceeded to draw my stockings over my little feet. The tears had quite dried now, yet the mournful thought of the invented dream was still haunting me a little. Presently Uncle [This term is often applied by children to old servants in Russia] Nicola came in—a neat little man who was always grave, methodical, and respectful, as well as a great friend of Karl's. He brought with him our clothes and boots—at least, boots for Woloda, and for myself the old detestable, be-ribanded shoes. In his presence I felt ashamed to cry, and, moreover, the morning sun was shining so gaily through the window, and Woloda, standing at the washstand as he mimicked Maria Ivanovna (my sister's governess), was laughing so loud and so long, that even the serious Nicola—a towel over his shoulder, the soap in one hand, and the basin in the other—could not help smiling as he said, "Will you please let me wash you, Vladimir Petrovitch?" I had cheered up completely.

"Are you nearly ready?" came Karl's voice from the schoolroom. The tone of that voice sounded stern now, and had nothing in it of the kindness which had just touched me so much. In fact, in the schoolroom Karl was altogether a different man from what he was at other times. There he was the tutor. I washed and dressed myself hurriedly, and, a brush still in my hand as I smoothed my wet hair, answered to his call. Karl, with spectacles on nose and a book in his hand, was sitting, as usual, between the door and one of the windows. To the left of the door were two shelves—one of them the children's (that is to say, ours), and the other one Karl's own. Upon ours were heaped all sorts of books—lesson books and play books—some standing up and some lying down. The only two standing decorously against the wall were two large volumes of a Histoire des Voyages, in red binding. On that shelf could be seen books thick and thin and books large and small, as well as covers without books and books without covers, since everything got crammed up together anyhow when play time arrived and we were told to put the "library" (as Karl called these shelves) in order. The collection of books on his own shelf was, if not so numerous as ours, at least more varied. Three of them in particular I remember, namely, a German pamphlet (minus a cover) on Manuring Cabbages in Kitchen-Gardens, a History of the Seven Years' War (bound in parchment and burnt at one corner), and a Course of Hydrostatics. Though Karl passed so much of his time in reading that he had injured his sight by doing so, he never read anything beyond these books and The Northern Bee.

Another article on Karl's shelf I remember well. This was a round piece of cardboard fastened by a screw to a wooden stand, with a sort of comic picture of a lady and a hairdresser glued to the cardboard. Karl was very clever at fixing pieces of cardboard together, and had devised this contrivance for shielding his weak eyes from any very strong light.

I can see him before me now—the tall figure in its wadded dressing-gown and red cap (a few grey hairs visible beneath the latter) sitting beside the table; the screen with the hairdresser shading his face; one hand holding a book, and the other one resting on the arm of the chair. Before him lie his watch, with a huntsman painted on the dial, a check cotton handkerchief, a round black snuff-box, and a green spectacle-case. The neatness and orderliness of all these articles show clearly that Karl Ivanitch has a clear conscience and a quiet mind.

Sometimes, when tired of running about the salon downstairs, I would steal on tiptoe to the schoolroom and find Karl sitting alone in his armchair as, with a grave and quiet expression on his face, he perused one of his favourite books. Yet sometimes, also, there were moments when he was not reading, and when the spectacles had slipped down his large aquiline nose, and the blue, half-closed eyes and faintly smiling lips seemed to be gazing before them with a curious expression. All would be quiet in the room—not a sound being audible save his regular breathing and the ticking of the watch with the hunter painted on the dial. He would not see me, and I would stand at the door and think: "Poor, poor old man! There are many of us, and we can play together and be happy, but he sits there all alone, and has nobody to be fond of him. Surely he speaks truth when he says that he is an orphan. And the story of his life, too—how terrible it is! I remember him telling it to Nicola. How dreadful to be in his position!" Then I would feel so sorry for him that I would go to him, and take his hand, and say, "Dear Karl Ivanitch!" and he would be visibly delighted whenever I spoke to him like this, and would look much brighter.

On the second wall of the schoolroom hung some maps—mostly torn, but glued together again by Karl's hand. On the third wall (in the middle of which stood the door) hung, on one side of the door, a couple of rulers (one of them ours—much bescratched, and the other one his—quite a new one), with, on the further side of the door, a blackboard on which our more serious faults were marked by circles and our lesser faults by crosses. To the left of the blackboard was the corner in which we had to kneel when naughty. How

94

well I remember that corner—the shutter on the stove, the ventilator above it, and the noise which it made when turned! Sometimes I would be made to stay in that corner till my back and knees were aching all over, and I would think to myself. "Has Karl Ivanitch forgotten me? He goes on sitting quietly in his arm-chair and reading his Hydrostatics, while I—!" Then, to remind him of my presence, I would begin gently turning the ventilator round. Or scratching some plaster off the wall; but if by chance an extra large piece fell upon the floor, the fright of it was worse than any punishment. I would glance round at Karl, but he would still be sitting there quietly, book in hand, and pretending that he had noticed nothing.

In the middle of the room stood a table, covered with a torn black oilcloth so much cut about with penknives that the edge of the table showed through. Round the table stood unpainted chairs which, through use, had attained a high degree of polish. The fourth and last wall contained three windows, from the first of which the view was as follows. Immediately beneath it there ran a high road on which every irregularity, every pebble, every rut was known and dear to me. Beside the road stretched a row of lime-trees, through which glimpses could be caught of a wattled fence, with a meadow with farm buildings on one side of it and a wood on the other—the whole bounded by the keeper's hut at the further end of the meadow. The next window to the right overlooked the part of the terrace where the "grownups" of the family used to sit before luncheon. Sometimes, when Karl was correcting our exercises, I would look out of that window and see Mamma's dark hair and the backs of some persons with her, and hear the murmur of their talking and laughter. Then I would feel vexed that I could not be there too, and think to myself, "When am I going to be grown up, and to have no more lessons, but sit with the people whom I love instead of with these horrid dialogues in my hand?" Then my anger would change to sadness, and I would fall into such a reverie that I never heard Karl when he scolded me for my mistakes.

At last, on the morning of which I am speaking, Karl Ivanitch took off his dressing-gown, put on his blue frockcoat with its creased and crumpled shoulders, adjusted his tie before the looking-glass, and took us down to greet Mamma.

II — MAMMA

Mamma was sitting in the drawing-room and making tea. In one hand she was holding the tea-pot, while with the other one she was drawing water from the urn and letting it drip into the tray. Yet though she appeared to be noticing what she doing, in reality she noted neither this fact nor our entry.

However vivid be one's recollection of the past, any attempt to recall the features of a beloved being shows them to one's vision as through a mist of tears—dim and blurred. Those tears are the tears of the imagination. When I try to recall Mamma as she was then, I see, true, her brown eyes, expressive always of love and kindness, the small mole on her neck below where the small hairs grow, her white embroidered collar, and the delicate, fresh hand which so often caressed me, and which I so often kissed; but her general appearance escapes me altogether.

To the left of the sofa stood an English piano, at which my dark-haired sister Lubotshka was sitting and playing with manifest effort (for her hands were rosy from a recent washing in cold water) Clementi's "Etudes." Then eleven years old, she was dressed in a short cotton frock and white lace-frilled trousers, and could take her octaves only in arpeggio. Beside her was sitting Maria Ivanovna, in a cap adorned with pink ribbons and a blue shawl. Her face was red and cross, and it assumed an expression even more severe when Karl Ivanitch entered the room. Looking angrily at him without answering his bow, she went on beating time with her foot and counting, "One, two, three—one, two, three," more loudly and commandingly than ever.

Karl Ivanitch paid no attention to this rudeness, but went, as usual, with German politeness to kiss Mamma's hand. She drew herself up, shook her head as though by the movement to chase away sad thoughts from her, and gave Karl her hand, kissing him on his wrinkled temple as he bent his head in salutation.

"I thank you, dear Karl Ivanitch," she said in German, and then, still using the same language asked him how we (the children) had slept. Karl Ivanitch was deaf in one ear, and the added noise of the piano now prevented him from hearing anything at all. He moved nearer to the sofa, and, leaning one hand upon the table and lifting his cap above his head, said with, a smile which in those days always seemed to me the perfection of politeness: "You, will excuse me, will you not, Natalia Nicolaevna?"

The reason for this was that, to avoid catching cold, Karl never took off his red cap, but invariably asked permission, on entering the drawing-room, to retain it on his head.

"Yes, pray replace it, Karl Ivanitch," said Mamma, bending towards him and raising her voice, "But I asked you whether the children had slept well?"

Still he did not hear, but, covering his bald head again with the red cap, went on smiling more than ever.

"Stop a moment, Mimi," said Mamma (now smiling also) to Maria Ivanovna. "It is impossible to hear anything."

How beautiful Mamma's face was when she smiled! It made her so infinitely more charming, and everything around her seemed to grow brighter! If in the more painful moments of my life I could have seen that smile before my eyes, I should never have known what grief is. In my opinion, it is in the smile of a face that the essence of what we call beauty lies. If the smile heightens the charm of the face, then the face is a beautiful one. If the smile does not alter the face, then the face is an ordinary one. But if the smile spoils the face, then the face is an ugly one indeed.

Mamma took my head between her hands, bent it gently backwards, looked at me gravely, and said: "You have been crying this morning?"

I did not answer. She kissed my eyes, and said again in German: "Why did you cry?"

When talking to us with particular intimacy she always used this language, which she knew to perfection.

"I cried about a dream, Mamma" I replied, remembering the invented vision, and trembling involuntarily at the recollection.

Karl Ivanitch confirmed my words, but said nothing as to the subject of the dream. Then, after a little conversation on the weather, in which Mimi also took part, Mamma laid some lumps of sugar on the tray for one or two of the more privileged servants, and crossed over to her embroidery frame, which stood near one of the windows.

"Go to Papa now, children," she said, "and ask him to come to me before he goes to the home farm."

Then the music, the counting, and the wrathful looks from Mimi began again, and we went off to see Papa. Passing through the room which had been known ever since Grandpapa's time as "the pantry," we entered the study.

III – PAPA

He was standing near his writing-table, and pointing angrily to some envelopes, papers, and little piles of coin upon it as he addressed some observations to the bailiff, Jakoff Michaelovitch, who was standing in his usual place (that is to say, between the door and the barometer) and rapidly closing and unclosing the fingers of the hand which he held behind his back. The more angry Papa grew, the more rapidly did those fingers twirl, and when Papa ceased speaking they came to rest also. Yet, as soon as ever Jakoff himself began to talk, they flew here, there, and everywhere with lightning rapidity. These movements always appeared to me an index of Jakoff's secret thoughts, though his face was invariably placid, and expressive alike of dignity and submissiveness, as who should say, "I am right, yet let it be as you wish." On seeing us, Papa said, "Directly—wait a moment," and looked towards the door as a hint for it to be shut.

"Gracious heavens! What can be the matter with you to-day, Jakoff?" he went on with a hitch of one shoulder (a habit of his). "This envelope here with the 800 roubles enclosed,"—Jacob took out a set of tablets, put down "800" and remained looking at the figures while he waited for what was to come next—"is for expenses during my absence. Do you understand? From the mill you ought to receive 1000 roubles. Is not that so? And from the Treasury mortgage you ought to receive some 8000 roubles. From the hay—of which, according to your calculations, we shall be able to sell 7000 poods [The pood = 40 lbs.]at 45 copecks a piece there should come in 3000. Consequently the sum-total that you ought to have in hand soon is—how much?—12,000 roubles. Is that right?"

"Precisely," answered Jakoff. Yet by the extreme rapidity with which his fingers were twitching I could see that he had an objection to make. Papa went on:

"Well, of this money you will send 10,000 roubles to the Petrovskoe local council. As for the money already at the office, you will remit it to me, and enter it as spent on this present date." Jakoff turned over the tablet marked "12,000," and put down "21,000"—seeming, by his action, to imply that 12,000 roubles had been turned over in the same fashion as he had turned the tablet. "And this envelope with the enclosed money," concluded Papa, "you will deliver for me to the person to whom it is addressed."

I was standing close to the table, and could see the address. It was "To Karl Ivanitch Mayer." Perhaps Papa had an idea that I had read something which I ought not, for he touched my shoulder with his hand and made me aware, by a slight movement, that I must withdraw from the table. Not sure whether the movement was meant for a caress or a command, I kissed the large, sinewy hand which rested upon my shoulder.

"Very well," said Jakoff. "And what are your orders about the accounts for the money from Chabarovska?" (Chabarovska was Mamma's village.)

"Only that they are to remain in my office, and not to be taken thence without my express instructions."

For a minute or two Jakoff was silent. Then his fingers began to twitch with extraordinary rapidity, and, changing the expression of deferential vacancy with which he had listened to his orders for one of shrewd intelligence, he turned his tablets back and spoke.

"Will you allow me to inform you, Peter Alexandritch," he said, with frequent pauses between his words, "that, however much you wish it, it is out of the question to repay the local council now. You enumerated some items, I think, as to what ought to come in from the mortgage, the mill, and the hay (he jotted down each of these items on his tablets again as he spoke). Yet I fear that we must have made a mistake somewhere in the accounts." Here he paused a while, and looked gravely at Papa.

"How so?"

"Well, will you be good enough to look for yourself? There is the account for the mill. The miller has been to me twice to ask for time, and I am afraid that he has no money whatever in hand. He is here now. Would you like to speak to him?"

"No. Tell me what he says," replied Papa, showing by a movement of his head that he had no desire to have speech with the miller.

"Well, it is easy enough to guess what he says. He declares that there is no grinding to be got now, and that his last remaining money has gone to pay for the dam. What good would it do for us to turn him out? As to what you were pleased to say about the mortgage, you yourself are aware that your money there is locked up and cannot be recovered at a moment's notice. I was sending a load of flour to Ivan Afanovitch to-day, and sent him a letter as well, to which he replies that he would have been glad to oblige you, Peter Alexandritch, were it not that the matter is out of his hands now, and that all the circumstances show that it would take you at least two months to withdraw the money. From the hay I understood you to estimate a return of 3000 roubles?" (Here Jakoff jotted down "3000" on his tablets, and then looked for a moment from the figures to Papa with a peculiar expression on his face.) "Well, surely you see for yourself how little that is? And even then we should lose if we were to sell the stuff now, for you must know that—"

It was clear that he would have had many other arguments to adduce had not Papa interrupted him.

"I cannot make any change in my arrangements," said Papa. "Yet if there should REALLY have to be any delay in the recovery of these sums, we could borrow what we wanted from the Chabarovska funds."

"Very well, sir." The expression of Jakoff's face and the way in which he twitched his fingers showed that this order had given him great satisfaction. He was a serf, and a most zealous, devoted one, but, like all good bailiffs, exacting and parsimonious to a degree in the interests of his master. Moreover, he had some queer notions of his own. He was forever endeavouring to increase his master's property at the expense of his mistress's, and to prove that it would be impossible to avoid using the rents from her estates for the benefit of Petrovskoe (my father's village, and the place where we lived). This point he had now gained and was delighted in consequence.

Papa then greeted ourselves, and said that if we stayed much longer in the country we should become lazy boys; that we were growing quite big now,

101

and must set about doing lessons in earnest,

"I suppose you know that I am starting for Moscow to-night?" he went on, "and that I am going to take you with me? You will live with Grandmamma, but Mamma and the girls will remain here. You know, too, I am sure, that Mamma's one consolation will be to hear that you are doing your lessons well and pleasing every one around you."

The preparations which had been in progress for some days past had made us expect some unusual event, but this news left us thunderstruck, Woloda turned red, and, with a shaking voice, delivered Mamma's message to Papa.

"So this was what my dream foreboded!" I thought to myself. "God send that there come nothing worse!" I felt terribly sorry to have to leave Mamma, but at the same rejoiced to think that I should soon be grown up, "If we are going to-day, we shall probably have no lessons to do, and that will be splendid. However, I am sorry for Karl Ivanitch, for he will certainly be dismissed now. That was why that envelope had been prepared for him. I think I would almost rather stay and do lessons here than leave Mamma or hurt poor Karl. He is miserable enough already."

As these thoughts crossed my mind I stood looking sadly at the black ribbons on my shoes. After a few words to Karl Ivanitch about the depression of the barometer and an injunction to Jakoff not to feed the hounds, since a farewell meet was to be held after luncheon, Papa disappointed my hopes by sending us off to lessons—though he also consoled us by promising to take us out hunting later.

On my way upstairs I made a digression to the terrace. Near the door leading on to it Papa's favourite hound, Milka, was lying in the sun and blinking her eyes.

"Miloshka," I cried as I caressed her and kissed her nose, "we are going away today. Good-bye. Perhaps we shall never see each other again." I was crying and laughing at the same time.

IV – LESSONS

Karl Ivanitch was in a bad temper. This was clear from his contracted brows, and from the way in which he flung his frockcoat into a drawer, angrily donned his old dressing-gown again, and made deep dints with his nails to mark the place in the book of dialogues to which we were to learn by heart. Woloda began working diligently, but I was too distracted to do anything at all. For a long while I stared vacantly at the book; but tears at the thought of the impending separation kept rushing to my eyes and preventing me from reading a single word. When at length the time came to repeat the dialogues to Karl (who listened to us with blinking eyes—a very bad sign), I had no sooner reached the place where some one asks, "Wo kommen Sie her?" ("Where do you come from?") and some one else answers him, "Ich komme vom Kaffeehaus" ("I come from the coffee-house"), than I burst into tears and, for sobbing, could not pronounce, "Haben Sie die Zeitung nicht gelesen?" ("Have you not read the newspaper?") at all. Next, when we came to our writing lesson, the tears kept falling from my eyes and, making a mess on the paper, as though some one had written on blotting-paper with water, Karl was very angry. He ordered me to go down upon my knees, declared that it was all obstinacy and "puppet-comedy playing" (a favourite expression of his) on my part, threatened me with the ruler, and commanded me to say that I was sorry. Yet for sobbing and crying I could not get a word out. At last—conscious, perhaps, that he was unjust—he departed to Nicola's pantry, and slammed the door behind him. Nevertheless their conversation there carried to the schoolroom.

"Have you heard that the children are going to Moscow, Nicola?" said Karl.

"Yes. How could I help hearing it?"

At this point Nicola seemed to get up for Karl said, "Sit down, Nicola," and then locked the door. However, I came out of my corner and crept to the door to listen.

"However much you may do for people, and however fond of them you may be, never expect any gratitude, Nicola," said Karl warmly. Nicola, who was shoe-cobbling by the window, nodded his head in assent.

"Twelve years have I lived in this house," went on Karl, lifting his eyes and his snuff-box towards the ceiling, "and before God I can say that I have loved them, and worked for them, even more than if they had been my own children. You recollect, Nicola, when Woloda had the fever? You recollect how, for nine days and nights, I never closed my eyes as I sat beside his bed? Yes, at that time I was 'the dear, good Karl Ivanitch'—I was wanted then; but now"—and he smiled ironically—"the children are growing up, and must go to study in earnest. Perhaps they never learnt anything with me, Nicola? Eh?"

"I am sure they did," replied Nicola, laying his awl down and straightening a piece of thread with his hands.

"No, I am wanted no longer, and am to be turned out. What good are promises and gratitude? Natalia Nicolaevna"—here he laid his hand upon his heart—"I love and revere, but what can SHE I do here? Her will is powerless in this house."

He flung a strip of leather on the floor with an angry gesture. "Yet I know who has been playing tricks here, and why I am no longer wanted. It is because I do not flatter and toady as certain people do. I am in the habit of speaking the truth in all places and to all persons," he continued proudly, "God be with these children, for my leaving them will benefit them little, whereas I—well, by God's help I may be able to earn a crust of bread somewhere. Nicola, eh?"

Nicola raised his head and looked at Karl as though to consider whether he would indeed be able to earn a crust of bread, but he said nothing. Karl said a great deal more of the same kind—in particular how much better his services had been appreciated at a certain general's where he had formerly lived (I regretted to hear that). Likewise he spoke of Saxony, his parents, his friend the tailor, Schonheit (beauty), and so on.

I sympathised with his distress, and felt dreadfully sorry that he and

Papa (both of whom I loved about equally) had had a difference. Then I returned to my corner, crouched down upon my heels, and fell to thinking how a reconciliation between them might be effected.

Returning to the study, Karl ordered me to get up and prepare to write from dictation. When I was ready he sat down with a dignified air in his armchair, and in a voice which seemed to come from a profound abyss began to dictate: "Von al-len Lei-den-shaf-ten die grau-samste ist. Have you written that?" He paused, took a pinch of snuff, and began again: "Die grausamste ist die Un-dank-bar-keit [The most cruel of all passions is ingratitude.] a capital U, mind."

The last word written, I looked at him, for him to go on.

"Punctum" (stop), he concluded, with a faintly perceptible smile, as he signed to us to hand him our copy-books.

Several times, and in several different tones, and always with an expression of the greatest satisfaction, did he read out that sentence, which expressed his predominant thought at the moment. Then he set us to learn a lesson in history, and sat down near the window. His face did not look so depressed now, but, on the contrary, expressed eloquently the satisfaction of a man who had avenged himself for an injury dealt him.

By this time it was a quarter to one o'clock, but Karl Ivanitch never thought of releasing us. He merely set us a new lesson to learn. My fatigue and hunger were increasing in equal proportions, so that I eagerly followed every sign of the approach of luncheon. First came the housemaid with a cloth to wipe the plates. Next, the sound of crockery resounded in the dining-room, as the table was moved and chairs placed round it. After that, Mimi, Lubotshka, and Katenka. (Katenka was Mimi's daughter, and twelve years old) came in from the garden, but Foka (the servant who always used to come and announce luncheon) was not yet to be seen. Only when he entered was it lawful to throw one's books aside and run downstairs.

Hark! Steps resounded on the staircase, but they were not Foka's. Foka's I had learnt to study, and knew the creaking of his boots well. The door opened, and a figure unknown to me made its appearance.

V – THE IDIOT

The man who now entered the room was about fifty years old, with a pale, attenuated face pitted with smallpox, long grey hair, and a scanty beard of a reddish hue. Likewise he was so tall that, on coming through the doorway, he was forced not only to bend his head, but to incline his whole body forward. He was dressed in a sort of smock that was much torn, and held in his hand a stout staff. As he entered he smote this staff upon the floor, and, contracting his brows and opening his mouth to its fullest extent, laughed in a dreadful, unnatural way. He had lost the sight of one eye, and its colourless pupil kept rolling about and imparting to his hideous face an even more repellent expression than it otherwise bore.

"Hullo, you are caught!" he exclaimed as he ran to Woloda with little short steps and, seizing him round the head, looked at it searchingly. Next he left him, went to the table, and, with a perfectly serious expression on his face, began to blow under the oil-cloth, and to make the sign of the cross over it, "O-oh, what a pity! O-oh, how it hurts! They are angry! They fly from me!" he exclaimed in a tearful choking voice as he glared at Woloda and wiped away the streaming tears with his sleeve. His voice was harsh and rough, all his movements hysterical and spasmodic, and his words devoid of sense or connection (for he used no conjunctions). Yet the tone of that voice was so heartrending, and his yellow, deformed face at times so sincere and pitiful in its expression, that, as one listened to him, it was impossible to repress a mingled sensation of pity, grief, and fear.

This was the idiot Grisha. Whence he had come, or who were his parents, or what had induced him to choose the strange life which he led, no one ever knew. All that I myself knew was that from his fifteenth year upwards he had been known as an imbecile who went barefooted both in winter and summer, visited convents, gave little images to any one who cared to take them, and spoke meaningless words which some people took for prophecies; that nobody remembered him as being different; that, at rare intervals he used to call at Grandmamma's house; and that by some people he was said to be the outcast son of rich parents and a pure, saintly soul, while others averred that he was a mere peasant and an idler.

At last the punctual and wished-for Foka arrived, and we went downstairs. Grisha followed us sobbing and continuing to talk nonsense, and knocking his staff on each step of the staircase. When we entered the drawing-room we found Papa and Mamma walking up and down there, with their hands clasped in each other's, and talking in low tones. Maria Ivanovna was sitting bolt upright in an arm-chair placed at tight angles to the sofa, and giving some sort of a lesson to the two girls sitting beside her. When Karl Ivanitch entered the room she looked at him for a moment, and then turned her eyes away with an expression which seemed to say, "You are beneath my notice, Karl Ivanitch." It was easy to see from the girls' eyes that they had important news to communicate to us as soon as an opportunity occurred (for to leave their seats and approach us first was contrary to Mimi's rules). It was for us to go to her and say, "Bon jour, Mimi," and then make her a low bow; after which we should possibly be permitted to enter into conversation with the girls.

What an intolerable creature that Mimi was! One could hardly say a word in her presence without being found fault with. Also whenever we wanted to speak in Russian, she would say, "Parlez, donc, francais," as though on purpose to annoy us, while, if there was any particularly nice dish at luncheon which we wished to enjoy in peace, she would keep on ejaculating, "Mangez, donc, avec du pain!" or, "Comment est-ce que vous tenez votre fourchette?" "What has SHE got to do with us?" I used to think to myself. "Let her teach the girls. WE have our Karl Ivanitch." I shared to the full his dislike of "certain people."

"Ask Mamma to let us go hunting too," Katenka whispered to me, as she caught me by the sleeve just when the elders of the family were making a move towards the dining-room.

"Very well. I will try."

Grisha likewise took a seat in the dining-room, but at a little table apart from the rest. He never lifted his eyes from his plate, but kept on sighing and making horrible grimaces, as he muttered to himself: "What a pity! It has flown away! The dove is flying to heaven! The stone lies on the tomb!" and so forth.

Ever since the morning Mamma had been absent-minded, and Grisha's presence, words, and actions seemed to make her more so.

"By the way, there is something I forgot to ask you," she said, as she handed Papa a plate of soup.

"What is it?"

"That you will have those dreadful dogs of yours tied up. They nearly worried poor Grisha to death when he entered the courtyard, and I am sure they will bite the children some day."

No sooner did Grisha hear himself mentioned that he turned towards our table and showed us his torn clothes. Then, as he went on with his meal, he said: "He would have let them tear me in pieces, but God would not allow it! What a sin to let the dogs loose—a great sin! But do not beat him, master; do not beat him! It is for God to forgive! It is past now!"

"What does he say?" said Papa, looking at him gravely and sternly. "I cannot understand him at all."

"I think he is saying," replied Mamma, "that one of the huntsmen set the dogs on him, but that God would not allow him to be torn in pieces. Therefore he begs you not to punish the man."

"Oh, is that it?" said Papa, "How does he know that I intended to punish the huntsman? You know, I am not very fond of fellows like this," he added in French, "and this one offends me particularly. Should it ever happen that—"

"Oh, don't say so," interrupted Mamma, as if frightened by some thought. "How can you know what he is?"

"I think I have plenty of opportunities for doing so, since no lack of them come to see you—all of them the same sort, and probably all with the same story."

I could see that Mamma's opinion differed from his, but that she did not mean to quarrel about it.

"Please hand me the cakes," she said to him, "Are they good to-day or not?"

"Yes, I AM angry," he went on as he took the cakes and put them where Mamma could not reach them, "very angry at seeing supposedly reasonable and educated people let themselves be deceived," and he struck the table with his fork.

"I asked you to hand me the cakes," she repeated with outstretched hand.

"And it is a good thing," Papa continued as he put the hand aside, "that the police run such vagabonds in. All they are good for is to play upon the nerves of certain people who are already not over-strong in that respect," and he smiled, observing that Mamma did not like the conversation at all. However, he handed her the cakes.

"All that I have to say," she replied, "is that one can hardly believe that a man who, though sixty years of age, goes barefooted winter and summer, and always wears chains of two pounds' weight, and never accepts the offers made to him to live a quiet, comfortable life—it is difficult to believe that such a man should act thus out of laziness." Pausing a moment, she added with a sigh: "As to predictions, je suis payee pour y croire, I told you, I think, that Grisha prophesied the very day and hour of poor Papa's death?"

"Oh, what HAVE you gone and done?" said Papa, laughing and putting his hand to his cheek (whenever he did this I used to look for something particularly comical from him). "Why did you call my attention to his feet? I looked at them, and now can eat nothing more."

Luncheon was over now, and Lubotshka and Katenka were winking at us, fidgeting about in their chairs, and showing great restlessness. The winking, of course, signified, "Why don't you ask whether we too may go to the hunt?" I nudged Woloda, and Woloda nudged me back, until at last I took heart of grace, and began (at first shyly, but gradually with more assurance) to ask if it would matter much if the girls too were allowed to enjoy the sport. Thereupon a consultation was held among the elder folks, and eventually leave was granted—Mamma, to make things still more delightful, saying that she would come too.

VI — PREPARATIONS FOR THE CHASE

During dessert Jakoff had been sent for, and orders given him to have ready the carriage, the hounds, and the saddle-horses—every detail being minutely specified, and every horse called by its own particular name. As Woloda's usual mount was lame, Papa ordered a "hunter" to be saddled for him; which term, "hunter" so horrified Mamma's ears, that she imagined it to be some kind of an animal which would at once run away and bring about Woloda's death. Consequently, in spite of all Papa's and Woloda's assurances (the latter glibly affirming that it was nothing, and that he liked his horse to go fast), poor Mamma continued to exclaim that her pleasure would be quite spoilt for her.

When luncheon was over, the grown-ups had coffee in the study, while we younger ones ran into the garden and went chattering along the undulating paths with their carpet of yellow leaves. We talked about Woloda's riding a hunter and said what a shame it was that Lubotshka, could not run as fast as Katenka, and what fun it would be if we could see Grisha's chains, and so forth; but of the impending separation we said not a word. Our chatter was interrupted by the sound of the carriage driving up, with a village urchin perched on each of its springs. Behind the carriage rode the huntsmen with the hounds, and they, again, were followed by the groom Ignat on the steed intended for Woloda, with my old horse trotting alongside. After running to the garden fence to get a sight of all these interesting objects, and indulging in a chorus of whistling and hallooing, we rushed upstairs to dress—our one aim being to make ourselves look as like the huntsmen as possible. The obvious way to do this was to tuck one's breeches inside one's boots. We lost no time over it all, for we were in a hurry to run to the entrance steps again there to feast our eyes upon the horses and hounds, and to have a chat with the huntsmen. The day was exceedingly warm while, though clouds of fantastic shape had been gathering on the horizon since morning and driving before a light breeze across the sun, it was clear that, for all their menacing blackness, they did not really intend to form a thunderstorm and spoil our last day's pleasure. Moreover, towards afternoon some of them broke, grew pale and elongated, and sank to the horizon again, while others of them changed to the likeness of white transparent fish-scales. In the east, over Maslovska, a single lurid mass was louring, but Karl Ivanitch (who always seemed to know the ways of the heavens) said that the weather would still continue to be fair and dry.

In spite of his advanced years, it was in quite a sprightly manner that Foka came out to the entrance steps, to give the order "Drive up." In fact, as he planted his legs firmly apart and took up his station between the lowest step and the spot where the coachman was to halt, his mien was that of a man who knew his duties and had no need to be reminded of them by anybody. Presently the ladies, also came out, and after a little discussions as to seats and the safety of the girls (all of which seemed to me wholly superfluous), they settled themselves in the vehicle, opened their parasols, and started. As the carriage was, driving away, Mamma pointed to the hunter and asked nervously "Is that the horse intended for Vladimir Petrovitch?" On the groom answering in the affirmative, she raised her hands in horror and turned her head away. As for myself, I was burning with impatience. Clambering on to the back of my steed (I was just tall enough to see between its ears), I proceeded to perform evolutions in the courtyard.

"Mind you don't ride over the hounds, sir," said one of the huntsmen.

"Hold your tongue. It is not the first time I have been one of the party." I retorted with dignity.

Although Woloda had plenty of pluck, he was not altogether free from apprehensions as he sat on the hunter. Indeed, he more than once asked as he patted it, "Is he quiet?" He looked very well on horseback—almost a grown-up young man, and held himself so upright in the saddle that I envied him since my shadow seemed to show that I could not compare with him in looks.

Presently Papa's footsteps sounded on the flagstones, the whip collected the hounds, and the huntsmen mounted their steeds. Papa's horse came up in charge of a groom, the hounds of his particular leash sprang up from their picturesque attitudes to fawn upon him, and Milka, in a collar studded with beads, came bounding joyfully from behind his heels to greet and sport with the other dogs. Finally, as soon as Papa had mounted we rode away.

VII — THE HUNT

AT the head of the cavalcade rode Turka, on a hog-backed roan. On his head he wore a shaggy cap, while, with a magnificent horn slung across his shoulders and a knife at his belt, he looked so cruel and inexorable that one would have thought he was going to engage in bloody strife with his fellow men rather than to hunt a small animal. Around the hind legs of his horse the hounds gambolled like a cluster of checkered, restless balls. If one of them wished to stop, it was only with the greatest difficulty that it could do so, since not only had its leash-fellow also to be induced to halt, but at once one of the huntsmen would wheel round, crack his whip, and shout to the delinquent,

"Back to the pack, there!"

Arrived at a gate, Papa told us and the huntsmen to continue our way along the road, and then rode off across a cornfield. The harvest was at its height. On the further side of a large, shining, yellow stretch of cornland lay a high purple belt of forest which always figured in my eyes as a distant, mysterious region behind which either the world ended or an uninhabited waste began. This expanse of corn-land was dotted with swathes and reapers, while along the lanes where the sickle had passed could be seen the backs of women as they stooped among the tall, thick grain or lifted armfuls of corn and rested them against the shocks. In one corner a woman was bending over a cradle, and the whole stubble was studded with sheaves and cornflowers. In another direction shirt-sleeved men were standing on waggons, shaking the soil from the stalks of sheaves, and stacking them for carrying. As soon as the foreman (dressed in a blouse and high boots, and carrying a tally-stick) caught sight of Papa, he hastened to take off his lamb's-wool cap and, wiping his red head, told the women to get up. Papa's chestnut horse went trotting along with a prancing gait as it tossed its head and swished its tail to and fro to drive away the gadflies and countless other insects which tormented its flanks, while his two greyhounds—their tails curved like sickles—went springing gracefully over the stubble. Milka was always first, but every now and then she would halt with a shake of her head to await the whipper-in. The chatter of the peasants; the rumbling of horses and waggons; the joyous cries of quails; the hum of insects as they hung suspended in the motionless air; the smell of the soil and grain and steam from our horses; the thousand different lights and shadows which the burning sun cast upon the yellowish-white cornland; the purple forest in the distance; the white gossamer threads which were floating in the air or resting on the soil-all these things I observed and heard and felt to the core.

Arrived at the Kalinovo wood, we found the carriage awaiting us there, with, beside it, a one-horse waggonette driven by the butler—a waggonette in which were a tea-urn, some apparatus for making ices, and many other attractive boxes and bundles, all packed in straw! There was no mistaking these signs, for they meant that we were going to have tea, fruit, and ices in the open air. This afforded us intense delight, since to drink tea in a wood and on the grass and where none else had ever drunk tea before seemed to us a treat beyond expressing.

When Turka arrived at the little clearing where the carriage was halted he took Papa's detailed instructions as to how we were to divide ourselves and where each of us was to go (though, as a matter of fact, he never acted according to such instructions, but always followed his own devices). Then he unleashed the hounds, fastened the leashes to his saddle, whistled to the pack, and disappeared among the young birch trees the liberated hounds jumping about him in high delight, wagging their tails, and sniffing and gambolling with one another as they dispersed themselves in different directions.

"Has anyone a pocket-handkerchief to spare?" asked Papa. I took mine from my pocket and offered it to him.

"Very well. Fasten it to this greyhound here."

"Gizana?" I asked, with the air of a connoisseur.

"Yes. Then run him along the road with you. When you come to a little clearing in the wood stop and look about you, and don't come back to me

114

without a hare."

Accordingly I tied my handkerchief round Gizana's soft neck, and set off running at full speed towards the appointed spot, Papa laughing as he shouted after me, "Hurry up, hurry up or you'll be late!"

Every now and then Gizana kept stopping, pricking up his ears, and listening to the hallooing of the beaters. Whenever he did this I was not strong enough to move him, and could do no more than shout, "Come on, come on!" Presently he set off so fast that I could not restrain him, and I encountered more than one fall before we reached our destination. Selecting there a level, shady spot near the roots of a great oak-tree, I lay down on the turf, made Gizana crouch beside me, and waited. As usual, my imagination far outstripped reality. I fancied that I was pursuing at least my third hare when, as a matter of fact, the first hound was only just giving tongue. Presently, however, Turka's voice began to sound through the wood in louder and more excited tones, the baying of a hound came nearer and nearer, and then another, and then a third, and then a fourth, deep throat joined in the rising and falling cadences of a chorus, until the whole had united their voices in one continuous, tumultuous burst of melody. As the Russian proverb expresses it, "The forest had found a tongue, and the hounds were burning as with fire."

My excitement was so great that I nearly swooned where I stood. My lips parted themselves as though smiling, the perspiration poured from me in streams, and, in spite of the tickling sensation caused by the drops as they trickled over my chin, I never thought of wiping them away. I felt that a crisis was approaching. Yet the tension was too unnatural to last. Soon the hounds came tearing along the edge of the wood, and then—behold, they were racing away from me again, and of hares there was not a sign to be seen! I looked in every direction and Gizana did the same—pulling at his leash at first and whining. Then he lay down again by my side, rested his muzzle on my knees, and resigned himself to disappointment. Among the naked roots of the oak-tree under which I was sitting. I could see countless ants swarming over the parched grey earth and winding among the acorns, withered oak-leaves, dry twigs, russet moss, and slender, scanty blades of grass. In serried files they kept pressing forward on the level track they had made for themselves—some carrying burdens, some not. I took a piece of twig and barred their way. Instantly it was curious to see how they made light of the obstacle. Some got past it by creeping underneath, and some by climbing over it. A few, however, there were (especially those weighted with loads) who were nonplussed what to do. They either halted and searched for a way round, or returned whence they had come, or climbed the adjacent herbage, with the evident intention of reaching my hand and going up the sleeve of my jacket. From this interesting spectacle my attention was distracted by the yellow wings of a butterfly which was fluttering alluringly before me. Yet I had scarcely noticed it before it flew away to a little distance and, circling over some half-faded blossoms of white clover, settled on one of them. Whether it was the sun's warmth that delighted it, or whether it was busy sucking nectar from the flower, at all events it seemed thoroughly comfortable. It scarcely moved its wings at all, and pressed itself down into the clover until I could hardly see its body. I sat with my chin on my hands and watched it with intense interest.

Suddenly Gizana sprang up and gave me such a violent jerk that I nearly rolled over. I looked round. At the edge of the wood a hare had just come into view, with one ear bent down and the other one sharply pricked. The blood rushed to my head, and I forgot everything else as I shouted, slipped the dog, and rushed towards the spot. Yet all was in vain. The hare stopped, made a rush, and was lost to view.

How confused I felt when at that moment Turka stepped from the undergrowth (he had been following the hounds as they ran along the edges of the wood)! He had seen my mistake (which had consisted in my not biding my time), and now threw me a contemptuous look as he said, "Ah, master!" And you should have heard the tone in which he said it! It would have been a relief to me if he had then and there suspended me to his saddle instead of the hare. For a while I could only stand miserably where I was, without attempting to recall the dog, and ejaculate as I slapped my knees, "Good heavens! What a fool I was!" I could hear the hounds retreating into the distance, and baying along the further side of the wood as they pursued the hare, while Turka rallied them with blasts on his gorgeous horn: yet I did not stir.

VIII — WE PLAY GAMES

THE hunt was over, a cloth had been spread in the shade of some young birch-trees, and the whole party was disposed around it. The butler, Gabriel, had stamped down the surrounding grass, wiped the plates in readiness, and unpacked from a basket a quantity of plums and peaches wrapped in leaves.

Through the green branches of the young birch-trees the sun glittered and threw little glancing balls of light upon the pattern of my napkin, my legs, and the bald moist head of Gabriel. A soft breeze played in the leaves of the trees above us, and, breathing softly upon my hair and heated face, refreshed me beyond measure. When we had finished the fruit and ices, nothing remained to be done around the empty cloth, so, despite the oblique, scorching rays of the sun, we rose and proceeded to play.

"Well, what shall it be?" said Lubotshka, blinking in the sunlight and skipping about the grass, "Suppose we play Robinson?"

"No, that's a tiresome game," objected Woloda, stretching himself lazily on the turf and gnawing some leaves, "Always Robinson! If you want to play at something, play at building a summerhouse."

Woloda was giving himself tremendous airs. Probably he was proud of having ridden the hunter, and so pretended to be very tired. Perhaps, also, he had too much hard-headedness and too little imagination fully to enjoy the game of Robinson. It was a game which consisted of performing various scenes from The Swiss Family Robinson, a book which we had recently been reading.

"Well, but be a good boy. Why not try and please us this time?" the girls answered. "You may be Charles or Ernest or the father, whichever you like best," added Katenka as she tried to raise him from the ground by pulling at his sleeve.

"No, I'm not going to; it's a tiresome game," said Woloda again, though smiling as if secretly pleased.

"It would be better to sit at home than not to play at ANYTHING," murmured Lubotshka, with tears in her eyes. She was a great weeper.

"Well, go on, then. Only, DON'T cry; I can't stand that sort of thing."

Woloda's condescension did not please us much. On the contrary, his lazy, tired expression took away all the fun of the game. When we sat on the ground and imagined that we were sitting in a boat and either fishing or rowing with all our might, Woloda persisted in sitting with folded hands or in anything but a fisherman's posture. I made a remark about it, but he replied that, whether we moved our hands or not, we should neither gain nor lose ground—certainly not advance at all, and I was forced to agree with him. Again, when I pretended to go out hunting, and, with a stick over my shoulder, set off into the wood, Woloda only lay down on his back with his hands under his head, and said that he supposed it was all the same whether he went or not. Such behaviour and speeches cooled our ardour for the game and were very disagreeable—the more so since it was impossible not to confess to oneself that Woloda was right, I myself knew that it was not only impossible to kill birds with a stick, but to shoot at all with such a weapon. Still, it was the game, and if we were once to begin reasoning thus, it would become equally impossible for us to go for drives on chairs. I think that even Woloda himself cannot at that moment have forgotten how, in the long winter evenings, we had been used to cover an arm-chair with a shawl and make a carriage of it—one of us being the coachman, another one the footman, the two girls the passengers, and three other chairs the trio of horses abreast. With what ceremony we used to set out, and with what adventures we used to meet on the way! How gaily and quickly those long winter evenings used to pass! If we were always to judge from reality, games would be nonsense; but if games were nonsense, what else would there be left to do?

IX — A FIRST ESSAY IN LOVE

PRETENDING to gather some "American fruit" from a tree, Lubotshka suddenly plucked a leaf upon which was a huge caterpillar, and throwing the insect with horror to the ground, lifted her hands and sprang away as though afraid it would spit at her. The game stopped, and we crowded our heads together as we stooped to look at the curiosity.

I peeped over Katenka's shoulder as she was trying to lift the caterpillar by placing another leaf in its way. I had observed before that the girls had a way of shrugging their shoulders whenever they were trying to put a loose garment straight on their bare necks, as well as that Mimi always grew angry on witnessing this manoeuvre and declared it to be a chambermaid's trick. As Katenka bent over the caterpillar she made that very movement, while at the same instant the breeze lifted the fichu on her white neck. Her shoulder was close to my lips, I looked at it and kissed it. She did not turn round, but Woloda remarked without raising his head, "What spooniness!" I felt the tears rising to my eyes, and could not take my gaze from Katenka. I had long been used to her fair, fresh face, and had always been fond of her, but now I looked at her more closely, and felt more fond of her, than I had ever done or felt before.

When we returned to the grown-ups, Papa informed us, to our great joy, that, at Mamma's entreaties, our departure was to be postponed until the following morning. We rode home beside the carriage—Woloda and I galloping near it, and vieing with one another in our exhibition of horsemanship and daring. My shadow looked longer now than it had done before, and from that I judged that I had grown into a fine rider. Yet my complacency was soon marred by an unfortunate occurrence. Desiring to outdo Woloda before the audience in the carriage, I dropped a little behind. Then with whip and spur I urged my steed forward, and at the same time assumed a natural, graceful attitude, with the intention of whooting past the carriage on the side on which Katenka was seated. My only doubt was whether to halloo or not as I did so. In the event, my infernal horse stopped so abruptly when just level with the carriage horses that I was pitched forward on to its neck and cut a very sorry figure!

X – THE SORT OF MAN MY FATHER WAS

Papa was a gentleman of the last century, with all the chivalrous character, self-reliance, and gallantry of the youth of that time. Upon the men of the present day he looked with a contempt arising partly from inborn pride and partly from a secret feeling of vexation that, in this age of ours, he could no longer enjoy the influence and success which had been his in his youth. His two principal failings were gambling and gallantry, and he had won or lost, in the course of his career, several millions of roubles.

Tall and of imposing figure, he walked with a curiously quick, mincing gait, as well as had a habit of hitching one of his shoulders. His eyes were small and perpetually twinkling, his nose large and aquiline, his lips irregular and rather oddly (though pleasantly) compressed, his articulation slightly defective and lisping, and his head quite bald. Such was my father's exterior from the days of my earliest recollection. It was an exterior which not only brought him success and made him a man a bonnes fortunes but one which pleased people of all ranks and stations. Especially did it please those whom he desired to please.

At all junctures he knew how to take the lead, for, though not deriving from the highest circles of society, he had always mixed with them, and knew how to win their respect. He possessed in the highest degree that measure of pride and self-confidence which, without giving offence, maintains a man in the opinion of the world. He had much originality, as well as the ability to use it in such a way that it benefited him as much as actual worldly position or fortune could have done. Nothing in the universe could surprise him, and though not of eminent attainments in life, he seemed born to have acquired them. He understood so perfectly how to make both himself and others forget and keep at a distance the seamy side of life, with all its petty troubles and vicissitudes, that it was impossible not to envy him. He was a connoisseur in everything which could give ease and pleasure, as well as knew how to make use of such knowledge. Likewise he prided himself on the brilliant connections which he had formed through my mother's family or through friends of his youth, and was secretly jealous of any one of a higher rank than himself—any one, that is to say, of a rank higher than a retired lieutenant of the Guards. Moreover, like all ex-officers, he refused to dress himself in the prevailing fashion, though he attired himself both originally and artistically—his invariable wear being light, loose-fitting suits, very fine shirts, and large collars and cuffs. Everything seemed to suit his upright figure and quiet, assured air. He was sensitive to the pitch of sentimentality, and, when reading a pathetic passage, his voice would begin to tremble and the tears to come into his eyes, until he had to lay the book aside. Likewise he was fond of music, and could accompany himself on the piano as he sang the love songs of his friend A— or gipsy songs or themes from operas; but he had no love for serious music, and would frankly flout received opinion by declaring that, whereas Beethoven's sonatas wearied him and sent him to sleep, his ideal of beauty was "Do not wake me, youth" as Semenoff sang it, or "Not one" as the gipsy Taninsha rendered that ditty. His nature was essentially one of those which follow public opinion concerning what is good, and consider only that good which the public declares to be so. [It may be noted that the author has said earlier in the chapter that his father possessed "much originality."] God only knows whether he had any moral convictions. His life was so full of amusement that probably he never had time to form any, and was too successful ever to feel the lack of them.

As he grew to old age he looked at things always from a fixed point of view, and cultivated fixed rules—but only so long as that point or those rules coincided with expediency. The mode of life which offered some passing degree of interest—that, in his opinion, was the right one and the only one that men ought to affect. He had great fluency of argument; and this, I think, increased the adaptability of his morals and enabled him to speak of one and the same act, now as good, and now, with abuse, as abominable.

XI – IN THE DRAWING-ROOM AND THE STUDY

Twilight had set in when we reached home. Mamma sat down to the piano, and we to a table, there to paint and draw in colours and pencil. Though I had only one cake of colour, and it was blue, I determined to draw a picture of the hunt. In exceedingly vivid fashion I painted a blue boy on a blue horse, and—but here I stopped, for I was uncertain whether it was possible also to paint a blue HARE. I ran to the study to consult Papa, and as he was busy reading he never lifted his eyes from his book when I asked, "Can there be blue hares?" but at once replied, "There can, my boy, there can." Returning to the table I painted in my blue hare, but subsequently thought it better to change it into a blue bush. Yet the blue bush did not wholly please me, so I changed it into a tree, and then into a rick, until, the whole paper having now become one blur of blue, I tore it angrily in pieces, and went off to meditate in the large arm-chair.

Mamma was playing Field's second concerto. Field, it may be said, had been her master. As I dozed, the music brought up before my imagination a kind of luminosity, with transparent dream-shapes. Next she played the "Sonate Pathetique" of Beethoven, and I at once felt heavy, depressed, and apprehensive. Mamma often played those two pieces, and therefore I well recollect the feelings they awakened in me. Those feelings were a reminiscence—of what? Somehow I seemed to remember something which had never been.

Opposite to me lay the study door, and presently I saw Jakoff enter it, accompanied by several long-bearded men in kaftans. Then the door shut again.

"Now they are going to begin some business or other," I thought. I believed the affairs transacted in that study to be the most important ones on earth. This opinion was confirmed by the fact that people only approached the door of that room on tiptoe and speaking in whispers. Presently Papa's resonant voice sounded within, and I also scented cigar smoke—always a very attractive thing to me. Next, as I dozed, I suddenly heard a creaking of boots that I knew, and, sure enough, saw Karl Ivanitch go on tiptoe, and with a depressed, but resolute, expression on his face and a written document in his hand, to the study door and knock softly. It opened, and then shut again behind him.

"I hope nothing is going to happen," I mused. "Karl Ivanitch is offended, and might be capable of anything—" and again I dozed off.

Nevertheless something DID happen. An hour later I was disturbed by the same creaking of boots, and saw Karl come out, and disappear up the stairs, wiping away a few tears from his cheeks with his pocket handkerchief as he went and muttering something between his teeth. Papa came out behind him and turned aside into the drawing-room.

"Do you know what I have just decided to do?" he asked gaily as he laid a hand upon Mamma's shoulder.

"What, my love?"

"To take Karl Ivanitch with the children. There will be room enough for him in the carriage. They are used to him, and he seems greatly attached to them. Seven hundred roubles a year cannot make much difference to us, and the poor devil is not at all a bad sort of a fellow." I could not understand why Papa should speak of him so disrespectfully.

"I am delighted," said Mamma, "and as much for the children's sake as his own. He is a worthy old man."

"I wish you could have seen how moved he was when I told him that he might look upon the 500 roubles as a present! But the most amusing thing of all is this bill which he has just handed me. It is worth seeing," and with a smile Papa gave Mamma a paper inscribed in Karl's handwriting. "Is it not capital?" he concluded.

The contents of the paper were as follows: [The joke of this bill consists chiefly in its being written in very bad Russian, with continual mistakes as to plural and singular, prepositions and so forth.]

"Two book for the children—70 copeck. Coloured paper, gold frames, and a pop-guns, blockheads [This word has a double meaning in Russian.] for cutting out several box for presents—6 roubles, 55 copecks. Several book and a bows, presents for the childrens—8 roubles, 16 copecks. A gold watches promised to me by Peter Alexandrovitch out of Moscow, in the years 18— for 140 roubles. Consequently Karl Mayer have to receive 139 rouble, 79 copecks, beside his wage."

If people were to judge only by this bill (in which Karl Ivanitch demanded repayment of all the money he had spent on presents, as well as the value of a present promised to himself), they would take him to have been a callous, avaricious egotist yet they would be wrong.

It appears that he had entered the study with the paper in his hand and a set speech in his head, for the purpose of declaiming eloquently to Papa on the subject of the wrongs which he believed himself to have suffered in our house, but that, as soon as ever he began to speak in the vibratory voice and with the expressive intonations which he used in dictating to us, his eloquence wrought upon himself more than upon Papa; with the result that, when he came to the point where he had to say, "however sad it will be for me to part with the children," he lost his self-command utterly, his articulation became choked, and he was obliged to draw his coloured pocket-handkerchief from his pocket.

"Yes, Peter Alexandrovitch," he said, weeping (this formed no part of the prepared speech), "I am grown so used to the children that I cannot think what I should do without them. I would rather serve you without salary than not at all," and with one hand he wiped his eyes, while with the other he presented the bill.

Although I am convinced that at that moment Karl Ivanitch was speaking with absolute sincerity (for I know how good his heart was), I confess that never to this day have I been able quite to reconcile his words with the bill.

"Well, if the idea of leaving us grieves you, you may be sure that the idea of dismissing you grieves me equally," said Papa, tapping him on the shoulder. Then, after a pause, he added, "But I have changed my mind, and you shall not leave us."

Just before supper Grisha entered the room. Ever since he had entered the house that day he had never ceased to sigh and weep—a portent, according to those who believed in his prophetic powers, that misfortune was impending for the household. He had now come to take leave of us, for to-morrow (so he said) he must be moving on. I nudged Woloda, and we moved towards the door.

"What is the matter?" he said.

"This—that if we want to see Grisha's chains we must go upstairs at once to the men-servants' rooms. Grisha is to sleep in the second one, so we can sit in the store-room and see everything."

"All right. Wait here, and I'll tell the girls."

The girls came at once, and we ascended the stairs, though the question as to which of us should first enter the store-room gave us some little trouble. Then we cowered down and waited.

XII – GRISHA

WE all felt a little uneasy in the thick darkness, so we pressed close to one another and said nothing. Before long Grisha arrived with his soft tread, carrying in one hand his staff and in the other a tallow candle set in a brass candlestick. We scarcely ventured to breathe.

"Our Lord Jesus Christ! Holy Mother of God! Father, Son, and Holy Ghost!" he kept repeating, with the different intonations and abbreviations which gradually become peculiar to persons who are accustomed to pronounce the words with great frequency.

Still praying, he placed his staff in a corner and looked at the bed; after which he began to undress. Unfastening his old black girdle, he slowly divested himself of his torn nankeen kaftan, and deposited it carefully on the back of a chair. His face had now lost its usual disquietude and idiocy. On the contrary, it had in it something restful, thoughtful, and even grand, while all his movements were deliberate and intelligent.

Next, he lay down quietly in his shirt on the bed, made the sign of the cross towards every side of him, and adjusted his chains beneath his shirt—an operation which, as we could see from his face, occasioned him considerable pain. Then he sat up again, looked gravely at his ragged shirt, and rising and taking the candle, lifted the latter towards the shrine where the images of the saints stood. That done, he made the sign of the cross again, and turned the candle upside down, when it went out with a hissing noise.

Through the window (which overlooked the wood) the moon (nearly full) was shining in such a way that one side of the tall white figure of the idiot stood out in the pale, silvery moonlight, while the other side was lost in the dark shadow which covered the floor, walls, and ceiling. In the courtyard the watchman was tapping at intervals upon his brass alarm plate. For a while Grisha stood silently before the images and, with his large hands pressed to his breast and his head bent forward, gave occasional sighs. Then with difficulty he knelt down and began to pray.

At first he repeated some well-known prayers, and only accented a word here and there. Next, he repeated thee same prayers, but louder and with increased accentuation. Lastly he repeated them again and with even greater emphasis, as well as with an evident effort to pronounce them in the old Slavonic Church dialect. Though disconnected, his prayers were very touching. He prayed for all his benefactors (so he called every one who had received him hospitably), with, among them, Mamma and ourselves. Next he prayed for himself, and besought God to forgive him his sins, at the same time repeating, "God forgive also my enemies!" Then, moaning with the effort, he rose from his knees—only to fall to the floor again and repeat his phrases afresh. At last he regained his feet, despite the weight of the chains, which rattled loudly whenever they struck the floor.

Woloda pinched me rudely in the leg, but I took no notice of that (except that I involuntarily touched the place with my hand), as I observed with a feeling of childish astonishment, pity, and respect the words and gestures of Grisha. Instead of the laughter and amusement which I had expected on entering the store-room, I felt my heart beating and overcome.

Grisha continued for some time in this state of religious ecstasy as he improvised prayers and repeated again and yet again, "Lord, have mercy upon me!" Each time that he said, "Pardon me, Lord, and teach me to do what Thou wouldst have done," he pronounced the words with added earnestness and emphasis, as though he expected an immediate answer to his petition, and then fell to sobbing and moaning once more. Finally, he went down on his knees again, folded his arms upon his breast, and remained silent. I ventured to put my head round the door (holding my breath as I did so), but Grisha still made no movement except for the heavy sighs which heaved his breast. In the moonlight I could see a tear glistening on the white patch of his blind eye.

"Yes, Thy will be done!" he exclaimed suddenly, with an expression which I cannot describe, as, prostrating himself with his forehead on the floor, he fell to sobbing like a child.

Much sand has run out since then, many recollections of the past have faded from my memory or become blurred in indistinct visions, and poor Grisha himself has long since reached the end of his pilgrimage; but the impression which he produced upon me, and the feelings which he aroused in my breast, will never leave my mind. O truly Christian Grisha, your faith was so strong that you could feel the actual presence of God; your love so great that the words fell of themselves from your lips. You had no reason to prove them, for you did so with your earnest praises of His majesty as you fell to the ground speechless and in tears!

Nevertheless the sense of awe with which I had listened to Grisha could not last for ever. I had now satisfied my curiosity, and, being cramped with sitting in one position so long, desired to join in the tittering and fun which I could hear going on in the dark store-room behind me. Some one took my hand and whispered, "Whose hand is this?" Despite the darkness, I knew by the touch and the low voice in my ear that it was Katenka. I took her by the arm, but she withdrew it, and, in doing so, pushed a cane chair which was standing near. Grisha lifted his head looked quietly about him, and, muttering a prayer, rose and made the sign of the cross towards each of the four corners of the room.

XIII — NATALIA SAVISHNA

In days gone by there used to run about the seignorial courtyard of the country-house at Chabarovska a girl called Natashka. She always wore a cotton dress, went barefooted, and was rosy, plump, and gay. It was at the request and entreaties of her father, the clarionet player Savi, that my grandfather had "taken her upstairs"—that is to say, made her one of his wife's female servants. As chamber-maid, Natashka so distinguished herself by her zeal and amiable temper that when Mamma arrived as a baby and required a nurse Natashka was honoured with the charge of her. In this new office the girl earned still further praises and rewards for her activity, trustworthiness, and devotion to her young mistress. Soon, however, the powdered head and buckled shoes of the young and active footman Foka (who had frequent opportunities of courting her, since they were in the same service) captivated her unsophisticated, but loving, heart. At last she ventured to go and ask my grandfather if she might marry Foka, but her master took the request in bad part, flew into a passion, and punished poor Natashka by exiling her to a farm which he owned in a remote quarter of the Steppes. At length, when she had been gone six months and nobody could be found to replace her, she was recalled to her former duties. Returned, and with her dress in rags, she fell at Grandpapa's feet, and besought him to restore her his favour and kindness, and to forget the folly of which she had been guilty—folly which, she assured him, should never recur again. And she kept her word.

From that time forth she called herself, not Natashka, but Natalia Savishna, and took to wearing a cap. All the love in her heart was now bestowed upon her young charge. When Mamma had a governess appointed for her education, Natalia was awarded the keys as housekeeper, and henceforth had the linen and provisions under her care. These new duties she fulfilled with equal fidelity and zeal. She lived only for her master's advantage. Everything in which she could detect fraud, extravagance, or waste she endeavoured to remedy to the best of her power. When Mamma married and wished in some way to reward Natalia Savishna for her twenty years of care and labour, she sent for her and, voicing in the tenderest terms her attachment and love, presented her with a stamped charter of her (Natalia's) freedom, [It will be remembered that this was in the days of serfdom] telling her at the same time that, whether she continued to serve in the household or not, she should always receive an annual pension of 300 roubles. Natalia listened in silence to this. Then, taking the document in her hands and regarding it with a frown, she muttered something between her teeth, and darted from the room, slamming the door behind her. Not understanding the reason for such strange conduct, Mamma followed her presently to her room, and found her sitting with streaming eyes on her trunk, crushing her pocket-handkerchief between her fingers, and looking mournfully at the remains of the document, which was lying torn to pieces on the floor.

"What is the matter, dear Natalia Savishna?" said Mamma, taking her hand.

"Nothing, ma'am," she replied; "only—only I must have displeased you somehow, since you wish to dismiss me from the house. Well, I will go."

She withdrew her hand and, with difficulty restraining her tears, rose to leave the room, but Mamma stopped her, and they wept a while in one another's arms.

Ever since I can remember anything I can remember Natalia Savishna and her love and tenderness; yet only now have I learnt to appreciate them at their full value. In early days it never occurred to me to think what a rare and wonderful being this old domestic was. Not only did she never talk, but she seemed never even to think, of herself. Her whole life was compounded of love and self-sacrifice. Yet so used was I to her affection and singleness of heart that I could not picture things otherwise. I never thought of thanking her, or of asking myself, "Is she also happy? Is she also contented?" Often on some pretext or another I would leave my lessons and run to her room, where, sitting down, I would begin to muse aloud as though she were not there. She was forever mending something, or tidying the shelves which lined her room, or marking linen, so that she took no heed of the nonsense which I talked— how that I meant to become a general, to marry a beautiful woman, to buy a chestnut horse, to, build myself a house of glass, to invite Karl Ivanitch's relatives to come and visit me from Saxony, and so forth; to all of which she would only reply, "Yes, my love, yes." Then, on my rising, and preparing to go, she would open a blue trunk which had pasted on the inside of its lid a coloured picture of a hussar which had once adorned a pomade bottle and a sketch made by Woloda, and take from it a fumigation pastille, which she would light and shake for my benefit, saying:

"These, dear, are the pastilles which your grandfather (now in Heaven) brought back from Otchakov after fighting against the Turks." Then she would add with a sigh: "But this is nearly the last one."

The trunks which filled her room seemed to contain almost everything in the world. Whenever anything was wanted, people said, "Oh, go and ask Natalia Savishna for it," and, sure enough, it was seldom that she did not produce the object required and say, "See what comes of taking care of everything!" Her trunks contained thousands of things which nobody in the house but herself would have thought of preserving.

Once I lost my temper with her. This was how it happened.

One day after luncheon I poured myself out a glass of kvass, and then dropped the decanter, and so stained the tablecloth.

"Go and call Natalia, that she may come and see what her darling has done," said Mamma.

Natalia arrived, and shook her head at me when she saw the damage I had done; but Mamma whispered something in her car, threw a look at myself, and then left the room.

I was just skipping away, in the sprightliest mood possible, when Natalia darted out upon me from behind the door with the tablecloth in her hand, and, catching hold of me, rubbed my face hard with the stained part of it, repeating, "Don't thou go and spoil tablecloths any more!"

I struggled hard, and roared with temper.

"What?" I said to myself as I fled to the drawing-room in a mist of tears,

"To think that Natalia Savishna-just plain Natalia-should say 'THOU' to me and rub my face with a wet tablecloth as though I were a mere servant-boy! It is abominable!"

Seeing my fury, Natalia departed, while I continued to strut about and plan how to punish the bold woman for her offence. Yet not more than a few moments had passed when Natalia returned and, stealing to my side, began to comfort me,

"Hush, then, my love. Do not cry. Forgive me my rudeness. It was wrong of me. You WILL pardon me, my darling, will you not? There, there, that's a dear," and she took from her handkerchief a cornet of pink paper containing two little cakes and a grape, and offered it me with a trembling hand. I could not look the kind old woman in the face, but, turning aside, took the paper, while my tears flowed the faster—though from love and shame now, not from anger.

XIV — THE PARTING

ON the day after the events described, the carriage and the luggage-cart drew up to the door at noon. Nicola, dressed for the journey, with his breeches tucked into his boots and an old overcoat belted tightly about him with a girdle, got into the cart and arranged cloaks and cushions on the seats. When he thought that they were piled high enough he sat down on them, but finding them still unsatisfactory, jumped up and arranged them once more.

"Nicola Dimitvitch, would you be so good as to take master's dressing-case with you?" said Papa's valet, suddenly standing up in the carriage, "It won't take up much room."

"You should have told me before, Michael Ivanitch," answered Nicola snappishly as he hurled a bundle with all his might to the floor of the cart. "Good gracious! Why, when my head is going round like a whirlpool, there you come along with your dressing-case!" and he lifted his cap to wipe away the drops of perspiration from his sunburnt brow.

The courtyard was full of bareheaded peasants in kaftans or simple shirts, women clad in the national dress and wearing striped handkerchiefs, and barefooted little ones—the latter holding their mothers' hands or crowding round the entrance-steps. All were chattering among themselves as they stared at the carriage. One of the postillions, an old man dressed in a winter cap and cloak, took hold of the pole of the carriage and tried it carefully, while the other postillion (a young man in a white blouse with pink gussets on the sleeves and a black lamb's-wool cap which he kept cocking first on one side and then on the other as he arranged his flaxen hair) laid his overcoat upon the box, slung the reins over it, and cracked his thonged whip as he looked now at his boots and now at the other drivers where they stood greasing the wheels of the cart—one driver lifting up each wheel in turn and the other driver applying the grease. Tired post-horses of various hues stood lashing away flies with their tails near the gate—some stamping their great hairy legs, blinking their eyes, and dozing, some leaning wearily against their neighbours, and others cropping the leaves and stalks of dark-green fern which grew near the entrance-steps. Some of the dogs were lying panting in the sun, while others were slinking under the vehicles to lick the grease from the wheels. The air was filled with a sort of dusty mist, and the horizon was lilac-grey in colour, though no clouds were to be seen, A strong wind from the south was raising volumes of dust from the roads and fields, shaking the poplars and birch-trees in the garden, and whirling their yellow leaves away. I myself was sitting at a window and waiting impatiently for these various preparations to come to an end.

As we sat together by the drawing-room table, to pass the last few moments en famille, it never occurred to me that a sad moment was impending. On the contrary, the most trivial thoughts were filling my brain. Which driver was going to drive the carriage and which the cart? Which of us would sit with Papa, and which with Karl Ivanitch? Why must I be kept forever muffled up in a scarf and padded boots?

"Am I so delicate? Am I likely to be frozen?" I thought to myself. "I wish it would all come to an end, and we could take our seats and start."

"To whom shall I give the list of the children's linen?" asked Natalia Savishna of Mamma as she entered the room with a paper in her hand and her eyes red with weeping.

"Give it to Nicola, and then return to say good-bye to them," replied Mamma. The old woman seemed about to say something more, but suddenly stopped short, covered her face with her handkerchief, and left the room. Something seemed to prick at my heart when I saw that gesture of hers, but impatience to be off soon drowned all other feeling, and I continued to listen indifferently to Papa and Mamma as they talked together. They were discussing subjects which evidently interested neither of them. What must be bought for the house? What would Princess Sophia or Madame Julie say? Would the roads be good?—and so forth.

Foka entered, and in the same tone and with the same air as though he were announcing luncheon said, "The carriages are ready." I saw Mamma tremble and turn pale at the announcement, just as though it were something unexpected.

Next, Foka was ordered to shut all the doors of the room. This amused me highly. As though we needed to be concealed from some one! When every one else was seated, Foka took the last remaining chair. Scarcely, however, had he done so when the door creaked and every one looked that way. Natalia Savishna entered hastily, and, without raising her eyes, sat own on the same chair as Foka. I can see them before me now-Foka's bald head and wrinkled, set face, and, beside him, a bent, kind figure in a cap from beneath which a few grey hairs were straggling. The pair settled themselves together on the chair, but neither of them looked comfortable.

I continued preoccupied and impatient. In fact, the ten minutes during which we sat there with closed doors seemed to me an hour. At last every one rose, made the sign of the cross, and began to say good-bye. Papa embraced Mamma, and kissed her again and again.

"But enough," he said presently. "We are not parting for ever."

"No, but it is-so-so sad!" replied Mamma, her voice trembling with emotion.

When I heard that faltering voice, and saw those quivering lips and tear-filled eyes, I forgot everything else in the world. I felt so ill and miserable that I would gladly have run away rather than bid her farewell. I felt, too, that when she was embracing Papa she was embracing us all. She clasped Woloda to her several times, and made the sign of the cross over him; after which I approached her, thinking that it was my turn. Nevertheless she took him again and again to her heart, and blessed him. Finally I caught hold of her, and, clinging to her, wept—wept, thinking of nothing in the world but my grief.

As we passed out to take our seats, other servants pressed round us in the hall to say good-bye. Yet their requests to shake hands with us, their resounding kisses on our shoulders, [The fashion in which inferiors salute their superiors in Russia.] and the odour of their greasy heads only excited in me a feeling akin to impatience with these tiresome people. The same feeling made me bestow nothing more than a very cross kiss upon Natalia's cap when she approached to take leave of me. It is strange that I should still retain a perfect recollection of these servants' faces, and be able to draw them with the most minute accuracy in my mind, while Mamma's face and attitude escape me entirely. It may be that it is because at that moment I had not the heart to look at her closely. I felt that if I did so our mutual grief would burst forth too unrestrainedly.

I was the first to jump into the carriage and to take one of the hinder seats. The high back of the carriage prevented me from actually seeing her, yet I knew by instinct that Mamma was still there.

"Shall I look at her again or not?" I said to myself. "Well, just for the last time," and I peeped out towards the entrance-steps. Exactly at that moment Mamma moved by the same impulse, came to the opposite side of the carriage, and called me by name. Hearing her voice behind me. I turned round, but so hastily that our heads knocked together. She gave a sad smile, and kissed me convulsively for the last time.

When we had driven away a few paces I determined to look at her once more. The wind was lifting the blue handkerchief from her head as, bent forward and her face buried in her hands, she moved slowly up the steps. Foka was supporting her. Papa said nothing as he sat beside me. I felt breathless with tears—felt a sensation in my throat as though I were going to choke, just as we came out on to the open road I saw a white handkerchief waving from the terrace. I waved mine in return, and the action of so doing calmed me a little. I still went on crying, but the thought that my tears were a proof of my affection helped to soothe and comfort me.

After a little while I began to recover, and to look with interest at objects which we passed and at the hind-quarters of the led horse which was trotting on my side. I watched how it would swish its tail, how it would lift one hoof after the other, how the driver's thong would fall upon its back, and how all its legs would then seem to jump together and the back-band, with the rings on it, to jump too—the whole covered with the horse's foam. Then I would look at the rolling stretches of ripe corn, at the dark ploughed fields where ploughs and peasants and horses with foals were working, at their footprints, and at the box of the carriage to see who was driving us; until, though my face was still wet with tears, my thoughts had strayed far from her with whom I had just parted—parted, perhaps, for ever. Yet ever and again something would recall her to my memory. I remembered too how, the evening before, I had found a mushroom under the birch-trees, how Lubotshka had quarrelled with Katenka as to whose it should be, and how they had both of them wept when taking leave of us. I felt sorry to be parted from them, and from Natalia Savishna, and from the birch-tree avenue, and from Foka. Yes, even the horrid Mimi I longed for. I longed for everything at home. And poor Mamma!—The tears rushed to my eyes again. Yet even this mood passed away before long.

XV – CHILDHOOD

HAPPY, happy, never-returning time of childhood! How can we help loving and dwelling upon its recollections? They cheer and elevate the soul, and become to one a source of higher joys.

Sometimes, when dreaming of bygone days, I fancy that, tired out with running about, I have sat down, as of old, in my high arm-chair by the tea-table. It is late, and I have long since drunk my cup of milk. My eyes are heavy with sleep as I sit there and listen. How could I not listen, seeing that Mamma is speaking to somebody, and that the sound of her voice is so melodious and kind? How much its echoes recall to my heart! With my eyes veiled with drowsiness I gaze at her wistfully. Suddenly she seems to grow smaller and smaller, and her face vanishes to a point; yet I can still see it—can still see her as she looks at me and smiles. Somehow it pleases me to see her grown so small. I blink and blink, yet she looks no larger than a boy reflected in the pupil of an eye. Then I rouse myself, and the picture fades. Once more I half-close my eyes, and cast about to try and recall the dream, but it has gone.

I rise to my feet, only to fall back comfortably into the armchair.

"There! You are failing asleep again, little Nicolas," says Mamma. "You had better go to by-by."

"No, I won't go to sleep, Mamma," I reply, though almost inaudibly, for pleasant dreams are filling all my soul. The sound sleep of childhood is weighing my eyelids down, and for a few moments I sink into slumber and oblivion until awakened by some one. I feel in my sleep as though a soft hand were caressing me. I know it by the touch, and, though still dreaming, I seize hold of it and press it to my lips. Every one else has gone to bed, and only one candle remains burning in the drawing-room. Mamma has said that she herself will wake me. She sits down on the arm of the chair in which I am asleep, with her soft hand stroking my hair, and I hear her beloved, well-known voice say in my ear:

"Get up, my darling. It is time to go by-by."

No envious gaze sees her now. She is not afraid to shed upon me the whole of her tenderness and love. I do not wake up, yet I kiss and kiss her hand.

"Get up, then, my angel."

She passes her other arm round my neck, and her fingers tickle me as they move across it. The room is quiet and in half-darkness, but the tickling has touched my nerves and I begin to awake. Mamma is sitting near me—that I can tell—and touching me; I can hear her voice and feel her presence. This at last rouses me to spring up, to throw my arms around her neck, to hide my head in her bosom, and to say with a sigh:

"Ah, dear, darling Mamma, how much I love you!"

She smiles her sad, enchanting smile, takes my head between her two hands, kisses me on the forehead, and lifts me on to her lap.

"Do you love me so much, then?" she says. Then, after a few moments' silence, she continues: "And you must love me always, and never forget me. If your Mamma should no longer be here, will you promise never to forget her—never, Nicolinka? and she kisses me more fondly than ever.

"Oh, but you must not speak so, darling Mamma, my own darling Mamma!" I exclaim as I clasp her knees, and tears of joy and love fall from my eyes.

How, after scenes like this, I would go upstairs, and stand before the ikons, and say with a rapturous feeling, "God bless Papa and Mamma!" and repeat a prayer for my beloved mother which my childish lips had learnt to lisp-the love of God and of her blending strangely in a single emotion!

After saying my prayers I would wrap myself up in the bedclothes. My heart would feel light, peaceful, and happy, and one dream would follow another. Dreams of what? They were all of them vague, but all of them full of pure love and of a sort of expectation of happiness. I remember, too, that I used to think about Karl Ivanitch and his sad lot. He was the only unhappy being whom I knew, and so sorry would I feel for him, and so much did I love him, that tears would fall from my eyes as I thought, "May God give him happiness, and enable me to help him and to lessen his sorrow. I could make any sacrifice for him!" Usually, also, there would be some favourite toy—a china dog or hare—stuck into the bed-corner behind the pillow, and it would please me to think how warm and comfortable and well cared-for it was there. Also, I would pray God to make every one happy, so that every one might be contented, and also to send fine weather to-morrow for our walk. Then I would turn myself over on to the other side, and thoughts and dreams would become jumbled and entangled together until at last I slept soundly and peacefully, though with a face wet with tears.

Do in after life the freshness and light-heartedness, the craving for love and for strength of faith, ever return which we experience in our childhood's years? What better time is there in our lives than when the two best of virtues—innocent gaiety and a boundless yearning for affection—are our sole objects of pursuit?

Where now are our ardent prayers? Where now are our best gifts—the pure tears of emotion which a guardian angel dries with a smile as he sheds upon us lovely dreams of ineffable childish joy? Can it be that life has left such heavy traces upon one's heart that those tears and ecstasies are for ever vanished? Can it be that there remains to us only the recollection of them?

XVI — VERSE-MAKING

RATHER less than a month after our arrival in Moscow I was sitting upstairs in my Grandmamma's house and doing some writing at a large table. Opposite to me sat the drawing master, who was giving a few finishing touches to the head of a turbaned Turk, executed in black pencil. Woloda, with outstretched neck, was standing behind the drawing master and looking over his shoulder. The head was Woloda's first production in pencil and to-day— Grandmamma's name-day—the masterpiece was to be presented to her.

"Aren't you going to put a little more shadow there?" said Woloda to the master as he raised himself on tiptoe and pointed to the Turk's neck.

"No, it is not necessary," the master replied as he put pencil and drawing-pen into a japanned folding box. "It is just right now, and you need not do anything more to it. As for you, Nicolinka," he added, rising and glancing askew at the Turk, "won't you tell us your great secret at last? What are you going to give your Grandmamma? I think another head would be your best gift. But good-bye, gentlemen," and taking his hat and cardboard he departed.

I too had thought that another head than the one at which I had been working would be a better gift; so, when we were told that Grandmamma's name-day was soon to come round and that we must each of us have a present ready for her, I had taken it into my head to write some verses in honour of the occasion, and had forthwith composed two rhymed couplets, hoping that the rest would soon materialise. I really do not know how the idea—one so peculiar for a child—came to occur to me, but I know that I liked it vastly, and answered all questions on the subject of my gift by declaring that I should soon have something ready for Grandmamma, but was not going to say what it was.

Contrary to my expectation, I found that, after the first two couplets executed in the initial heat of enthusiasm, even my most strenuous efforts refused to produce another one. I began to read different poems in our books, but neither Dimitrieff nor Derzhavin could help me. On the contrary, they only confirmed my sense of incompetence. Knowing, however, that Karl Ivanitch was fond of writing verses, I stole softly upstairs to burrow among his papers, and found, among a number of German verses, some in the Russian language which seemed to have come from his own pen.

To L

Remember near

Remember far,

Remember me.

To-day be faithful, and for ever—

Aye, still beyond the grave—remember

That I have well loved thee.

"KARL MAYER."

These verses (which were written in a fine, round hand on thin letter-paper) pleased me with the touching sentiment with which they seemed to be inspired. I learnt them by heart, and decided to take them as a model. The thing was much easier now. By the time the name-day had arrived I had completed a twelve-couplet congratulatory ode, and sat down to the table in our school-room to copy them out on vellum.

Two sheets were soon spoiled—not because I found it necessary to alter anything (the verses seemed to me perfect), but because, after the third line, the tail-end of each successive one would go curving upward and making it plain to all the world that the whole thing had been written with a want of adherence to the horizontal—a thing which I could not bear to see.

The third sheet also came out crooked, but I determined to make it do.

In my verses I congratulated Grandmamma, wished her many happy returns, and concluded thus:

"Endeavouring you to please and cheer,

We love you like our Mother dear."

This seemed to me not bad, yet it offended my ear somehow.

"Lo-ve you li-ike our Mo-ther dear," I repeated to myself. "What other rhyme could I use instead of 'dear'? Fear? Steer? Well, it must go at that. At least the verses are better than Karl Ivanitch's."

Accordingly I added the last verse to the rest. Then I went into our bedroom and recited the whole poem aloud with much feeling and gesticulation. The verses were altogether guiltless of metre, but I did not stop to consider that. Yet the last one displeased me more than ever. As I sat on my bed I thought:

"Why on earth did I write 'like our Mother dear'? She is not here, and therefore she need never have been mentioned. True, I love and respect Grandmamma, but she is not quite the same as—Why DID I write that? What did I go and tell a lie for? They may be verses only, yet I needn't quite have done that."

At that moment the tailor arrived with some new clothes for us.

"Well, so be it!" I said in much vexation as I crammed the verses hastily under my pillow and ran down to adorn myself in the new Moscow garments.

They fitted marvellously-both the brown jacket with yellow buttons (a garment made skin-tight and not "to allow room for growth," as in the country) and the black trousers (also close-fitting so that they displayed the figure and lay smoothly over the boots).

"At last I have real trousers on!" I thought as I looked at my legs with the utmost satisfaction. I concealed from every one the fact that the new clothes were horribly tight and uncomfortable, but, on the contrary, said that, if there were a fault, it was that they were not tight enough. For a long while I stood before the looking-glass as I combed my elaborately pomaded head, but, try as I would, I could not reduce the topmost hairs on the crown to order. As soon as ever I left off combing them, they sprang up again and radiated in different directions, thus giving my face a ridiculous expression.

Karl Ivanitch was dressing in another room, and I heard some one bring him his blue frockcoat and under-linen. Then at the door leading downstairs I heard a maid-servant's voice, and went to see what she wanted. In her hand she held a well-starched shirt which she said she had been sitting up all night to get ready. I took it, and asked if Grandmamma was up yet.

"Oh yes, she has had her coffee, and the priest has come. My word, but you look a fine little fellow!" added the girl with a smile at my new clothes.

This observation made me blush, so I whirled round on one leg, snapped my fingers, and went skipping away, in the hope that by these manoeuvres I should make her sensible that even yet she had not realised quite what a fine fellow I was.

However, when I took the shirt to Karl I found that he did not need it, having taken another one. Standing before a small looking-glass, he tied his cravat with both hands—trying, by various motions of his head, to see whether it fitted him comfortably or not—and then took us down to see Grandmamma. To this day I cannot help laughing when I remember what a smell of pomade the three of us left behind us on the staircase as we descended.

Karl was carrying a box which he had made himself, Woloda, his drawing, and I my verses, while each of us also had a form of words ready with which to present his gift. Just as Karl opened the door, the priest put on his vestment and began to say prayers.

During the ceremony Grandmamma stood leaning over the back of a chair, with her head bent down. Near her stood Papa. He turned and smiled at us as we hurriedly thrust our presents behind our backs and tried to remain unobserved by the door. The whole effect of a surprise, upon which we had been counting, was entirely lost. When at last every one had made the sign of the cross I became intolerably oppressed with a sudden, invincible, and deadly attack of shyness, so that the courage to, offer my present completely failed me. I hid myself behind Karl Ivanitch, who solemnly congratulated Grandmamma and, transferring his box from his right hand to his left, presented it to her. Then he withdrew a few steps to make way for Woloda. Grandmamma seemed highly pleased with the box (which was adorned with a gold border), and smiled in the most friendly manner in order to express her gratitude. Yet it was evident that, she did not know where to set the box down, and this probably accounts for the fact that she handed it to Papa, at the same time bidding him observe how beautifully it was made.

His curiosity satisfied, Papa handed the box to the priest, who also seemed particularly delighted with it, and looked with astonishment, first at the article itself, and then at the artist who could make such wonderful things. Then Woloda presented his Turk, and received a similarly flattering ovation on all sides.

It was my turn now, and Grandmamma turned to me with her kindest smile. Those who have experienced what embarrassment is know that it is a feeling which grows in direct proportion to delay, while decision decreases in similar measure. In other words the longer the condition lasts, the more invincible does it become, and the smaller does the power of decision come to be.

My last remnants of nerve and energy had forsaken me while Karl and Woloda had been offering their presents, and my shyness now reached its culminating point, I felt the blood rushing from my heart to my head, one blush succeeding another across my face, and drops of perspiration beginning to stand out on my brow and nose. My ears were burning, I trembled from head to foot, and, though I kept changing from one foot to the other, I remained rooted where I stood.

"Well, Nicolinka, tell us what you have brought?" said Papa. "Is it a box or a drawing?"

There was nothing else to be done. With a trembling hand held out the folded, fatal paper, but my voiced failed me completely and I stood before Grandmamma in silence. I could not get rid of the dreadful idea that, instead of a display of the expected drawing, some bad verses of mine were about to be read aloud before every one, and that the words "our Mother dear" would clearly prove that I had never loved, but had only forgotten, her. How shall I express my sufferings when Grandmamma began to read my poetry aloud?—when, unable to decipher it, she stopped half-way and looked at Papa with a smile (which I took to be one of ridicule)?—when she did not pronounce it as I had meant it to be pronounced?—and when her weak sight not allowing her to finish it, she handed the paper to Papa and requested him to read it all over again from the beginning? I fancied that she must have done this last because she did not like to read such a lot of stupid, crookedly written stuff herself, yet wanted to point out to Papa my utter lack of feeling. I expected him to slap me in the face with the verses and say, "You bad boy! So you have forgotten your Mamma! Take that for it!" Yet nothing of the sort happened. On the contrary, when the whole had been read, Grandmamma said, "Charming!" and kissed me on the forehead. Then our presents, together with two cambric pocket-handkerchiefs and a snuff-box engraved with Mamma's portrait, were laid on the table attached to the great Voltairian arm-chair in which Grandmamma always sat.

"The Princess Barbara Ilinitsha!" announced one of the two footmen who used to stand behind Grandmamma's carriage, but Grandmamma was looking thoughtfully at the portrait on the snuff-box, and returned no answer.

"Shall I show her in, madam?" repeated the footman.

XVII – THE PRINCESS KORNAKOFF

"Yes, show her in," said Grandmamma, settling herself as far back in her arm-chair as possible. The Princess was a woman of about forty-five, small and delicate, with a shrivelled skin and disagreeable, greyish-green eyes, the expression of which contradicted the unnaturally suave look of the rest of her face. Underneath her velvet bonnet, adorned with an ostrich feather, was visible some reddish hair, while against the unhealthy colour of her skin her eyebrows and eyelashes looked even lighter and redder that they would other wise have done. Yet, for all that, her animated movements, small hands, and peculiarly dry features communicated something aristocratic and energetic to her general appearance. She talked a great deal, and, to judge from her eloquence, belonged to that class of persons who always speak as though some one were contradicting them, even though no one else may be saying a word. First she would raise her voice, then lower it and then take on a fresh access of vivacity as she looked at the persons present, but not participating in the conversation, with an air of endeavouring to draw them into it.

Although the Princess kissed Grandmamma's hand and repeatedly called her "my good Aunt," I could see that Grandmamma did not care much about her, for she kept raising her eyebrows in a peculiar way while listening to the Princess's excuses why Prince Michael had been prevented from calling, and congratulating Grandmamma "as he would like so-much to have done." At length, however, she answered the Princess's French with Russian, and with a sharp accentuation of certain words.

"I am much obliged to you for your kindness," she said. "As for Prince Michael's absence, pray do not mention it. He has so much else to do. Besides, what pleasure could he find in coming to see an old woman like me?" Then, without allowing the Princess time to reply, she went on: "How are your children my dear?"

"Well, thank God, Aunt, they grow and do their lessons and play—particularly my eldest one, Etienne, who is so wild that it is almost impossible to keep him in order. Still, he is a clever and promising boy. Would you believe it, cousin," (this last to Papa, since Grandmamma altogether uninterested in the Princess's children, had turned to us, taken my verses out from beneath the presentation box, and unfolded them again), "would you believe it, but one day not long ago—" and leaning over towards Papa, the Princess related something or other with great vivacity. Then, her tale concluded, she laughed, and, with a questioning look at Papa, went on:

"What a boy, cousin! He ought to have been whipped, but the trick was so spirited and amusing that I let him off." Then the Princess looked at Grandmamma and laughed again.

"Ah! So you WHIP your children, do you" said Grandmamma, with a significant lift of her eyebrows, and laying a peculiar stress on the word "WHIP."

"Alas, my good Aunt," replied the Princess in a sort of tolerant tone and with another glance at Papa, "I know your views on the subject, but must beg to be allowed to differ with them. However much I have thought over and read and talked about the matter, I have always been forced to come to the conclusion that children must be ruled through FEAR. To make something of a child, you must make it FEAR something. Is it not so, cousin? And what, pray, do children fear so much as a rod?"

As she spoke she seemed, to look inquiringly at Woloda and myself, and I confess that I did not feel altogether comfortable.

"Whatever you may say," she went on, "a boy of twelve, or even of fourteen, is still a child and should be whipped as such; but with girls, perhaps, it is another matter."

"How lucky it is that I am not her son!" I thought to myself.

"Oh, very well," said Grandmamma, folding up my verses and replacing them beneath the box (as though, after that exposition of views, the Princess was unworthy of the honour of listening to such a production). "Very well, my dear," she repeated, "But please tell me how, in return, you can look for any delicate sensibility from your children?"

Evidently Grandmamma thought this argument unanswerable, for she cut the subject short by adding:

"However, it is a point on which people must follow their own opinions."

The Princess did not choose to reply, but smiled condescendingly, and as though out of indulgence to the strange prejudices of a person whom she only PRETENDED to revere.

"Oh, by the way, pray introduce me to your young people," she went on presently as she threw us another gracious smile.

Thereupon we rose and stood looking at the Princess, without in the least knowing what we ought to do to show that we were being introduced.

"Kiss the Princess's hand," said Papa.

"Well, I hope you will love your old aunt," she said to Woloda, kissing his hair, "even though we are not near relatives. But I value friendship far more than I do degrees of relationship," she added to Grandmamma, who nevertheless, remained hostile, and replied:

"Eh, my dear? Is that what they think of relationships nowadays?"

"Here is my man of the world," put in Papa, indicating Woloda; "and here is my poet," he added as I kissed the small, dry hand of the Princess, with a vivid picture in my mind of that same hand holding a rod and applying it vigorously.

"WHICH one is the poet?" asked the Princess.

"This little one," replied Papa, smiling; "the one with the tuft of hair on his top-knot."

"Why need he bother about my tuft?" I thought to myself as I retired into a corner. "Is there nothing else for him to talk about?"

I had strange ideas on manly beauty. I considered Karl Ivanitch one of the handsomest men in the world, and myself so ugly that I had no need to deceive myself on that point. Therefore any remark on the subject of my exterior offended me extremely. I well remember how, one day after luncheon (I was then six years of age), the talk fell upon my personal appearance, and how Mamma tried to find good features in my face, and said that I had clever eyes and a charming smile; how, nevertheless, when Papa had examined me, and proved the contrary, she was obliged to confess that I was ugly; and how, when the meal was over and I went to pay her my respects, she said as she patted my cheek; "You know, Nicolinka, nobody will ever love you for your face alone, so you must try all the more to be a good and clever boy."

Although these words of hers confirmed in me my conviction that I was not handsome, they also confirmed in me an ambition to be just such a boy as she had indicated. Yet I had my moments of despair at my ugliness, for I thought that no human being with such a large nose, such thick lips, and such small grey eyes as mine could ever hope to attain happiness on this earth. I used to ask God to perform a miracle by changing me into a beauty, and would have given all that I possessed, or ever hoped to possess, to have a handsome face.

XVIII — PRINCE IVAN IVANOVITCH

When the Princess had heard my verses and overwhelmed the writer of them with praise, Grandmamma softened to her a little. She began to address her in French and to cease calling her "my dear." Likewise she invited her to return that evening with her children. This invitation having been accepted, the Princess took her leave. After that, so many other callers came to congratulate Grandmamma that the courtyard was crowded all day long with carriages.

"Good morning, my dear cousin," was the greeting of one guest in particular as he entered the room and kissed Grandmamma's hand. He was a man of seventy, with a stately figure clad in a military uniform and adorned with large epaulettes, an embroidered collar, and a white cross round the neck. His face, with its quiet and open expression, as well as the simplicity and ease of his manners, greatly pleased me, for, in spite of the thin half-circle of hair which was all that was now left to him, and the want of teeth disclosed by the set of his upper lip, his face was a remarkably handsome one.

Thanks to his fine character, handsome exterior, remarkable valour, influential relatives, and, above all, good fortune, Prince, Ivan Ivanovitch had early made himself a career. As that career progressed, his ambition had met with a success which left nothing more to be sought for in that direction. From his earliest youth upward he had prepared himself to fill the exalted station in the world to which fate actually called him later; wherefore, although in his prosperous life (as in the lives of all) there had been failures, misfortunes, and cares, he had never lost his quietness of character, his elevated tone of thought, or his peculiarly moral, religious bent of mind. Consequently, though he had won the universal esteem of his fellows, he had done so less through his important position than through his perseverance and integrity. While not of specially distinguished intellect, the eminence of his station (whence he could afford to look down upon all petty questions) had caused him to adopt high points of view. Though in reality he was kind and sympathetic, in manner he appeared cold and haughty—probably for the reason that he had forever to be on his guard against the endless claims and petitions of people who wished to profit through his influence. Yet even then his coldness was mitigated by the polite condescension of a man well accustomed to move in the highest circles of society. Well-educated, his culture was that of a youth of the end of the last century. He had read everything, whether philosophy or belles lettres, which that age had produced in France, and loved to quote from Racine, Corneille, Boileau, Moliere, Montaigne, and Fenelon. Likewise he had gleaned much history from Segur, and much of the old classics from French translations of them; but for mathematics, natural philosophy, or contemporary literature he cared nothing whatever. However, he knew how to be silent in conversation, as well as when to make general remarks on authors whom he had never read—such as Goethe, Schiller, and Byron. Moreover, despite his exclusively French education, he was simple in speech and hated originality (which he called the mark of an untutored nature). Wherever he lived, society was a necessity to him, and, both in Moscow and the country he had his reception days, on which practically "all the town" called upon him. An introduction from him was a passport to every drawing-room; few young and pretty ladies in society objected to offering him their rosy cheeks for a paternal salute; and people even in the highest positions felt flattered by invitations to his parties.

The Prince had few friends left now like Grandmamma—that is to say, few friends who were of the same standing as himself, who had had the same sort of education, and who saw things from the same point of view: wherefore he greatly valued his intimate, long-standing friendship with her, and always showed her the highest respect.

I hardly dared to look at the Prince, since the honour paid him on all sides, the huge epaulettes, the peculiar pleasure with which Grandmamma received him, and the fact that he alone, seemed in no way afraid of her, but addressed her with perfect freedom (even being so daring as to call her "cousin"), awakened in me a feeling of reverence for his person almost equal to that which I felt for Grandmamma herself.

On being shown my verses, he called me to his side, and said:

"Who knows, my cousin, but that he may prove to be a second

Derzhavin?" Nevertheless he pinched my cheek so hard that I was only prevented from crying by the thought that it must be meant for a caress.

Gradually the other guests dispersed, and with them Papa and Woloda. Thus only Grandmamma, the Prince, and myself were left in the drawing-room.

"Why has our dear Natalia Nicolaevna not come to-day," asked the Prince after a silence.

"Ah, my friend," replied Grandmamma, lowering her voice and laying a hand upon the sleeve of his uniform, "she would certainly have come if she had been at liberty to do what she likes. She wrote to me that Peter had proposed bringing her with him to town, but that she had refused, since their income had not been good this year, and she could see no real reason why the whole family need come to Moscow, seeing that Lubotshka was as yet very young and that the boys were living with me—a fact, she said, which made her feel as safe about them as though she had been living with them herself."

"True, it is good for the boys to be here," went on Grandmamma, yet in a tone which showed clearly that she did not think it was so very good, "since it was more than time that they should be sent to Moscow to study, as well as to learn how to comport themselves in society. What sort of an education could they have got in the country? The eldest boy will soon be thirteen, and the second one eleven. As yet, my cousin, they are quite untaught, and do not know even how to enter a room."

"Nevertheless," said the Prince, "I cannot understand these complaints of ruined fortunes. He has a very handsome income, and Natalia has Chabarovska, where we used to act plays, and which I know as well as I do my own hand. It is a splendid property, and ought to bring in an excellent return."

"Well," said Grandmamma with a sad expression on her face, "I do not mind telling you, as my most intimate friend, that all this seems to me a mere pretext on his part for living alone, for strolling about from club to club, for attending dinner-parties, and for resorting to—well, who knows what? She suspects nothing; you know her angelic sweetness and her implicit trust of him in everything. He had only to tell her that the children must go to Moscow and that she must be left behind in the country with a stupid governess for company, for her to believe him! I almost think that if he were to say that the children must be whipped just as the Princess Barbara whips hers, she would believe even that!" and Grandmamma leant back in her armchair with an expression of contempt. Then, after a moment of silence, during which she took her handkerchief out of her pocket to wipe away a few tears which had stolen down her cheeks, she went, on:

"Yes, my friend, I often think that he cannot value and understand her properly, and that, for all her goodness and love of him and her endeavours to conceal her grief (which, however as I know only too well, exists). She cannot really be happy with him. Mark my words if he does not—" Here Grandmamma buried her face in the handkerchief.

"Ah, my dear old friend," said the Prince reproachfully. "I think you are unreasonable. Why grieve and weep over imagined evils? That is not right. I have known him a long time, and feel sure that he is an attentive, kind, and excellent husband, as well as (which is the chief thing of all) a perfectly honourable man."

At this point, having been an involuntary auditor of a conversation not meant for my ears, I stole on tiptoe out of the room, in a state of great distress.

XIX – THE IWINS

"Woloda, Woloda! The Iwins are just coming." I shouted on seeing from the window three boys in blue overcoats, and followed by a young tutor, advancing along the pavement opposite our house.

The Iwins were related to us, and of about the same age as ourselves. We had made their acquaintance soon after our arrival in Moscow. The second brother, Seriosha, had dark curly hair, a turned-up, strongly pronounced nose, very bright red lips (which, never being quite shut, showed a row of white teeth), beautiful dark-blue eyes, and an uncommonly bold expression of face. He never smiled but was either wholly serious or laughing a clear, merry, agreeable laugh. His striking good looks had captivated me from the first, and I felt an irresistible attraction towards him. Only to see him filled me with pleasure, and at one time my whole mental faculties used to be concentrated in the wish that I might do so. If three or four days passed without my seeing him I felt listless and ready to cry. Awake or asleep, I was forever dreaming of him. On going to bed I used to see him in my dreams, and when I had shut my eyes and called up a picture of him I hugged the vision as my choicest delight. So much store did I set upon this feeling for my friend that I never mentioned it to any one. Nevertheless, it must have annoyed him to see my admiring eyes constantly fixed upon him, or else he must have felt no reciprocal attraction, for he always preferred to play and talk with Woloda. Still, even with that I felt satisfied, and wished and asked for nothing better than to be ready at any time to make any sacrifice for him. Likewise, over and above the strange fascination which he exercised upon me, I always felt another sensation, namely, a dread of making him angry, of offending him, of displeasing him. Was this because his face bore such a haughty expression, or because I, despising my own exterior, over-rated the beautiful in others, or, lastly (and most probably), because it is a common sign of affection? At all events, I felt as much fear, of him as I did love. The first time that he spoke to me I was so overwhelmed with sudden happiness that I turned pale, then red, and could not utter a word. He had an ugly habit of blinking when considering anything seriously, as well as of twitching his nose and eyebrows. Consequently every one thought that this habit marred his face. Yet I thought it such a nice one that I involuntarily adopted it for myself, until, a few days after I had made his acquaintance, Grandmamma suddenly asked me whether my eyes were hurting me, since I was winking like an owl! Never a word of affection passed between us, yet he felt his power over me, and unconsciously but tyrannically, exercised it in all our childish intercourse. I used to long to tell him all that was in my heart, yet was too much afraid of him to be frank in any way, and, while submitting myself to his will, tried to appear merely careless and indifferent. Although at times his influence seemed irksome and intolerable, to throw it off was beyond my strength.

I often think with regret of that fresh, beautiful feeling of boundless, disinterested love which came to an end without having ever found self-expression or return. It is strange how, when a child, I always longed to be like grown-up people, and yet how I have often longed, since childhood's days, for those days to come back to me! Many times, in my relations with Seriosha, this wish to resemble grown-up people put a rude check upon the love that was waiting to expand, and made me repress it. Not only was I afraid of kissing him, or of taking his hand and saying how glad I was to see him, but I even dreaded calling him "Seriosha" and always said "Sergius" as every one else did in our house. Any expression of affection would have seemed like evidence of childishness, and any one who indulged in it, a baby. Not having yet passed through those bitter experiences which enforce upon older years circumspection and coldness, I deprived myself of the pure delight of a fresh, childish instinct for the absurd purpose of trying to resemble grown-up people.

I met the Iwins in the ante-room, welcomed them, and then ran to tell Grandmamma of their arrival with an expression as happy as though she were certain to be equally delighted. Then, never taking my eyes off Seriosha, I conducted the visitors to the drawing-room, and eagerly followed every movement of my favourite. When Grandmamma spoke to and fixed her penetrating glance upon him, I experienced that mingled sensation of pride and solicitude which an artist might feel when waiting for revered lips to pronounce a judgment upon his work.

With Grandmamma's permission, the Iwins' young tutor, Herr Frost, accompanied us into the little back garden, where he seated himself upon a bench, arranged his legs in a tasteful attitude, rested his brass-knobbed cane between them, lighted a cigar, and assumed the air of a man well-pleased with himself. He was a German, but of a very different sort to our good Karl Ivanitch. In the first place, he spoke both Russian and French correctly, though with a hard accent Indeed, he enjoyed—especially among the ladies— the reputation of being a very accomplished fellow. In the second place, he wore a reddish moustache, a large gold pin set with a ruby, a black satin tie, and a very fashionable suit. Lastly, he was young, with a handsome, self-satisfied face and fine muscular legs. It was clear that he set the greatest store upon the latter, and thought them beyond compare, especially as regards the favour of the ladies. Consequently, whether sitting or standing, he always tried to exhibit them in the most favourable light. In short, he was a type of the young German-Russian whose main desire is to be thought perfectly gallant and gentlemanly.

In the little garden merriment reigned. In fact, the game of "robbers" never went better. Yet an incident occurred which came near to spoiling it. Seriosha was the robber, and in pouncing upon some travellers he fell down and knocked his leg so badly against a tree that I thought the leg must be broken. Consequently, though I was the gendarme and therefore bound to apprehend him, I only asked him anxiously, when I reached him, if he had hurt himself very much. Nevertheless this threw him into a passion, and made him exclaim with fists clenched and in a voice which showed by its faltering what pain he was enduring, "Why, whatever is the matter? Is this playing the game properly? You ought to arrest me. Why on earth don't you do so?" This he repeated several times, and then, seeing Woloda and the elder Iwin (who were taking the part of the travellers) jumping and running about the path, he suddenly threw himself upon them with a shout and loud laughter to effect their capture. I cannot express my wonder and delight at this valiant behaviour of my hero. In spite of the severe pain, he had not only refrained from crying, but had repressed the least symptom of suffering and kept his eye fixed upon the game! Shortly after this occurrence another boy, Ilinka Grap, joined our party. We went upstairs, and Seriosha gave me an opportunity of still further appreciating and taking delight in his manly bravery and fortitude. This was how it was.

Ilinka was the son of a poor foreigner who had been under certain obligations to my Grandpapa, and now thought it incumbent upon him to send his son to us as frequently as possible. Yet if he thought that the acquaintance would procure his son any advancement or pleasure, he was entirely mistaken, for not only were we anything but friendly to Ilinka, but it was seldom that we noticed him at all except to laugh at him. He was a boy of thirteen, tall and thin, with a pale, birdlike face, and a quiet, good-tempered expression. Though poorly dressed, he always had his head so thickly pomaded that we used to declare that on warm days it melted and ran down his neck. When I think of him now, it seems to me that he was a very quiet, obliging, and good-tempered boy, but at the time I thought him a creature so contemptible that he was not worth either attention or pity.

Upstairs we set ourselves to astonish each other with gymnastic tours de force. Ilinka watched us with a faint smile of admiration, but refused an invitation to attempt a similar feat, saying that he had no strength.

Seriosha was extremely captivating. His face and eyes glowed with laughter as he surprised us with tricks which we had never seen before. He jumped over three chairs put together, turned somersaults right across the room, and finally stood on his head on a pyramid of Tatistchev's dictionaries, moving his legs about with such comical rapidity that it was impossible not to help bursting with merriment.

After this last trick he pondered for a moment (blinking his eyes as usual), and then went up to Ilinka with a very serious face.

"Try and do that," he said. "It is not really difficult."

Ilinka, observing that the general attention was fixed upon him, blushed, and said in an almost inaudible voice that he could not do the feat.

"Well, what does he mean by doing nothing at all? What a girl the fellow is! He has just GOT to stand on his head," and Seriosha, took him by the hand.

"Yes, on your head at once! This instant, this instant!" every one shouted as we ran upon Ilinka and dragged him to the dictionaries, despite his being visibly pale and frightened.

"Leave me alone! You are tearing my jacket!" cried the unhappy victim, but his exclamations of despair only encouraged us the more. We were dying with laughter, while the green jacket was bursting at every seam.

Woloda and the eldest Iwin took his head and placed it on the dictionaries, while Seriosha, and I seized his poor, thin legs (his struggles had stripped them upwards to the knees), and with boisterous, laughter held them uptight—the youngest Iwin superintending his general equilibrium.

Suddenly a moment of silence occurred amid our boisterous laughter—a moment during which nothing was to be heard in the room but the panting of the miserable Ilinka. It occurred to me at that moment that, after all, there was nothing so very comical and pleasant in all this.

"Now, THAT'S a boy!" cried Seriosha, giving Ilinka a smack with his hand. Ilinka said nothing, but made such desperate movements with his legs to free himself that his foot suddenly kicked Seriosha in the eye: with the result that, letting go of Ilinka's leg and covering the wounded member with one hand, Seriosha hit out at him with all his might with the other one. Of course Ilinka's legs slipped down as, sinking exhausted to the floor and half-suffocated with tears, he stammered out:

"Why should you bully me so?"

The poor fellow's miserable figure, with its streaming tears, ruffled hair, and crumpled trousers revealing dirty boots, touched us a little, and we stood silent and trying to smile.

Seriosha was the first to recover himself.

"What a girl! What a gaby!" he said, giving Ilinka a slight kick. "He can't take things in fun a bit. Well, get up, then."

"You are an utter beast! That's what YOU are!" said Ilinka, turning miserably away and sobbing.

"Oh, oh! Would it still kick and show temper, then?" cried Seriosha, seizing a dictionary and throwing it at the unfortunate boy's head. Apparently it never occurred to Ilinka to take refuge from the missile; he merely guarded his head with his hands.

"Well, that's enough now," added Seriosha, with a forced laugh. "You DESERVE to be hurt if you can't take things in fun. Now let's go downstairs."

I could not help looking with some compassion at the miserable creature on the floor as, his face buried in the dictionary, he lay there sobbing almost as though he were in a fit.

"Oh, Sergius!" I said. "Why have you done this?"

"Well, you did it too! Besides, I did not cry this afternoon when I knocked my leg and nearly broke it."

"True enough," I thought. "Ilinka is a poor whining sort of a chap, while Seriosha is a boy—a REAL boy."

It never occurred to my mind that possibly poor Ilinka was suffering far less from bodily pain than from the thought that five companions for whom he may have felt a genuine liking had, for no reason at all, combined to hurt and humiliate him.

I cannot explain my cruelty on this occasion. Why did I not step forward to comfort and protect him? Where was the pitifulness which often made me burst into tears at the sight of a young bird fallen from its nest, or of a puppy being thrown over a wall, or of a chicken being killed by the cook for soup?

Can it be that the better instinct in me was overshadowed by my affection for Seriosha and the desire to shine before so brave a boy? If so, how contemptible were both the affection and the desire! They alone form dark spots on the pages of my youthful recollections.

XX – PREPARATIONS FOR THE PARTY

To judge from the extraordinary activity in the pantry, the shining cleanliness which imparted such a new and festal guise to certain articles in the salon and drawing-room which I had long known as anything but resplendent, and the arrival of some musicians whom Prince Ivan would certainly not have sent for nothing, no small amount of company was to be expected that evening.

At the sound of every vehicle which chanced to pass the house I ran to the window, leaned my head upon my arms, and peered with impatient curiosity into the street.

At last a carriage stopped at our door, and, in the full belief that this must be the Iwins, who had promised to come early, I at once ran downstairs to meet them in the hall.

But, instead of the Iwins, I beheld from behind the figure of the footman who opened the door two female figures-one tall and wrapped in a blue cloak trimmed with marten, and the other one short and wrapped in a green shawl from beneath which a pair of little feet, stuck into fur boots, peeped forth.

Without paying any attention to my presence in the hall (although I thought it my duty, on the appearance of these persons to salute them), the shorter one moved towards the taller, and stood silently in front of her. Thereupon the tall lady untied the shawl which enveloped the head of the little one, and unbuttoned the cloak which hid her form; until, by the time that the footmen had taken charge of these articles and removed the fur boots, there stood forth from the amorphous chrysalis a charming girl of twelve, dressed in a short muslin frock, white pantaloons, and smart black satin shoes. Around her, white neck she wore a narrow black velvet ribbon, while her head was covered with flaxen curls which so perfectly suited her beautiful face in front and her bare neck and shoulders behind that I, would have believed nobody, not even Karl Ivanitch, if he, or she had told me that they only hung so nicely because, ever since the morning, they had been screwed up in fragments of a Moscow newspaper and then warmed with a hot iron. To me it seemed as though she must have been born with those curls.

The most prominent feature in her face was a pair of unusually large half-veiled eyes, which formed a strange, but pleasing, contrast to the small mouth. Her lips were closed, while her eyes looked so grave that the general expression of her face gave one the impression that a smile was never to be looked for from her: wherefore, when a smile did come, it was all the more pleasing.

Trying to escape notice, I slipped through the door of the salon, and then thought it necessary to be seen pacing to and fro, seemingly engaged in thought, as though unconscious of the arrival of guests.

BY the time, however, that the ladies had advanced to the middle of the salon I seemed suddenly to awake from my reverie and told them that Grandmamma was in the drawing room, Madame Valakhin, whose face pleased me extremely (especially since it bore a great resemblance to her daughter's), stroked my head kindly.

Grandmamma seemed delighted to see Sonetchka. She invited her to come to her, put back a curl which had fallen over her brow, and looking earnestly at her said, "What a charming child!"

Sonetchka blushed, smiled, and, indeed, looked so charming that I myself blushed as I looked at her.

"I hope you are going to enjoy yourself here, my love," said Grandmamma. "Pray be as merry and dance as much as ever you can. See, we have two beaux for her already," she added, turning to Madame Valakhin, and stretching out her hand to me.

This coupling of Sonetchka and myself pleased me so much that I blushed again.

Feeling, presently, that my embarrassment was increasing, and hearing the sound of carriages approaching, I thought it wise to retire. In the hall I encountered the Princess Kornakoff, her son, and an incredible number of daughters. They had all of them the same face as their mother, and were very ugly. None of them arrested my attention. They talked in shrill tones as they took off their cloaks and boas, and laughed as they bustled about—probably at the fact that there were so many of them!

Etienne was a boy of fifteen, tall and plump, with a sharp face, deep-set bluish eyes, and very large hands and feet for his age. Likewise he was awkward, and had a nervous, unpleasing voice. Nevertheless he seemed very pleased with himself, and was, in my opinion, a boy who could well bear being beaten with rods.

For a long time we confronted one another without speaking as we took stock of each other. When the flood of dresses had swept past I made shift to begin a conversation by asking him whether it had not been very close in the carriage.

"I don't know," he answered indifferently. "I never ride inside it, for it makes me feel sick directly, and Mamma knows that. Whenever we are driving anywhere at night-time I always sit on the box. I like that, for then one sees everything. Philip gives me the reins, and sometimes the whip too, and then the people inside get a regular—well, you know," he added with a significant gesture "It's splendid then."

"Master Etienne," said a footman, entering the hall, "Philip wishes me to ask you where you put the whip."

"Where I put it? Why, I gave it back to him."

"But he says that you did not."

"Well, I laid it across the carriage-lamps!"

"No, sir, he says that you did not do that either. You had better confess that you took it and lashed it to shreds. I suppose poor Philip will have to make good your mischief out of his own pocket." The footman (who looked a grave and honest man) seemed much put out by the affair, and determined to sift it to the bottom on Philip's behalf.

Out of delicacy I pretended to notice nothing and turned aside, but the other footmen present gathered round and looked approvingly at the old servant.

"Hm—well, I DID tear it in pieces," at length confessed Etienne, shrinking from further explanations. "However, I will pay for it. Did you ever hear anything so absurd?" he added to me as he drew me towards the drawing-room.

"But excuse me, sir; HOW are you going to pay for it? I know your ways of paying. You have owed Maria Valericana twenty copecks these eight months now, and you have owed me something for two years, and Peter for—"

"Hold your tongue, will you!" shouted the young fellow, pale with rage, "I shall report you for this."

"Oh, you may do so," said the footman. "Yet it is not fair, your highness," he added, with a peculiar stress on the title, as he departed with the ladies' wraps to the cloak-room. We ourselves entered the salon.

"Quite right, footman," remarked someone approvingly from the ball behind us.

Grandmamma had a peculiar way of employing, now the second person singular, now the second person plural, in order to indicate her opinion of people. When the young Prince Etienne went up to her she addressed him as "YOU," and altogether looked at him with such an expression of contempt that, had I been in his place, I should have been utterly crestfallen. Etienne, however, was evidently not a boy of that sort, for he not only took no notice of her reception of him, but none of her person either. In fact, he bowed to the company at large in a way which, though not graceful, was at least free from embarrassment.

Sonetchka now claimed my whole attention. I remember that, as I stood in the salon with Etienne and Woloda, at a spot whence we could both see and be seen by Sonetchka, I took great pleasure in talking very loud (and all my utterances seemed to me both bold and comical) and glancing towards the door of the drawing-room, but that, as soon as ever we happened to move to another spot whence we could neither see nor be seen by her, I became dumb, and thought the conversation had ceased to be enjoyable. The rooms were now full of people—among them (as at all children's parties) a number of elder children who wished to dance and enjoy themselves very much, but who pretended to do everything merely in order to give pleasure to the mistress of the house.

When the Iwins arrived I found that, instead of being as delighted as usual to meet Seriosha, I felt a kind of vexation that he should see and be seen by Sonetchka.

XXI – BEFORE THE MAZURKA

"HULLO, Woloda! So we are going to dance to-night," said Seriosha, issuing from the drawing-room and taking out of his pocket a brand new pair of gloves. "I suppose it IS necessary to put on gloves?"

"Goodness! What shall I do? We have no gloves," I thought to myself. "I must go upstairs and search about." Yet though I rummaged in every drawer, I only found, in one of them, my green travelling mittens, and, in another, a single lilac-coloured glove, a thing which could be of no use to me, firstly, because it was very old and dirty, secondly, because it was much too large for me, and thirdly (and principally), because the middle finger was wanting—Karl having long ago cut it off to wear over a sore nail.

However, I put it on—not without some diffident contemplation of the blank left by the middle finger and of the ink-stained edges round the vacant space.

"If only Natalia Savishna had been here," I reflected, "we should certainly have found some gloves. I can't go downstairs in this condition. Yet, if they ask me why I am not dancing, what am I to say? However, I can't remain here either, or they will be sending upstairs to fetch me. What on earth am I to do?" and I wrung my hands.

"What are you up to here?" asked Woloda as he burst into the room. "Go and engage a partner. The dancing will be beginning directly."

"Woloda," I said despairingly, as I showed him my hand with two fingers thrust into a single finger of the dirty glove, "Woloda, you, never thought of this."

"Of what?" he said impatiently. "Oh, of gloves," he added with a careless glance at my hand. "That's nothing. We can ask Grandmamma what she thinks about it," and without further ado he departed downstairs. I felt a trifle relieved by the coolness with which he had met a situation which seemed to me so grave, and hastened back to the drawing-room, completely forgetful of the unfortunate glove which still adorned my left hand.

Cautiously approaching Grandmamma's arm-chair, I asked her in a whisper:

"Grandmamma, what are we to do? We have no gloves."

"What, my love?"

"We have no gloves," I repeated, at the same time bending over towards her and laying both hands on the arm of her chair.

"But what is that?" she cried as she caught hold of my left hand. "Look, my dear!" she continued, turning to Madame Valakhin. "See how smart this young man has made himself to dance with your daughter!"

As Grandmamma persisted in retaining hold of my hand and gazing with a mock air of gravity and interrogation at all around her, curiosity was soon aroused, and a general roar of laughter ensued.

I should have been infuriated at the thought that Seriosha was present to see this, as I scowled with embarrassment and struggled hard to free my hand, had it not been that somehow Sonetchka's laughter (and she was laughing to such a degree that the tears were standing in her eyes and the curls dancing about her lovely face) took away my feeling of humiliation. I felt that her laughter was not satirical, but only natural and free; so that, as we laughed together and looked at one another, there seemed to begin a kind of sympathy between us. Instead of turning out badly, therefore, the episode of the glove served only to set me at my ease among the dreaded circle of guests, and to make me cease to feel oppressed with shyness. The sufferings of shy people proceed only from the doubts which they feel concerning the opinions of their fellows. No sooner are those opinions expressed (whether flattering or the reverse) than the agony disappears.

How lovely Sonetchka looked when she was dancing a quadrille as my vis-a-vis, with, as her partner, the loutish Prince Etienne! How charmingly she smiled when, en chaine, she accorded me her hand! How gracefully the curls, around her head nodded to the rhythm, and how naively she executed

168

the jete assemble with her little feet!

In the fifth figure, when my partner had to leave me for the other side and I, counting the beats, was getting ready to dance my solo, she pursed her lips gravely and looked in another direction; but her fears for me were groundless. Boldly I performed the chasse en avant and chasse en arriere glissade, until, when it came to my turn to move towards her and I, with a comic gesture, showed her the poor glove with its crumpled fingers, she laughed heartily, and seemed to move her tiny feet more enchantingly than ever over the parquetted floor.

How well I remember how we formed the circle, and how, without withdrawing her hand from mine, she scratched her little nose with her glove! All this I can see before me still. Still can I hear the quadrille from "The Maids of the Danube" to which we danced that night.

The second quadrille, I danced with Sonetchka herself; yet when we went to sit down together during the interval, I felt overcome with shyness and as though I had nothing to say. At last, when my silence had lasted so long that I began to be afraid that she would think me a stupid boy, I decided at all hazards to counteract such a notion.

"Vous etes une habitante de Moscou?" I began, and, on receiving an affirmative answer, continued. "Et moi, je n'ai encore jamais frequente la capitale" (with a particular emphasis on the word "frequente"). Yet I felt that, brilliant though this introduction might be as evidence of my profound knowledge of the French language, I could not long keep up the conversation in that manner. Our turn for dancing had not yet arrived, and silence again ensued between us. I kept looking anxiously at her in the hope both of discerning what impression I had produced and of her coming to my aid.

"Where did you get that ridiculous glove of yours?" she asked me all of a sudden, and the question afforded me immense satisfaction and relief. I replied that the glove belonged to Karl Ivanitch, and then went on to speak ironically of his appearance, and to describe how comical he looked in his red cap, and how he and his green coat had once fallen plump off a horse into a pond.

The quadrille was soon over. Yet why had I spoken ironically of poor Karl Ivanitch? Should I, forsooth, have sunk in Sonetchka's esteem if, on the contrary, I had spoken of him with the love and respect which I undoubtedly bore him?

The quadrille ended, Sonetchka said, "Thank you," with as lovely an expression on her face as though I had really conferred, upon her a favour. I was delighted. In fact I hardly knew myself for joy and could not think whence I derived such case and confidence and even daring.

"Nothing in the world can abash me now," I thought as I wandered carelessly about the salon. "I am ready for anything."

Just then Seriosha came and requested me to be his vis-a-vis.

"Very well," I said. "I have no partner as yet, but I can soon find one."

Glancing round the salon with a confident eye, I saw that every lady was engaged save one—a tall girl standing near the drawing-room door. Yet a grown-up young man was approaching her-probably for the same purpose as myself! He was but two steps from her, while I was at the further end of the salon. Doing a glissade over the polished floor, I covered the intervening space, and in a brave, firm voice asked the favour of her hand in the quadrille. Smiling with a protecting air, the young lady accorded me her hand, and the tall young man was left without a partner. I felt so conscious of my strength that I paid no attention to his irritation, though I learnt later that he had asked somebody who the awkward, undity boy was who, had taken away his lady from him.

XXII – THE MAZURKA

AFTERWARDS the same young man formed one of the first couple in a mazurka. He sprang to his feet, took his partner's hand, and then, instead of executing the pas de Basques which Mimi had taught us, glided forward till he arrived at a corner of the room, stopped, divided his feet, turned on his heels, and, with a spring, glided back again. I, who had found no partner for this particular dance and was sitting on the arm of Grandmamma's chair, thought to myself:

"What on earth is he doing? That is not what Mimi taught us. And there are the Iwins and Etienne all dancing in the same way-without the pas de Basques! Ah! and there is Woloda too! He too is adopting the new style, and not so badly either. And there is Sonetchka, the lovely one! Yes, there she comes!" I felt immensely happy at that moment.

The mazurka came to an end, and already some of the guests were saying good-bye to Grandmamma. She was evidently tired, yet she assured them that she felt vexed at their early departure. Servants were gliding about with plates and trays among the dancers, and the musicians were carelessly playing the same tune for about the thirteenth time in succession, when the young lady whom I had danced with before, and who was just about to join in another mazurka, caught sight of me, and, with a kindly smile, led me to Sonetchka. And one of the innumerable Kornakoff princesses, at the same time asking me, "Rose or Hortie?"

"Ah, so it's YOU!" said Grandmamma as she turned round in her armchair. "Go and dance, then, my boy."

Although I would fain have taken refuge behind the armchair rather than leave its shelter, I could not refuse; so I got up, said, "Rose," and looked at Sonetchka. Before I had time to realise it, however, a hand in a white glove laid itself on mine, and the Kornakoff girl stepped forth with a pleased smile and evidently no suspicion that I was ignorant of the steps of the dance. I only knew that the pas de Basques (the only figure of it which I had been taught) would be out of place. However, the strains of the mazurka falling upon my ears, and imparting their usual impulse to my acoustic nerves (which, in their turn, imparted their usual impulse to my feet), I involuntarily, and to the amazement of the spectators, began executing on tiptoe the sole (and fatal) pas which I had been taught.

So long as we went straight ahead I kept fairly right, but when it came to turning I saw that I must make preparations to arrest my course. Accordingly, to avoid any appearance of awkwardness, I stopped short, with the intention of imitating the "wheel about" which I had seen the young man perform so neatly.

Unfortunately, just as I divided my feet and prepared to make a spring, the Princess Kornakoff looked sharply round at my legs with such an expression of stupefied amazement and curiosity that the glance undid me. Instead of continuing to dance, I remained moving my legs up and down on the same spot, in a sort of extraordinary fashion which bore no relation whatever either to form or rhythm. At last I stopped altogether. Every-one was looking at me—some with curiosity, some with astonishment, some with disdain, and some with compassion, Grandmamma alone seemed unmoved.

"You should not dance if you don't know the step," said Papa's angry voice in my ear as, pushing me gently aside, he took my partner's hand, completed the figures with her to the admiration of every one, and finally led her back to, her place. The mazurka was at an end.

Ah me! What had I done to be punished so heavily?

"Every one despises me, and will always despise me," I thought to myself. "The way is closed for me to friendship, love, and fame! All, all is lost!"

Why had Woloda made signs to me which every one saw, yet which could in no way help me? Why had that disgusting princess looked at my legs? Why had Sonetchka—she was a darling, of course!—yet why, oh why, had she smiled at that moment?

Why had Papa turned red and taken my hand? Can it be that he was ashamed of me?

Oh, it was dreadful! Alas, if only Mamma had been there she would never have blushed for her Nicolinka!

How on the instant that dear image led my imagination captive! I seemed to see once more the meadow before our house, the tall lime-trees in the garden, the clear pond where the ducks swain, the blue sky dappled with white clouds, the sweet-smelling ricks of hay. How those memories—aye, and many another quiet, beloved recollection—floated through my mind at that time!

XXIII — AFTER THE MAZURKA

At supper the young man whom I have mentioned seated himself beside me at the children's table, and treated me with an amount of attention which would have flattered my self-esteem had I been able, after the occurrence just related, to give a thought to anything beyond my failure in the mazurka. However, the young man seemed determined to cheer me up. He jested, called me "old boy," and finally (since none of the elder folks were looking at us) began to help me to wine, first from one bottle and then from another and to force me to drink it off quickly.

By the time (towards the end of supper) that a servant had poured me out a quarter of a glass of champagne, and the young man had straightway bid him fill it up and urged me to drink the beverage off at a draught, I had begun to feel a grateful warmth diffusing itself through my body. I also felt well-disposed towards my kind patron, and began to laugh heartily at everything. Suddenly the music of the Grosvater dance struck up, and every one rushed from the table. My friendship with the young man had now outlived its day; so, whereas he joined a group of the older folks, I approached Madame Valakhin to hear what she and her daughter had to say to one another.

"Just HALF-an-hour more?" Sonetchka was imploring her.

"Impossible, my dearest."

"Yet, only to please me—just this ONCE?" Sonetchka went on persuasively.

"Well, what if I should be ill to-morrow through all this dissipation?" rejoined her mother, and was incautious enough to smile.

"There! You DO consent, and we CAN stay after all!" exclaimed Sonetchka, jumping for joy.

"What is to be done with such a girl?" said Madame. "Well, run away and dance. See," she added on perceiving myself, "here is a cavalier ready waiting for you."

Sonetchka gave me her hand, and we darted off to the salon. The wine, added to Sonetchka's presence and gaiety, had at once made me forget all about the unfortunate end of the mazurka. I kept executing the most splendid feats with my legs—now imitating a horse as he throws out his hoofs in the trot, now stamping like a sheep infuriated at a dog, and all the while laughing regardless of appearances.

Sonetchka also laughed unceasingly, whether we were whirling round in a circle or whether we stood still to watch an old lady whose painful movements with her feet showed the difficulty she had in walking. Finally Sonetchka nearly died of merriment when I jumped half-way to the ceiling in proof of my skill.

As I passed a mirror in Grandmamma's boudoir and glanced at myself I could see that my face was all in a perspiration and my hair dishevelled—the top-knot, in particular, being more erect than ever. Yet my general appearance looked so happy, healthy, and good-tempered that I felt wholly pleased with myself.

"If I were always as I am now," I thought, "I might yet be able to please people with my looks." Yet as soon as I glanced at my partner's face again, and saw there not only the expression of happiness, health, and good temper which had just pleased me in my own, but also a fresh and enchanting beauty besides, I felt dissatisfied with myself again. I understood how silly of me it was to hope to attract the attention of such a wonderful being as Sonetchka. I could not hope for reciprocity—could not even think of it, yet my heart was overflowing with happiness. I could not imagine that the feeling of love which was filling my soul so pleasantly could require any happiness still greater, or wish for more than that that happiness should never cease. I felt perfectly contented. My heart beat like that of a dove, with the blood constantly flowing back to it, and I almost wept for joy.

As we passed through the hall and peered into a little dark store-room beneath the staircase I thought: "What bliss it would be if I could pass the rest of my life with her in that dark corner, and never let anybody know that we were there!"

"It HAS been a delightful evening, hasn't it?" I asked her in a low, tremulous voice. Then I quickened my steps—as much out of fear of what I had said as out of fear of what I had meant to imply.

"Yes, VERY!" she answered, and turned her face to look at me with an expression so kind that I ceased to be afraid. I went on:

"Particularly since supper. Yet if you could only know how I regret" (I had nearly said) "how miserable I am at your going, and to think that we shall see each other no more!"

"But why SHOULDN'T we?" she asked, looking gravely at the corner of her pocket-handkerchief, and gliding her fingers over a latticed screen which we were passing. "Every Tuesday and Friday I go with Mamma to the Iverskoi Prospect. I suppose you go for walks too sometimes?"

"Well, certainly I shall ask to go for one next Tuesday, and, if they won't take me I shall go by myself—even without my hat, if necessary. I know the way all right."

"Do you know what I have just thought of?" she went on. "You know, I call some of the boys who come to see us THOU. Shall you and I call each other THOU too? Wilt THOU?" she added, bending her head towards me and looking me straight in the eyes.

At this moment a more lively section of the Grosvater dance began.

"Give me your hand," I said, under the impression that the music and din would drown my exact words, but she smilingly replied, "THY hand, not YOUR hand." Yet the dance was over before I had succeeded in saying THOU, even though I kept conning over phrases in which the pronoun could be employed—and employed more than once. All that I wanted was the courage to say it.

"Wilt THOU?" and "THY hand" sounded continually in my ears, and caused in me a kind of intoxication I could hear and see nothing but Sonetchka. I watched her mother take her curls, lay them flat behind her

176

ears (thus disclosing portions of her forehead and temples which I had not yet seen), and wrap her up so completely in the green shawl that nothing was left visible but the tip of her nose. Indeed, I could see that, if her little rosy fingers had not made a small, opening near her mouth, she would have been unable to breathe. Finally I saw her leave her mother's arm for an instant on the staircase, and turn and nod to us quickly before she disappeared through the doorway.

Woloda, the Iwins, the young Prince Etienne, and myself were all of us in love with Sonetchka and all of us standing on the staircase to follow her with our eyes. To whom in particular she had nodded I do not know, but at the moment I firmly believed it to be myself. In taking leave of the Iwins, I spoke quite unconcernedly, and even coldly, to Seriosha before I finally shook hands with him. Though he tried to appear absolutely indifferent, I think that he understood that from that day forth he had lost both my affection and his power over me, as well as that he regretted it.

XXIV — IN BED

"How could I have managed to be so long and so passionately devoted to Seriosha?" I asked myself as I lay in bed that night. "He never either understood, appreciated, or deserved my love. But Sonetchka! What a darling SHE is! 'Wilt THOU?'—'THY hand'!"

I crept closer to the pillows, imagined to myself her lovely face, covered my head over with the bedclothes, tucked the counterpane in on all sides, and, thus snugly covered, lay quiet and enjoying the warmth until I became wholly absorbed in pleasant fancies and reminiscences.

If I stared fixedly at the inside of the sheet above me I found that I could see her as clearly as I had done an hour ago could talk to her in my thoughts, and, though it was a conversation of irrational tenor, I derived the greatest delight from it, seeing that "THOU" and "THINE" and "for THEE" and "to THEE" occurred in it incessantly. These fancies were so vivid that I could not sleep for the sweetness of my emotion, and felt as though I must communicate my superabundant happiness to some one.

"The darling!" I said, half-aloud, as I turned over; then, "Woloda, are you asleep?"

"No," he replied in a sleepy voice. "What's the matter?"

"I am in love, Woloda—terribly in love with Sonetchka"

"Well? Anything else?" he replied, stretching himself.

"Oh, but you cannot imagine what I feel just now, as I lay covered over with the counterpane, I could see her and talk to her so clearly that it was marvellous! And, do you know, while I was lying thinking about her—I don't know why it was, but all at once I felt so sad that I could have cried."

Woloda made a movement of some sort.

"One thing only I wish for," I continued; "and that is that I could always be with her and always be seeing her. Just that. You are in love too, I believe. Confess that you are."

It was strange, but somehow I wanted every one to be in love with Sonetchka, and every one to tell me that they were so.

"So that's how it is with you? " said Woloda, turning round to me. "Well, I can understand it."

"I can see that you cannot sleep," I remarked, observing by his bright eyes that he was anything but drowsy. "Well, cover yourself over SO" (and I pulled the bedclothes over him), "and then let us talk about her. Isn't she splendid? If she were to say to me, 'Nicolinka, jump out of the window,' or 'jump into the fire,' I should say, 'Yes, I will do it at once and rejoice in doing it.' Oh, how glorious she is!"

I went on picturing her again and again to my imagination, and, to enjoy the vision the better, turned over on my side and buried my head in the pillows, murmuring, "Oh, I want to cry, Woloda."

"What a fool you are!" he said with a slight laugh. Then, after a moment's silence he added: "I am not like you. I think I would rather sit and talk with her."

"Ah! Then you ARE in love with her!" I interrupted.

"And then," went on Woloda, smiling tenderly, "kiss her fingers and eyes and lips and nose and feet—kiss all of her."

"How absurd!" I exclaimed from beneath the pillows.

"Ah, you don't understand things," said Woloda with contempt.

"I DO understand. It's you who don't understand things, and you talk rubbish, too," I replied, half-crying.

"Well, there is nothing to cry about," he concluded. "She is only a girl."

XXV – THE LETTER

ON the 16th of April, nearly six months after the day just described, Papa entered our schoolroom and told us that that night we must start with him for our country house. I felt a pang at my heart when I heard the news, and my thoughts at once turned to Mamma. The cause of our unexpected departure was the following letter:

"PETROVSKOE, 12th April.

"Only this moment (i.e. at ten o'clock in the evening) have I received your dear letter of the 3rd of April, but as usual, I answer it at once. Fedor brought it yesterday from town, but, as it was late, he did not give it to Mimi till this morning, and Mimi (since I was unwell) kept it from me all day. I have been a little feverish. In fact, to tell the truth, this is the fourth day that I have been in bed.

"Yet do not be uneasy. I feel almost myself again now, and if Ivan Vassilitch should allow me, I think of getting up to-morrow.

"On Friday last I took the girls for a drive, and, close to the little bridge by the turning on to the high road (the place which always makes me nervous), the horses and carriage stuck fast in the mud. Well, the day being fine, I thought that we would walk a little up the road until the carriage should be extricated, but no sooner had we reached the chapel than I felt obliged to sit down, I was so tired, and in this way half-an-hour passed while help was being sent for to get the carriage dug out. I felt cold, for I had only thin boots on, and they had been wet through. After luncheon too, I had alternate cold and hot fits, yet still continued to follow our ordinary routine.

"When tea was over I sat down to the piano to play a duct with Lubotshka, (you would be astonished to hear what progress she has made!), but imagine my surprise when I found that I could not count the beats! Several times I began to do so, yet always felt confused in my head, and kept hearing strange noises in my ears. I would begin 'One-two-three—' and then suddenly go on '-eight-fifteen,' and so on, as though I were talking nonsense and could not help it. At last Mimi came to my assistance and forced me to retire to bed. That was how my illness began, and it was all through my own fault. The next day I had a good deal of fever, and our good Ivan Vassilitch came. He has not left us since, but promises soon to restore me to the world.

"What a wonderful old man he is! While I was feverish and delirious he sat the whole night by my bedside without once closing his eyes; and at this moment (since he knows I am busy writing) he is with the girls in the divannaia, and I can hear him telling them German stories, and them laughing as they listen to him.

"'La Belle Flamande,' as you call her, is now spending her second week here as my guest (her mother having gone to pay a visit somewhere), and she is most attentive and attached to me. She even tells me her secret affairs. Under different circumstances her beautiful face, good temper, and youth might have made a most excellent girl of her, but in the society in which according to her own account, she moves she will be wasted. The idea has more than once occurred to me that, had I not had so many children of my own, it would have been a deed of mercy to have adopted her.

"Lubotshka had meant to write to you herself, but she has torn up three sheets of paper, saying: 'I know what a quizzer Papa always is. If he were to find a single fault in my letter he would show it to everybody.' Katenka is as charming as usual, and Mimi, too, is good, but tiresome.

"Now let me speak of more serious matters. You write to me that your affairs are not going well this winter, and that you wish to break into the revenues of Chabarovska. It seems to me strange that you should think it necessary to ask my consent. Surely what belongs to me belongs no less to you? You are so kind-hearted, dear, that, for fear of worrying me, you conceal the real state of things, but I can guess that you have lost a great deal at cards, as also that you are afraid of my being angry at that. Yet, so long as you can tide over this crisis, I shall not think much of it, and you need not be uneasy, I have grown accustomed to no longer relying, so far as the children are concerned, upon your gains at play, nor yet—excuse me for saying so—upon your income. Therefore your losses cause me as little anxiety as your gains give me pleasure. What I really grieve over is your unhappy passion itself for gambling—a passion which bereaves me of part of your tender affection and obliges me to tell you such bitter truths as (God knows with what pain) I am now telling you. I never cease to beseech Him that He may preserve us, not from poverty (for what is poverty?), but from the terrible juncture which would arise should the interests of the children, which I am called upon to protect, ever come into collision with our own. Hitherto God has listened to my prayers. You have never yet overstepped the limit beyond which we should be obliged either to sacrifice property which would no longer belong to us, but to the children, or—It is terrible to think of, but the dreadful misfortune at which I hint is forever hanging over our heads. Yes, it is the heavy cross which God has given us both to carry.

"Also, you write about the children, and come back to our old point of difference by asking my consent to your placing them at a boarding-school. You know my objection to that kind of education. I do not know, dear, whether you will accede to my request, but I nevertheless beseech you, by your love for me, to give me your promise that never so long as I am alive, nor yet after my death (if God should see fit to separate us), shall such a thing be done.

"Also you write that our affairs render it indispensable for you to visit St. Petersburg. The Lord go with you! Go and return as, soon as possible. Without you we shall all of us be lonely.

"Spring is coming in beautifully. We keep the door on to the terrace always open now, while the path to the orangery is dry and the peach-trees are in full blossom. Only here and there is there a little snow remaining. The swallows are arriving, and to-day Lubotshka brought me the first flowers. The doctor says that in about three days' time I shall be well again and able to take the open air and to enjoy the April sun. Now, au revoir, my dearest one. Do not be alarmed, I beg of you, either on account of my illness or on account of your losses at play. End the crisis as soon as possible, and then return here with the children for the summer. I am making wonderful plans for our passing of it, and I only need your presence to realise them."

The rest of the letter was written in French, as well as in a strange, uncertain hand, on another piece of paper. I transcribe it word for word:

"Do not believe what I have just written to you about my illness. It is more serious than any one knows. I alone know that I shall never leave my bed again. Do not, therefore, delay a minute in coming here with the children. Perhaps it may yet be permitted me to embrace and bless them. It is my last wish that it should be so. I know what a terrible blow this will be to you, but you would have had to hear it sooner or later—if not from me, at least from others. Let us try to, bear the Calamity with fortitude, and place our trust in the mercy of God. Let us submit ourselves to His will. Do not think that what I am writing is some delusion of my sick imagination. On the contrary, I am perfectly clear at this moment, and absolutely calm. Nor must you comfort yourself with the false hope that these are the unreal, confused feelings of a despondent spirit, for I feel indeed, I know, since God has deigned to reveal it to me—that I have now but a very short time to live. Will my love for you and the children cease with my life? I know that that can never be. At this moment I am too full of that love to be capable of believing that such a feeling (which constitutes a part of my very existence) can ever, perish. My soul can never lack its love for you; and I know that that love will exist for ever, since such a feeling could never have been awakened if it were not to be eternal. I shall no longer be with you, yet I firmly believe that my love will cleave to you always, and from that thought I glean such comfort that I await the approach of death calmly and without fear. Yes, I am calm, and God knows that I have ever looked, and do look now, upon death as no more than the passage to a better life. Yet why do tears blind my eyes? Why should the children lose a mother's love? Why must you, my husband, experience such a heavy and unlooked-for blow? Why must I die when your love was making life so inexpressibly happy for me?

"But His holy will be done!

"The tears prevent my writing more. It may be that I shall never see you again. I thank you, my darling beyond all price, for all the felicity with which you have surrounded me in this life. Soon I shall appear before God Himself to pray that He may reward you. Farewell, my dearest! Remember that, if I am no longer here, my love will none the less NEVER AND NOWHERE fail you. Farewell, Woloda—farewell, my pet! Farewell, my Benjamin, my little Nicolinka! Surely they will never forget me?"

With this letter had come also a French note from Mimi, in which the latter said:

"The sad circumstances of which she has written to you are but too surely confirmed by the words of the doctor. Yesterday evening she ordered the letter to be posted at once, but, thinking at she did so in delirium, I waited until this morning, with the intention of sealing and sending it then. Hardly had I done so when Natalia Nicolaevna asked me what I had done with the letter and told me to burn it if not yet despatched. She is forever speaking of it, and saying that it will kill you. Do not delay your departure for an instant if you wish to see the angel before she leaves us. Pray excuse this scribble, but I have not slept now for three nights. You know how much I love her."

Later I heard from Natalia Savishna (who passed the whole of the night of the 11th April at Mamma's bedside) that, after writing the first part of the letter, Mamma laid it down upon the table beside her and went to sleep for a while.

"I confess," said Natalia Savishna, "that I too fell asleep in the arm-chair, and let my knitting slip from my hands. Suddenly, towards one o'clock in the morning, I heard her saying something; whereupon I opened my eyes and looked at her. My darling was sitting up in bed, with her hands clasped together and streams of tears gushing from her eyes.

"'It is all over now,' she said, and hid her face in her hands.

"I sprang to my feet, and asked what the matter was.

"'Ah, Natalia Savishna, if you could only know what I have just seen!' she said; yet, for all my asking, she would say no more, beyond commanding me to hand her the letter. To that letter she added something, and then said that it must be sent off directly. From that moment she grew, rapidly worse."

XXVI — WHAT AWAITED US AT THE COUNTRY-HOUSE

On the 18th of April we descended from the carriage at the front door of the house at Petrovskoe. All the way from Moscow Papa had been preoccupied, and when Woloda had asked him "whether Mamma was ill" he had looked at him sadly and nodded an affirmative. Nevertheless he had grown more composed during the journey, and it was only when we were actually approaching the house that his face again began to grow anxious, until, as he leaped from the carriage and asked Foka (who had run breathlessly to meet us), "How is Natalia Nicolaevna now?" his voice, was trembling, and his eyes had filled with tears. The good, old Foka looked at us, and then lowered his gaze again. Finally he said as he opened the hall-door and turned his head aside: "It is the sixth day since she has not left her bed."

Milka (who, as we afterwards learned, had never ceased to whine from the day when Mamma was taken ill) came leaping, joyfully to meet Papa, and barking a welcome as she licked his hands, but Papa put her aside, and went first to the drawing-room, and then into the divannaia, from which a door led into the bedroom. The nearer he approached the latter, the more, did his movements express the agitation that he felt. Entering the divannaia he crossed it on tiptoe, seeming to hold his breath. Even then he had to stop and make the sign of the cross before he could summon up courage to turn the handle. At the same moment Mimi, with dishevelled hair and eyes red with weeping came hastily out of the corridor.

"Ah, Peter Alexandritch!" she said in a whisper and with a marked expression of despair. Then, observing that Papa was trying to open the door, she whispered again:

"Not here. This door is locked. Go round to the door on the other side."

Oh, how terribly all this wrought upon my imagination, racked as it was by grief and terrible forebodings!

So we went round to the other side. In the corridor we met the gardener, Akim, who had been wont to amuse us with his grimaces, but at this moment I could see nothing comical in him. Indeed, the sight of his thoughtless, indifferent face struck me more painfully than anything else. In the maidservants' hall, through which we had to pass, two maids were sitting at their work, but rose to salute us with an expression so mournful that I felt completely overwhelmed.

Passing also through Mimi's room, Papa opened the door of the bedroom, and we entered. The two windows on the right were curtained over, and close to them was seated, Natalia Savishna, spectacles on nose and engaged in darning stockings. She did not approach us to kiss me as she had been used to do, but just rose and looked at us, her tears beginning to flow afresh. Somehow it frightened me to see every one, on beholding us, begin to cry, although they had been calm enough before.

On the left stood the bed behind a screen, while in the great arm-chair the doctor lay asleep. Beside the bed a young, fair-haired and remarkably beautiful girl in a white morning wrapper was applying ice to Mamma's head, but Mamma herself I could not see. This girl was "La Belle Flamande" of whom Mamma had written, and who afterwards played so important a part in our family life. As we entered she disengaged one of her hands, straightened the pleats of her dress on her bosom, and whispered, "She is insensible." Though I was in an agony of grief, I observed at that moment every little detail.

It was almost dark in the room, and very hot, while the air was heavy with the mingled, scent of mint, eau-de-cologne, camomile, and Hoffman's pastilles. The latter ingredient caught my attention so strongly that even now I can never hear of it, or even think of it, without my memory carrying me back to that dark, close room, and all the details of that dreadful time.

Mamma's eyes were wide open, but they could not see us. Never shall I forget the terrible expression in them—the expression of agonies of suffering!

Then we were taken away.

When, later, I was able to ask Natalia Savishna about Mamma's last moments she told me the following:

"After you were taken out of the room, my beloved one struggled for a long time, as though some one were trying to strangle her. Then at last she laid her head back upon the pillow, and slept softly, peacefully, like an angel from Heaven. I went away for a moment to see about her medicine, and just as I entered the room again my darling was throwing the bedclothes from off her and calling for your Papa. He stooped over her, but strength failed her to say what she wanted to. All she could do was to open her lips and gasp, 'My God, my God! The children, the children!' I would have run to fetch you, but Ivan Vassilitch stopped me, saying that it would only excite her—it were best not to do so. Then suddenly she stretched her arms out and dropped them again. What she meant by that gesture the good God alone knows, but I think that in it she was blessing you—you the children whom she could not see. God did not grant her to see her little ones before her death. Then she raised herself up—did my love, my darling—yes, just so with her hands, and exclaimed in a voice which I cannot bear to remember, 'Mother of God, never forsake them!'"

"Then the pain mounted to her heart, and from her eyes it as, plain that she suffered terribly, my poor one! She sank back upon the pillows, tore the bedclothes with her teeth, and wept—wept—"

"Yes and what then?" I asked but Natalia Savishna could say no more. She turned away and cried bitterly.

Mamma had expired in terrible agonies.

XXVII — GRIEF

LATE the following evening I thought I would like to look at her once more; so, conquering an involuntary sense of fear, I gently opened the door of the salon and entered on tiptoe.

In the middle of the room, on a table, lay the coffin, with wax candles burning all round it on tall silver candelabra. In the further corner sat the chanter, reading the Psalms in a low, monotonous voice. I stopped at the door and tried to look, but my eyes were so weak with crying, and my nerves so terribly on edge, that I could distinguish nothing. Every object seemed to mingle together in a strange blur—the candles, the brocade, the velvet, the great candelabra, the pink satin cushion trimmed with lace, the chaplet of flowers, the ribboned cap, and something of a transparent, wax-like colour. I mounted a chair to see her face, yet where it should have been I could see only that wax-like, transparent something. I could not believe it to be her face. Yet, as I stood grazing at it, I at last recognised the well-known, beloved features. I shuddered with horror to realise that it WAS she. Why were those eyes so sunken? What had laid that dreadful paleness upon her cheeks, and stamped the black spot beneath the transparent skin on one of them? Why was the expression of the whole face so cold and severe? Why were the lips so white, and their outline so beautiful, so majestic, so expressive of an unnatural calm that, as I looked at them, a chill shudder ran through my hair and down my back?

Somehow, as I gazed, an irrepressible, incomprehensible power seemed to compel me to keep my eyes fixed upon that lifeless face. I could not turn away, and my imagination began to picture before me scenes of her active life and happiness. I forgot that the corpse lying before me now—the THING at which I was gazing unconsciously as at an object which had nothing in common with my dreams—was SHE. I fancied I could see her—now here, now there, alive, happy, and smiling. Then some well-known feature in the face at which I was gazing would suddenly arrest my attention, and in a flash

I would recall the terrible reality and shudder-though still unable to turn my eyes away.

Then again the dreams would replace reality—then again the reality put to flight the dreams. At last the consciousness of both left me, and for a while I became insensible.

How long I remained in that condition I do not know, nor yet how it occurred. I only know that for a time I lost all sense of existence, and experienced a kind of vague blissfulness which though grand and sweet, was also sad. It may be that, as it ascended to a better world, her beautiful soul had looked down with longing at the world in which she had left us—that it had seen my sorrow, and, pitying me, had returned to earth on the wings of love to console and bless me with a heavenly smile of compassion.

The door creaked as the chanter entered who was to relieve his predecessor. The noise awakened me, and my first thought was that, seeing me standing on the chair in a posture which had nothing touching in its aspect, he might take me for an unfeeling boy who had climbed on to the chair out of mere curiosity: wherefore I hastened to make the sign of the cross, to bend down my head, and to burst out crying. As I recall now my impressions of that episode I find that it was only during my moments of self-forgetfulness that my grief was wholehearted. True, both before and after the funeral I never ceased to cry and to look miserable, yet I feel conscience-stricken when I recall that grief of mine, seeing that always present in it there was an element of conceit—of a desire to show that I was more grieved than any one else, of an interest which I took in observing the effect, produced upon others by my tears, and of an idle curiosity leading me to remark Mimi's bonnet and the faces of all present. The mere circumstance that I despised myself for not feeling grief to the exclusion of everything else, and that I endeavoured to conceal the fact, shows that my sadness was insincere and unnatural. I took a delight in feeling that I was unhappy, and in trying to feel more so. Consequently this egotistic consciousness completely annulled any element of sincerity in my woe.

That night I slept calmly and soundly (as is usual after any great emotion), and awoke with my tears dried and my nerves restored. At ten o'clock we were summoned to attend the pre-funeral requiem.

The room was full of weeping servants and peasants who had come to bid farewell to their late mistress. During the service I myself wept a great deal, made frequent signs of the cross, and performed many genuflections, but I did not pray with, my soul, and felt, if anything, almost indifferent. My thoughts were chiefly centred upon the new coat which I was wearing (a garment which was tight and uncomfortable) and upon how to avoid soiling my trousers at the knees. Also I took the most minute notice of all present.

Papa stood at the head of the coffin. He was as white as snow, and only with difficulty restrained his tears. His tall figure in its black frockcoat, his pale, expressive face, the graceful, assured manner in which, as usual, he made the sign of the cross or bowed until he touched the floor with his hand [A custom of the Greek funeral rite.] or took the candle from the priest or went to the coffin—all were exceedingly effective; yet for some reason or another I felt a grudge against him for that very ability to appear effective at such a moment. Mimi stood leaning against the wall as though scarcely able to support herself. Her dress was all awry and covered with feathers, and her cap cocked to one side, while her eyes were red with weeping, her legs trembling under her, and she sobbed incessantly in a heartrending manner as ever and again she buried her face in her handkerchief or her hands. I imagine that she did this to check her continual sobbing without being seen by the spectators. I remember, too, her telling Papa, the evening before, that Mamma's death had come upon her as a blow from which she could never hope to recover; that with Mamma she had lost everything; but that "the angel," as she called my mother, had not forgotten her when at the point of death, since she had declared her wish to render her (Mimi's) and Katenka's fortunes secure for ever. Mimi had shed bitter tears while relating this, and very likely her sorrow, if not wholly pure and disinterested, was in the main sincere. Lubotshka, in black garments and suffused with tears, stood with her head bowed upon her breast. She rarely looked at the coffin, yet whenever she did so her face expressed a sort of childish fear. Katenka stood near her mother, and, despite her lengthened face, looked as lovely as ever. Woloda's frank nature was frank also in grief. He stood looking grave and as though he were staring at some object with fixed eyes. Then suddenly his lips would begin to quiver, and he would hastily make the sign of the cross, and bend his head again.

Such of those present as were strangers I found intolerable. In fact, the phrases of condolence with which they addressed Papa (such, for instance, as that "she is better off now" "she was too good for this world," and so on) awakened in me something like fury. What right had they to weep over or to talk about her? Some of them, in referring to ourselves, called us "orphans"— just as though it were not a matter of common knowledge that children who have lost their mother are known as orphans! Probably (I thought) they liked to be the first to give us that name, just as some people find pleasure in being the first to address a newly-married girl as "Madame."

In a far corner of the room, and almost hidden by the open door, of the dining-room, stood a grey old woman with bent knees. With hands clasped together and eyes lifted to heaven, she prayed only—not wept. Her soul was in the presence of God, and she was asking Him soon to reunite her to her whom she had loved beyond all beings on this earth, and whom she steadfastly believed that she would very soon meet again.

"There stands one who SINCERELY loved her," I thought to myself, and felt ashamed.

The requiem was over. They uncovered the face of the deceased, and all present except ourselves went to the coffin to give her the kiss of farewell.

One of the last to take leave of her departed mistress was a peasant woman who was holding by the hand a pretty little girl of five whom she had brought with her, God knows for what reason. Just at a moment when I chanced to drop my wet handkerchief and was stooping to pick it up again, a loud, piercing scream startled me, and filled me with such terror that, were I to live a hundred years more, I should never forget it. Even now the recollection always sends a cold shudder through my frame. I raised my head. Standing on the chair near the coffin was the peasant woman, while struggling and fighting in her arms was the little girl, and it was this same poor child who had screamed with such dreadful, desperate frenzy as, straining her terrified face away, she still, continued to gaze with dilated eyes at the face of the corpse. I too screamed in a voice perhaps more dreadful still, and ran headlong from the room.

Only now did I understand the source of the strong, oppressive smell which, mingling with the scent of the incense, filled the chamber, while the thought that the face which, but a few days ago, had been full of freshness and beauty—the face which I loved more than anything else in all the world—was now capable of inspiring horror at length revealed to me, as though for the first time, the terrible truth, and filled my soul with despair.

XXVIII — SAD RECOLLECTIONS

Mamma was no longer with us, but our life went on as usual. We went to bed and got up at the same times and in the same rooms; breakfast, luncheon, and supper continued to be at their usual hours; everything remained standing in its accustomed place; nothing in the house or in our mode of life was altered: only, she was not there.

Yet it seemed to me as though such a misfortune ought to have changed everything. Our old mode of life appeared like an insult to her memory. It recalled too vividly her presence.

The day before the funeral I felt as though I should like to rest a little after luncheon, and accordingly went to Natalia Savishna's room with the intention of installing myself comfortably under the warm, soft down of the quilt on her bed. When I entered I found Natalia herself lying on the bed and apparently asleep, but, on hearing my footsteps, she raised herself up, removed the handkerchief which had been protecting her face from the flies, and, adjusting her cap, sat forward on the edge of the bed. Since it frequently happened that I came to lie down in her room, she guessed my errand at once, and said:

"So you have come to rest here a little, have you? Lie down, then, my dearest."

"Oh, but what is the matter with you, Natalia Savishna?" I exclaimed as I forced her back again. "I did not come for that. No, you are tired yourself, so you LIE down."

"I am quite rested now, darling," she said (though I knew that it was many a night since she had closed her eyes). "Yes, I am indeed, and have no wish to sleep again," she added with a deep sigh.

I felt as though I wanted to speak to her of our misfortune, since I knew her sincerity and love, and thought that it would be a consolation to me to weep with her.

"Natalia Savishna," I said after a pause, as I seated myself upon the bed, "who would ever have thought of this?"

The old woman looked at me with astonishment, for she did not quite understand my question.

"Yes, who would ever have thought of it?" I repeated.

"Ah, my darling," she said with a glance of tender compassion, "it is not only 'Who would ever have thought of it?' but 'Who, even now, would ever believe it?' I am old, and my bones should long ago have gone to rest rather than that I should have lived to see the old master, your Grandpapa, of blessed memory, and Prince Nicola Michaelovitch, and his two brothers, and your sister Amenka all buried before me, though all younger than myself— and now my darling, to my never-ending sorrow, gone home before me! Yet it has been God's will. He took her away because she was worthy to be taken, and because He has need of the good ones."

This simple thought seemed to me a consolation, and I pressed closer to Natalia. She laid her hands upon my head as she looked upward with eyes expressive of a deep, but resigned, sorrow. In her soul was a sure and certain hope that God would not long separate her from the one upon whom the whole strength of her love had for many years been concentrated.

"Yes, my dear," she went on, "it is a long time now since I used to nurse and fondle her, and she used to call me Natasha. She used to come jumping upon me, and caressing and kissing me, and say, 'MY Nashik, MY darling, MY ducky,' and I used to answer jokingly, 'Well, my love, I don't believe that you DO love me. You will be a grown-up young lady soon, and going away to be married, and will leave your Nashik forgotten.' Then she would grow thoughtful and say, 'I think I had better not marry if my Nashik cannot go with me, for I mean never to leave her.' Yet, alas! She has left me now! Who was there in the world she did not love? Yes, my dearest, it must never be POSSIBLE for you to forget your Mamma. She was not a being of earth—she was an angel from Heaven. When her soul has entered the heavenly kingdom she will continue to love you and to be proud of you even there."

"But why do you say 'when her soul has entered the heavenly kingdom'?"

I asked. "I believe it is there now."

"No, my dearest," replied Natalia as she lowered her voice and pressed herself yet closer to me, "her soul is still here," and she pointed upwards. She spoke in a whisper, but with such an intensity of conviction that I too involuntarily raised my eyes and looked at the ceiling, as though expecting to see something there. "Before the souls of the just enter Paradise they have to undergo forty trials for forty days, and during that time they hover around their earthly home." [A Russian popular legend.]

She went on speaking for some time in this strain—speaking with the same simplicity and conviction as though she were relating common things which she herself had witnessed, and to doubt which could never enter into any one's head. I listened almost breathlessly, and though I did not understand all she said, I never for a moment doubted her word.

"Yes, my darling, she is here now, and perhaps looking at us and listening to what we are saying," concluded Natalia. Raising her head, she remained silent for a while. At length she wiped away the tears which were streaming from her eyes, looked me straight in the face, and said in a voice trembling with emotion:

"Ah, it is through many trials that God is leading me to Him. Why, indeed, am I still here? Whom have I to live for? Whom have I to love?"

"Do you not love US, then?" I asked sadly, and half-choking with my tears.

"Yes, God knows that I love you, my darling; but to love any one as I loved HER—that I cannot do."

She could say no more, but turned her head aside and wept bitterly. As for me, I no longer thought of going to sleep, but sat silently with her and mingled my tears with hers.

Presently Foka entered the room, but, on seeing our emotion and not wishing to disturb us, stopped short at the door.

"Do you want anything, my good Foka?" asked Natalia as she wiped away her tears.

"If you please, half-a-pound of currants, four pounds of sugar, and three pounds of rice for the kutia." [Cakes partaken of by the mourners at a Russian funeral.]

"Yes, in one moment," said Natalia as she took a pinch of snuff and hastened to her drawers. All traces of the grief, aroused by our conversation disappeared on, the instant that she had duties to fulfil, for she looked upon those duties as of paramount importance.

"But why FOUR pounds?" she objected as she weighed the sugar on a steelyard. "Three and a half would be sufficient," and she withdrew a few lumps. "How is it, too, that, though I weighed out eight pounds of rice yesterday, more is wanted now? No offence to you, Foka, but I am not going to waste rice like that. I suppose Vanka is glad that there is confusion in the house just now, for he thinks that nothing will be looked after, but I am not going to have any careless extravagance with my master's goods. Did one ever hear of such a thing? Eight pounds!"

"Well, I have nothing to do with it. He says it is all gone, that's all."

"Hm, hm! Well, there it is. Let him take it."

I was struck by the sudden transition from the touching sensibility with which she had just been speaking to me to this petty reckoning and captiousness. Yet, thinking it over afterwards, I recognised that it was merely because, in spite of what was lying on her heart, she retained the habit of duty, and that it was the strength of that habit which enabled her to pursue her functions as of old. Her grief was too strong and too true to require any pretence of being unable to fulfil trivial tasks, nor would she have understood that any one could so pretend. Vanity is a sentiment so entirely at variance with genuine grief, yet a sentiment so inherent in human nature, that even the most poignant sorrow does not always drive it wholly forth. Vanity mingled with grief shows itself in a desire to be recognised as unhappy or resigned; and this ignoble desire—an aspiration which, for all that we may not acknowledge it is rarely absent, even in cases of the utmost affliction—

takes off greatly from the force, the dignity, and the sincerity of grief. Natalia Savishna had been so sorely smitten by her misfortune that not a single wish of her own remained in her soul—she went on living purely by habit.

Having handed over the provisions to Foka, and reminded him of the refreshments which must be ready for the priests, she took up her knitting and seated herself by my side again. The conversation reverted to the old topic, and we once more mourned and shed tears together. These talks with Natalia I repeated every day, for her quiet tears and words of devotion brought me relief and comfort. Soon, however, a parting came. Three days after the funeral we returned to Moscow, and I never saw her again.

Grandmamma received the sad tidings only on our return to her house, and her grief was extraordinary. At first we were not allowed to see her, since for a whole week she was out of her mind, and the doctors were afraid for her life. Not only did she decline all medicine whatsoever, but she refused to speak to anybody or to take nourishment, and never closed her eyes in sleep. Sometimes, as she sat alone in the arm-chair in her room, she would begin laughing and crying at the same time, with a sort of tearless grief, or else relapse into convulsions, and scream out dreadful, incoherent words in a horrible voice. It was the first dire sorrow which she had known in her life, and it reduced her almost to distraction. She would begin accusing first one person, and then another, of bringing this misfortune upon her, and rail at and blame them with the most extraordinary virulence. Finally she would rise from her arm-chair, pace the room for a while, and end by falling senseless to the floor.

Once, when I went to her room, she appeared to be sitting quietly in her chair, yet with an air which struck me as curious. Though her eyes were wide open, their glance was vacant and meaningless, and she seemed to gaze in my direction without seeing me. Suddenly her lips parted slowly in a smile, and she said in a touchingly, tender voice: "Come here, then, my dearest one; come here, my angel." Thinking that it was myself she was addressing, I moved towards her, but it was not I whom she was beholding at that moment. "Oh, my love," she went on, "if only you could know how distracted I have been, and how delighted I am to see you once more!" I understood then that she believed herself to be looking upon Mamma, and halted where I was. "They told me you were gone," she concluded with a frown; "but what nonsense! As if you could die before ME!" and she laughed a terrible, hysterical laugh.

Only those who can love strongly can experience an overwhelming grief. Yet their very need of loving sometimes serves to throw off their grief from them and to save them. The moral nature of man is more tenacious of life than the physical, and grief never kills.

After a time Grandmamma's power of weeping came back to her, and she began to recover. Her first thought when her reason returned was for us children, and her love for us was greater than ever. We never left her armchair, and she would talk of Mamma, and weep softly, and caress us.

Nobody who saw her grief could say that it was consciously exaggerated, for its expression was too strong and touching; yet for some reason or another my sympathy went out more to Natalia Savishna, and to this day I am convinced that nobody loved and regretted Mamma so purely and sincerely as did that simple-hearted, affectionate being.

With Mamma's death the happy time of my childhood came to an end, and a new epoch—the epoch of my boyhood—began; but since my memories of Natalia Savishna (who exercised such a strong and beneficial influence upon the bent of my mind and the development of my sensibility) belong rather to the first period, I will add a few words about her and her death before closing this portion of my life.

I heard later from people in the village that, after our return to Moscow, she found time hang very heavy on her hands. Although the drawers and shelves were still under her charge, and she never ceased to arrange and rearrange them—to take things out and to dispose of them afresh—she sadly missed the din and bustle of the seignorial mansion to which she had been accustomed from her childhood up. Consequently grief, the alteration in her mode of life, and her lack of activity soon combined to develop in her a malady to which she had always been more or less subject.

Scarcely more than a year after Mamma's death dropsy showed itself, and she took to her bed. I can imagine how sad it must have been for her to go on living—still more, to die—alone in that great empty house at Petrovskoe, with no relations or any one near her. Every one there esteemed and loved her, but she had formed no intimate friendships in the place, and was rather proud of the fact. That was because, enjoying her master's confidence as she did, and having so much property under her care, she considered that intimacies would lead to culpable indulgence and condescension. Consequently (and perhaps, also, because she had nothing really in common with the other servants) she kept them all at a distance, and used to say that she "recognised neither kinsman nor godfather in the house, and would permit of no exceptions with regard to her master's property."

Instead, she sought and found consolation in fervent prayers to God. Yet sometimes, in those moments of weakness to which all of us are subject, and when man's best solace is the tears and compassion of his fellow-creatures, she would take her old dog Moska on to her bed, and talk to it, and weep softly over it as it answered her caresses by licking her hands, with its yellow eyes fixed upon her. When Moska began to whine she would say as she quieted it: "Enough, enough! I know without thy telling me that my time is near." A month before her death she took out of her chest of drawers some fine white calico, white cambric, and pink ribbon, and, with the help of the maidservants, fashioned the garments in which she wished to be buried. Next she put everything on her shelves in order and handed the bailiff an inventory which she had made out with scrupulous accuracy. All that she kept back was a couple of silk gowns, an old shawl, and Grandpapa's military uniform—things which had been presented to her absolutely, and which, thanks to her care and orderliness, were in an excellent state of preservation—particularly the handsome gold embroidery on the uniform.

Just before her death, again, she expressed a wish that one of the gowns (a pink one) should be made into a robe de chambre for Woloda; that the other one (a many-coloured gown) should be made into a similar garment for myself; and that the shawl should go to Lubotshka. As for the uniform, it was to devolve either to Woloda or to myself, according as the one or the other of us should first become an officer. All the rest of her property (save only forty roubles, which she set aside for her commemorative rites and to defray the costs of her burial) was to pass to her brother, a person with whom, since he lived a dissipated life in a distant province, she had had no intercourse during her lifetime. When, eventually, he arrived to claim the inheritance, and found that its sum-total only amounted to twenty-five roubles in notes, he refused to believe it, and declared that it was impossible that his sister-a woman who for sixty years had had sole charge in a wealthy house, as well as all her life had been penurious and averse to giving away even the smallest thing should have left no more: yet it was a fact.

Though Natalia's last illness lasted for two months, she bore her sufferings with truly Christian fortitude. Never did she fret or complain, but, as usual, appealed continually to God. An hour before the end came she made her final confession, received the Sacrament with quiet joy, and was accorded extreme unction. Then she begged forgiveness of every one in the house for any wrong she might have done them, and requested the priest to send us word of the number of times she had blessed us for our love of her, as well as of how in her last moments she had implored our forgiveness if, in her ignorance, she had ever at any time given us offence. "Yet a thief have I never been. Never have I used so much as a piece of thread that was not my own." Such was the one quality which she valued in herself.

Dressed in the cap and gown prepared so long beforehand, and with her head resting, upon the cushion made for the purpose, she conversed with the priest up to the very last moment, until, suddenly, recollecting that she had left him nothing for the poor, she took out ten roubles, and asked him to distribute them in the parish. Lastly she made the sign of the cross, lay down, and expired—pronouncing with a smile of joy the name of the Almighty.

She quitted life without a pang, and, so far from fearing death, welcomed it as a blessing. How often do we hear that said, and how seldom is it a reality! Natalia Savishna had no reason to fear death for the simple reason that she died in a sure and certain faith and in strict obedience to the commands of the Gospel. Her whole life had been one of pure, disinterested love, of utter self-negation. Had her convictions been of a more enlightened order, her life directed to a higher aim, would that pure soul have been the more worthy of love and reverence? She accomplished the highest and best achievement in this world: she died without fear and without repining.

They buried her where she had wished to lie—near the little mausoleum which still covers Mamma's tomb. The little mound beneath which she sleeps is overgrown with nettles and burdock, and surrounded by a black railing, but I never forget, when leaving the mausoleum, to approach that railing, and to salute the plot of earth within by bowing reverently to the ground.

Sometimes, too, I stand thoughtfully between the railing and the mausoleum, and sad memories pass through my mind. Once the idea came to me as I stood there: "Did Providence unite me to those two beings solely in order to make me regret them my life long?"

BOYHOOD

I. A SLOW JOURNEY

Again two carriages stood at the front door of the house at Petrovskoe. In one of them sat Mimi, the two girls, and their maid, with the bailiff, Jakoff, on the box, while in the other—a britchka—sat Woloda, myself, and our servant Vassili. Papa, who was to follow us to Moscow in a few days, was standing bareheaded on the entrance-steps. He made the sign of the cross at the windows of the carriages, and said:

"Christ go with you! Good-bye."

Jakoff and our coachman (for we had our own horses) lifted their caps in answer, and also made the sign of the cross.

"Amen. God go with us!"

The carriages began to roll away, and the birch-trees of the great avenue filed out of sight.

I was not in the least depressed on this occasion, for my mind was not so much turned upon what I had left as upon what was awaiting me. In proportion as the various objects connected with the sad recollections which had recently filled my imagination receded behind me, those recollections lost their power, and gave place to a consolatory feeling of life, youthful vigour, freshness, and hope.

Seldom have I spent four days more—well, I will not say gaily, since I should still have shrunk from appearing gay—but more agreeably and pleasantly than those occupied by our journey.

No longer were my eyes confronted with the closed door of Mamma's room (which I had never been able to pass without a pang), nor with the covered piano (which nobody opened now, and at which I could never look without trembling), nor with mourning dresses (we had each of us on our ordinary travelling clothes), nor with all those other objects which recalled to me so vividly our irreparable loss, and forced me to abstain from any manifestation of merriment lest I should unwittingly offend against HER memory.

On the contrary, a continual succession of new and exciting objects and places now caught and held my attention, and the charms of spring awakened in my soul a soothing sense of satisfaction with the present and of blissful hope for the future.

Very early next morning the merciless Vassili (who had only just entered our service, and was therefore, like most people in such a position, zealous to a fault) came and stripped off my counterpane, affirming that it was time for me to get up, since everything was in readiness for us to continue our journey. Though I felt inclined to stretch myself and rebel—though I would gladly have spent another quarter of an hour in sweet enjoyment of my morning slumber—Vassili's inexorable face showed that he would grant me no respite, but that he was ready to tear away the counterpane twenty times more if necessary. Accordingly I submitted myself to the inevitable and ran down into the courtyard to wash myself at the fountain.

In the coffee-room, a tea-kettle was already surmounting the fire which Milka the ostler, as red in the face as a crab, was blowing with a pair of bellows. All was grey and misty in the courtyard, like steam from a smoking dunghill, but in the eastern sky the sun was diffusing a clear, cheerful radiance, and making the straw roofs of the sheds around the courtyard sparkle with the night dew. Beneath them stood our horses, tied to mangers, and I could hear the ceaseless sound of their chewing. A curly-haired dog which had been spending the night on a dry dunghill now rose in lazy fashion and, wagging its tail, walked slowly across the courtyard.

The bustling landlady opened the creaking gates, turned her meditative cows into the street (whence came the lowing and bellowing of other cattle), and exchanged a word or two with a sleepy neighbour. Philip, with his shirt-sleeves rolled up, was working the windlass of a draw-well, and sending sparkling fresh water coursing into an oaken trough, while in the pool beneath it some early-rising ducks were taking a bath. It gave me pleasure to watch his strongly-marked, bearded face, and the veins and muscles as they stood out upon his great powerful hands whenever he made an extra effort. In the room behind the partition-wall where Mimi and the girls had slept (yet so near to ourselves that we had exchanged confidences overnight) movements now became audible, their maid kept passing in and out with clothes, and, at last the door opened and we were summoned to breakfast. Woloda, however, remained in a state of bustle throughout as he ran to fetch first one article and then another and urged the maid to hasten her preparations.

The horses were put to, and showed their impatience by tinkling their bells. Parcels, trunks, dressing-cases, and boxes were replaced, and we set about taking our seats. Yet, every time that we got in, the mountain of luggage in the britchka seemed to have grown larger than before, and we had much ado to understand how things had been arranged yesterday, and how we should sit now. A tea-chest, in particular, greatly inconvenienced me, but Vassili declared that "things will soon right themselves," and I had no choice but to believe him.

The sun was just rising, covered with dense white clouds, and every object around us was standing out in a cheerful, calm sort of radiance. The whole was beautiful to look at, and I felt comfortable and light of heart.

Before us the road ran like a broad, sinuous ribbon through cornfields glittering with dew. Here and there a dark bush or young birch-tree cast a long shadow over the ruts and scattered grass-tufts of the track. Yet even the monotonous din of our carriage-wheels and collar-bells could not drown the joyous song of soaring larks, nor the combined odour of moth-eaten cloth, dust, and sourness peculiar to our britchka overpower the fresh scents of the morning. I felt in my heart that delightful impulse to be up and doing which is a sign of sincere enjoyment.

As I had not been able to say my prayers in the courtyard of the inn, but had nevertheless been assured once that on the very first day when I omitted to perform that ceremony some misfortune would overtake me, I now hastened to rectify the omission. Taking off my cap, and stooping down in a corner of the britchka, I duly recited my orisons, and unobtrusively signed the sign of the cross beneath my coat. Yet all the while a thousand different objects were distracting my attention, and more than once I inadvertently repeated a prayer twice over.

Soon on the little footpath beside the road became visible some slowly moving figures. They were pilgrims. On their heads they had dirty handkerchiefs, on their backs wallets of birch-bark, and on their feet bundles of soiled rags and heavy bast shoes. Moving their staffs in regular rhythm, and scarcely throwing us a glance, they pressed onwards with heavy tread and in single file.

"Where have they come from?" I wondered to myself, "and whither are they bound? Is it a long pilgrimage they are making?" But soon the shadows they cast on the road became indistinguishable from the shadows of the bushes which they passed.

Next a carriage-and-four could be seen approaching us. In two seconds the faces which looked out at us from it with smiling curiosity had vanished. How strange it seemed that those faces should have nothing in common with me, and that in all probability they would never meet my eyes again!

Next came a pair of post-horses, with the traces looped up to their collars. On one of them a young postillion-his lamb's wool cap cocked to one side-was negligently kicking his booted legs against the flanks of his steed as he sang a melancholy ditty. Yet his face and attitude seemed to me to express such perfect carelessness and indolent ease that I imagined it to be the height of happiness to be a postillion and to sing melancholy songs.

Far off, through a cutting in the road, there soon stood out against the light-blue sky, the green roof of a village church. Presently the village itself became visible, together with the roof of the manor-house and the garden attached to it. Who lived in that house? Children, parents, teachers? Why should we not call there and make the acquaintance of its inmates?

Next we overtook a file of loaded waggons—a procession to which our vehicles had to yield the road.

"What have you got in there?" asked Vassili of one waggoner who was dangling his legs lazily over the splashboard of his conveyance and flicking his whip about as he gazed at us with a stolid, vacant look; but he only made answer when we were too far off to catch what he said.

"And what have YOU got?" asked Vassili of a second waggoner who was lying at full length under a new rug on the driving-seat of his vehicle. The red poll and red face beneath it lifted themselves up for a second from the folds of the rug, measured our britchka with a cold, contemptuous look, and lay down again; whereupon I concluded that the driver was wondering to himself who we were, whence we had come, and whither we were going.

These various objects of interest had absorbed so much of my time that, as yet, I had paid no attention to the crooked figures on the verst posts as we passed them in rapid succession; but in time the sun began to burn my head and back, the road to become increasingly dusty, the impedimenta in the carriage to grow more and more uncomfortable, and myself to feel more and more cramped. Consequently, I relapsed into devoting my whole faculties to the distance-posts and their numerals, and to solving difficult mathematical problems for reckoning the time when we should arrive at the next posting-house.

"Twelve versts are a third of thirty-six, and in all there are forty-one to Lipetz. We have done a third and how much, then?", and so forth, and so forth.

"Vassili," was my next remark, on observing that he was beginning to nod on the box-seat, "suppose we change seats? Will you?" Vassili agreed, and had no sooner stretched himself out in the body of the vehicle than he began to snore. To me on my new perch, however, a most interesting spectacle now became visible—namely, our horses, all of which were familiar to me down to the smallest detail.

"Why is Diashak on the right today, Philip, not on the left?" I asked knowingly. "And Nerusinka is not doing her proper share of the pulling."

"One could not put Diashak on the left," replied Philip, altogether ignoring my last remark. "He is not the kind of horse to put there at all. A horse like the one on the left now is the right kind of one for the job."

After this fragment of eloquence, Philip turned towards Diashak and began to do his best to worry the poor animal by jogging at the reins, in spite of the fact that Diashak was doing well and dragging the vehicle almost unaided. This Philip continued to do until he found it convenient to breathe and rest himself awhile and to settle his cap askew, though it had looked well enough before.

I profited by the opportunity to ask him to let me have the reins to hold, until, the whole six in my hand, as well as the whip, I had attained complete happiness. Several times I asked whether I was doing things right, but, as usual, Philip was never satisfied, and soon destroyed my felicity.

The heat increased until a hand showed itself at the carriage window, and waved a bottle and a parcel of eatables; whereupon Vassili leapt briskly from the britchka, and ran forward to get us something to eat and drink.

When we arrived at a steep descent, we all got out and ran down it to a little bridge, while Vassili and Jakoff followed, supporting the carriage on either side, as though to hold it up in the event of its threatening to upset.

After that, Mimi gave permission for a change of seats, and sometimes Woloda or myself would ride in the carriage, and Lubotshka or Katenka in the britchka. This arrangement greatly pleased the girls, since much more fun went on in the britchka. Just when the day was at its hottest, we got out at a wood, and, breaking off a quantity of branches, transformed our vehicle into a bower. This travelling arbour then bustled on to catch the carriage up, and had the effect of exciting Lubotshka to one of those piercing shrieks of delight which she was in the habit of occasionally emitting.

At last we drew near the village where we were to halt and dine. Already we could perceive the smell of the place—the smell of smoke and tar and sheep-and distinguish the sound of voices, footsteps, and carts. The bells on our horses began to ring less clearly than they had done in the open country, and on both sides the road became lined with huts—dwellings with straw roofs, carved porches, and small red or green painted shutters to the windows, through which, here and there, was a woman's face looking inquisitively out. Peasant children clad in smocks only stood staring open-eyed or, stretching out their arms to us, ran barefooted through the dust to climb on to the luggage behind, despite Philip's menacing gestures. Likewise, red-haired waiters came darting around the carriages to invite us, with words and signs, to select their several hostelries as our halting-place.

Presently a gate creaked, and we entered a courtyard. Four hours of rest and liberty now awaited us.

II. THE THUNDERSTORM

The sun was sinking towards the west, and his long, hot rays were burning my neck and cheeks beyond endurance, while thick clouds of dust were rising from the road and filling the whole air. Not the slightest wind was there to carry it away. I could not think what to do. Neither the dust-blackened face of Woloda dozing in a corner, nor the motion of Philip's back, nor the long shadow of our britchka as it came bowling along behind us brought me any relief. I concentrated my whole attention upon the distance-posts ahead and the clouds which, hitherto dispersed over the sky, were now assuming a menacing blackness, and beginning to form themselves into a single solid mass.

From time to time distant thunder could be heard—a circumstance which greatly increased my impatience to arrive at the inn where we were to spend the night. A thunderstorm always communicated to me an inexpressibly oppressive feeling of fear and gloom.

Yet we were still ten versts from the next village, and in the meanwhile the large purple cloudbank—arisen from no one knows where—was advancing steadily towards us. The sun, not yet obscured, was picking out its fuscous shape with dazzling light, and marking its front with grey stripes running right down to the horizon. At intervals, vivid lightning could be seen in the distance, followed by low rumbles which increased steadily in volume until they merged into a prolonged roll which seemed to embrace the entire heavens. At length, Vassili got up and covered over the britchka, the coachman wrapped himself up in his cloak and lifted his cap to make the sign of the cross at each successive thunderclap, and the horses pricked up their ears and snorted as though to drink in the fresh air which the flying clouds were outdistancing. The britchka began to roll more swiftly along the dusty road, and I felt uneasy, and as though the blood were coursing more quickly through my veins. Soon the clouds had veiled the face of the sun, and though he threw a last gleam of light to the dark and terrifying horizon, he had no choice but to disappear behind them.

Suddenly everything around us seemed changed, and assumed a gloomy aspect. A wood of aspen trees which we were passing seemed to be all in a tremble, with its leaves showing white against the dark lilac background of the clouds, murmuring together in an agitated manner. The tops of the larger trees began to bend to and fro, and dried leaves and grass to whirl about in eddies over the road. Swallows and white-breasted swifts came darting around the britchka and even passing in front of the forelegs of the horses. While rooks, despite their outstretched wings, were laid, as it were, on their keels by the wind. Finally, the leather apron which covered us began to flutter about and to beat against the sides of the conveyance.

The lightning flashed right into the britchka as, cleaving the obscurity for a second, it lit up the grey cloth and silk galloon of the lining and Woloda's figure pressed back into a corner.

Next came a terrible sound which, rising higher and higher, and spreading further and further, increased until it reached its climax in a deafening thunderclap which made us tremble and hold our breaths. "The wrath of God"—what poetry there is in that simple popular conception!

The pace of the vehicle was continually increasing, and from Philip's and Vassili's backs (the former was tugging furiously at the reins) I could see that they too were alarmed.

Bowling rapidly down an incline, the britchka cannoned violently against a wooden bridge at the bottom. I dared not stir and expected destruction every moment.

Crack! A trace had given way, and, in spite of the ceaseless, deafening thunderclaps, we had to pull up on the bridge.

Leaning my head despairingly against the side of the britchka, I followed with a beating heart the movements of Philip's great black fingers as he tied up the broken trace and, with hands and the butt-end of the whip, pushed the harness vigorously back into its place.

My sense of terror was increasing with the violence of the thunder.

Indeed, at the moment of supreme silence which generally precedes the greatest intensity of a storm, it mounted to such a height that I felt as though another quarter of an hour of this emotion would kill me.

Just then there appeared from beneath the bridge a human being who, clad in a torn, filthy smock, and supported on a pair of thin shanks bare of muscles, thrust an idiotic face, a tremulous, bare, shaven head, and a pair of red, shining stumps in place of hands into the britchka.

"M-my lord! A copeck for—for God's sake!" groaned a feeble voice as at each word the wretched being made the sign of the cross and bowed himself to the ground.

I cannot describe the chill feeling of horror which penetrated my heart at that moment. A shudder crept through all my hair, and my eyes stared in vacant terror at the outcast.

Vassili, who was charged with the apportioning of alms during the journey, was busy helping Philip, and only when everything had been put straight and Philip had resumed the reins again had he time to look for his purse. Hardly had the britchka begun to move when a blinding flash filled the welkin with a blaze of light which brought the horses to their haunches. Then, the flash was followed by such an ear-splitting roar that the very vault of heaven seemed to be descending upon our heads. The wind blew harder than ever, and Vassili's cloak, the manes and tails of the horses, and the carriage-apron were all slanted in one direction as they waved furiously in the violent blast.

Presently, upon the britchka's top there fell some large drops of rain— "one, two, three:" then suddenly, and as though a roll of drums were being beaten over our heads, the whole countryside resounded with the clatter of the deluge.

From Vassili's movements, I could see that he had now got his purse open, and that the poor outcast was still bowing and making the sign of the cross as he ran beside the wheels of the vehicle, at the imminent risk of being run over, and reiterated from time to time his plea, "For-for God's sake!"

At last a copeck rolled upon the ground, and the miserable creature—his mutilated arms, with their sleeves wet through and through, held out before him—stopped perplexed in the roadway and vanished from my sight.

The heavy rain, driven before the tempestuous wind, poured down in pailfuls and, dripping from Vassili's thick cloak, formed a series of pools on the apron. The dust became changed to a paste which clung to the wheels, and the ruts became transformed into muddy rivulets.

At last, however, the lightning grew paler and more diffuse, and the thunderclaps lost some of their terror amid the monotonous rattling of the downpour. Then the rain also abated, and the clouds began to disperse. In the region of the sun, a lightness appeared, and between the white-grey clouds could be caught glimpses of an azure sky.

Finally, a dazzling ray shot across the pools on the road, shot through the threads of rain—now falling thin and straight, as from a sieve—, and fell upon the fresh leaves and blades of grass. The great cloud was still louring black and threatening on the far horizon, but I no longer felt afraid of it—I felt only an inexpressibly pleasant hopefulness in proportion, as trust in life replaced the late burden of fear. Indeed, my heart was smiling like that of refreshed, revivified Nature herself.

Vassili took off his cloak and wrung the water from it. Woloda flung back the apron, and I stood up in the britchka to drink in the new, fresh, balm-laden air. In front of us was the carriage, rolling along and looking as wet and resplendent in the sunlight as though it had just been polished. On one side of the road boundless oatfields, intersected in places by small ravines which now showed bright with their moist earth and greenery, stretched to the far horizon like a checkered carpet, while on the other side of us an aspen wood, intermingled with hazel bushes, and parquetted with wild thyme in joyous profusion, no longer rustled and trembled, but slowly dropped rich, sparkling diamonds from its newly-bathed branches on to the withered leaves of last year.

From above us, from every side, came the happy songs of little birds calling to one another among the dripping brushwood, while clear from the inmost depths of the wood sounded the voice of the cuckoo. So delicious was the wondrous scent of the wood, the scent which follows a thunderstorm in spring, the scent of birch-trees, violets, mushrooms, and thyme, that I could no longer remain in the britchka. Jumping out, I ran to some bushes, and, regardless of the showers of drops discharged upon me, tore off a few sprigs of thyme, and buried my face in them to smell their glorious scent.

Then, despite the mud which had got into my boots, as also the fact that my stockings were soaked, I went skipping through the puddles to the window of the carriage.

"Lubotshka! Katenka!" I shouted as I handed them some of the thyme, "Just look how delicious this is!"

The girls smelt it and cried, "A-ah!" but Mimi shrieked to me to go away, for fear I should be run over by the wheels.

"Oh, but smell how delicious it is!" I persisted.

III. A NEW POINT OF VIEW

Katenka was with me in the britchka; her lovely head inclined as she gazed pensively at the roadway. I looked at her in silence and wondered what had brought the unchildlike expression of sadness to her face which I now observed for the first time there.

"We shall soon be in Moscow," I said at last. "How large do you suppose it is?"

"I don't know," she replied.

"Well, but how large do you IMAGINE? As large as Serpukhov?"

"What do you say?"

"Nothing."

Yet the instinctive feeling which enables one person to guess the thoughts of another and serves as a guiding thread in conversation soon made Katenka feel that her indifference was disagreeable to me; wherefore she raised her head presently, and, turning round, said:

"Did your Papa tell you that we girls too were going to live at your Grandmamma's?"

"Yes, he said that we should ALL live there."

"ALL live there?"

"Yes, of course. We shall have one half of the upper floor, and you the other half, and Papa the wing; but we shall all of us dine together with Grandmamma downstairs."

"But Mamma says that your Grandmamma is so very grave and so easily made angry?"

"No, she only SEEMS like that at first. She is grave, but not bad-tempered. On the contrary, she is both kind and cheerful. If you could only have seen the ball at her house!"

"All the same, I am afraid of her. Besides, who knows whether we—"

Katenka stopped short, and once again became thoughtful.

"What?" I asked with some anxiety.

"Nothing, I only said that—"

"No. You said, 'Who knows whether we—'"

"And YOU said, didn't you, that once there was ever such a ball at Grandmamma's?"

"Yes. It is a pity you were not there. There were heaps of guests—about a thousand people, and all of them princes or generals, and there was music, and I danced—But, Katenka" I broke off, "you are not listening to me?"

"Oh yes, I am listening. You said that you danced—?"

"Why are you so serious?"

"Well, one cannot ALWAYS be gay."

"But you have changed tremendously since Woloda and I first went to Moscow. Tell me the truth, now: why are you so odd?" My tone was resolute.

"AM I so odd?" said Katenka with an animation which showed me that my question had interested her. "I don't see that I am so at all."

"Well, you are not the same as you were before," I continued. "Once upon a time any one could see that you were our equal in everything, and that you loved us like relations, just as we did you; but now you are always serious, and keep yourself apart from us."

"Oh, not at all."

"But let me finish, please," I interrupted, already conscious of a slight tickling in my nose—the precursor of the tears which usually came to my eyes whenever I had to vent any long pent-up feeling. "You avoid us, and talk to no one but Mimi, as though you had no wish for our further acquaintance."

"But one cannot always remain the same—one must change a little sometimes," replied Katenka, who had an inveterate habit of pleading some such fatalistic necessity whenever she did not know what else to say.

I recollect that once, when having a quarrel with Lubotshka, who had called her "a stupid girl," she (Katenka) retorted that EVERYBODY could not be wise, seeing that a certain number of stupid people was a necessity in the world. However, on the present occasion, I was not satisfied that any such inevitable necessity for "changing sometimes" existed, and asked further:

"WHY is it necessary?"

"Well, you see, we MAY not always go on living together as we are doing now," said Katenka, colouring slightly, and regarding Philip's back with a grave expression on her face. "My Mamma was able to live with your mother because she was her friend; but will a similar arrangement always suit the Countess, who, they say, is so easily offended? Besides, in any case, we shall have to separate SOME day. You are rich—you have Petrovskoe, while we are poor—Mamma has nothing."

"You are rich," "we are poor"—both the words and the ideas which they connoted seemed to me extremely strange. Hitherto, I had conceived that only beggars and peasants were poor and could not reconcile in my mind the idea of poverty and the graceful, charming Katenka. I felt that Mimi and her daughter ought to live with us ALWAYS and to share everything that we possessed. Things ought never to be otherwise. Yet, at this moment, a thousand new thoughts with regard to their lonely position came crowding into my head, and I felt so remorseful at the notion that we were rich and they poor, that I coloured up and could not look Katenka in the face.

"Yet what does it matter," I thought, "that we are well off and they are not? Why should that necessitate a separation? Why should we not share in common what we possess?" Yet, I had a feeling that I could not talk to Katenka on the subject, since a certain practical instinct, opposed to all logical reasoning, warned me that, right though she possibly was, I should do wrong to tell her so.

"It is impossible that you should leave us. How could we ever live apart?"

"Yet what else is there to be done? Certainly I do not WANT to do it;

yet, if it HAS to be done, I know what my plan in life will be."

"Yes, to become an actress! How absurd!" I exclaimed (for I knew that to enter that profession had always been her favourite dream).

"Oh no. I only used to say that when I was a little girl."

"Well, then? What?"

"To go into a convent and live there. Then I could walk out in a black dress and velvet cap!" cried Katenka.

Has it ever befallen you, my readers, to become suddenly aware that your conception of things has altered—as though every object in life had unexpectedly turned a side towards you of which you had hitherto remained unaware? Such a species of moral change occurred, as regards myself, during this journey, and therefore from it I date the beginning of my boyhood. For the first time in my life, I then envisaged the idea that we—i.e. our family—were not the only persons in the world; that not every conceivable interest was centred in ourselves; and that there existed numbers of people who had nothing in common with us, cared nothing for us, and even knew nothing of our existence. No doubt I had known all this before—only I had not known it then as I knew it now; I had never properly felt or understood it.

Thought merges into conviction through paths of its own, as well as, sometimes, with great suddenness and by methods wholly different from those which have brought other intellects to the same conclusion. For me the conversation with Katenka—striking deeply as it did, and forcing me to reflect on her future position—constituted such a path. As I gazed at the towns and villages through which we passed, and in each house of which lived at least one family like our own, as well as at the women and children who stared with curiosity at our carriages and then became lost to sight for ever, and the peasants and workmen who did not even look at us, much less make us any obeisance, the question arose for the first time in my thoughts, "Whom else do they care for if not for us?" And this question was followed by others, such as, "To what end do they live?" "How do they educate their children?" "Do they teach their children and let them play? What are their names?" and so forth.

IV. IN MOSCOW

From the time of our arrival in Moscow, the change in my conception of objects, of persons, and of my connection with them became increasingly perceptible. When at my first meeting with Grandmamma, I saw her thin, wrinkled face and faded eyes, the mingled respect and fear with which she had hitherto inspired me gave place to compassion, and when, laying her cheek against Lubotshka's head, she sobbed as though she saw before her the corpse of her beloved daughter, my compassion grew to love.

I felt deeply sorry to see her grief at our meeting, even though I knew that in ourselves we represented nothing in her eyes, but were dear to her only as reminders of our mother—that every kiss which she imprinted upon my cheeks expressed the one thought, "She is no more—she is dead, and I shall never see her again."

Papa, who took little notice of us here in Moscow, and whose face was perpetually preoccupied on the rare occasions when he came in his black dress-coat to take formal dinner with us, lost much in my eyes at this period, in spite of his turned-up ruffles, robes de chambre, overseers, bailiffs, expeditions to the estate, and hunting exploits.

Karl Ivanitch—whom Grandmamma always called "Uncle," and who (Heaven knows why!) had taken it into his head to adorn the bald pate of my childhood's days with a red wig parted in the middle—now looked to me so strange and ridiculous that I wondered how I could ever have failed to observe the fact before. Even between the girls and ourselves there seemed to have sprung up an invisible barrier. They, too, began to have secrets among themselves, as well as to evince a desire to show off their ever-lengthening skirts even as we boys did our trousers and ankle-straps. As for Mimi, she appeared at luncheon, the first Sunday, in such a gorgeous dress and with so many ribbons in her cap that it was clear that we were no longer en campagne, and that everything was now going to be different.

V. MY ELDER BROTHER

I was only a year and some odd months younger than Woloda, and from the first we had grown up and studied and played together. Hitherto, the difference between elder and younger brother had never been felt between us, but at the period of which I am speaking, I began to have a notion that I was not Woloda's equal either in years, in tastes, or in capabilities. I even began to fancy that Woloda himself was aware of his superiority and that he was proud of it, and, though, perhaps, I was wrong, the idea wounded my conceit—already suffering from frequent comparison with him. He was my superior in everything—in games, in studies, in quarrels, and in deportment. All this brought about an estrangement between us and occasioned me moral sufferings which I had never hitherto experienced.

When for the first time Woloda wore Dutch pleated shirts, I at once said that I was greatly put out at not being given similar ones, and each time that he arranged his collar, I felt that he was doing so on purpose to offend me. But, what tormented me most of all was the idea that Woloda could see through me, yet did not choose to show it.

Who has not known those secret, wordless communications which spring from some barely perceptible smile or movement—from a casual glance between two persons who live as constantly together as do brothers, friends, man and wife, or master and servant—particularly if those two persons do not in all things cultivate mutual frankness? How many half-expressed wishes, thoughts, and meanings which one shrinks from revealing are made plain by a single accidental glance which timidly and irresolutely meets the eye!

However, in my own case I may have been deceived by my excessive capacity for, and love of, analysis. Possibly Woloda did not feel at all as I did. Passionate and frank, but unstable in his likings, he was attracted by the most diverse things, and always surrendered himself wholly to such attraction. For instance, he suddenly conceived a passion for pictures, spent all his money on their purchase, begged Papa, Grandmamma, and his drawing master to add to their number, and applied himself with enthusiasm to art. Next came a sudden rage for curios, with which he covered his table, and for which he ransacked the whole house. Following upon that, he took to violent novel-reading—procuring such works by stealth, and devouring them day and night. Involuntarily I was influenced by his whims, for, though too proud to imitate him, I was also too young and too lacking in independence to choose my own way. Above all, I envied Woloda his happy, nobly frank character, which showed itself most strikingly when we quarrelled. I always felt that he was in the right, yet could not imitate him. For instance, on one occasion when his passion for curios was at its height, I went to his table and accidentally broke an empty many-coloured smelling-bottle.

"Who gave you leave to touch my things?" asked Woloda, chancing to enter the room at that moment and at once perceiving the disorder which I had occasioned in the orderly arrangement of the treasures on his table. "And where is that smelling bottle? Perhaps you—?"

"I let it fall, and it smashed to pieces; but what does that matter?"

"Well, please do me the favour never to DARE to touch my things again," he said as he gathered up the broken fragments and looked at them vexedly.

"And will YOU please do me the favour never to ORDER me to do anything whatever," I retorted. "When a thing's broken, it's broken, and there is no more to be said." Then I smiled, though I hardly felt like smiling.

"Oh, it may mean nothing to you, but to me it means a good deal," said Woloda, shrugging his shoulders (a habit he had caught from Papa). "First of all you go and break my things, and then you laugh. What a nuisance a little boy can be!"

"LITTLE boy, indeed? Then YOU, I suppose, are a man, and ever so wise?"

"I do not intend to quarrel with you," said Woloda, giving me a slight push. "Go away."

"Don't you push me!"

"Go away."

"I say again—don't you push me!"

Woloda took me by the hand and tried to drag me away from the table, but I was excited to the last degree, and gave the table such a push with my foot that I upset the whole concern, and brought china and crystal ornaments and everything else with a crash to the floor.

"You disgusting little brute!" exclaimed Woloda, trying to save some of his falling treasures.

"At last all is over between us," I thought to myself as I strode from the room. "We are separated now for ever."

It was not until evening that we again exchanged a word. Yet I felt guilty, and was afraid to look at him, and remained at a loose end all day.

Woloda, on the contrary, did his lessons as diligently as ever, and passed the time after luncheon in talking and laughing with the girls. As soon, again, as afternoon lessons were over I left the room, for it would have been terribly embarrassing for me to be alone with my brother. When, too, the evening class in history was ended I took my notebook and moved towards the door. Just as I passed Woloda, I pouted and pulled an angry face, though in reality I should have liked to have made my peace with him. At the same moment he lifted his head, and with a barely perceptible and good-humouredly satirical smile looked me full in the face. Our eyes met, and I saw that he understood me, while he, for his part, saw that I knew that he understood me; yet a feeling stronger than myself obliged me to turn away from him.

"Nicolinka," he said in a perfectly simple and anything but mock-pathetic way, "you have been angry with me long enough. I am sorry if I offended you," and he tendered me his hand.

It was as though something welled up from my heart and nearly choked me. Presently it passed away, the tears rushed to my eyes, and I felt immensely relieved.

"I too am so-rry, Wo-lo-da," I said, taking his hand. Yet he only looked at me with an expression as though he could not understand why there should be tears in my eyes.

VI. MASHA

None of the changes produced in my conception of things were so striking as the one which led me to cease to see in one of our chambermaids a mere servant of the female sex, but, on the contrary, a WOMAN upon whom depended, to a certain extent, my peace of mind and happiness. From the time of my earliest recollection I can remember Masha an inmate of our house, yet never until the occurrence of which I am going to speak—an occurrence which entirely altered my impression of her—had I bestowed the smallest attention upon her. She was twenty-five years old, while I was but fourteen. Also, she was very beautiful. But I hesitate to give a further description of her lest my imagination should once more picture the bewitching, though deceptive, conception of her which filled my mind during the period of my passion. To be frank, I will only say that she was extraordinarily handsome, magnificently developed, and a woman—as also that I was but fourteen.

At one of those moments when, lesson-book in hand, I would pace the room, and try to keep strictly to one particular crack in the floor as I hummed a fragment of some tune or repeated some vague formula—in short, at one of those moments when the mind leaves off thinking and the imagination gains the upper hand and yearns for new impressions—I left the schoolroom, and turned, with no definite purpose in view, towards the head of the staircase.

Somebody in slippers was ascending the second flight of stairs. Of course I felt curious to see who it was, but the footsteps ceased abruptly, and then I heard Masha's voice say:

"Go away! What nonsense! What would Maria Ivanovna think if she were to come now?"

"Oh, but she will not come," answered Woloda's voice in a whisper.

"Well, go away, you silly boy," and Masha came running up, and fled past me.

I cannot describe the way in which this discovery confounded me.

Nevertheless the feeling of amazement soon gave place to a kind of sympathy with Woloda's conduct. I found myself wondering less at the conduct itself than at his ability to behave so agreeably. Also, I found myself involuntarily desiring to imitate him.

Sometimes I would pace the landing for an hour at a time, with no other thought in my head than to watch for movements from above. Yet, although I longed beyond all things to do as Woloda had done, I could not bring myself to the point. At other times, filled with a sense of envious jealousy, I would conceal myself behind a door and listen to the sounds which came from the maidservants' room, until the thought would occur to my mind, "How if I were to go in now and, like Woloda, kiss Masha? What should I say when she asked me—ME with the huge nose and the tuft on the top of my head— what I wanted?" Sometimes, too, I could hear her saying to Woloda,

"That serves you right! Go away! Nicolas Petrovitch never comes in here with such nonsense." Alas! she did not know that Nicolas Petrovitch was sitting on the staircase just below and feeling that he would give all he possessed to be in "that bold fellow Woloda's" place! I was shy by nature, and rendered worse in that respect by a consciousness of my own ugliness. I am certain that nothing so much influences the development of a man as his exterior—though the exterior itself less than his belief in its plainness or beauty.

Yet I was too conceited altogether to resign myself to my fate. I tried to comfort myself much as the fox did when he declared that the grapes were sour. That is to say, I tried to make light of the satisfaction to be gained from making such use of a pleasing exterior as I believed Woloda to employ (satisfaction which I nevertheless envied him from my heart), and endeavoured with every faculty of my intellect and imagination to console myself with a pride in my isolation.

VII. SMALL SHOT

"Good gracious! Powder!" exclaimed Mimi in a voice trembling with alarm. "Whatever are you doing? You will set the house on fire in a moment, and be the death of us all!" Upon that, with an indescribable expression of firmness, Mimi ordered every one to stand aside, and, regardless of all possible danger from a premature explosion, strode with long and resolute steps to where some small shot was scattered about the floor, and began to trample upon it.

When, in her opinion, the peril was at least lessened, she called for Michael and commanded him to throw the "powder" away into some remote spot, or, better still, to immerse it in water; after which she adjusted her cap and returned proudly to the drawing-room, murmuring as she went, "At least I can say that they are well looked after."

When Papa issued from his room and took us to see Grandmamma we found Mimi sitting by the window and glancing with a grave, mysterious, official expression towards the door. In her hand she was holding something carefully wrapped in paper. I guessed that that something was the small shot, and that Grandmamma had been informed of the occurrence. In the room also were the maidservant Gasha (who, to judge by her angry flushed face, was in a state of great irritation) and Doctor Blumenthal—the latter a little man pitted with smallpox, who was endeavouring by tacit, pacificatory signs with his head and eyes to reassure the perturbed Gasha. Grandmamma was sitting a little askew and playing that variety of "patience" which is called "The Traveller"—two unmistakable signs of her displeasure.

"How are you to-day, Mamma?" said Papa as he kissed her hand respectfully. "Have you had a good night?"

"Yes, very good, my dear; you KNOW that I always enjoy sound health," replied Grandmamma in a tone implying that Papa's inquiries were out of place and highly offensive. "Please give me a clean pocket-handkerchief," she added to Gasha.

"I HAVE given you one, madam," answered Gasha, pointing to the snow-white cambric handkerchief which she had just laid on the arm of Grandmamma's chair.

"No, no; it's a nasty, dirty thing. Take it away and bring me a CLEAN one, my dear."

Gasha went to a cupboard and slammed the door of it back so violently that every window rattled. Grandmamma glared angrily at each of us, and then turned her attention to following the movements of the servant. After the latter had presented her with what I suspected to be the same handkerchief as before, Grandmamma continued:

"And when do you mean to cut me some snuff, my dear?"

"When I have time."

"What do you say?"

"To-day."

"If you don't want to continue in my service you had better say so at once. I would have sent you away long ago had I known that you wished it."

"It wouldn't have broken my heart if you had!" muttered the woman in an undertone.

Here the doctor winked at her again, but she returned his gaze so firmly and wrathfully that he soon lowered it and went on playing with his watch-key.

"You see, my dear, how people speak to me in my own house!" said Grandmamma to Papa when Gasha had left the room grumbling.

"Well, Mamma, I will cut you some snuff myself," replied Papa, though evidently at a loss how to proceed now that he had made this rash promise.

"No, no, I thank you. Probably she is cross because she knows that no one except herself can cut the snuff just as I like it. Do you know, my dear," she went on after a pause, "that your children very nearly set the house on fire this morning?"

Papa gazed at Grandmamma with respectful astonishment.

"Yes, they were playing with something or another. Tell him the story," she added to Mimi.

Papa could not help smiling as he took the shot in his hand.

"This is only small shot, Mamma," he remarked, "and could never be dangerous."

"I thank you, my dear, for your instruction, but I am rather too old for that sort of thing."

"Nerves, nerves!" whispered the doctor.

Papa turned to us and asked us where we had got the stuff, and how we could dare to play with it.

"Don't ask THEM, ask that useless 'Uncle,' rather," put in Grandmamma, laying a peculiar stress upon the word "UNCLE." "What else is he for?"

"Woloda says that Karl Ivanitch gave him the powder himself," declared Mimi.

"Then you can see for yourself what use he is," continued Grandmamma. "And where IS he—this precious 'Uncle'? How is one to get hold of him? Send him here."

"He has gone an errand for me," said Papa.

"That is not at all right," rejoined Grandmamma. "He ought ALWAYS to be here. True, the children are yours, not mine, and I have nothing to do with them, seeing that you are so much cleverer than I am; yet all the same I think it is time we had a regular tutor for them, and not this 'Uncle' of a German—a stupid fellow who knows only how to teach them rude manners and Tyrolean songs! Is it necessary, I ask you, that they should learn Tyrolean songs? However, there is no one for me to consult about it, and you must do just as you like."

The word "NOW" meant "NOW THAT THEY HAVE NO MOTHER," and suddenly awakened sad recollections in Grandmamma's heart. She threw a glance at the snuff-box bearing Mamma's portrait and sighed.

"I thought of all this long ago," said Papa eagerly, "as well as taking your advice on the subject. How would you like St. Jerome to superintend their lessons?"

"Oh, I think he would do excellently, my friend," said Grandmamma in a mollified tone, "He is at least a tutor comme il faut, and knows how to instruct des enfants de bonne maison. He is not a mere 'Uncle' who is good only for taking them out walking."

"Very well; I will talk to him to-morrow," said Papa. And, sure enough, two days later saw Karl Ivanitch forced to retire in favour of the young Frenchman referred to.

VIII. KARL IVANITCH'S HISTORY

THE evening before the day when Karl was to leave us for ever, he was standing (clad, as usual, in his wadded dressing-gown and red cap) near the bed in his room, and bending down over a trunk as he carefully packed his belongings.

His behaviour towards us had been very cool of late, and he had seemed to shrink from all contact with us. Consequently, when I entered his room on the present occasion, he only glanced at me for a second and then went on with his occupation. Even though I proceeded to jump on to his bed (a thing hitherto always forbidden me to do), he said not a word; and the idea that he would soon be scolding or forgiving us no longer—no longer having anything to do with us—reminded me vividly of the impending separation. I felt grieved to think that he had ceased to love us and wanted to show him my grief.

"Will you let me help you?" I said, approaching him.

He looked at me for a moment and turned away again. Yet the expression of pain in his eyes showed that his coldness was not the result of indifference, but rather of sincere and concentrated sorrow.

"God sees and knows everything," he said at length, raising himself to his full height and drawing a deep sigh. "Yes, Nicolinka," he went on, observing, the expression of sincere pity on my face, "my fate has been an unhappy one from the cradle, and will continue so to the grave. The good that I have done to people has always been repaid with evil; yet, though I shall receive no reward here, I shall find one THERE" (he pointed upwards). "Ah, if only you knew my whole story, and all that I have endured in this life!—I who have been a bootmaker, a soldier, a deserter, a factory hand, and a teacher! Yet now—now I am nothing, and, like the Son of Man, have nowhere to lay my head." Sitting down upon a chair, he covered his eyes with his hand.

Seeing that he was in the introspective mood in which a man pays no attention to his listener as he cons over his secret thoughts, I remained silent, and, seating myself upon the bed, continued to watch his kind face.

"You are no longer a child. You can understand things now, and I will tell you my whole story and all that I have undergone. Some day, my children, you may remember the old friend who loved you so much—"

He leant his elbow upon the table by his side, took a pinch of snuff, and, in the peculiarly measured, guttural tone in which he used to dictate us our lessons, began the story of his career.

Since he many times in later years repeated the whole to me again— always in the same order, and with the same expressions and the same unvarying intonation—I will try to render it literally, and without omitting the innumerable grammatical errors into which he always strayed when speaking in Russian. Whether it was really the history of his life, or whether it was the mere product of his imagination—that is to say, some narrative which he had conceived during his lonely residence in our house, and had at last, from endless repetition, come to believe in himself—or whether he was adorning with imaginary facts the true record of his career, I have never quite been able to make out. On the one hand, there was too much depth of feeling and practical consistency in its recital for it to be wholly incredible, while, on the other hand, the abundance of poetical beauty which it contained tended to raise doubts in the mind of the listener.

"Me vere very unhappy from ze time of my birth," he began with a profound sigh. "Ze noble blot of ze Countess of Zomerblat flows in my veins. Me vere born six veek after ze vetting. Ze man of my Mutter (I called him 'Papa') vere farmer to ze Count von Zomerblat. He coult not forget my Mutter's shame, ant loaft me not. I had a youngster broser Johann ant two sister, pot me vere strange petween my own family. Ven Johann mate several silly trick Papa sayt, 'Wit sis chilt Karl I am never to have one moment tranquil!' and zen he scoltet ant ponishet me. Ven ze sister quarrellet among zemselves Papa sayt, 'Karl vill never be one opedient poy,' ant still scoltet ant ponishet me. My goot Mamma alone loaft ant tenteret me. Often she sayt to me, 'Karl, come in my room,' ant zere she kisset me secretly. 'Poorly, poorly

Karl!' she sayt. 'Nopoty loaf you, pot I will not exchange you for somepoty in ze worlt, One zing your Mutter pegs you, to rememper,' sayt she to me, 'learn vell, ant be efer one honest man; zen Got will not forsake you.' Ant I triet so to become. Ven my fourteen year hat expiret, ant me coult partake of ze Holy Sopper, my Mutter sayt to my Vater, 'Karl is one pig poy now, Kustaf. Vat shall we do wis him?' Ant Papa sayt, 'Me ton't know.' Zen Mamma sayt, 'Let us give him to town at Mister Schultzen's, and he may pea Schumacher,' ant my Vater sayt, 'Goot!' Six year ant seven mons livet I in town wis ze Mister Shoemaker, ant he loaft me. He sayt, 'Karl are one goot vorkman, ant shall soon become my Geselle.' Pot-man makes ze proposition, ant Got ze deposition. In ze year 1796 one conscription took place, ant each which vas serviceable, from ze eighteens to ze twenty-first year, hat to go to town.

"My Fater and my broser Johann come to town, ant ve go togezer to throw ze lot for which shoult pe Soldat. Johann drew ze fatal nomper, and me vas not necessary to pe Soldat. Ant Papa sayt, 'I have only vun son, ant wis him I must now separate!'

"Den I take his hant, ant says, 'Why say you so, Papa? Come wis me, ant I will say you somesing.' Ant Papa come, ant we seat togezer at ze publics-house, ant me sayt, 'Vaiter, give us one Bierkrug,' ant he gives us one. We trink altogezer, and broser Johann also trink. 'Papa,' sayt me, 'ton't say zat you have only one son, ant wis it you must separate, My heart was breaking ven you say sis. Broser Johann must not serve; ME shall pe Soldat. Karl is for nopoty necessary, and Karl shall pe Soldat.'

"'You is one honest man, Karl,' sayt Papa, ant kiss me. Ant me was Soldat."

IX. CONTINUATION OF KARL'S NARRATIVE

"Zat was a terrible time, Nicolinka," continued Karl Ivanitch, "ze time of Napoleon. He vanted to conquer Germany, ant we protected our Vaterland to ze last trop of plot. Me vere at Ulm, me vere at Austerlitz, me vere at Wagram."

"Did you really fight?" I asked with a gaze of astonishment "Did you really kill anybody?"

Karl instantly reassured me on this point,

"Vonce one French grenadier was left behint, ant fell to ze grount. I sprang forvarts wis my gon, ant vere about to kill him, aber der Franzose warf sein Gewehr hin und rief, 'Pardon'—ant I let him loose.

"At Wagram, Napoleon cut us open, ant surrountet us in such a way as zere vas no helping. Sree days hat we no provisions, ant stoot in ze vater op to ze knees. Ze evil Napoleon neiser let us go loose nor catchet us.

"On ze fours day zey took us prisoners—zank Got! ant sent us to one fortress. Upon me vas one blue trousers, uniforms of very goot clos, fifteen of Thalers, ant one silver clock which my Vater hat given me, Ze Frans Soldaten took from me everysing. For my happiness zere vas sree tucats on me which my Mamma hat sewn in my shirt of flannel. Nopoty fount zem.

"I liket not long to stay in ze fortresses, ant resoluted to ron away. Von day, von pig holitay, says I to the sergeant which hat to look after us, 'Mister Sergeant, to-day is a pig holitay, ant me vants to celeprate it. Pring here, if you please, two pottle Mateira, ant we shall trink zem wis each oser.' Ant ze sergeant says, 'Goot!' Ven ze sergeant pring ze Mateira ant we trink it out to ze last trop, I taket his hant ant says, 'Mister Sergeant, perhaps you have still one Vater and one Mutter?' He says, 'So I have, Mister Mayer.' 'My Vater ant Mutter not seen me eight year,' I goes on to him, 'ant zey know not if I am yet alive or if my bones be reposing in ze grave. Oh, Mister Sergeant, I have two tucats which is in my shirt of flannel. Take zem, ant let me loose! You will pe my penefactor, ant my Mutter will be praying for you all her life to ze Almighty Got!'

"Ze sergeant emptiet his glass of Mateira, ant says, 'Mister Mayer, I loaf and pity you very much, pot you is one prisoner, ant I one soldat.' So I take his hant ant says, 'Mister Sergeant!'

"Ant ze sergeant says, 'You is one poor man, ant I will not take your money, pot I will help you. Ven I go to sleep, puy one pail of pranty for ze Soldaten, ant zey will sleep. Me will not look after you.' Sis was one goot man. I puyet ze pail of pranty, ant ven ze Soldaten was trunken me tresset in one olt coat, ant gang in silence out of ze doon.

"I go to ze wall, ant will leap down, pot zere is vater pelow, ant I will not spoil my last tressing, so I go to ze gate.

"Ze sentry go up and town wis one gon, ant look at me. 'Who goes zere?' ant I was silent. 'Who goes zere ze second time?' ant I was silent. 'Who goes zere ze third time?' ant I ron away, I sprang in ze vater, climp op to ze oser site, ant walk on.

"Ze entire night I ron on ze vay, pot ven taylight came I was afrait zat zey woult catch me, ant I hit myself in ze high corn. Zere I kneelet town, zanket ze Vater in Heaven for my safety, ant fall asleep wis a tranquil feeling.

"I wakenet op in ze evening, ant gang furser. At once one large German carriage, wis two raven-black horse, came alongside me. In ze carriage sit one well-tresset man, smoking pipe, ant look at me. I go slowly, so zat ze carriage shall have time to pass me, pot I go slowly, ant ze carriage go slowly, ant ze man look at me. I go quick, ant ze carriage go quick, ant ze man stop its two horses, ant look at me. 'Young man,' says he, 'where go you so late?' I says, 'I go to Frankfort.' 'Sit in ze carriage—zere is room enough, ant I will trag you,' he says. 'Bot why have you nosing about you? Your boots is dirty, ant your beart not shaven.' I seated wis him, ant says, 'Ich bin one poor man, ant I would like to pusy myself wis somesing in a manufactory. My tressing is dirty because I fell in ze mud on ze roat.'

"'You tell me ontruse, young man,' says he. 'Ze roat is kvite dry now.' I

234

was silent. 'Tell me ze whole truse,' goes on ze goot man—'who you are, ant vere you go to? I like your face, ant ven you is one honest man, so I will help you.' Ant I tell all.

"'Goot, young man!' he says. 'Come to my manufactory of rope, ant I will give you work ant tress ant money, ant you can live wis os.' I says, 'Goot!'

"I go to ze manufactory of rope, ant ze goot man says to his voman, 'Here is one yong man who defended his Vaterland, ant ron away from prisons. He has not house nor tresses nor preat. He will live wis os. Give him clean linen, ant norish him.'

"I livet one ant a half year in ze manufactory of rope, ant my lantlort loaft me so much zat he would not let me loose. Ant I felt very goot.

"I were zen handsome man—yong, of pig stature, with blue eyes and romische nose—ant Missis L— (I like not to say her name—she was ze voman of my lantlort) was yong ant handsome laty. Ant she fell in loaf wis me."

Here Karl Ivanitch made a long pause, lowered his kindly blue eyes, shook his head quietly, and smiled as people always do under the influence of a pleasing recollection.

"Yes," he resumed as he leant back in his arm-chair and adjusted his dressing-gown, "I have experiencet many sings in my life, pot zere is my witness,"—here he pointed to an image of the Saviour, embroidered on wool, which was hanging over his bed—"zat nopoty in ze worlt can say zat Karl Ivanitch has been one dishonest man, I would not repay black ingratitude for ze goot which Mister L— dit me, ant I resoluted to ron away. So in ze evening, ven all were asleep, I writet one letter to my lantlort, ant laid it on ze table in his room. Zen I taket my tresses, tree Thaler of money, ant go mysteriously into ze street. Nopoty have seen me, ant I go on ze roat."

X. CONCLUSION OF KARL'S NARRATIVE

"I had not seen my Mamma for nine year, ant I know not whether she lived or whether her bones had long since lain in ze dark grave. Ven I come to my own country and go to ze town I ask, 'Where live Kustaf Mayer who was farmer to ze Count von Zomerblat?' ant zey answer me, 'Graf Zomerblat is deat, ant Kustaf Mayer live now in ze pig street, ant keep a public-house.' So I tress in my new waistcoat and one noble coat which ze manufacturist presented me, arranged my hairs nice, ant go to ze public-house of my Papa. Sister Mariechen vas sitting on a pench, and she ask me what I want. I says, 'Might I trink one glass of pranty?' ant she says, 'Vater, here is a yong man who wish to trink one glass of pranty.' Ant Papa says, 'Give him ze glass.' I set to ze table, trink my glass of pranty, smoke my pipe, ant look at Papa, Mariechen, ant Johann (who also come into ze shop). In ze conversation Papa says, 'You know, perhaps, yong man, where stants our army?' and I say, 'I myself am come from ze army, ant it stants now at Wien.' 'Our son,' says Papa, 'is a Soldat, ant now is it nine years since he wrote never one wort, and we know not whether he is alive or dead. My voman cry continually for him.' I still fumigate the pipe, ant say, 'What was your son's name, and where servet he? Perhaps I may know him.' 'His name was Karl Mayer, ant he servet in ze Austrian Jagers.' 'He were of pig stature, ant a handsome man like yourself,' puts in Mariechen. I say, 'I know your Karl.' 'Amalia,' exclaimet my Vater. 'Come here! Here is yong man which knows our Karl!'—ant my dear Mutter comes out from a back door. I knew her directly. 'You know our Karl?' says she, ant looks at me, ant, white all over, trembles. 'Yes, I haf seen him,' I says, without ze corage to look at her, for my heart did almost burst. 'My Karl is alive?' she cry. 'Zen tank Got! Vere is he, my Karl? I woult die in peace if I coult see him once more—my darling son! Bot Got will not haf it so.' Then she cried, and I coult no longer stant it. 'Darling Mamma!' I say, 'I am your son, I am your Karl!'—and she fell into my arms."

Karl Ivanitch covered his eyes, and his lips were quivering.

"'Mutter,' sagte ich, 'ich bin ihr Sohn, ich bin ihr Karl!'—und sie sturtzte mir in die Arme!'" he repeated, recovering a little and wiping the tears from his eyes.

"Bot Got did not wish me to finish my tays in my own town. I were pursuet by fate. I livet in my own town only sree mons. One Suntay I sit in a coffee-house, ant trinket one pint of Pier, ant fumigated my pipe, ant speaket wis some frients of Politik, of ze Emperor Franz, of Napoleon, of ze war—ant anypoty might say his opinion. But next to us sits a strange chentleman in a grey Uberrock, who trink coffee, fumigate the pipe, ant says nosing. Ven the night watchman shoutet ten o'clock I taket my hat, paid ze money, and go home. At ze middle of ze night some one knock at ze door. I rise ant says, 'Who is zere?' 'Open!' says someone. I shout again, 'First say who is zere, ant I will open.' 'Open in the name of the law!' say the someone behint the door. I now do so. Two Soldaten wis gons stant at ze door, ant into ze room steps ze man in ze grey Uberrock, who had sat with us in ze coffeehouse. He were Spion! 'Come wis me,' says ze Spion, 'Very goot!' say I. I dresset myself in boots, trousers, ant coat, ant go srough ze room. Ven I come to ze wall where my gon hangs I take it, ant says, 'You are a Spion, so defent you!' I give one stroke left, one right, ant one on ze head. Ze Spion lay precipitated on ze floor! Zen I taket my cloak-bag ant money, ant jompet out of ze vintow. I vent to Ems, where I was acquainted wis one General Sasin, who loaft me, givet me a passport from ze Embassy, ant taket me to Russland to learn his chiltren. Ven General Sasin tiet, your Mamma callet for me, ant says, 'Karl Ivanitch, I gif you my children. Loaf them, ant I will never leave you, ant will take care for your olt age.' Now is she teat, ant all is forgotten! For my twenty year full of service I most now go into ze street ant seek for a try crust of preat for my olt age! Got sees all sis, ant knows all sis. His holy will be done! Only-only, I yearn for you, my children!"—and Karl drew me to him, and kissed me on the forehead.

XI. ONE MARK ONLY

The year of mourning over, Grandmamma recovered a little from her grief, and once more took to receiving occasional guests, especially children of the same age as ourselves.

On the 13th of December—Lubotshka's birthday—the Princess Kornakoff and her daughters, with Madame Valakhin, Sonetchka, Ilinka Grap, and the two younger Iwins, arrived at our house before luncheon.

Though we could hear the sounds of talking, laughter, and movements going on in the drawing-room, we could not join the party until our morning lessons were finished. The table of studies in the schoolroom said, "Lundi, de 2 a 3, maitre d'Histoire et de Geographie," and this infernal maitre d'Histoire we must await, listen to, and see the back of before we could gain our liberty. Already it was twenty minutes past two, and nothing was to be heard of the tutor, nor yet anything to be seen of him in the street, although I kept looking up and down it with the greatest impatience and with an emphatic longing never to see the maitre again.

"I believe he is not coming to-day," said Woloda, looking up for a moment from his lesson-book.

"I hope he is not, please the Lord!" I answered, but in a despondent tone. "Yet there he DOES come, I believe, all the same!"

"Not he! Why, that is a GENTLEMAN," said Woloda, likewise looking out of the window, "Let us wait till half-past two, and then ask St. Jerome if we may put away our books."

"Yes, and wish them au revoir," I added, stretching my arms, with the book clasped in my hands, over my head. Having hitherto idled away my time, I now opened the book at the place where the lesson was to begin, and started to learn it. It was long and difficult, and, moreover, I was in the mood when one's thoughts refuse to be arrested by anything at all. Consequently I made no progress. After our last lesson in history (which always seemed to me a peculiarly arduous and wearisome subject) the history master had complained to St. Jerome of me because only two good marks stood to my credit in the register—a very small total. St. Jerome had then told me that if I failed to gain less than THREE marks at the next lesson I should be severely punished. The next lesson was now imminent, and I confess that I felt a little nervous.

So absorbed, however, did I become in my reading that the sound of goloshes being taken off in the ante-room came upon me almost as a shock. I had just time to look up when there appeared in the doorway the servile and (to me) very disgusting face and form of the master, clad in a blue frockcoat with brass buttons.

Slowly he set down his hat and books and adjusted the folds of his coat (as though such a thing were necessary!), and seated himself in his place.

"Well, gentlemen," he said, rubbing his hands, "let us first of all repeat the general contents of the last lesson: after which I will proceed to narrate the succeeding events of the middle ages."

This meant "Say over the last lesson." While Woloda was answering the master with the entire ease and confidence which come of knowing a subject well, I went aimlessly out on to the landing, and, since I was not allowed to go downstairs, what more natural than that I should involuntarily turn towards the alcove on the landing? Yet before I had time to establish myself in my usual coign of vantage behind the door I found myself pounced upon by Mimi—always the cause of my misfortunes!

"YOU here?" she said, looking severely, first at myself, and then at the maidservants' door, and then at myself again.

I felt thoroughly guilty, firstly, because I was not in the schoolroom, and secondly, because I was in a forbidden place. So I remained silent, and, dropping my head, assumed a touching expression of contrition.

"Indeed, this is TOO bad!" Mimi went on, "What are you doing here?"

Still I said nothing.

"Well, it shall not rest where it is," she added, tapping the banister with her yellow fingers. "I shall inform the Countess."

It was five minutes to three when I re-entered the schoolroom. The master, as though oblivious of my presence or absence, was explaining the new lesson to Woloda. When he had finished doing this, and had put his books together (while Woloda went into the other room to fetch his ticket), the comforting idea occurred to me that perhaps the whole thing was over now, and that the master had forgotten me.

But suddenly he turned in my direction with a malicious smile, and said as he rubbed his hands anew, "I hope you have learnt your lesson?"

"Yes," I replied.

"Would you be so kind, then, as to tell me something about St. Louis' Crusade?" he went on, balancing himself on his chair and looking gravely at his feet. "Firstly, tell me something about the reasons which induced the French king to assume the cross" (here he raised his eyebrows and pointed to the inkstand); "then explain to me the general characteristics of the Crusade" (here he made a sweeping gesture with his hand, as though to seize hold of something with it); "and lastly, expound to me the influence of this Crusade upon the European states in general" (drawing the copy books to the left side of the table) "and upon the French state in particular" (drawing one of them to the right, and inclining his head in the same direction).

I swallowed a few times, coughed, bent forward, and was silent. Then, taking a pen from the table, I began to pick it to pieces, yet still said nothing.

"Allow me the pen—I shall want it," said the master. "Well?"

"Louis the-er-Saint was-was-a very good and wise king."

"What?"

"King, He took it into his head to go to Jerusalem, and handed over the reins of government to his mother."

"What was her name?

240

"B-b-b-lanka."

"What? Belanka?"

I laughed in a rather forced manner.

"Well, is that all you know?" he asked again, smiling.

I had nothing to lose now, so I began chattering the first thing that came into my head. The master remained silent as he gathered together the remains of the pen which I had left strewn about the table, looked gravely past my ear at the wall, and repeated from time to time, "Very well, very well." Though I was conscious that I knew nothing whatever and was expressing myself all wrong, I felt much hurt at the fact that he never either corrected or interrupted me.

"What made him think of going to Jerusalem?" he asked at last, repeating some words of my own.

"Because—because—that is to say—"

My confusion was complete, and I relapsed into silence, I felt that, even if this disgusting history master were to go on putting questions to me, and gazing inquiringly into my face, for a year, I should never be able to enunciate another syllable. After staring at me for some three minutes, he suddenly assumed a mournful cast of countenance, and said in an agitated voice to Woloda (who was just re-entering the room):

"Allow me the register. I will write my remarks."

He opened the book thoughtfully, and in his fine caligraphy marked FIVE for Woloda for diligence, and the same for good behaviour. Then, resting his pen on the line where my report was to go, he looked at me and reflected. Suddenly his hand made a decisive movement and, behold, against my name stood a clearly-marked ONE, with a full stop after it! Another movement and in the behaviour column there stood another one and another full stop! Quietly closing the book, the master then rose, and moved towards the door as though unconscious of my look of entreaty, despair, and reproach.

"Michael Lavionitch!" I said.

"No!" he replied, as though knowing beforehand what I was about to say. "It is impossible for you to learn in that way. I am not going to earn my money for nothing."

He put on his goloshes and cloak, and then slowly tied a scarf about his neck. To think that he could care about such trifles after what had just happened to me! To him it was all a mere stroke of the pen, but to me it meant the direst misfortune.

"Is the lesson over?" asked St. Jerome, entering.

"Yes."

"And was the master pleased with you?"

"Yes."

"How many marks did he give you?"

"Five."

"And to Nicholas?"

I was silent.

"I think four," said Woloda. His idea was to save me for at least today. If punishment there must be, it need not be awarded while we had guests.

"Voyons, Messieurs!" (St. Jerome was forever saying "Voyons!") "Faites votre toilette, et descendons."

XII. THE KEY

We had hardly descended and greeted our guests when luncheon was announced. Papa was in the highest of spirits since for some time past he had been winning. He had presented Lubotshka with a silver tea service, and suddenly remembered, after luncheon, that he had forgotten a box of bonbons which she was to have too.

"Why send a servant for it? YOU had better go, Koko," he said to me jestingly. "The keys are in the tray on the table, you know. Take them, and with the largest one open the second drawer on the right. There you will find the box of bonbons. Bring it here."

"Shall I get you some cigars as well?" said I, knowing that he always smoked after luncheon.

"Yes, do; but don't touch anything else."

I found the keys, and was about to carry out my orders, when I was seized with a desire to know what the smallest of the keys on the bunch belonged to.

On the table I saw, among many other things, a padlocked portfolio, and at once felt curious to see if that was what the key fitted. My experiment was crowned with success. The portfolio opened and disclosed a number of papers. Curiosity so strongly urged me also to ascertain what those papers contained that the voice of conscience was stilled, and I began to read their contents. . . .

My childish feeling of unlimited respect for my elders, especially for Papa, was so strong within me that my intellect involuntarily refused to draw any conclusions from what I had seen. I felt that Papa was living in a sphere completely apart from, incomprehensible by, and unattainable for, me, as well as one that was in every way excellent, and that any attempt on my part to criticise the secrets of his life would constitute something like sacrilege.

For this reason, the discovery which I made from Papa's portfolio left no clear impression upon my mind, but only a dim consciousness that I had done wrong. I felt ashamed and confused.

The feeling made me eager to shut the portfolio again as quickly as possible, but it seemed as though on this unlucky day I was destined to experience every possible kind of adversity. I put the key back into the padlock and turned it round, but not in the right direction. Thinking that the portfolio was now locked, I pulled at the key and, oh horror! found my hand come away with only the top half of the key in it! In vain did I try to put the two halves together, and to extract the portion that was sticking in the padlock. At last I had to resign myself to the dreadful thought that I had committed a new crime—one which would be discovered to-day as soon as ever Papa returned to his study! First of all, Mimi's accusation on the staircase, and then that one mark, and then this key! Nothing worse could happen now. This very evening I should be assailed successively by Grandmamma (because of Mimi's denunciation), by St. Jerome (because of the solitary mark), and by Papa (because of the matter of this key)—yes, all in one evening!

"What on earth is to become of me? What have I done?" I exclaimed as I paced the soft carpet. "Well," I went on with sudden determination, "what MUST come, MUST—that's all;" and, taking up the bonbons and the cigars, I ran back to the other part of the house.

The fatalistic formula with which I had concluded (and which was one that I often heard Nicola utter during my childhood) always produced in me, at the more difficult crises of my life, a momentarily soothing, beneficial effect. Consequently, when I re-entered the drawing-room, I was in a rather excited, unnatural mood, yet one that was perfectly cheerful.

XIII. THE TRAITRESS

After luncheon we began to play at round games, in which I took a lively part. While indulging in "cat and mouse", I happened to cannon rather awkwardly against the Kornakoffs' governess, who was playing with us, and, stepping on her dress, tore a large hole in it. Seeing that the girls—particularly Sonetchka—were anything but displeased at the spectacle of the governess angrily departing to the maidservants' room to have her dress mended, I resolved to procure them the satisfaction a second time. Accordingly, in pursuance of this amiable resolution, I waited until my victim returned, and then began to gallop madly round her, until a favourable moment occurred for once more planting my heel upon her dress and reopening the rent. Sonetchka and the young princesses had much ado to restrain their laughter, which excited my conceit the more, but St. Jerome, who had probably divined my tricks, came up to me with the frown which I could never abide in him, and said that, since I seemed disposed to mischief, he would have to send me away if I did not moderate my behaviour.

However, I was in the desperate position of a person who, having staked more than he has in his pocket, and feeling that he can never make up his account, continues to plunge on unlucky cards—not because he hopes to regain his losses, but because it will not do for him to stop and consider. So, I merely laughed in an impudent fashion and flung away from my monitor.

After "cat and mouse", another game followed in which the gentlemen sit on one row of chairs and the ladies on another, and choose each other for partners. The youngest princess always chose the younger Iwin, Katenka either Woloda or Ilinka, and Sonetchka Seriosha—nor, to my extreme astonishment, did Sonetchka seem at all embarrassed when her cavalier went and sat down beside her. On the contrary, she only laughed her sweet, musical laugh, and made a sign with her head that he had chosen right. Since nobody chose me, I always had the mortification of finding myself left over, and of hearing them say, "Who has been left out? Oh, Nicolinka. Well, DO take him, somebody."

Consequently, whenever it came to my turn to guess who had chosen me, I had to go either to my sister or to one of the ugly elder princesses. Sonetchka seemed so absorbed in Seriosha that in her eyes I clearly existed no longer. I do not quite know why I called her "the traitress" in my thoughts, since she had never promised to choose me instead of Seriosha, but, for all that, I felt convinced that she was treating me in a very abominable fashion. After the game was finished, I actually saw "the traitress" (from whom I nevertheless could not withdraw my eyes) go with Seriosha and Katenka into a corner, and engage in secret confabulation. Stealing softly round the piano which masked the conclave, I beheld the following:

Katenka was holding up a pocket-handkerchief by two of its corners, so as to form a screen for the heads of her two companions. "No, you have lost! You must pay the forfeit!" cried Seriosha at that moment, and Sonetchka, who was standing in front of him, blushed like a criminal as she replied, "No, I have NOT lost! HAVE I, Mademoiselle Katherine?" "Well, I must speak the truth," answered Katenka, "and say that you HAVE lost, my dear." Scarcely had she spoken the words when Seriosha embraced Sonetchka, and kissed her right on her rosy lips! And Sonetchka smiled as though it were nothing, but merely something very pleasant!

Horrors! The artful "traitress!"

XIV. THE RETRIBUTION

Instantly, I began to feel a strong contempt for the female sex in general and Sonetchka in particular. I began to think that there was nothing at all amusing in these games—that they were only fit for girls, and felt as though I should like to make a great noise, or to do something of such extraordinary boldness that every one would be forced to admire it. The opportunity soon arrived. St. Jerome said something to Mimi, and then left the room, I could hear his footsteps ascending the staircase, and then passing across the schoolroom, and the idea occurred to me that Mimi must have told him her story about my being found on the landing, and thereupon he had gone to look at the register. (In those days, it must be remembered, I believed that St. Jerome's whole aim in life was to annoy me.) Some where I have read that, not infrequently, children of from twelve to fourteen years of age—that is to say, children just passing from childhood to adolescence—are addicted to incendiarism, or even to murder. As I look back upon my childhood, and particularly upon the mood in which I was on that (for myself) most unlucky day, I can quite understand the possibility of such terrible crimes being committed by children without any real aim in view—without any real wish to do wrong, but merely out of curiosity or under the influence of an unconscious necessity for action. There are moments when the human being sees the future in such lurid colours that he shrinks from fixing his mental eye upon it, puts a check upon all his intellectual activity, and tries to feel convinced that the future will never be, and that the past has never been. At such moments—moments when thought does not shrink from manifestations of will, and the carnal instincts alone constitute the springs of life—I can understand that want of experience (which is a particularly predisposing factor in this connection) might very possibly lead a child, aye, without fear or hesitation, but rather with a smile of curiosity on its face, to set fire to the house in which its parents and brothers and sisters (beings whom it tenderly loves) are lying asleep. It would be under the same influence of momentary absence of thought—almost absence of mind—that a peasant boy of seventeen might catch sight of the edge of a newly-sharpened axe reposing near the bench on which his aged father was lying asleep, face downwards, and suddenly raise the implement in order to observe with unconscious curiosity how the blood would come spurting out upon the floor if he made a wound in the sleeper's neck. It is under the same influence—the same absence of thought, the same instinctive curiosity—that a man finds delight in standing on the brink of an abyss and thinking to himself, "How if I were to throw myself down?" or in holding to his brow a loaded pistol and wondering, "What if I were to pull the trigger?" or in feeling, when he catches sight of some universally respected personage, that he would like to go up to him, pull his nose hard, and say, "How do you do, old boy?"

Under the spell, then, of this instinctive agitation and lack of reflection I was moved to put out my tongue, and to say that I would not move, when St. Jerome came down and told me that I had behaved so badly that day, as well as done my lessons so ill, that I had no right to be where I was, and must go upstairs directly.

At first, from astonishment and anger, he could not utter a word.

"C'est bien!" he exclaimed eventually as he darted towards me. "Several times have I promised to punish you, and you have been saved from it by your Grandmamma, but now I see that nothing but the cane will teach you obedience, and you shall therefore taste it."

This was said loud enough for every one to hear. The blood rushed to my heart with such vehemence that I could feel that organ beating violently—could feel the colour rising to my cheeks and my lips trembling. Probably I looked horrible at that moment, for, avoiding my eye, St. Jerome stepped forward and caught me by the hand. Hardly feeling his touch, I pulled away my hand in blind fury, and with all my childish might struck him.

"What are you doing?" said Woloda, who had seen my behaviour, and now approached me in alarm and astonishment.

"Let me alone!" I exclaimed, the tears flowing fast. "Not a single one of you loves me or understands how miserable I am! You are all of you odious and disgusting!" I added bluntly, turning to the company at large.

At this moment St. Jerome—his face pale, but determined—approached me again, and, with a movement too quick to admit of any defence, seized my hands as with a pair of tongs, and dragged me away. My head swam with excitement, and I can only remember that, so long as I had strength to do it, I fought with head and legs; that my nose several times collided with a pair of knees; that my teeth tore some one's coat; that all around me I could hear the shuffling of feet; and that I could smell dust and the scent of violets with which St. Jerome used to perfume himself.

Five minutes later the door of the store-room closed behind me.

"Basil," said a triumphant but detestable voice, "bring me the cane."

XV. DREAMS

Could I at that moment have supposed that I should ever live to survive the misfortunes of that day, or that there would ever come a time when I should be able to look back upon those misfortunes composedly?

As I sat there thinking over what I had done, I could not imagine what the matter had been with me. I only felt with despair that I was for ever lost.

At first the most profound stillness reigned around me—at least, so it appeared to me as compared with the violent internal emotion which I had been experiencing; but by and by I began to distinguish various sounds. Basil brought something downstairs which he laid upon a chest outside. It sounded like a broom-stick. Below me I could hear St. Jerome's grumbling voice (probably he was speaking of me), and then children's voices and laughter and footsteps; until in a few moments everything seemed to have regained its normal course in the house, as though nobody knew or cared to know that here was I sitting alone in the dark store-room!

I did not cry, but something lay heavy, like a stone, upon my heart. Ideas and pictures passed with extraordinary rapidity before my troubled imagination, yet through their fantastic sequence broke continually the remembrance of the misfortune which had befallen me as I once again plunged into an interminable labyrinth of conjectures as to the punishment, the fate, and the despair that were awaiting me. The thought occurred to me that there must be some reason for the general dislike—even contempt—which I fancied to be felt for me by others. I was firmly convinced that every one, from Grandmamma down to the coachman Philip, despised me, and found pleasure in my sufferings. Next an idea struck me that perhaps I was not the son of my father and mother at all, nor Woloda's brother, but only some unfortunate orphan who had been adopted by them out of compassion, and this absurd notion not only afforded me a certain melancholy consolation, but seemed to me quite probable. I found it comforting to think that I was unhappy, not through my own fault, but because I was fated to be so from my birth, and conceived that my destiny was very much like poor Karl Ivanitch's.

"Why conceal the secret any longer, now that I have discovered it?" I reflected. "To-morrow I will go to Papa and say to him, 'It is in vain for you to try and conceal from me the mystery of my birth. I know it already.' And he will answer me, 'What else could I do, my good fellow? Sooner or later you would have had to know that you are not my son, but were adopted as such. Nevertheless, so long as you remain worthy of my love, I will never cast you out.' Then I shall say, 'Papa, though I have no right to call you by that name, and am now doing so for the last time, I have always loved you, and shall always retain that love. At the same time, while I can never forget that you have been my benefactor, I cannot remain longer in your house. Nobody here loves me, and St. Jerome has wrought my ruin. Either he or I must go forth, since I cannot answer for myself. I hate the man so that I could do anything—I could even kill him.' Papa will begin to entreat me, but I shall make a gesture, and say, 'No, no, my friend and benefactor! We cannot live together. Let me go'—and for the last time I shall embrace him, and say in French, 'O mon pere, O mon bienfaiteur, donne moi, pour la derniere fois, ta benediction, et que la volonte de Dieu soit faite!'"

I sobbed bitterly at these thoughts as I sat on a trunk in that dark storeroom. Then, suddenly recollecting the shameful punishment which was awaiting me, I would find myself back again in actuality, and the dreams had fled. Soon, again, I began to fancy myself far away from the house and alone in the world. I enter a hussar regiment and go to war. Surrounded by the foe on every side, I wave my sword, and kill one of them and wound another—then a third,—then a fourth. At last, exhausted with loss of blood and fatigue, I fall to the ground and cry, "Victory!" The general comes to look for me, asking, "Where is our saviour?" whereupon I am pointed out to him. He embraces me, and, in his turn, exclaims with tears of joy, "Victory!" I recover and, with my arm in a black sling, go to walk on the boulevards. I am a general now. I meet the Emperor, who asks, "Who is this young man who has been wounded?" He is told that it is the famous hero Nicolas; whereupon he approaches me and says, "My thanks to you! Whatsoever you may ask for, I will grant it." To this I bow respectfully, and, leaning on my sword, reply, "I am happy, most august Emperor, that I have been able to shed my blood for my country. I would gladly have died for it. Yet, since you are so generous as to grant any wish of mine, I venture to ask of you permission to annihilate my enemy, the foreigner St. Jerome" And then I step fiercely before St. Jerome and say, "YOU were the cause of all my fortunes! Down now on your knees!"

Unfortunately this recalled to my mind the fact that at any moment the REAL St. Jerome might be entering with the cane; so that once more I saw myself, not a general and the saviour of my country, but an unhappy, pitiful creature.

Then the idea of God occurred to me, and I asked Him boldly why He had punished me thus, seeing that I had never forgotten to say my prayers, either morning or evening. Indeed, I can positively declare that it was during that hour in the store-room that I took the first step towards the religious doubt which afterwards assailed me during my youth (not that mere misfortune could arouse me to infidelity and murmuring, but that, at moments of utter contrition and solitude, the idea of the injustice of Providence took root in me as readily as bad seed takes root in land well soaked with rain). Also, I imagined that I was going to die there and then, and drew vivid pictures of St. Jerome's astonishment when he entered the store-room and found a corpse there instead of myself! Likewise, recollecting what Natalia Savishna had told me of the forty days during which the souls of the departed must hover around their earthly home, I imagined myself flying through the rooms of Grandmamma's house, and seeing Lubotshka's bitter tears, and hearing Grandmamma's lamentations, and listening to Papa and St. Jerome talking together. "He was a fine boy," Papa would say with tears in his eyes. "Yes," St. Jerome would reply, "but a sad scapegrace and good-for-nothing." "But you should respect the dead," would expostulate Papa. "YOU were the cause of his death; YOU frightened him until he could no longer bear the thought of the humiliation which you were about to inflict upon him. Away from me, criminal!" Upon that St. Jerome would fall upon his knees and implore forgiveness, and when the forty days were ended my soul would fly to Heaven, and see there something wonderfully beautiful, white, and transparent, and know that it was Mamma.

And that something would embrace and caress me. Yet, all at once, I should feel troubled, and not know her. "If it be you," I should say to her, "show yourself more distinctly, so that I may embrace you in return." And her voice would answer me, "Do you not feel happy thus?" and I should reply, "Yes, I do, but you cannot REALLY caress me, and I cannot REALLY kiss your hand like this." "But it is not necessary," she would say. "There can be happiness here without that,"—and I should feel that it was so, and we should ascend together, ever higher and higher, until—Suddenly I feel as though I am being thrown down again, and find myself sitting on the trunk in the dark store-room (my cheeks wet with tears and my thoughts in a mist), yet still repeating the words, "Let us ascend together, higher and higher." Indeed, it was a long, long while before I could remember where I was, for at that moment my mind's eye saw only a dark, dreadful, illimitable void. I tried to renew the happy, consoling dream which had been thus interrupted by the return to reality, but, to my surprise, I found that, as soon as ever I attempted to re-enter former dreams, their continuation became impossible, while—which astonished me even more—they no longer gave me pleasure.

XVI. "KEEP ON GRINDING, AND YOU'LL HAVE FLOUR"

I PASSED the night in the store-room, and nothing further happened, except that on the following morning—a Sunday—I was removed to a small chamber adjoining the schoolroom, and once more shut up. I began to hope that my punishment was going to be limited to confinement, and found my thoughts growing calmer under the influence of a sound, soft sleep, the clear sunlight playing upon the frost crystals of the windowpanes, and the familiar noises in the street.

Nevertheless, solitude gradually became intolerable. I wanted to move about, and to communicate to some one all that was lying upon my heart, but not a living creature was near me. The position was the more unpleasant because, willy-nilly, I could hear St. Jerome walking about in his room, and softly whistling some hackneyed tune. Somehow, I felt convinced that he was whistling not because he wanted to, but because he knew it annoyed me.

At two o'clock, he and Woloda departed downstairs, and Nicola brought me up some luncheon. When I told him what I had done and what was awaiting me he said:

"Pshaw, sir! Don't be alarmed. 'Keep on grinding, and you'll have flour.'"

Although this expression (which also in later days has more than once helped me to preserve my firmness of mind) brought me a little comfort, the fact that I received, not bread and water only, but a whole luncheon, and even dessert, gave me much to think about. If they had sent me no dessert, it would have meant that my punishment was to be limited to confinement; whereas it was now evident that I was looked upon as not yet punished—that I was only being kept away from the others, as an evil-doer, until the due time of punishment. While I was still debating the question, the key of my prison turned, and St. Jerome entered with a severe, official air.

"Come down and see your Grandmamma," he said without looking at me.

I should have liked first to have brushed my jacket, since it was covered with dust, but St. Jerome said that that was quite unnecessary, since I was in such a deplorable moral condition that my exterior was not worth considering. As he led me through the salon, Katenka, Lubotshka, and Woloda looked at me with much the same expression as we were wont to look at the convicts who on certain days filed past my grandmother's house. Likewise, when I approached Grandmamma's arm-chair to kiss her hand, she withdrew it, and thrust it under her mantilla.

"Well, my dear," she began after a long pause, during which she regarded me from head to foot with the kind of expression which makes one uncertain where to look or what to do, "I must say that you seem to value my love very highly, and afford me great consolation." Then she went on, with an emphasis on each word, "Monsieur St. Jerome, who, at my request, undertook your education, says that he can no longer remain in the house. And why? Simply because of you." Another pause ensued. Presently she continued in a tone which clearly showed that her speech had been prepared beforehand, "I had hoped that you would be grateful for all his care, and for all the trouble that he has taken with you, that you would have appreciated his services; but you—you baby, you silly boy!—you actually dare to raise your hand against him! Very well, very good. I am beginning to think that you cannot understand kind treatment, but require to be treated in a very different and humiliating fashion. Go now directly and beg his pardon," she added in a stern and peremptory tone as she pointed to St. Jerome, "Do you hear me?"

I followed the direction of her finger with my eye, but on that member alighting upon St. Jerome's coat, I turned my head away, and once more felt my heart beating violently as I remained where I was.

"What? Did you not hear me when I told you what to do?"

I was trembling all over, but I would not stir.

"Koko," went on my grandmother, probably divining my inward sufferings, "Koko," she repeated in a voice tender rather than harsh, "is this you?"

"Grandmamma, I cannot beg his pardon for—" and I stopped suddenly, for I felt the next word refuse to come for the tears that were choking me.

"But I ordered you, I begged of you, to do so. What is the matter with you?"

"I-I-I will not—I cannot!" I gasped, and the tears, long pent up and accumulated in my breast, burst forth like a stream which breaks its dikes and goes flowing madly over the country.

"C'est ainsi que vous obeissez a votre seconde mere, c'est ainsi que vous reconnaissez ses bontes!" remarked St. Jerome quietly, "A genoux!"

"Good God! If SHE had seen this!" exclaimed Grandmamma, turning from me and wiping away her tears. "If she had seen this! It may be all for the best, yet she could never have survived such grief—never!" and Grandmamma wept more and more. I too wept, but it never occurred to me to ask for pardon.

"Tranquillisez-vous au nom du ciel, Madame la Comtesse," said St. Jerome, but Grandmamma heard him not. She covered her face with her hands, and her sobs soon passed to hiccups and hysteria. Mimi and Gasha came running in with frightened faces, salts and spirits were applied, and the whole house was soon in a ferment.

"You may feel pleased at your work," said St. Jerome to me as he led me from the room.

"Good God! What have I done?" I thought to myself. "What a terribly bad boy I am!"

As soon as St. Jerome, bidding me go into his room, had returned to Grandmamma, I, all unconscious of what I was doing, ran down the grand staircase leading to the front door. Whether I intended to drown myself, or whether merely to run away from home, I do not remember. I only know that I went blindly on, my face covered with my hands that I might see nothing.

"Where are you going to?" asked a well-known voice. "I want you, my boy."

I would have passed on, but Papa caught hold of me, and said sternly:

"Come here, you impudent rascal. How could you dare to do such a thing as to touch the portfolio in my study?" he went on as he dragged me into his room. "Oh! you are silent, eh?" and he pulled my ear.

"Yes, I WAS naughty," I said. "I don't know myself what came over me then."

"So you don't know what came over you—you don't know, you don't know?" he repeated as he pulled my ear harder and harder. "Will you go and put your nose where you ought not to again—will you, will you?"

Although my ear was in great pain, I did not cry, but, on the contrary, felt a sort of morally pleasing sensation. No sooner did he let go of my ear than I seized his hand and covered it with tears and kisses.

"Please whip me!" I cried, sobbing. "Please hurt me the more and more, for I am a wretched, bad, miserable boy!"

"Why, what on earth is the matter with you?" he said, giving me a slight push from him.

"No, I will not go away!" I continued, seizing his coat. "Every one else hates me—I know that, but do YOU listen to me and protect me, or else send me away altogether. I cannot live with HIM. He tries to humiliate me—he tells me to kneel before him, and wants to strike me. I can't stand it. I'm not a baby. I can't stand it—I shall die, I shall kill myself. HE told Grandmamma that I was naughty, and now she is ill—she will die through me. It is all his fault. Please let me—W-why should-he-tor-ment me?"

The tears choked my further speech. I sat down on the sofa, and, with my head buried on Papa's knees, sobbed until I thought I should die of grief.

"Come, come! Why are you such a water-pump?" said Papa compassionately, as he stooped over me.

"He is such a bully! He is murdering me! I shall die! Nobody loves me at all!" I gasped almost inaudibly, and went into convulsions.

Papa lifted me up, and carried me to my bedroom, where I fell asleep.

When I awoke it was late. Only a solitary candle burned in the room, while beside the bed there were seated Mimi, Lubotshka, and our doctor. In their faces I could discern anxiety for my health, so, although I felt so well after my twelve-hours' sleep that I could have got up directly, I thought it best to let them continue thinking that I was unwell.

XVII. HATRED

Yes, it was the real feeling of hatred that was mine now—not the hatred of which one reads in novels, and in the existence of which I do not believe—the hatred which finds satisfaction in doing harm to a fellow-creature, but the hatred which consists of an unconquerable aversion to a person who may be wholly deserving of your esteem, yet whose very hair, neck, walk, voice, limbs, movements, and everything else are disgusting to you, while all the while an incomprehensible force attracts you towards him, and compels you to follow his slightest acts with anxious attention.

This was the feeling which I cherished for St. Jerome, who had lived with us now for a year and a half.

Judging coolly of the man at this time of day, I find that he was a true Frenchman, but a Frenchman in the better acceptation of the term. He was fairly well educated, and fulfilled his duties to us conscientiously, but he had the peculiar features of fickle egotism, boastfulness, impertinence, and ignorant self-assurance which are common to all his countrymen, as well as entirely opposed to the Russian character.

All this set me against him, Grandmamma had signified to him her dislike for corporal punishment, and therefore he dared not beat us, but he frequently THREATENED us, particularly myself, with the cane, and would utter the word fouetter as though it were fouatter in an expressive and detestable way which always gave me the idea that to whip me would afford him the greatest possible satisfaction.

I was not in the least afraid of the bodily pain, for I had never experienced it. It was the mere idea that he could beat me that threw me into such paroxysms of wrath and despair.

True, Karl Ivanitch sometimes (in moments of exasperation) had recourse to a ruler or to his braces, but that I can look back upon without anger. Even if he had struck me at the time of which I am now speaking (namely, when

I was fourteen years old), I should have submitted quietly to the correction, for I loved him, and had known him all my life, and looked upon him as a member of our family, but St. Jerome was a conceited, opinionated fellow for whom I felt merely the unwilling respect which I entertained for all persons older than myself. Karl Ivanitch was a comical old "Uncle" whom I loved with my whole heart, but who, according to my childish conception of social distinctions, ranked below us, whereas St. Jerome was a well-educated, handsome young dandy who was for showing himself the equal of any one.

Karl Ivanitch had always scolded and punished us coolly, as though he thought it a necessary, but extremely disagreeable, duty. St. Jerome, on the contrary, always liked to emphasise his part as JUDGE when correcting us, and clearly did it as much for his own satisfaction as for our good. He loved authority. Nevertheless, I always found his grandiloquent French phrases (which he pronounced with a strong emphasis on all the final syllables) inexpressibly disgusting, whereas Karl, when angry, had never said anything beyond, "What a foolish puppet-comedy it is!" or "You boys are as irritating as Spanish fly!" (which he always called "Spaniard" fly). St. Jerome, however, had names for us like "mauvais sujet," "villain," "garnement," and so forth—epithets which greatly offended my self-respect. When Karl Ivanitch ordered us to kneel in the corner with our faces to the wall, the punishment consisted merely in the bodily discomfort of the position, whereas St. Jerome, in such cases, always assumed a haughty air, made a grandiose gesture with his hand, and exclaiming in a pseudo-tragic tone, "A genoux, mauvais sujet!" ordered us to kneel with our faces towards him, and to crave his pardon. His punishment consisted in humiliation.

However, on the present occasion the punishment never came, nor was the matter ever referred to again. Yet, I could not forget all that I had gone through—the shame, the fear, and the hatred of those two days. From that time forth, St. Jerome appeared to give me up in despair, and took no further trouble with me, yet I could not bring myself to treat him with indifference. Every time that our eyes met I felt that my look expressed only too plainly my dislike, and, though I tried hard to assume a careless air, he seemed to divine my hypocrisy, until I was forced to blush and turn away.

In short, it was a terrible trial to me to have anything to do with him.

XVIII. THE MAIDSERVANTS' ROOM

I BEGAN to feel more and more lonely, until my chief solace lay in solitary reflection and observation. Of the favourite subject of my reflections I shall speak in the next chapter. The scene where I indulged in them was, for preference, the maidservants' room, where a plot suitable for a novel was in progress—a plot which touched and engrossed me to the highest degree. The heroine of the romance was, of course, Masha. She was in love with Basil, who had known her before she had become a servant in our house, and who had promised to marry her some day. Unfortunately, fate, which had separated them five years ago, and afterwards reunited them in Grandmamma's abode, next proceeded to interpose an obstacle between them in the shape of Masha's uncle, our man Nicola, who would not hear of his niece marrying that "uneducated and unbearable fellow," as he called Basil. One effect of the obstacle had been to make the otherwise slightly cool and indifferent Basil fall as passionately in love with Masha as it is possible for a man to be who is only a servant and a tailor, wears a red shirt, and has his hair pomaded. Although his methods of expressing his affection were odd (for instance, whenever he met Masha he always endeavoured to inflict upon her some bodily pain, either by pinching her, giving her a slap with his open hand, or squeezing her so hard that she could scarcely breathe), that affection was sincere enough, and he proved it by the fact that, from the moment when Nicola refused him his niece's hand, his grief led him to drinking, and to frequenting taverns, until he proved so unruly that more than once he had to be sent to undergo a humiliating chastisement at the police-station.

Nevertheless, these faults of his and their consequences only served to elevate him in Masha's eyes, and to increase her love for him. Whenever he was in the hands of the police, she would sit crying the whole day, and complain to Gasha of her hard fate (Gasha played an active part in the affairs of these unfortunate lovers). Then, regardless of her uncle's anger and blows, she would stealthily make her way to the police-station, there to visit and console her swain.

Excuse me, reader, for introducing you to such company. Nevertheless, if the cords of love and compassion have not wholly snapped in your soul, you will find, even in that maidservants' room, something which may cause them to vibrate again.

So, whether you please to follow me or not, I will return to the alcove on the staircase whence I was able to observe all that passed in that room. From my post I could see the stove-couch, with, upon it, an iron, an old cap-stand with its peg bent crooked, a wash-tub, and a basin. There, too, was the window, with, in fine disorder before it, a piece of black wax, some fragments of silk, a half-eaten cucumber, a box of sweets, and so on. There, too, was the large table at which SHE used to sit in the pink cotton dress which I admired so much and the blue handkerchief which always caught my attention so. She would be sewing-though interrupting her work at intervals to scratch her head a little, to bite the end of her thread, or to snuff the candle—and I would think to myself: "Why was she not born a lady—she with her blue eyes, beautiful fair hair, and magnificent bust? How splendid she would look if she were sitting in a drawing-room and dressed in a cap with pink ribbons and a silk gown—not one like Mimi's, but one like the gown which I saw the other day on the Tverski Boulevard!" Yes, she would work at the embroidery-frame, and I would sit and look at her in the mirror, and be ready to do whatsoever she wanted—to help her on with her mantle or to hand her food. As for Basil's drunken face and horrid figure in the scanty coat with the red shirt showing beneath it, well, in his every gesture, in his every movement of his back, I seemed always to see signs of the humiliating chastisements which he had undergone.

"Ah, Basil! AGAIN?" cried Masha on one occasion as she stuck her needle into the pincushion, but without looking up at the person who was entering.

"What is the good of a man like HIM?" was Basil's first remark.

"Yes. If only he would say something DECISIVE! But I am powerless in the matter—I am all at odds and ends, and through his fault, too."

"Will you have some tea?" put in Madesha (another servant).

"No, thank you.—But why does he hate me so, that old thief of an uncle of yours? Why? Is it because of the clothes I wear, or of my height, or of my walk, or what? Well, damn and confound him!" finished Basil, snapping his fingers.

"We must be patient," said Masha, threading her needle.

"You are so—"

"It is my nerves that won't stand it, that's all."

At this moment the door of Grandmamma's room banged, and Gasha's angry voice could be heard as she came up the stairs.

"There!" she muttered with a gesture of her hands. "Try to please people when even they themselves do not know what they want, and it is a cursed life—sheer hard labour, and nothing else! If only a certain thing would happen!—though God forgive me for thinking it!"

"Good evening, Agatha Michaelovna," said Basil, rising to greet her.

"You here?" she answered brusquely as she stared at him, "That is not very much to your credit. What do you come here for? Is the maids' room a proper place for men?"

"I wanted to see how you were," said Basil soothingly.

"I shall soon be breathing my last—THAT'S how I am!" cried Gasha, still greatly incensed.

Basil laughed.

"Oh, there's nothing to laugh at when I say that I shall soon be dead. But that's how it will be, all the same. Just look at the drunkard! Marry her, would he? The fool! Come, get out of here!" and, with a stamp of her foot on the floor, Gasha retreated to her own room, and banged the door behind her until the window rattled again. For a while she could be heard scolding at everything, flinging dresses and other things about, and pulling the ears of her favourite cat. Then the door opened again, and puss, mewing pitifully, was flung forth by the tail.

"I had better come another time for tea," said Basil in a whisper—"at some better time for our meeting."

"No, no!" put in Madesha. "I'll go and fetch the urn at once."

"I mean to put an end to things soon," went on Basil, seating himself beside Masha as soon as ever Madesha had left the room. "I had much better go straight to the Countess, and say 'so-and-so' or I will throw up my situation and go off into the world. Oh dear, oh dear!"

"And am I to remain here?"

"Ah, there's the difficulty—that's what I feel so badly about, You have been my sweetheart so long, you see. Ah, dear me!"

"Why don't you bring me your shirts to wash, Basil?" asked Masha after a pause, during which she had been inspecting his wrist-bands.

At this moment Grandmamma's bell rang, and Gasha issued from her room again.

"What do you want with her, you impudent fellow?" she cried as she pushed Basil (who had risen at her entrance) before her towards the door. "First you lead a girl on, and then you want to lead her further still. I suppose it amuses you to see her tears. There's the door, now. Off you go! We want your room, not your company. And what good can you see in him?" she went on, turning to Masha. "Has not your uncle been walking into you to-day already? No; she must stick to her promise, forsooth! 'I will have no one but Basil,' Fool that you are!"

"Yes, I WILL have no one but him! I'll never love any one else! I could kill myself for him!" poor Masha burst out, the tears suddenly gushing forth.

For a while I stood watching her as she wiped away those tears. Then I fell to contemplating Basil attentively, in the hope of finding out what there was in him that she found so attractive; yet, though I sympathised with her sincerely in her grief, I could not for the life of me understand how such a charming creature as I considered her to be could love a man like him.

"When I become a man," I thought to myself as I returned to my room,

"Petrovskoe shall be mine, and Basil and Masha my servants. Some day, when I am sitting in my study and smoking a pipe, Masha will chance to pass the door on her way to the kitchen with an iron, and I shall say, 'Masha, come here,' and she will enter, and there will be no one else in the room. Then suddenly Basil too will enter, and, on seeing her, will cry, 'My sweetheart is lost to me!' and Masha will begin to weep, Then I shall say, 'Basil, I know that you love her, and that she loves you. Here are a thousand roubles for you. Marry her, and may God grant you both happiness!' Then I shall leave them together."

Among the countless thoughts and fancies which pass, without logic or sequence, through the mind and the imagination, there are always some which leave behind them a mark so profound that, without remembering their exact subject, we can at least recall that something good has passed through our brain, and try to retain and reproduce its effect. Such was the mark left upon my consciousness by the idea of sacrificing my feelings to Masha's happiness, seeing that she believed that she could attain it only through a union with Basil.

XIX. BOYHOOD

PERHAPS people will scarcely believe me when I tell them what were the dearest, most constant, objects of my reflections during my boyhood, so little did those objects consort with my age and position. Yet, in my opinion, contrast between a man's actual position and his moral activity constitutes the most reliable sign of his genuineness.

During the period when I was leading a solitary and self-centred moral life, I was much taken up with abstract thoughts on man's destiny, on a future life, and on the immortality of the soul, and, with all the ardour of inexperience, strove to make my youthful intellect solve those questions—the questions which constitute the highest level of thought to which the human intellect can tend, but a final decision of which the human intellect can never succeed in attaining.

I believe the intellect to take the same course of development in the individual as in the mass, as also that the thoughts which serve as a basis for philosophical theories are an inseparable part of that intellect, and that every man must be more or less conscious of those thoughts before he can know anything of the existence of philosophical theories. To my own mind those thoughts presented themselves with such clarity and force that I tried to apply them to life, in the fond belief that I was the first to have discovered such splendid and invaluable truths.

Sometimes I would suppose that happiness depends, not upon external causes themselves, but only upon our relation to them, and that, provided a man can accustom himself to bearing suffering, he need never be unhappy. To prove the latter hypothesis, I would (despite the horrible pain) hold out a Tatistchev's dictionary at arm's length for five minutes at a time, or else go into the store-room and scourge my back with cords until the tears involuntarily came to my eyes!

Another time, suddenly bethinking me that death might find me at any hour or any minute, I came to the conclusion that man could only be happy by using the present to the full and taking no thought for the future. Indeed, I wondered how people had never found that out before. Acting under the influence of the new idea, I laid my lesson-books aside for two or three days, and, reposing on my bed, gave myself up to novel-reading and the eating of gingerbread-and-honey which I had bought with my last remaining coins.

Again, standing one day before the blackboard and smearing figures on it with honey, I was struck with the thought, "Why is symmetry so agreeable to the eye? What is symmetry? Of course it is an innate sense," I continued; "yet what is its basis? Perhaps everything in life is symmetry? But no. On the contrary, this is life"—and I drew an oblong figure on the board—"and after life the soul passes to eternity"—here I drew a line from one end of the oblong figure to the edge of the board. "Why should there not be a corresponding line on the other side? If there be an eternity on one side, there must surely be a corresponding one on the other? That means that we have existed in a previous life, but have lost the recollection of it."

This conclusion—which seemed to me at the time both clear and novel, but the arguments for which it would be difficult for me, at this distance of time, to piece together—pleased me extremely, so I took a piece of paper and tried to write it down. But at the first attempt such a rush of other thoughts came whirling though my brain that I was obliged to jump up and pace the room. At the window, my attention was arrested by a driver harnessing a horse to a water-cart, and at once my mind concentrated itself upon the decision of the question, "Into what animal or human being will the spirit of that horse pass at death?" Just at that moment, Woloda passed through the room, and smiled to see me absorbed in speculative thoughts. His smile at once made me feel that all that I had been thinking about was utter nonsense.

I have related all this as I recollect it in order to show the reader the nature of my cogitations. No philosophical theory attracted me so much as scepticism, which at one period brought me to a state of mind verging upon insanity. I took the fancy into my head that no one nor anything really existed in the world except myself—that objects were not objects at all, but that images of them became manifest only so soon as I turned my attention upon them, and vanished again directly that I ceased to think about them. In short, this idea of mine (that real objects do not exist, but only one's conception of them) brought me to Schelling's well-known theory. There were moments when the influence of this idea led me to such vagaries as, for instance, turning sharply round, in the hope that by the suddenness of the movement I should come in contact with the void which I believed to be existing where I myself purported to be!

What a pitiful spring of moral activity is the human intellect! My faulty reason could not define the impenetrable. Consequently it shattered one fruitless conviction after another—convictions which, happily for my after life, I never lacked the courage to abandon as soon as they proved inadequate. From all this weary mental struggle I derived only a certain pliancy of mind, a weakening of the will, a habit of perpetual moral analysis, and a diminution both of freshness of sentiment and of clearness of thought. Usually abstract thinking develops man's capacity for apprehending the bent of his mind at certain moments and laying it to heart, but my inclination for abstract thought developed my consciousness in such a way that often when I began to consider even the simplest matter, I would lose myself in a labyrinthine analysis of my own thoughts concerning the matter in question. That is to say, I no longer thought of the matter itself, but only of what I was thinking about it. If I had then asked myself, "Of what am I thinking?" the true answer would have been, "I am thinking of what I am thinking;" and if I had further asked myself, "What, then, are the thoughts of which I am thinking?" I should have had to reply, "They are attempts to think of what I am thinking concerning my own thoughts"—and so on. Reason, with me, had to yield to excess of reason. Every philosophical discovery which I made so flattered my conceit that I often imagined myself to be a great man discovering new truths for the benefit of humanity. Consequently, I looked down with proud dignity upon my fellow-mortals. Yet, strange to state, no sooner did I come in contact with those fellow-mortals than I became filled with a stupid shyness of them, and, the higher I happened to be standing in my own opinion, the less did I feel capable of making others perceive my consciousness of my own dignity, since I could not rid myself of a sense of diffidence concerning even the simplest of my words and acts.

XX. WOLODA

THE further I advance in the recital of this period of my life, the more difficult and onerous does the task become. Too rarely do I find among the reminiscences of that time any moments full of the ardent feeling of sincerity which so often and so cheeringly illumined my childhood. Gladly would I pass in haste over my lonely boyhood, the sooner to arrive at the happy time when once again a tender, sincere, and noble friendship marked with a gleam of light at once the termination of that period and the beginning of a phase of my youth which was full of the charm of poetry. Therefore, I will not pursue my recollections from hour to hour, but only throw a cursory glance at the most prominent of them, from the time to which I have now carried my tale to the moment of my first contact with the exceptional personality that was fated to exercise such a decisive influence upon my character and ideas.

Woloda was about to enter the University. Tutors came to give him lessons independently of myself, and I listened with envy and involuntary respect as he drew boldly on the blackboard with white chalk and talked about "functions," "sines," and so forth—all of which seemed to me terms pertaining to unattainable wisdom. At length, one Sunday before luncheon all the tutors—and among them two professors—assembled in Grandmamma's room, and in the presence of Papa and some friends put Woloda through a rehearsal of his University examination—in which, to Grandmamma's delight, he gave evidence of no ordinary amount of knowledge.

Questions on different subjects were also put to me, but on all of them I showed complete ignorance, while the fact that the professors manifestly endeavoured to conceal that ignorance from Grandmamma only confused me the more. Yet, after all, I was only fifteen, and so had a year before me in which to prepare for the examinations. Woloda now came downstairs for luncheon only, and spent whole days and evenings over his studies in his own room—to which he kept, not from necessity, but because he preferred its seclusion. He was very ambitious, and meant to pass the examinations, not by halves, but with flying colours.

The first day arrived. Woloda was wearing a new blue frockcoat with brass buttons, a gold watch, and shiny boots. At the door stood Papa's phaeton, which Nicola duly opened; and presently, when Woloda and St. Jerome set out for the University, the girls—particularly Katenka—could be seen gazing with beaming faces from the window at Woloda's pleasing figure as it sat in the carriage. Papa said several times, "God go with him!" and Grandmamma, who also had dragged herself to the window, continued to make the sign of the cross as long as the phaeton was visible, as well as to murmur something to herself.

When Woloda returned, every one eagerly crowded round him. "How many marks? Were they good ones?" "Yes." But his happy face was an answer in itself. He had received five marks-the maximum! The next day, he sped on his way with the same good wishes and the same anxiety for his success, and was welcomed home with the same eagerness and joy.

This lasted for nine days. On the tenth day there was to be the last and most difficult examination of all—the one in divinity.

We all stood at the window, and watched for him with greater impatience than ever. Two o'clock, and yet no Woloda.

"Here they come, Papa! Here they come!" suddenly screamed Lubotshka as she peered through the window.

Sure enough the phaeton was driving up with St. Jerome and Woloda—the latter no longer in his grey cap and blue frockcoat, but in the uniform of a student of the University, with its embroidered blue collar, three-cornered hat, and gilded sword.

"Ah! If only SHE had been alive now!" exclaimed Grandmamma on seeing Woloda in this dress, and swooned away.

Woloda enters the anteroom with a beaming face, and embraces myself, Lubotshka, Mimi, and Katenka—the latter blushing to her ears. He hardly knows himself for joy. And how smart he looks in that uniform! How well

270

the blue collar suits his budding, dark moustache! What a tall, elegant figure is his, and what a distinguished walk!

On that memorable day we all lunched together in Grandmamma's room. Every face expressed delight, and with the dessert which followed the meal the servants, with grave but gratified faces, brought in bottles of champagne.

Grandmamma, for the first time since Mamma's death, drank a full glass of the wine to Woloda's health, and wept for joy as she looked at him.

Henceforth Woloda drove his own turn-out, invited his own friends, smoked, and went to balls. On one occasion, I even saw him sharing a couple of bottles of champagne with some guests in his room, and the whole company drinking a toast, with each glass, to some mysterious being, and then quarrelling as to who should have the bottom of the bottle!

Nevertheless he always lunched at home, and after the meal would stretch himself on a sofa and talk confidentially to Katenka: yet from what I overheard (while pretending, of course, to pay no attention) I gathered that they were only talking of the heroes and heroines of novels which they had read, or else of jealousy and love, and so on. Never could I understand what they found so attractive in these conversations, nor why they smiled so happily and discussed things with such animation.

Altogether I could see that, in addition to the friendship natural to persons who had been companions from childhood, there existed between Woloda and Katenka a relation which differentiated them from us, and united them mysteriously to one another.

XXI. KATENKA AND LUBOTSHKA

Katenka was now sixteen years old—quite a grown-up girl; and although at that age the angular figures, the bashfulness, and the gaucherie peculiar to girls passing from childhood to youth usually replace the comely freshness and graceful, half-developed bloom of childhood, she had in no way altered. Still the blue eyes with their merry glance were hers, the well-shaped nose with firm nostrils and almost forming a line with the forehead, the little mouth with its charming smile, the dimples in the rosy cheeks, and the small white hands. To her, the epithet of "girl," pure and simple, was pre-eminently applicable, for in her the only new features were a new and "young-lady-like" arrangement of her thick flaxen hair and a youthful bosom—the latter an addition which at once caused her great joy and made her very bashful.

Although Lubotshka and she had grown up together and received the same education, they were totally unlike one another. Lubotshka was not tall, and the rickets from which she had suffered had shaped her feet in goose fashion and made her figure very bad. The only pretty feature in her face was her eyes, which were indeed wonderful, being large and black, and instinct with such an extremely pleasing expression of mingled gravity and naivete that she was bound to attract attention. In everything she was simple and natural, so that, whereas Katenka always looked as though she were trying to be like some one else, Lubotshka looked people straight in the face, and sometimes fixed them so long with her splendid black eyes that she got blamed for doing what was thought to be improper. Katenka, on the contrary, always cast her eyelids down, blinked, and pretended that she was short-sighted, though I knew very well that her sight was excellent. Lubotshka hated being shown off before strangers, and when a visitor offered to kiss her she invariably grew cross, and said that she hated "affection"; whereas, when strangers were present, Katenka was always particularly endearing to Mimi, and loved to walk about the room arm in arm with another girl. Likewise, though Lubotshka was a terrible giggler, and sometimes ran about the room in convulsions of gesticulating laughter, Katenka always covered her mouth with her hands or her pocket-handkerchief when she wanted to laugh. Lubotshka, again, loved to have grown-up men to talk to, and said that some day she meant to marry a hussar, but Katenka always pretended that all men were horrid, and that she never meant to marry any one of them, while as soon as a male visitor addressed her she changed completely, as though she were nervous of something. Likewise, Lubotshka was continually at loggerheads with Mimi because the latter wanted her to have her stays so tight that she could not breathe or eat or drink in comfort, while Katenka, on the contrary, would often insert her finger into her waistband to show how loose it was, and always ate very little. Lubotshka liked to draw heads; Katenka only flowers and butterflies. The former could play Field's concertos and Beethoven's sonatas excellently, whereas the latter indulged in variations and waltzes, retarded the time, and used the pedals continuously—not to mention the fact that, before she began, she invariably struck three chords in arpeggio.

Nevertheless, in those days I thought Katenka much the grander person of the two, and liked her the best.

XXII. PAPA

Papa had been in a particularly good humour ever since Woloda had passed into the University, and came much oftener to dine with Grandmamma. However, I knew from Nicola that he had won a great deal lately. Occasionally, he would come and sit with us in the evening before going to the club. He used to sit down to the piano and bid us group ourselves around him, after which he would beat time with his thin boots (he detested heels, and never wore them), and make us sing gipsy songs. At such times you should have seen the quaint enthusiasm of his beloved Lubotshka, who adored him!

Sometimes, again, he would come to the schoolroom and listen with a grave face as I said my lessons; yet by the few words which he would let drop when correcting me, I could see that he knew even less about the subject than I did. Not infrequently, too, he would wink at us and make secret signs when Grandmamma was beginning to scold us and find fault with us all round. "So much for us children!" he would say. On the whole, however, the impossible pinnacle upon which my childish imagination had placed him had undergone a certain abasement. I still kissed his large white hand with a certain feeling of love and respect, but I also allowed myself to think about him and to criticise his behaviour until involuntarily thoughts occurred to me which alarmed me by their presence. Never shall I forget one incident in particular which awakened thoughts of this kind, and caused me intense astonishment. Late one evening, he entered the drawing-room in his black dress-coat and white waistcoat, to take Woloda (who was still dressing in his bedroom) to a ball. Grandmamma was also in her bedroom, but had given orders that, before setting out, Woloda was to come and say goodbye to her (it was her invariable custom to inspect him before he went to a ball, and to bless him and direct him as to his behaviour). The room where we were was lighted by a solitary lamp. Mimi and Katenka were walking up and down, and Lubotshka was playing Field's Second Concerto (Mamma's favourite piece) at the piano. Never was there such a family likeness as between Mamma and my sister—not so much in the face or the stature as in the hands, the walk, the voice, the favourite expressions, and, above all, the way of playing the piano and the whole demeanour at the instrument. Lubotshka always arranged her dress when sitting down just as Mamma had done, as well as turned the leaves like her, tapped her fingers angrily and said "Dear me!" whenever a difficult passage did not go smoothly, and, in particular, played with the delicacy and exquisite purity of touch which in those days caused the execution of Field's music to be known characteristically as "jeu perle" and to lie beyond comparison with the humbug of our modern virtuosi.

Papa entered the room with short, soft steps, and approached Lubotshka. On seeing him she stopped playing.

"No, go on, Luba, go on," he said as he forced her to sit down again. She went on playing, while Papa, his head on his hand, sat near her for a while. Then suddenly he gave his shoulders a shrug, and, rising, began to pace the room. Every time that he approached the piano he halted for a moment and looked fixedly at Lubotshka. By his walk and his every movement, I could see that he was greatly agitated. Once, when he stopped behind Lubotshka, he kissed her black hair, and then, wheeling quickly round, resumed his pacing. The piece finished, Lubotshka went up to him and said, "Was it well played?" whereupon, without answering, he took her head in his two hands, and kissed her forehead and eyes with such tenderness as I had never before seen him display.

"Why, you are crying!" cried Lubotshka suddenly as she ceased to toy with his watch-chain and stared at him with her great black eyes. "Pardon me, darling Papa! I had quite forgotten that it was dear Mamma's piece which I was playing."

"No, no, my love; play it often," he said in a voice trembling with emotion. "Ah, if you only knew how much good it does me to share your tears!"

He kissed her again, and then, mastering his feelings and shrugging his shoulders, went to the door leading to the corridor which ran past Woloda's room.

"Waldemar, shall you be ready soon?" he cried, halting in the middle of the passage. Just then Masha came along.

"Why, you look prettier every day," he said to her. She blushed and passed on.

"Waldemar, shall you be ready soon?" he cried again, with a cough and a shake of his shoulders, just as Masha slipped away and he first caught sight of me.

I loved Papa, but the intellect is independent of the heart, and often gives birth to thoughts which offend and are harsh and incomprehensible to the feelings. And it was thoughts of this kind that, for all I strove to put them away, arose at that moment in my mind.

XXIII. GRANDMAMMA

Grandmamma was growing weaker every day. Her bell, Gasha's grumbling voice, and the slamming of doors in her room were sounds of constant occurrence, and she no longer received us sitting in the Voltairian arm-chair in her boudoir, but lying on the bed in her bedroom, supported on lace-trimmed cushions. One day when she greeted us, I noticed a yellowish-white swelling on her hand, and smelt the same oppressive odour which I had smelt five years ago in Mamma's room. The doctor came three times a day, and there had been more than one consultation. Yet the character of her haughty, ceremonious bearing towards all who lived with her, and particularly towards Papa, never changed in the least. She went on emphasising certain words, raising her eyebrows, and saying "my dear," just as she had always done.

Then for a few days we did not see her at all, and one morning St. Jerome proposed to me that Woloda and I should take Katenka and Lubotshka for a drive during the hours generally allotted to study. Although I observed that the street was lined with straw under the windows of Grandmamma's room, and that some men in blue stockings [Undertaker's men.] were standing at our gate, the reason never dawned upon me why we were being sent out at that unusual hour. Throughout the drive Lubotshka and I were in that particularly merry mood when the least trifle, the least word or movement, sets one off laughing.

A pedlar went trotting across the road with a tray, and we laughed. Some ragged cabmen, brandishing their reins and driving at full speed, overtook our sledge, and we laughed again. Next, Philip's whip got caught in the side of the vehicle, and the way in which he said, "Bother the thing!" as he drove to disentangle it almost killed us with mirth. Mimi looked displeased, and said that only silly people laughed for no reason at all, but Lubotshka—her face purple with suppressed merriment—needed but to give me a sly glance, and we again burst out into such Homeric laughter, when our eyes met, that the tears rushed into them and we could not stop our paroxysms, although they nearly choked us. Hardly, again, had we desisted a little when I looked at

Lubotshka once more, and gave vent to one of the slang words which we then affected among ourselves—words which always called forth hilarity; and in a moment we were laughing again.

Just as we reached home, I was opening my mouth to make a splendid grimace at Lubotshka when my eye fell upon a black coffin-cover which was leaning against the gate—and my mouth remained fixed in its gaping position.

"Your Grandmamma is dead," said St. Jerome as he met us. His face was very pale.

Throughout the whole time that Grandmamma's body was in the house I was oppressed with the fear of death, for the corpse served as a forcible and disagreeable reminder that I too must die some day—a feeling which people often mistake for grief. I had no sincere regret for Grandmamma, nor, I think, had any one else, since, although the house was full of sympathising callers, nobody seemed to mourn for her from their hearts except one mourner whose genuine grief made a great impression upon me, seeing that the mourner in question was—Gasha! She shut herself up in the garret, tore her hair and refused all consolation, saying that, now that her mistress was dead, she only wished to die herself.

I again assert that, in matters of feeling, it is the unexpected effects that constitute the most reliable signs of sincerity.

Though Grandmamma was no longer with us, reminiscences and gossip about her long went on in the house. Such gossip referred mostly to her will, which she had made shortly before her death, and of which, as yet, no one knew the contents except her bosom friend, Prince Ivan Ivanovitch. I could hear the servants talking excitedly together, and making innumerable conjectures as to the amount left and the probable beneficiaries: nor can I deny that the idea that we ourselves were probably the latter greatly pleased me.

Six weeks later, Nicola—who acted as regular news-agent to the house—informed me that Grandmamma had left the whole of her fortune to Lubotshka, with, as her trustee until her majority, not Papa, but Prince Ivan Ivanovitch!

278

XXIV. MYSELF

Only a few months remained before I was to matriculate for the University, yet I was making such good progress that I felt no apprehensions, and even took a pleasure in my studies. I kept in good heart, and learnt my lessons fluently and intelligently. The faculty I had selected was the mathematical one—probably, to tell the truth, because the terms "tangent," "differentials," "integrals," and so forth, pleased my fancy.

Though stout and broad-shouldered, I was shorter than Woloda, while my ugliness of face still remained and tormented me as much as ever. By way of compensation, I tried to appear original. Yet one thing comforted me, namely, that Papa had said that I had "an INTELLIGENT face." I quite believed him.

St. Jerome was not only satisfied with me, but actually had taken to praising me. Consequently, I had now ceased to hate him. In fact, when, one day, he said that, with my "capacities" and my "intellect," it would be shameful for me not to accomplish this, that, or the other thing, I believe I almost liked him.

I had long ago given up keeping observation on the maidservants' room, for I was now ashamed to hide behind doors. Likewise, I confess that the knowledge of Masha's love for Basil had greatly cooled my ardour for her, and that my passion underwent a final cure by their marriage—a consummation to which I myself contributed by, at Basil's request, asking Papa's consent to the union.

When the newly-married couple brought trays of cakes and sweetmeats to Papa as a thank-offering, and Masha, in a cap with blue ribbons, kissed each of us on the shoulder in token of her gratitude, I merely noticed the scent of the rose pomade on her hair, but felt no other sensation.

In general, I was beginning to get the better of my youthful defects, with the exception of the principal one—the one of which I shall often again have to speak in relating my life's history—namely, the tendency to abstract thought.

XXV. WOLODA'S FRIENDS

Although, when in the society of Woloda's friends, I had to play a part that hurt my pride, I liked sitting in his room when he had visitors, and silently watching all they did. The two who came most frequently to see him were a military adjutant called Dubkoff and a student named Prince Nechludoff. Dubkoff was a little dark-haired, highly-strung man who, though short of stature and no longer in his first youth, had a pleasing and invariably cheerful air. His was one of those limited natures which are agreeable through their very limitations; natures which cannot regard matters from every point of view, but which are nevertheless attracted by everything. Usually the reasoning of such persons is false and one-sided, yet always genuine and taking; wherefore their narrow egotism seems both amiable and excusable. There were two other reasons why Dubkoff had charms for Woloda and myself—namely, the fact that he was of military appearance, and, secondly (and principally), the fact that he was of a certain age—an age with which young people are apt to associate that quality of "gentlemanliness" which is so highly esteemed at their time of life. However, he was in very truth un homme comme il faut. The only thing which I did not like about it all was that, in his presence, Woloda always seemed ashamed of my innocent behaviour, and still more so of my youthfulness. As for Prince Nechludoff, he was in no way handsome, since neither his small grey eyes, his low, projecting forehead, nor his disproportionately long hands and feet could be called good features. The only good points about him were his unusually tall stature, his delicate colouring, and his splendid teeth. Nevertheless, his face was of such an original, energetic character (owing to his narrow, sparkling eyes and ever-changing expression—now stern, now childlike, now smiling indeterminately) that it was impossible to help noticing it. As a rule he was very shy, and would blush to the ears at the smallest trifle, but it was a shyness altogether different from mine, seeing that, the more he blushed, the more determined-looking he grew, as though he were vexed at his own weakness.

Although he was on very good terms with Woloda and Dubkoff,

it was clearly chance which had united them thus, since their tastes were entirely dissimilar. Woloda and Dubkoff seemed to be afraid of anything like serious consideration or emotion, whereas Nechludoff was beyond all things an enthusiast, and would often, despite their sarcastic remarks, plunge into dissertations on philosophical matters or matters of feeling. Again, the two former liked talking about the fair objects of their adoration (these were always numerous, and always shared by the friends in common), whereas Nechludoff invariably grew annoyed when taxed with his love for a certain red-haired lady.

Again, Woloda and Dubkoff often permitted themselves to criticise their relatives, and to find amusement in so doing, but Nechludoff flew into a tremendous rage when on one occasion they referred to some weak points in the character of an aunt of his whom he adored. Finally, after supper Woloda and Dubkoff would usually go off to some place whither Nechludoff would not accompany them; wherefore they called him "a dainty girl."

The very first time that I ever saw Prince Nechludoff I was struck with his exterior and conversation. Yet, though I could discern a great similarity between his disposition and my own (or perhaps it was because I COULD so discern it), the impression which he produced upon me at first was anything but agreeable. I liked neither his quick glance, his hard voice, his proud bearing, nor (least of all) the utter indifference with which he treated me. Often, when conversing, I burned to contradict him, to punish his pride by confuting him, to show him that I was clever in spite of his disdainful neglect of my presence. But I was invariably prevented from doing so by my shyness.

XXVI. DISCUSSIONS

Woloda was lying reading a French novel on the sofa when I paid my usual visit to his room after my evening lessons. He looked up at me for a moment from his book, and then went on reading. This perfectly simple and natural movement, however, offended me. I conceived that the glance implied a question why I had come and a wish to hide his thoughts from me (I may say that at that period a tendency to attach a meaning to the most insignificant of acts formed a prominent feature in my character). So I went to the table and also took up a book to read. Yet, even before I had actually begun reading, the idea struck me how ridiculous it was that, although we had never seen one another all day, we should have not a word to exchange.

"Are you going to stay in to-night, Woloda?"

"I don't know. Why?"

"Oh, because—" Seeing that the conversation did not promise to be a success, I took up my book again, and began to read. Yet it was a strange thing that, though we sometimes passed whole hours together without speaking when we were alone, the mere presence of a third—sometimes of a taciturn and wholly uninteresting person—sufficed to plunge us into the most varied and engrossing of discussions. The truth was that we knew one another too well, and to know a person either too well or too little acts as a bar to intimacy.

"Is Woloda at home?" came in Dubkoff's voice from the ante-room.

"Yes!" shouted Woloda, springing up and throwing aside his book.

Dubkoff and Nechludoff entered.

"Are you coming to the theatre, Woloda?"

"No, I have no time," he replied with a blush.

"Oh, never mind that. Come along."

"But I haven't got a ticket."

"Tickets, as many as you like, at the entrance."

"Very well, then; I'll be back in a minute," said Woloda evasively as he left the room. I knew very well that he wanted to go, but that he had declined because he had no money, and had now gone to borrow five roubles of one of the servants—to be repaid when he got his next allowance.

"How do you do, DIPLOMAT?" said Dubkoff to me as he shook me by the hand. Woloda's friends had called me by that nickname since the day when Grandmamma had said at luncheon that Woloda must go into the army, but that she would like to see me in the diplomatic service, dressed in a black frock-coat, and with my hair arranged a la coq (the two essential requirements, in her opinion, of a DIPLOMAT).

"Where has Woloda gone to?" asked Nechludoff.

"I don't know," I replied, blushing to think that nevertheless they had probably guessed his errand.

"I suppose he has no money? Yes, I can see I am right, O diplomatist," he added, taking my smile as an answer in the affirmative. "Well, I have none, either. Have you any, Dubkoff?"

"I'll see," replied Dubkoff, feeling for his pocket, and rummaging gingerly about with his squat little fingers among his small change. "Yes, here are five copecks-twenty, but that's all," he concluded with a comic gesture of his hand.

At this point Woloda re-entered.

"Are we going?"

"No."

"What an odd fellow you are!" said Nechludoff. "Why don't you say that you have no money? Here, take my ticket."

"But what are you going to do?"

"He can go into his cousin's box," said Dubkoff.

"No, I'm not going at all," replied Nechludoff.

"Why?"

"Because I hate sitting in a box."

"And for what reason?"

"I don't know. Somehow I feel uncomfortable there."

"Always the same! I can't understand a fellow feeling uncomfortable when he is sitting with people who are fond of him. It is unnatural, mon cher."

"But what else is there to be done si je suis tant timide? You never blushed in your life, but I do at the least trifle," and he blushed at that moment.

"Do you know what that nervousness of yours proceeds from?" said Dubkoff in a protecting sort of tone, "D'un exces d'amour propre, mon cher."

"What do you mean by 'exces d'amour propre'?" asked Nechludoff, highly offended. "On the contrary, I am shy just because I have TOO LITTLE amour propre. I always feel as though I were being tiresome and disagreeable, and therefore—"

"Well, get ready, Woloda," interrupted Dubkoff, tapping my brother on the shoulder and handing him his cloak. "Ignaz, get your master ready."

"Therefore," continued Nechludoff, "it often happens with me that—"

But Dubkoff was not listening. "Tra-la-la-la," and he hummed a popular air.

"Oh, but I'm not going to let you off," went on Nechludoff. "I mean to prove to you that my shyness is not the result of conceit."

"You can prove it as we go along."

"But I have told you that I am NOT going."

"Well, then, stay here and prove it to the DIPLOMAT, and he can tell us all about it when we return."

"Yes, that's what I WILL do," said Nechludoff with boyish obstinacy, "so hurry up with your return."

"Well, do you think I am egotistic?" he continued, seating himself beside me.

True, I had a definite opinion on the subject, but I felt so taken aback by this unexpected question that at first I could make no reply.

"Yes, I DO think so," I said at length in a faltering voice, and colouring at the thought that at last the moment had come when I could show him that I was clever. "I think that EVERYBODY is egotistic, and that everything we do is done out of egotism."

"But what do you call egotism?" asked Nechludoff—smiling, as I thought, a little contemptuously.

"Egotism is a conviction that we are better and cleverer than any one else," I replied.

"But how can we ALL be filled with this conviction?" he inquired.

"Well, I don't know if I am right or not—certainly no one but myself seems to hold the opinion—but I believe that I am wiser than any one else in the world, and that all of you know it."

"At least I can say for myself," observed Nechludoff, "that I have met a FEW people whom I believe to excel me in wisdom."

"It is impossible," I replied with conviction.

"Do you really think so?" he said, looking at me gravely.

"Yes, really," I answered, and an idea crossed my mind which I proceeded to expound further. "Let me prove it to you. Why do we love ourselves better than any one else? Because we think ourselves BETTER than any one else—more worthy of our own love. If we THOUGHT others better than ourselves, we should LOVE them better than ourselves: but that is never the case. And even if it were so, I should still be right," I added with an involuntary smile of complacency.

For a few minutes Nechludoff was silent.

"I never thought you were so clever," he said with a smile so goodhumoured and charming that I at once felt happy.

Praise exercises an all-potent influence, not only upon the feelings, but also upon the intellect; so that under the influence of that agreeable sensation I straightway felt much cleverer than before, and thoughts began to rush with extraordinary rapidity through my head. From egotism we passed insensibly to the theme of love, which seemed inexhaustible. Although our reasonings might have sounded nonsensical to a listener (so vague and one-sided were they), for ourselves they had a profound significance. Our minds were so perfectly in harmony that not a chord was struck in the one without awakening an echo in the other, and in this harmonious striking of different chords we found the greatest delight. Indeed, we felt as though time and language were insufficient to express the thoughts which seethed within us.

XXVII. THE BEGINNING OF OUR FRIENDSHIP

From that time forth, a strange, but exceedingly pleasant, relation subsisted between Dimitri Nechludoff and myself. Before other people he paid me scanty attention, but as soon as ever we were alone, we would sit down together in some comfortable corner and, forgetful both of time and of everything around us, fall to reasoning.

We talked of a future life, of art, service, marriage, and education; nor did the idea ever occur to us that very possibly all we said was shocking nonsense. The reason why it never occurred to us was that the nonsense which we talked was good, sensible nonsense, and that, so long as one is young, one can appreciate good nonsense, and believe in it. In youth the powers of the mind are directed wholly to the future, and that future assumes such various, vivid, and alluring forms under the influence of hope—hope based, not upon the experience of the past, but upon an assumed possibility of happiness to come—that such dreams of expected felicity constitute in themselves the true happiness of that period of our life. How I loved those moments in our metaphysical discussions (discussions which formed the major portion of our intercourse) when thoughts came thronging faster and faster, and, succeeding one another at lightning speed, and growing more and more abstract, at length attained such a pitch of elevation that one felt powerless to express them, and said something quite different from what one had intended at first to say! How I liked those moments, too, when, carried higher and higher into the realms of thought, we suddenly felt that we could grasp its substance no longer and go no further!

At carnival time Nechludoff was so much taken up with one festivity and another that, though he came to see us several times a day, he never addressed a single word to me. This offended me so much that once again I found myself thinking him a haughty, disagreeable fellow, and only awaited an opportunity to show him that I no longer valued his company or felt any particular affection for him. Accordingly, the first time that he spoke to me after the carnival, I said that I had lessons to do, and went upstairs, but a quarter of an hour later some one opened the schoolroom door, and Nechludoff entered.

"Am I disturbing you?" he asked.

"No," I replied, although I had at first intended to say that I had a great deal to do.

"Then why did you run away just now? It is a long while since we had a talk together, and I have grown so accustomed to these discussions that I feel as though something were wanting."

My anger had quite gone now, and Dimitri stood before me the same good and lovable being as before.

"You know, perhaps, why I ran away?" I said.

"Perhaps I do," he answered, taking a seat near me. "However, though it is possible I know why, I cannot say it straight out, whereas YOU can."

"Then I will do so. I ran away because I was angry with you—well, not angry, but grieved. I always have an idea that you despise me for being so young."

"Well, do you know why I always feel so attracted towards you?" he replied, meeting my confession with a look of kind understanding, "and why I like you better than any of my other acquaintances or than any of the people among whom I mostly have to live? It is because I found out at once that you have the rare and astonishing gift of sincerity."

"Yes, I always confess the things of which I am most ashamed—but only to people in whom I trust," I said.

"Ah, but to trust a man you must be his friend completely, and we are not friends yet, Nicolas. Remember how, when we were speaking of friendship, we agreed that, to be real friends, we ought to trust one another implicitly."

"I trust you in so far as that I feel convinced that you would never repeat a word of what I might tell you," I said.

"Yet perhaps the most interesting and important thoughts of all are just those which we never tell one another, while the mean thoughts (the thoughts which, if we only knew that we had to confess them to one another, would probably never have the hardihood to enter our minds)—Well, do you know what I am thinking of, Nicolas?" he broke off, rising and taking my hand with a smile. "I propose (and I feel sure that it would benefit us mutually) that we should pledge our word to one another to tell each other EVERYTHING. We should then really know each other, and never have anything on our consciences. And, to guard against outsiders, let us also agree never to speak of one another to a third person. Suppose we do that?"

"I agree," I replied. And we did it. What the result was shall be told hereafter.

Kerr has said that every attachment has two sides: one loves, and the other allows himself to be loved; one kisses, and the other surrenders his cheek. That is perfectly true. In the case of our own attachment it was I who kissed, and Dimitri who surrendered his cheek—though he, in his turn, was ready to pay me a similar salute. We loved equally because we knew and appreciated each other thoroughly, but this did not prevent him from exercising an influence over me, nor myself from rendering him adoration.

It will readily be understood that Nechludoff's influence caused me to adopt his bent of mind, the essence of which lay in an enthusiastic reverence for ideal virtue and a firm belief in man's vocation to perpetual perfection. To raise mankind, to abolish vice and misery, seemed at that time a task offering no difficulties. To educate oneself to every virtue, and so to achieve happiness, seemed a simple and easy matter.

Only God Himself knows whether those blessed dreams of youth were ridiculous, or whose the fault was that they never became realised.

YOUTH

I. WHAT I CONSIDER TO HAVE BEEN THE BEGINNING OF MY YOUTH

I have said that my friendship with Dimitri opened up for me a new view of my life and of its aim and relations. The essence of that view lay in the conviction that the destiny of man is to strive for moral improvement, and that such improvement is at once easy, possible, and lasting. Hitherto, however, I had found pleasure only in the new ideas which I discovered to arise from that conviction, and in the forming of brilliant plans for a moral, active future, while all the time my life had been continuing along its old petty, muddled, pleasure-seeking course, and the same virtuous thoughts which I and my adored friend Dimitri ("my own marvellous Mitia," as I used to call him to myself in a whisper) had been wont to exchange with one another still pleased my intellect, but left my sensibility untouched. Nevertheless there came a moment when those thoughts swept into my head with a sudden freshness and force of moral revelation which left me aghast at the amount of time which I had been wasting, and made me feel as though I must at once—that very second—apply those thoughts to life, with the firm intention of never again changing them.

It is from that moment that I date the beginning of my youth.

I was then nearly sixteen. Tutors still attended to give me lessons, St. Jerome still acted as general supervisor of my education, and, willy-nilly, I was being prepared for the University. In addition to my studies, my occupations included certain vague dreamings and ponderings, a number of gymnastic exercises to make myself the finest athlete in the world, a good deal of aimless, thoughtless wandering through the rooms of the house (but more especially along the maidservants' corridor), and much looking at myself in the mirror. From the latter, however, I always turned away with a vague feeling of depression, almost of repulsion. Not only did I feel sure that my exterior was ugly, but I could derive no comfort from any of the usual consolations under such circumstances. I could not say, for instance, that I had at least an expressive, clever, or refined face, for there was nothing whatever expressive about it. Its features were of the most humdrum, dull, and unbecoming type, with small grey eyes which seemed to me, whenever I regarded them in the mirror, to be stupid rather than clever. Of manly bearing I possessed even less, since, although I was not exactly small of stature, and had, moreover, plenty of strength for my years, every feature in my face was of the meek, sleepy-looking, indefinite type. Even refinement was lacking in it, since, on the contrary, it precisely resembled that of a simple-looking moujik, while I also had the same big hands and feet as he. At the time, all this seemed to me very shameful.

II. SPRINGTIME

Easter of the year when I entered the University fell late in April, so that the examinations were fixed for St. Thomas's Week, [Easter week.] and I had to spend Good Friday in fasting and finally getting myself ready for the ordeal.

Following upon wet snow (the kind of stuff which Karl Ivanitch used to describe as "a child following, its father"), the weather had for three days been bright and mild and still. Not a clot of snow was now to be seen in the streets, and the dirty slush had given place to wet, shining pavements and coursing rivulets. The last icicles on the roofs were fast melting in the sunshine, buds were swelling on the trees in the little garden, the path leading across the courtyard to the stables was soft instead of being a frozen ridge of mud, and mossy grass was showing green between the stones around the entrance-steps. It was just that particular time in spring when the season exercises the strongest influence upon the human soul—when clear sunlight illuminates everything, yet sheds no warmth, when rivulets run trickling under one's feet, when the air is charged with an odorous freshness, and when the bright blue sky is streaked with long, transparent clouds.

For some reason or another the influence of this early stage in the birth of spring always seems to me more perceptible and more impressive in a great town than in the country. One sees less, but one feels more. I was standing near the window—through the double frames of which the morning sun was throwing its mote-flecked beams upon the floor of what seemed to me my intolerably wearisome schoolroom—and working out a long algebraical equation on the blackboard. In one hand I was holding a ragged, long-suffering "Algebra" and in the other a small piece of chalk which had already besmeared my hands, my face, and the elbows of my jacket. Nicola, clad in an apron, and with his sleeves rolled up, was picking out the putty from the window-frames with a pair of nippers, and unfastening the screws. The window looked out upon the little garden. At length his occupation and the noise which he was making over it arrested my attention. At the moment I was in a very cross, dissatisfied frame of mind, for nothing seemed to be going right with me. I had made a mistake at the very beginning of my algebra, and so should have to work it out again; twice I had let the chalk drop. I was conscious that my hands and face were whitened all over; the sponge had rolled away into a corner; and the noise of Nicola's operations was fast getting on my nerves. I had a feeling as though I wanted to fly into a temper and grumble at some one, so I threw down chalk and "Algebra" alike, and began to pace the room. Then suddenly I remembered that to-day we were to go to confession, and that therefore I must refrain from doing anything wrong. Next, with equal suddenness I relapsed into an extraordinarily goodhumoured frame of mind, and walked across to Nicola.

"Let me help you, Nicola," I said, trying to speak as pleasantly as I possibly could. The idea that I was performing a meritorious action in thus suppressing my ill-temper and offering to help him increased my good-humour all the more.

By this time the putty had been chipped out, and the screws removed, yet, though Nicola pulled with might and main at the cross-piece, the window-frame refused to budge.

"If it comes out as soon as he and I begin to pull at it together," I thought, "it will be rather a shame, as then I shall have nothing more of the kind to do to-day."

Suddenly the frame yielded a little at one side, and came out.

"Where shall I put it?" I said.

"Let ME see to it, if you please," replied Nicola, evidently surprised as well as, seemingly, not over-pleased at my zeal. "We must not leave it here, but carry it away to the lumber-room, where I keep all the frames stored and numbered."

"Oh, but I can manage it," I said as I lifted it up. I verily believe that if the lumber-room had been a couple of versts away, and the frame twice as heavy as it was, I should have been the more pleased. I felt as though I wanted

294

to tire myself out in performing this service for Nicola. When I returned to the room the bricks and screws had been replaced on the windowsill, and Nicola was sweeping the debris, as well as a few torpid flies, out of the open window. The fresh, fragrant air was rushing into and filling all the room, while with it came also the dull murmur of the city and the twittering of sparrows in the garden. Everything was in brilliant light, the room looked cheerful, and a gentle spring breeze was stirring Nicola's hair and the leaves of my "Algebra." Approaching the window, I sat down upon the sill, turned my eyes downwards towards the garden, and fell into a brown study.

Something new to me, something extraordinarily potent and unfamiliar, had suddenly invaded my soul. The wet ground on which, here and there, a few yellowish stalks and blades of bright-green grass were to be seen; the little rivulets glittering in the sunshine, and sweeping clods of earth and tiny chips of wood along with them; the reddish twigs of the lilac, with their swelling buds, which nodded just beneath the window; the fussy twitterings of birds as they fluttered in the bush below; the blackened fence shining wet from the snow which had lately melted off it; and, most of all, the raw, odorous air and radiant sunlight—all spoke to me, clearly and unmistakably, of something new and beautiful, of something which, though I cannot repeat it here as it was then expressed to me, I will try to reproduce so far as I understood it. Everything spoke to me of beauty, happiness, and virtue—as three things which were both easy and possible for me—and said that no one of them could exist without the other two, since beauty, happiness, and virtue were one. "How did I never come to understand that before?" I cried to myself. "How did I ever manage to be so wicked? Oh, but how good, how happy, I could be—nay, I WILL be—in the future! At once, at once—yes, this very minute—I will become another being, and begin to live differently!" For all that, I continued sitting on the window-sill, continued merely dreaming, and doing nothing. Have you ever, on a summer's day, gone to bed in dull, rainy weather, and, waking just at sunset, opened your eyes and seen through the square space of the window—the space where the linen blind is blowing up and down, and beating its rod upon the window-sill—the rain-soaked, shadowy, purple vista of an avenue of lime-trees, with a damp garden path lit up by the clear, slanting beams of the sun, and then suddenly heard the joyous sounds of bird life in the garden, and seen insects flying to and fro at the open window, and glittering in the sunlight, and smelt the fragrance of the rain-washed air, and thought to yourself, "Am I not ashamed to be lying in bed on such an evening as this?" and, leaping joyously to your feet, gone out into the garden and revelled in all that welter of life? If you have, then you can imagine for yourself the overpowering sensation which was then possessing me.

III. DREAMS

"To-day I will make my confession and purge myself of every sin," I thought to myself. "Nor will I ever commit another one." At this point I recalled all the peccadilloes which most troubled my conscience. "I will go to church regularly every Sunday, as well as read the Gospel at the close of every hour throughout the day. What is more, I will set aside, out of the cheque which I shall receive each month after I have gone to the University, two-and-a-half roubles" (a tenth of my monthly allowance) "for people who are poor but not exactly beggars, yet without letting any one know anything about it. Yes, I will begin to look out for people like that—orphans or old women—at once, yet never tell a soul what I am doing for them.

"Also, I will have a room here of my very own (St. Jerome's, probably), and look after it myself, and keep it perfectly clean. I will never let any one do anything for me, for every one is just a human being like myself. Likewise I will walk every day, not drive, to the University. Even if some one gives me a drozhki [Russian phaeton.] I will sell it, and devote the money to the poor. Everything I will do exactly and always" (what that "always" meant I could not possibly have said, but at least I had a vivid consciousness of its connoting some kind of prudent, moral, and irreproachable life). "I will get up all my lectures thoroughly, and go over all the subjects beforehand, so that at the end of my first course I may come out top and write a thesis. During my second course also I will get up everything beforehand, so that I may soon be transferred to the third course, and at eighteen come out top in the examinations, and receive two gold medals, and go on to be Master of Arts, and Doctor, and the first scholar in Europe. Yes, in all Europe I mean to be the first scholar.—Well, what next?" I asked myself at this point. Suddenly it struck me that dreams of this sort were a form of pride—a sin which I should have to confess to the priest that very evening, so I returned to the original thread of my meditations. "When getting up my lectures I will go to the Vorobievi Gori, [Sparrow Hills—a public park near Moscow.] and choose some spot under a tree, and read my lectures over there. Sometimes I will take with me something to eat—cheese or a pie from Pedotti's, or something of the kind. After that I will sleep a little, and then read some good book or other, or else draw pictures or play on some instrument (certainly I must learn to play the flute). Perhaps SHE too will be walking on the Vorobievi Gori, and will approach me one day and say, 'Who are you?' and I shall look at her, oh, so sadly, and say that I am the son of a priest, and that I am happy only when I am there alone, quite alone. Then she will give me her hand, and say something to me, and sit down beside me. So every day we shall go to the same spot, and be friends together, and I shall kiss her. But no! That would not be right! On the contrary, from this day forward I never mean to look at a woman again. Never, never again do I mean to walk with a girl, nor even to go near one if I can help it. Yet, of course, in three years' time, when I have come of age, I shall marry. Also, I mean to take as much exercise as ever I can, and to do gymnastics every day, so that, when I have turned twenty-five, I shall be stronger even than Rappo. On my first day's training I mean to hold out half a pood [The Pood = 40 Russian pounds.] at arm's length for five minutes, and the next day twenty-one pounds, and the third day twenty-two pounds, and so on, until at last I can hold out four poods in each hand, and be stronger even than a porter. Then, if ever any one should try to insult me or should begin to speak disrespectfully of HER, I shall take him so, by the front of his coat, and lift him up an arshin [The arshin = 2 feet 3 inches.] or two with one hand, and just hold him there, so that he may feel my strength and cease from his conduct. Yet that too would not be right. No, no, it would not matter; I should not hurt him, merely show him that I—"

Let no one blame me because the dreams of my youth were as foolish as those of my childhood and boyhood. I am sure that, even if it be my fate to live to extreme old age and to continue my story with the years, I, an old man of seventy, shall be found dreaming dreams just as impossible and childish as those I am dreaming now. I shall be dreaming of some lovely Maria who loves me, the toothless old man, as she might love a Mazeppa; of some imbecile son who, through some extraordinary chance, has suddenly become a minister of state; of my suddenly receiving a windfall of a million of roubles. I am sure that there exists no human being, no human age, to whom or to which that gracious, consolatory power of dreaming is totally a stranger.

Yet, save for the one general feature of magic and impossibility, the dreams of each human being, of each age of man, have their own distinguishing characteristics. At the period upon which I look as having marked the close of my boyhood and the beginning of my youth, four leading sentiments formed the basis of my dreams. The first of those sentiments was love for HER—for an imaginary woman whom I always pictured the same in my dreams, and whom I somehow expected to meet some day and somewhere. This she of mine had a little of Sonetchka in her, a little of Masha as Masha could look when she stood washing linen over the clothes-tub, and a little of a certain woman with pearls round her fair white neck whom I had once seen long, long ago at a theatre, in a box below our own. My second sentiment was a craving for love. I wanted every one to know me and to love me. I wanted to be able to utter my name—Nicola Irtenieff—and at once to see every one thunderstruck at it, and come crowding round me and thanking me for something or another, I hardly knew what. My third sentiment was the expectation of some extraordinary, glorious happiness that was impending—some happiness so strong and assured as to verge upon ecstasy. Indeed, so firmly persuaded was I that very, very soon some unexpected chance would suddenly make me the richest and most famous man in the world that I lived in constant, tremulous expectation of this magic good fortune befalling me. I was always thinking to myself that "IT is beginning," and that I should go on thereafter to attain everything that a man could wish for. Consequently, I was for ever hurrying from place to place, in the belief that "IT" must be "beginning" just where I happened not to be. Lastly, my fourth and principal sentiment of all was abhorrence of myself, mingled with regret—yet a regret so blended with the certain expectation of happiness to which I have referred that it had in it nothing of sorrow. It seemed to me that it would be so easy and natural for me to tear myself away from my past and to remake it—to forget all that had been, and to begin my life, with all its relations, anew—that the past never troubled me, never clung to me at all. I even found a certain pleasure in detesting the past, and in seeing it in a darker light than the true one. This note of regret and of a curious longing for perfection were the chief mental impressions which I gathered from that new stage of my growth—impressions which imparted new principles to my view of myself, of men, and of God's world. O good and consoling voice, which in later days, in sorrowful days when my soul yielded silently to the sway of life's falseness and depravity, so often raised a sudden, bold protest against all iniquity, as well as mercilessly exposed the past, commanded, nay, compelled, me to love only the pure vista of the present, and promised me all that was fair and happy in the future! O good and consoling voice! Surely the day will never come when you are silent?

IV. OUR FAMILY CIRCLE

PAPA was seldom at home that spring. Yet, whenever he was so, he seemed extraordinarily cheerful as he either strummed his favourite pieces on the piano or looked roguishly at us and made jokes about us all, not excluding even Mimi. For instance, he would say that the Tsarevitch himself had seen Mimi at the rink, and fallen so much in love with her that he had presented a petition to the Synod for divorce; or else that I had been granted an appointment as secretary to the Austrian ambassador—a piece of news which he imparted to us with a perfectly grave face. Next, he would frighten Katenka with some spiders (of which she was very much afraid), engage in an animated conversation with our friends Dubkoff and Nechludoff, and tell us and our guests, over and over again, his plans for the year. Although these plans changed almost from day to day, and were for ever contradicting one another, they seemed so attractive that we were always glad to listen to them, and Lubotshka, in particular, would glue her eyes to his face, so as not to lose a single word. One day his plan would be that he should leave my brother and myself at the University, and go and live with Lubotshka in Italy for two years. Next, the plan would be that he should buy an estate on the south coast of the Crimea, and take us for an annual visit there; next, that we should migrate en masse to St. Petersburg; and so forth. Yet, in addition to this unusual cheerfulness of his, another change had come over him of late—a change which greatly surprised me. This was that he had had some fashionable clothes made—an olive-coloured frockcoat, smart trousers with straps at the sides, and a long wadded greatcoat which fitted him to perfection. Often, too, there was a delightful smell of scent about him when he came home from a party—more especially when he had been to see a lady of whom Mimi never spoke but with a sigh and a face that seemed to say: "Poor orphans! How dreadful! It is a good thing that SHE is gone now!" and so on, and so on. From Nicola (for Papa never spoke to us of his gambling) I had learnt that he (Papa) had been very fortunate in play that winter, and so had won an extraordinary amount of money, all of which he had placed in the bank after vowing that he would play no more that spring. Evidently, it was his fear of being unable to resist again doing so that was rendering him anxious to leave for the country as soon as possible. Indeed, he ended by deciding not to wait until I had entered the University, but to take the girls to Petrovskoe immediately after Easter, and to leave Woloda and myself to follow them at a later season.

All that winter, until the opening of spring, Woloda had been inseparable from Dubkoff, while at the same time the pair of them had cooled greatly towards Dimitri. Their chief amusements (so I gathered from conversations overheard) were continual drinking of champagne, sledge-driving past the windows of a lady with whom both of them appeared to be in love, and dancing with her—not at children's parties, either, but at real balls! It was this last fact which, despite our love for one another, placed a vast gulf between Woloda and myself. We felt that the distance between a boy still taking lessons under a tutor and a man who danced at real, grown-up balls was too great to allow of their exchanging mutual ideas. Katenka, too, seemed grown-up now, and read innumerable novels; so that the idea that she would some day be getting married no longer seemed to me a joke. Yet, though she and Woloda were thus grown-up, they never made friends with one another, but, on the contrary, seemed to cherish a mutual contempt. In general, when Katenka was at home alone, nothing but novels amused her, and they but slightly; but as soon as ever a visitor of the opposite sex called, she at once grew lively and amiable, and used her eyes for saying things which I could not then understand. It was only later, when she one day informed me in conversation that the only thing a girl was allowed to indulge in was coquetry—coquetry of the eyes, I mean—that I understood those strange contortions of her features which to every one else had seemed a matter for no surprise at all. Lubotshka also had begun to wear what was almost a long dress—a dress which almost concealed her goose-shaped feet; yet she still remained as ready a weeper as ever. She dreamed now of marrying, not a hussar, but a singer or an instrumentalist, and accordingly applied herself to her music with greater diligence than ever. St. Jerome, who knew that he was going to remain with us only until my examinations were over, and so had obtained for himself a new post in the family of some count or another, now looked with contempt upon the members of our household. He stayed indoors very little, took to smoking cigarettes (then all the rage), and was for ever whistling lively tunes on the edge of a card. Mimi daily grew more and more despondent, as though, now that we were beginning to grow up, she looked for nothing good from any one or anything.

When, on the day of which I am speaking, I went in to luncheon I found only Mimi, Katenka, Lubotshka, and St. Jerome in the dining-room. Papa was away, and Woloda in his own room, doing some preparation work for his examinations in company with a party of his comrades: wherefore he had requested that lunch should be sent to him there. Of late, Mimi had usually taken the head of the table, and as none of us had any respect for her, luncheon had lost most of its refinement and charm. That is to say, the meal was no longer what it had been in Mamma's or our grandmother's time, namely, a kind of rite which brought all the family together at a given hour and divided the day into two halves. We allowed ourselves to come in as late as the second course, to drink wine in tumblers (St. Jerome himself set us the example), to roll about on our chairs, to depart without saying grace, and so on. In fact, luncheon had ceased to be a family ceremony. In the old days at Petrovskoe, every one had been used to wash and dress for the meal, and then to repair to the drawing-room as the appointed hour (two o'clock) drew near, and pass the time of waiting in lively conversation. Just as the clock in the servants' hall was beginning to whirr before striking the hour, Foka would enter with noiseless footsteps, and, throwing his napkin over his arm and assuming a dignified, rather severe expression, would say in loud, measured tones: "Luncheon is ready!" Thereupon, with pleased, cheerful faces, we would form a procession—the elders going first and the juniors following, and, with much rustling of starched petticoats and subdued creaking of boots and shoes—would proceed to the dining-room, where, still talking in undertones, the company would seat themselves in their accustomed places. Or, again, at Moscow, we would all of us be standing before the table ready-laid in the hall, talking quietly among ourselves as we waited for our grandmother, whom the butler, Gabriel, had gone to acquaint with the fact that luncheon was ready. Suddenly the door would open, there would come the faint swish of a dress and the sound of footsteps, and our grandmother—dressed in a mob-cap trimmed with a quaint old lilac bow, and wearing either a smile or a severe expression on her face according as the state of her health inclined her—would issue from her room. Gabriel would hasten to precede her to her arm-chair, the other chairs would make a scraping sound, and, with a feeling as though a cold shiver (the precursor of appetite) were running down one's back, one would seize upon one's damp, starched napkin, nibble a morsel or two of bread, and, rubbing one's hands softly under the table, gaze with eager, radiant impatience at the steaming plates of soup which the butler was beginning to dispense in order of ranks and ages or according to the favour of our grandmother.

On the present occasion, however, I was conscious of neither excitement nor pleasure when I went in to luncheon. Even the mingled chatter of Mimi, the girls, and St. Jerome about the horrible boots of our Russian tutor, the pleated dresses worn by the young Princesses Kornakoff, and so forth (chatter which at any other time would have filled me with a sincerity of contempt which I should have been at no pains to conceal—at all events so far as Lubotshka and Katenka were concerned), failed to shake the benevolent frame of mind into which I had fallen. I was unusually good-humoured that day, and listened to everything with a smile and a studied air of kindness. Even when I asked for the kvas I did so politely, while I lost not a moment in agreeing with St. Jerome when he told me that it was undoubtedly more correct to say "Je peux" than "Je puis." Yet, I must confess to a certain disappointment at finding that no one paid any particular attention to my politeness and good-humour. After luncheon, Lubotshka showed me a paper on which she had written down a list of her sins: upon which I observed that, although the idea was excellent so far as it went, it would be still better for her to write down her sins on her SOUL—"a very different matter."

"Why is it 'a very different matter'?" asked Lubotshka.

"Never mind: that is all right; you do not understand me," and I went upstairs to my room, telling St. Jerome that I was going to work, but in reality purposing to occupy the hour and a half before confession time in writing down a list of my daily tasks and duties which should last me all my life, together with a statement of my life's aim, and the rules by which I meant unswervingly to be guided.

304

V. MY RULES

I TOOK some sheets of paper, and tried, first of all, to make a list of my tasks and duties for the coming year. The paper needed ruling, but, as I could not find the ruler, I had to use a Latin dictionary instead. The result was that, when I had drawn the pen along the edge of the dictionary and removed the latter, I found that, in place of a line, I had only made an oblong smudge on the paper, since the dictionary was not long enough to reach across it, and the pen had slipped round the soft, yielding corner of the book. Thereupon I took another piece of paper, and, by carefully manipulating the dictionary, contrived to rule what at least RESEMBLED lines. Dividing my duties into three sections—my duties to myself, my duties to my neighbour, and my duties to God—I started to indite a list of the first of those sections, but they seemed to me so numerous, and therefore requiring to be divided into so many species and subdivisions, that I thought I had better first of all write down the heading of "Rules of My Life" before proceeding to their detailed inscription. Accordingly, I proceeded to write "Rules of My Life" on the outside of the six sheets of paper which I had made into a sort of folio, but the words came out in such a crooked and uneven scrawl that for long I sat debating the question, "Shall I write them again?"—for long, sat in agonised contemplation of the ragged handwriting and disfigured title-page. Why was it that all the beauty and clarity which my soul then contained came out so misshapenly on paper (as in life itself) just when I was wishing to apply those qualities to what I was thinking at the moment?

"The priest is here, so please come downstairs and hear his directions," said Nicola as he entered.

Hurriedly concealing my folio under the table-cloth, I looked at myself in the mirror, combed my hair upwards (I imagined this to give me a pensive air), and descended to the divannaia, [Room with divans, or ante-room] where the table stood covered with a cloth and had an ikon and candles placed upon it. Papa entered just as I did, but by another door: whereupon the priest—a grey-headed old monk with a severe, elderly face—blessed him, and Papa kissed his small, squat, wizened hand. I did the same.

"Go and call Woldemar," said Papa. "Where is he? Wait a minute, though. Perhaps he is preparing for the Communion at the University?"

"No, he is with the Prince," said Katenka, and glanced at Lubotshka. Suddenly the latter blushed for some reason or another, and then frowned. Finally, pretending that she was not well, she left the room, and I followed her. In the drawing-room she halted, and began to pencil something fresh on her paper of peccadilloes.

"Well, what new sin have you gone and committed?" I asked.

"Nothing," she replied with another blush. All at once we heard Dimitri's voice raised in the hall as he took his leave of Woloda.

"It seems to me you are always experiencing some new temptation," said Katenka, who had entered the room behind us, and now stood looking at Lubotshka.

What was the matter with my sister I could not conceive, but she was now so agitated that the tears were starting from her eyes. Finally her confusion grew uncontrollable, and vented itself in rage against both herself and Katenka, who appeared to be teasing her.

"Any one can see that you are a FOREIGNER!" she cried (nothing offended Katenka so much as to be called by that term, which is why Lubotshka used it). "Just because I have the secret of which you know," she went on, with anger ringing through her tone, "you purposely go and upset me! Please do understand that it is no joking matter."

"Do you know what she has gone and written on her paper, Nicolinka?" cried Katenka, much infuriated by the term "foreigner." "She has written down that—"

"Oh, I never could have believed that you could be so cruel!" exclaimed Lubotshka, now bursting into open sobbing as she moved away from us. "You chose that moment on purpose! You spend your whole time in trying to make me sin! I'll never go to YOU again for sympathy and advice!"

VI. CONFESSION

With these and other disjointed impressions in my mind, I returned to the divannaia. As soon as every one had reassembled, the priest rose and prepared to read the prayer before confession. The instant that the silence was broken by the stern, expressive voice of the monk as he recited the prayer—and more especially when he addressed to us the words: "Reveal thou all thy sins without shame, concealment, or extenuation, and let thy soul be cleansed before God: for if thou concealest aught, then great will be thy sin"—the same sensation of reverent awe came over me as I had felt during the morning. I even took a certain pleasure in recognising this condition of mine, and strove to preserve it, not only by restraining all other thoughts from entering my brain, but also by consciously exerting myself to feel no other sensation than this same one of reverence.

Papa was the first to go to confession. He remained a long, long time in the room which had belonged to our grandmother, and during that time the rest of us kept silence in the divannaia, or only whispered to one another on the subject of who should precede whom. At length, the voice of the priest again reading the prayer sounded from the doorway, and then Papa's footsteps. The door creaked as he came out, coughing and holding one shoulder higher than the other, in his usual way, and for the moment he did not look at any of us.

"YOU go now, Luba," he said presently, as he gave her cheek a mischievous pinch. "Mind you tell him everything. You are my greatest sinner, you know."

Lubotshka went red and pale by turns, took her memorandum paper out of her apron, replaced it, and finally moved away towards the doorway with her head sunk between her shoulders as though she expected to receive a blow upon it from above. She was not long gone, and when she returned her shoulders were shaking with sobs.

At length—next after the excellent Katenka (who came out of the doorway with a smile on her face)—my turn arrived. I entered the dimly-lighted room with the same vague feeling of awe, the same conscious eagerness to arouse that feeling more and more in my soul, that had possessed me up to the present moment. The priest, standing in front of a reading-desk, slowly turned his face to me.

I was not more than five minutes in the room, but came out from it happy and (so I persuaded myself) entirely cleansed—a new, a morally reborn individual. Despite the fact that the old surroundings of my life now struck me as unfamiliar (even though the rooms, the furniture, and my own figure—would to heavens that I could have changed my outer man for the better in the same way that I believed myself to have changed my inner I—were the same as before), I remained in that comfortable attitude of mine until the very moment of bedtime.

Yet, no sooner had I begun to grow drowsy with the conning over of my sins than in a flash I recollected a particularly shameful sin which I had suppressed at confession time. Instantly the words of the prayer before confession came back to my memory and began sounding in my ears. My peace was gone for ever. "For if thou concealest aught, then great will be thy sin." Each time that the phrase recurred to me I saw myself a sinner for whom no punishment was adequate. Long did I toss from side to side as I considered my position, while expecting every moment to be visited with the divine wrath—to be struck with sudden death, perhaps!—an insupportable thought! Then suddenly the reassuring thought occurred to me: "Why should I not drive out to the monastery when the morning comes, and see the priest again, and make a second confession?" Thereafter I grew calmer.

VII. THE EXPEDITION TO THE MONASTERY

Several times that night I woke in terror at the thought that I might be oversleeping myself, and by six o'clock was out of bed, although the dawn was hardly peeping in at the window. I put on my clothes and boots (all of which were lying tumbled and unbrushed beside the bed, since Nicola, of course had not been in yet to tidy them up), and, without a prayer said or my face washed, emerged, for the first time in my life, into the street ALONE.

Over the way, behind the green roof of a large building, the dim, cold dawn was beginning to blush red. The keen frost of the spring morning which had stiffened the pools and mud and made them crackle under my feet now nipped my face and hands also. Not a cab was to be seen, though I had counted upon one to make the journey out and home the quicker. Only a file of waggons was rumbling along the Arbat Prospect, and a couple of bricklayers talking noisily together as they strode along the pavement. However, after walking a verst or so I began to meet men and women taking baskets to market or going with empty barrels to fetch the day's water supply; until at length, at the cross streets near the Arbat Gate, where a pieman had set up his stall and a baker was just opening his shop, I espied an old cabman shaking himself after indulging in a nap on the box of his be-scratched old blue-painted, hobble-de-hoy wreck of a drozhki. He seemed barely awake as he asked twenty copecks as the fare to the monastery and back, but came to himself a moment afterwards, just as I was about to get in, and, touching up his horse with the spare end of the reins, started to drive off and leave me. "My horse wants feeding," he growled, "I can't take you, barin.[Sir]"

With some difficulty and a promise of FORTY copecks I persuaded him to stop. He eyed me narrowly as he pulled up, but nevertheless said: "Very well. Get in, barin." I must confess that I had some qualms lest he should drive me to a quiet corner somewhere, and then rob me, but I caught hold of the collar of his ragged driving-coat, close to where his wrinkled neck showed sadly lean above his hunched-up back, and climbed on to the blue-painted, curved, rickety scat. As we set off along Vozdvizhenka Street, I noticed that the back of the drozhki was covered with a strip of the same greenish material as that of which his coat was made. For some reason or another this reassured me, and I no longer felt nervous of being taken to a quiet spot and robbed.

The sun had risen to a good height, and was gilding the cupolas of the churches, when we arrived at the monastery. In the shade the frost had not yet given, but in the open roadway muddy rivulets of water were coursing along, and it was through fast-thawing mire that the horse went clip-clopping his way. Alighting, and entering the monastery grounds, I inquired of the first monk whom I met where I could find the priest whom I was seeking.

"His cell is over there," replied the monk as he stopped a moment and pointed towards a little building up to which a flight of steps led.

"I respectfully thank you," I said, and then fell to wondering what all the monks (who at that moment began to come filing out of the church) must be thinking of me as they glanced in my direction. I was neither a grown-up nor a child, while my face was unwashed, my hair unbrushed, my clothes tumbled, and my boots unblacked and muddy. To what class of persons were the brethren assigning me—for they stared at me hard enough? Nevertheless I proceeded in the direction which the young priest had pointed out to me.

An old man with bushy grey eyebrows and a black cassock met me on the narrow path to the cells, and asked me what I wanted. For a brief moment I felt inclined to say "Nothing," and then run back to the drozhki and drive away home; but, for all its beetling brows, the face of the old man inspired confidence, and I merely said that I wished to see the priest (whom I named).

"Very well, young sir; I will take you to him," said the old man as he turned round. Clearly he had guessed my errand at a stroke. "The father is at matins at this moment, but he will soon be back," and, opening a door, the old man led me through a neat hall and corridor, all lined with clean matting, to a cell.

"Please to wait here," he added, and then, with a kind, reassuring glance, departed.

310

The little room in which I found myself was of the smallest possible dimensions, but extremely neat and clean. Its furniture only consisted of a small table (covered with a cloth, and placed between two equally small casement-windows, in which stood two pots of geraniums), a stand of ikons, with a lamp suspended in front of them, a bench, and two chairs. In one corner hung a wall clock, with little flowers painted on its dial, and brass weights to its chains, while upon two nails driven into a screen (which, fastened to the ceiling with whitewashed pegs, probably concealed the bed) hung a couple of cassocks. The windows looked out upon a whitewashed wall, about two arshins distant, and in the space between them there grew a small lilac-bush.

Not a sound penetrated from without, and in the stillness the measured, friendly stroke of the clock's pendulum seemed to beat quite loudly. The instant that I found myself alone in this calm retreat all other thoughts and recollections left my head as completely as though they had never been there, and I subsided into an inexpressibly pleasing kind of torpor. The rusty alpaca cassocks with their frayed linings, the worn black leather bindings of the books with their metal clasps, the dull-green plants with their carefully watered leaves and soil, and, above all, the abrupt, regular beat of the pendulum, all spoke to me intimately of some new life hitherto unknown to me—a life of unity and prayer, of calm, restful happiness.

"The months, the years, may pass," I thought to myself, "but he remains alone—always at peace, always knowing that his conscience is pure before God, that his prayer will be heard by Him." For fully half an hour I sat on that chair, trying not to move, not even to breathe loudly, for fear I should mar the harmony of the sounds which were telling me so much, and ever the pendulum continued to beat the same—now a little louder to the right, now a little softer to the left.

VIII. THE SECOND CONFESSION

Suddenly the sound of the priest's footsteps roused me from this reverie.

"Good morning to you," he said as he smoothed his grey hair with his hand. "What can I do for you?"

I besought him to give me his blessing, and then kissed his small, wizened hand with great fervour. After I had explained to him my errand he said nothing, but moved away towards the ikons, and began to read the exhortation: whereupon I overcame my shame, and told him all that was in my heart. Finally he laid his hands upon my head, and pronounced in his even, resonant voice the words: "My son, may the blessing of Our Heavenly Father be upon thee, and may He always preserve thee in faithfulness, loving-kindness, and meekness. Amen."

I was entirely happy. Tears of joy coursed down my face as I kissed the hem of his cassock and then raised my head again. The face of the priest expressed perfect tranquillity. So keenly did I feel the joy of reconciliation that, fearing in any way to dispel it, I took hasty leave of him, and, without looking to one side of me or the other (in order that my attention might not be distracted), left the grounds and re-entered the rickety, battered drozhki. Yet the joltings of the vehicle and the variety of objects which flitted past my eyes soon dissipated that feeling, and I became filled with nothing but the idea that the priest must have thought me the finest-spirited young man he had ever met, or ever would meet, in the whole of his life. Indeed, I reflected, there could not be many such as myself—of that I felt sure, and the conviction produced in me the kind of complacency which craves for self-communication to another. I had a great desire to unbosom myself to some one, and as there was no one else to speak to, I addressed myself to the cabman.

"Was I very long gone?" I asked him.

"No, not very long," he replied. He seemed to have grown more cheerful under the influence of the sunshine. "Yet now it is a good while past my horse's feeding-time. You see, I am a night cabman."

"Well, I only seemed to myself to be about a minute," I went on. "Do you know what I went there for?" I added, changing my seat to the well of the drozhki, so as to be nearer the driver.

"What business is it of mine? I drive a fare where he tells me to go," he replied.

"Yes, but, all the same, what do you think I went there for?" I persisted.

"I expect some one you know is going to be buried there, so you went to see about a plot for the grave."

"No, no, my friend. Still, DO you know what I went there for?"

"No, of course I cannot tell, barin," he repeated.

His voice seemed to me so kind that I decided to edify him by relating the cause of my expedition, and even telling him of the feeling which I had experienced.

"Shall I tell you?" I said. "Well, you see,"—and I told him all, as well as inflicted upon him a description of my fine sentiments. To this day I blush at the recollection.

"Well, well!" said the cabman non-committally, and for a long while afterwards he remained silent and motionless, except that at intervals he adjusted the skirt of his coat each time that it was jerked from beneath his leg by the joltings of his huge boot on the drozhki's step. I felt sure that he must be thinking of me even as the priest had done. That is to say, that he must be thinking that no such fine-spirited young man existed in the world as I. Suddenly he shot at me:

"I tell you what, barin. You ought to keep God's affairs to yourself."

"What?" I said.

"Those affairs of yours—they are God's business," he repeated, mumbling

313

the words with his toothless lips.

"No, he has not understood me," I thought to myself, and said no more to him till we reached home.

Although it was not my original sense of reconciliation and reverence, but only a sort of complacency at having experienced such a sense, that lasted in me during the drive home (and that, too, despite the distraction of the crowds of people who now thronged the sunlit streets in every direction), I had no sooner reached home than even my spurious complacency was shattered, for I found that I had not the forty copecks wherewith to pay the cabman! To the butler, Gabriel, I already owed a small debt, and he refused to lend me any more. Seeing me twice run across the courtyard in quest of the money, the cabman must have divined the reason, for, leaping from his drozhki, he—notwithstanding that he had seemed so kind—began to bawl aloud (with an evident desire to punch my head) that people who do not pay for their cab-rides are swindlers.

None of my family were yet out of bed, so that, except for the servants, there was no one from whom to borrow the forty copecks. At length, on my most sacred, sacred word of honour to repay (a word to which, as I could see from his face, he did not altogether trust), Basil so far yielded to his fondness for me and his remembrance of the many services I had done him as to pay the cabman. Thus all my beautiful feelings ended in smoke. When I went upstairs to dress for church and go to Communion with the rest I found that my new clothes had not yet come home, and so I could not wear them. Then I sinned headlong. Donning my other suit, I went to Communion in a sad state of mental perturbation, and filled with complete distrust of all my finer impulses.

IX. HOW I PREPARED MYSELF FOR THE EXAMINATIONS

On the Thursday in Easter week Papa, my sister, Katenka, and Mimi went away into the country, and no one remained in my grandmother's great house but Woloda, St. Jerome, and myself. The frame of mind which I had experienced on the day of my confession and during my subsequent expedition to the monastery had now completely passed away, and left behind it only a dim, though pleasing, memory which daily became more and more submerged by the impressions of this emancipated existence.

The folio endorsed "Rules of My Life" lay concealed beneath a pile of school-books. Although the idea of the possibility of framing rules, for every occasion in my life and always letting myself be guided by them still pleased me (since it appeared an idea at once simple and magnificent, and I was determined to make practical application of it), I seemed somehow to have forgotten to put it into practice at once, and kept deferring doing so until such and such a moment. At the same time, I took pleasure in the thought that every idea which now entered my head could be allotted precisely to one or other of my three sections of tasks and duties—those for or to God, those for or to my neighbour, and those for or to myself. "I can always refer everything to them," I said to myself, "as well as the many, many other ideas which occur to me on one subject or another." Yet at this period I often asked myself, "Was I better and more truthful when I only believed in the power of the human intellect, or am I more so now, when I am losing the faculty of developing that power, and am in doubt both as to its potency and as to its importance?" To this I could return no positive answer.

The sense of freedom, combined with the spring-like feeling of vague expectation to which I have referred already, so unsettled me that I could not keep myself in hand—could make none but the sorriest of preparations for my University ordeal. Thus I was busy in the schoolroom one morning, and fully aware that I must work hard, seeing that to-morrow was the day of my examination in a subject of which I had the two whole questions still to read up; yet no sooner had a breath of spring come wafted through the window than I felt as though there were something quite different that I wished to recall to my memory. My hands laid down my book, my feet began to move of themselves, and to set me walking up and down the room, and my head felt as though some one had suddenly touched in it a little spring and set some machine in motion—so easily and swiftly and naturally did all sorts of pleasing fancies of which I could catch no more than the radiancy begin coursing through it. Thus one hour, two hours, elapsed unperceived. Even if I sat down determinedly to my book, and managed to concentrate my whole attention upon what I was reading, suddenly there would sound in the corridor the footsteps of a woman and the rustle of her dress. Instantly everything would escape my mind, and I would find it impossible to remain still any longer, however much I knew that the woman could only be either Gasha or my grandmother's old sewing-maid moving about in the corridor. "Yet suppose it should be SHE all at once?" I would say to myself. "Suppose IT is beginning now, and I were to lose it?" and, darting out into the corridor, I would find, each time, that it was only Gasha. Yet for long enough afterwards I could not recall my attention to my studies. A little spring had been touched in my head, and a strange mental ferment started afresh. Again, that evening I was sitting alone beside a tallow candle in my room. Suddenly I looked up for a moment—to snuff the candle, or to straighten myself in my chair—and at once became aware of nothing but the darkness in the corners and the blank of the open doorway. Then, I also became conscious how still the house was, and felt as though I could do nothing else than go on listening to that stillness, and gazing into the black square of that open doorway, and gradually sinking into a brown study as I sat there without moving. At intervals, however, I would get up, and go downstairs, and begin wandering through the empty rooms. Once I sat a long while in the small drawing-room as I listened to Gasha playing "The Nightingale" (with two fingers) on the piano in the large drawing-room, where a solitary candle burned. Later, when the moon was bright, I felt obliged to get out of bed and to lean out of the window, so that I might gaze into the garden, and at the lighted roof of the Shaposnikoff mansion, the straight tower of our parish church, and the dark shadows of the fence and the lilac-bush where they lay black upon the path. So long did I remain there that, when I at length returned to bed, it was ten o'clock in the morning before I could open my eyes again.

In short, had it not been for the tutors who came to give me lessons, as well as for St. Jerome (who at intervals, and very grudgingly, applied a spur to my self-conceit) and, most of all, for the desire to figure as "clever" in the eyes of my friend Nechludoff (who looked upon distinctions in University examinations as a matter of first-rate importance)—had it not been for all these things, I say, the spring and my new freedom would have combined to make me forget everything I had ever learnt, and so to go through the examinations to no purpose whatsoever.

X. THE EXAMINATION IN HISTORY

ON the 16th of April I entered, for the first time, and under the wing of St. Jerome, the great hall of the University. I had driven there with St. Jerome in our smart phaeton and wearing the first frockcoat of my life, while the whole of my other clothes—even down to my socks and linen—were new and of a grander sort. When a Swiss waiter relieved me of my greatcoat, and I stood before him in all the beauty of my attire, I felt almost sorry to dazzle him so. Yet I had no sooner entered the bright, carpeted, crowded hall, and caught sight of hundreds of other young men in gymnasium [The Russian gymnasium = the English grammar or secondary school.] uniforms or frockcoats (of whom but a few threw me an indifferent glance), as well as, at the far end, of some solemn-looking professors who were seated on chairs or walking carelessly about among some tables, than I at once became disabused of the notion that I should attract the general attention, while the expression of my face, which at home, and even in the vestibule of the University buildings, had denoted only a kind of vague regret that I should have to present so important and distinguished an appearance, became exchanged for an expression of the most acute nervousness and dejection. However, I soon picked up again when I perceived sitting at one of the desks a very badly, untidily dressed gentleman who, though not really old, was almost entirely grey. He was occupying a seat quite at the back of the hall and a little apart from the rest, so I hastened to sit down beside him, and then fell to looking at the candidates for examination, and to forming conclusions about them. Many different figures and faces were there to be seen there; yet, in my opinion, they all seemed to divide themselves into three classes. First of all, there were youths like myself, attending for examination in the company of their parents or tutors. Among such I could see the youngest Iwin (accompanied by Frost) and Ilinka Grap (accompanied by his old father). All youths of this class wore the early beginnings of beards, sported prominent linen, sat quietly in their places, and never opened the books and notebooks which they had brought with them, but gazed at the professors and examination tables with ill-concealed nervousness. The second class of candidates were young men in gymnasium uniforms. Several of them had attained to the dignity of shaving, and most of them knew one another. They talked loudly, called the professors by their names and surnames, occupied themselves in getting their subjects ready, exchanged notebooks, climbed over desks, fetched themselves pies and sandwiches from the vestibule, and ate them then and there merely lowering their heads to the level of a desk for propriety's sake. Lastly, the third class of candidates (which seemed a small one) consisted of oldish men—some of them in frock coats, but the majority in jackets, and with no linen to be seen. These preserved a serious demeanour, sat by themselves, and had a very dingy look. The man who had afforded me consolation by being worse dressed than myself belonged to this class. Leaning forward upon his elbows, and running his fingers through his grey, dishevelled hair as he read some book or another, he had thrown me only a momentary glance—and that not a very friendly one—from a pair of glittering eyes. Then, as I sat down, he had frowned grimly, and stuck a shiny elbow out to prevent me from coming any nearer. On the other hand, the gymnasium men were over-sociable, and I felt rather afraid of their proximity. One of them did not hesitate to thrust a book into my hands, saying, "Give that to that fellow over there, will you?" while another of them exclaimed as he pushed past me, "By your leave, young fellow!" and a third made use of my shoulder as a prop when he wanted to scramble over a desk. All this seemed to me a little rough and unpleasant, for I looked upon myself as immensely superior to such fellows, and considered that they ought not to treat me with such familiarity. At length, the names began to be called out. The gymnasium men walked out boldly, answered their questions (apparently) well, and came back looking cheerful. My own class of candidates were much more diffident, as well as appeared to answer worse. Of the oldish men, some answered well, and some very poorly. When the name "Semenoff" was called out my neighbour with the grey hair and glittering eyes jostled me roughly, stepped over my legs, and went up to one of the examiners' tables. It was plain from the aspect of the professors that he answered well and with assurance, yet, on returning to his place, he did not wait to see where he was placed on the list, but quietly collected his notebooks and departed. Several times I shuddered at the sound of the voice calling out the names, but my turn did not come in exact alphabetical order, though already names had begun to be called beginning with "I."

"Ikonin and Tenieff!" suddenly shouted some one from the professors' end of the hall.

"Go on, Ikonin! You are being called," said a tall, red-faced gymnasium student near me. "But who is this BARtenieff or MORtenieff or somebody? I don't know him."

"It must be you," whispered St. Jerome loudly in my ear.

"MY name is IRtenieff," I said to the red-faced student. "Do you think that was the name they were calling out?"

"Yes. Why on earth don't you go up?" he replied. "Lord, what a dandy!" he added under his breath, yet not so quietly but that I failed to hear the words as they came wafted to me from below the desk. In front of me walked Ikonin—a tall young man of about twenty-five, who was one of those whom I had classed as oldish men. He wore a tight brown frockcoat and a blue satin tie, and had wisps of flaxen hair carefully brushed over his collar in the peasant style. His appearance had already caught my attention when we were sitting among the desks, and had given me an impression that he was not bad-looking. Also I had noticed that he was very talkative. Yet what struck me most about his physiognomy was a tuft, of queer red hairs which he had under his chin, as well as, still more, a strange habit of continually unbuttoning his waistcoat and scratching his chest under his shirt.

Behind the table to which we were summoned sat three Professors, none of whom acknowledged our salutations. A youngish professor was shuffling a bundle of tickets like a pack of cards; another one, with a star on his frockcoat, was gazing hard at a gymnasium student, who was repeating something at great speed about Charles the Great, and adding to each of his sentences the word nakonetz [= the English colloquialism "you know."] while a third one—an old man in spectacles—proceeded to bend his head down as we approached, and, peering at us through his glasses, pointed silently to the tickets. I felt his glance go over both myself and Ikonin, and also felt sure that something about us had displeased him (perhaps it was Ikonin's red hairs), for, after taking another look at the pair of us, he motioned impatiently to us to be quick in taking our tickets. I felt vexed and offended—firstly, because none of the professors had responded to our bows, and, secondly, because they evidently coupled me with Ikonin under the one denomination of "candidates," and so were condemning me in advance on account of Ikonin's red hairs. I took my ticket boldly and made ready to answer, but the professor's eye passed over my head and alighted upon Ikonin. Accordingly, I occupied myself in reading my ticket. The questions printed on it were all familiar to me, so, as I silently awaited my turn, I gazed at what was passing near me, Ikonin seemed in no way diffident—rather the reverse, for, in reaching for his ticket, he threw his body half-way across the table. Then he gave his long hair a shake, and rapidly conned over what was written on his ticket. I think he had just opened his mouth to answer when the professor with the star dismissed the gymnasium student with a word of commendation, and then turned and looked at Ikonin. At once the latter seemed taken back, and stopped short. For about two minutes there was a dead silence.

"Well?" said the professor in the spectacles.

Once more Ikonin opened his mouth, and once more remained silent.

"Come! You are not the only one to be examined. Do you mean to answer or do you not?" said the youngish professor, but Ikonin did not even look at him. He was gazing fixedly at his ticket and uttered not a single word. The professor in the spectacles scanned him through his glasses, then over them, then without them (for, indeed, he had time to take them off, to wipe their lenses carefully, and to replace them). Still not a word from Ikonin. All at once, however, a smile spread itself over his face, and he gave his long hair another shake. Next he reached across the table, laid down his ticket, looked at each of the professors in turn and then at myself, and finally, wheeling round on his heels, made a gesture with his hand and returned to the desks. The professors stared blankly at one another.

"Bless the fellow!" said the youngish professor. "What an original!"

It was now my turn to move towards the table, but the professors went on talking in undertones among themselves, as though they were unaware of my presence. At the moment, I felt firmly persuaded that the three of them were engrossed solely with the question of whether I should merely PASS the examination or whether I should pass it WELL, and that it was only swagger which made them pretend that they did not care either way, and behave as though they had not seen me.

When at length the professor in the spectacles turned to me with an air of indifference, and invited me to answer, I felt hurt, as I looked at him, to think that he should have so undeceived me: wherefore I answered brokenly at first. In time, however, things came easier to my tongue, and, inasmuch as all the questions bore upon Russian history (which I knew thoroughly), I ended with eclat, and even went so far, in my desire to convince the professors that I was not Ikonin and that they must not in anyway confound me with him, as to offer to draw a second ticket. The professor in the spectacles, however, merely nodded his head, said "That will do," and marked something in his register. On returning to the desks, I at once learnt from the gymnasium men (who somehow seemed to know everything) that I had been placed fifth.

XI. MY EXAMINATION IN MATHEMATICS

AT the subsequent examinations, I made several new acquaintances in addition to the Graps (whom I considered unworthy of my notice) and Iwin (who for some reason or other avoided me). With some of these new friends I grew quite intimate, and even Ikonin plucked up sufficient courage to inform me, when we next met, that he would have to undergo re-examination in history—the reason for his failure this time being that the professor of that faculty had never forgiven him for last year's examination, and had, indeed, "almost killed" him for it. Semenoff (who was destined for the same faculty as myself—the faculty of mathematics) avoided every one up to the very close of the examinations. Always leaning forward upon his elbows and running his fingers through his grey hair, he sat silent and alone. Nevertheless, when called up for examination in mathematics (he had no companion to accompany him), he came out second. The first place was taken by a student from the first gymnasium—a tall, dark, lanky, pale-faced fellow who wore a black folded cravat and had his cheeks and forehead dotted all over with pimples. His hands were shapely and slender, but their nails were so bitten to the quick that the finger-ends looked as though they had been tied round with strips of thread. All this seemed to me splendid, and wholly becoming to a student of the first gymnasium. He spoke to every one, and we all made friends with him. To me in particular his walk, his every movement, his lips, his dark eyes, all seemed to have in them something extraordinary and magnetic.

On the day of the mathematical examination I arrived earlier than usual at the hall. I knew the syllabus well, yet there were two questions in the algebra which my tutor had managed to pass over, and which were therefore quite unknown to me. If I remember rightly, they were the Theory of Combinations and Newton's Binomial. I seated myself on one of the back benches and pored over the two questions, but, inasmuch as I was not accustomed to working in a noisy room, and had even less time for preparation than I had anticipated, I soon found it difficult to take in all that I was reading.

"Here he is. This way, Nechludoff," said Woloda's familiar voice behind me.

I turned and saw my brother and Dimitri—their gowns unbuttoned, and their hands waving a greeting to me—threading their way through the desks. A moment's glance would have sufficed to show any one that they were second-course students—persons to whom the University was as a second home. The mere look of their open gowns expressed at once disdain for the "mere candidate" and a knowledge that the "mere candidate's" soul was filled with envy and admiration of them. I was charmed to think that every one near me could now see that I knew two real second-course students: wherefore I hastened to meet them half-way.

Woloda, of course, could not help vaunting his superiority a little.

"Hullo, you smug!" he said. "Haven't you been examined yet?"

"No."

"Well, what are you reading? Aren't you sufficiently primed?"

"Yes, except in two questions. I don't understand them at all."

"Eh, what?"—and Woloda straightway began to expound to me Newton's Binomial, but so rapidly and unintelligibly that, suddenly reading in my eyes certain misgivings as to the soundness of his knowledge, he glanced also at Dimitri's face. Clearly, he saw the same misgivings there, for he blushed hotly, though still continuing his involved explanations.

"No; hold on, Woloda, and let me try and do it," put in Dimitri at length, with a glance at the professors' corner as he seated himself beside me.

I could see that my friend was in the best of humours. This was always the case with him when he was satisfied with himself, and was one of the things in him which I liked best. Inasmuch as he knew mathematics well and could speak clearly, he hammered the question so thoroughly into my head that I can remember it to this day. Hardly had he finished when St. Jerome said to me in a loud whisper, "A vous, Nicolas," and I followed Ikonin out from among the desks without having had an opportunity of going through the OTHER question of which I was ignorant. At the table which we now approached were seated two professors, while before the blackboard stood a gymnasium student, who was working some formula aloud, and knocking bits off the end of the chalk with his too vigorous strokes. He even continued writing after one of the Professors had said to him "Enough!" and bidden us draw our tickets. "Suppose I get the Theory of Combinations?" I thought to myself as my tremulous fingers took a ticket from among a bundle wrapped in torn paper. Ikonin, for his part, reached across the table with the same assurance, and the same sidelong movement of his whole body, as he had done at the previous examination. Taking the topmost ticket without troubling to make further selection, he just glanced at it, and then frowned angrily.

"I always draw this kind of thing," he muttered.

I looked at mine. Horrors! It was the Theory of Combinations!

"What have you got?" whispered Ikonin at this point.

I showed him.

"Oh, I know that," he said.

"Will you make an exchange, then?"

"No. Besides, it would be all the same for me if I did," he contrived to whisper just as the professor called us up to the blackboard. "I don't feel up to anything to-day."

"Then everything is lost!" I thought to myself. Instead of the brilliant result which I had anticipated I should be for ever covered with shame—more so even than Ikonin! Suddenly, under the very eyes of the professor, Ikonin turned to me, snatched my ticket out of my hands, and handed me his own. I looked at his ticket. It was Newton's Binomial!

The professor was a youngish man, with a pleasant, clever expression of face—an effect chiefly due to the prominence of the lower part of his forehead.

"What? Are you exchanging tickets, gentlemen?" he said.

"No. He only gave me his to look at, professor," answered Ikonin—and,

325

sure enough, the word "professor" was the last word that he uttered there. Once again, he stepped backwards towards me from the table, once again he looked at each of the professors in turn and then at myself, once again he smiled faintly, and once again he shrugged his shoulders as much as to say, "It is no use, my good sirs." Then he returned to the desks. Subsequently, I learnt that this was the third year he had vainly attempted to matriculate.

I answered my question well, for I had just read it up; and the professor, kindly informing me that I had done even better than was required, placed me fifth.

XII. MY EXAMINATION IN LATIN

All went well until my examination in Latin. So far, a gymnasium student stood first on the list, Semenoff second, and myself third. On the strength of it I had begun to swagger a little, and to think that, for all my youth, I was not to be despised.

From the first day of the examinations, I had heard every one speak with awe of the Professor of Latin, who appeared to be some sort of a wild beast who battened on the financial ruin of young men (of those, that is to say, who paid their own fees) and spoke only in the Greek and Latin tongues. However, St. Jerome, who had coached me in Latin, spoke encouragingly, and I myself thought that, since I could translate Cicero and certain parts of Horace without the aid of a lexicon, I should do no worse than the rest. Yet things proved otherwise. All the morning the air had been full of rumours concerning the tribulations of candidates who had gone up before me: rumours of how one young fellow had been accorded a nought, another one a single mark only, a third one greeted with abuse and threatened with expulsion, and so forth. Only Semenoff and the first gymnasium student had, as usual, gone up quietly, and returned to their seats with five marks credited to their names. Already I felt a prescience of disaster when Ikonin and myself found ourselves summoned to the little table at which the terrible professor sat in solitary grandeur.

The terrible professor turned out to be a little thin, bilious-looking man with hair long and greasy and a face expressive of extraordinary sullenness. Handing Ikonin a copy of Cicero's Orations, he bid him translate. To my great astonishment Ikonin not only read off some of the Latin, but even managed to construe a few lines to the professor's prompting. At the same time, conscious of my superiority over such a feeble companion, I could not help smiling a little, and even looking rather contemptuous, when it came to a question of analysis, and Ikonin, as on previous occasions, plunged into a silence which promised never to end. I had hoped to please the professor by that knowing, slightly sarcastic smile of mine, but, as a matter of fact, I contrived to do quite the contrary.

"Evidently you know better than he, since you are laughing," he said to me in bad Russian. "Well, we shall see. Tell me the answer, then."

Later I learnt that the professor was Ikonin's guardian, and that Ikonin actually lived with him. I lost no time in answering the question in syntax which had been put to Ikonin, but the professor only pulled a long face and turned away from me.

"Well, your turn will come presently, and then we shall see how much you know," he remarked, without looking at me, but proceeding to explain to Ikonin the point on which he had questioned him.

"That will do," he added, and I saw him put down four marks to Ikonin in his register. "Come!" I thought to myself. "He cannot be so strict after all."

When Ikonin had taken his departure the professor spent fully five minutes—five minutes which seemed to me five hours—in setting his books and tickets in order, in blowing his nose, in adjusting and sprawling about on his chair, in gazing down the hall, and in looking here, there, and everywhere—in doing everything, in fact, except once letting his eye rest upon me. Yet even that amount of dissimulation did not seem to satisfy him, for he next opened a book, and pretended to read it, for all the world as though I were not there at all. I moved a little nearer him, and gave a cough.

"Ah, yes! You too, of course! Well, translate me something," he remarked, handing me a book of some kind. "But no; you had better take this," and, turning over the leaves of a Horace, he indicated to me a passage which I should never have imagined possible of translation.

"I have not prepared this," I said.

"Oh! Then you only wish to answer things which you have got by heart, do you? Indeed? No, no; translate me that."

I started to grope for the meaning of the passage, but each questioning look which I threw at the professor was met by a shake of the head, a profound sigh, and an exclamation of "No, no!" Finally he banged the book to with such a snap that he caught his finger between the covers. Angrily releasing it, he handed me a ticket containing questions in grammar, and, flinging himself back in his chair, maintained a menacing silence. I should have tried to answer the questions had not the expression of his face so clogged my tongue that nothing seemed to come from it right.

"No, no! That's not it at all!" he suddenly exclaimed in his horrible accent as he altered his posture to one of leaning forward upon the table and playing with the gold signet-ring which was nearly slipping from the little finger of his left hand. "That is not the way to prepare for serious study, my good sir. Fellows like yourself think that, once they have a gown and a blue collar to their backs, they have reached the summit of all things and become students. No, no, my dear sir. A subject needs to be studied FUNDAMENTALLY," and so on, and so on.

During this speech (which was uttered with a clipped sort of intonation) I went on staring dully at his lowered eyelids. Beginning with a fear lest I should lose my place as third on the list, I went on to fear lest I should pass at all. Next, these feelings became reinforced by a sense of injustice, injured self-respect, and unmerited humiliation, while the contempt which I felt for the professor as some one not quite (according to my ideas) "comme il faut"—a fact which I deduced from the shortness, strength, and roundness of his nails—flared up in me more and more and turned all my other feelings to sheer animosity. Happening, presently, to glance at me, and to note my quivering lips and tear-filled eyes, he seemed to interpret my agitation as a desire to be accorded my marks and dismissed: wherefore, with an air of relenting, he said (in the presence of another professor who had just approached):

"Very well; I will accord you a 'pass'" (which signified two marks), "although you do not deserve it. I do so simply out of consideration for your youth, and in the hope that, when you begin your University career, you will learn to be less light-minded."

The concluding phrase, uttered in the hearing of the other professor (who at once turned his eyes upon me, as though remarking, "There! You see, young man!") completed my discomfiture. For a moment, a mist swam before my eyes—a mist in which the terrible professor seemed to be far away, as he sat at his table while for an instant a wild idea danced through my brain. "What if I DID do such a thing?" I thought to myself. "What would come of it?" However, I did not do the thing in question, but, on the contrary, made a bow of peculiar reverence to each of the professors, and with a slight smile on my face—presumably the same smile as that with which I had derided Ikonin—turned away from the table.

This piece of unfairness affected me so powerfully at the time that, had I been a free agent, I should have attended for no more examinations. My ambition was gone (since now I could not possibly be third), and I therefore let the other examinations pass without any exertion, or even agitation, on my part. In the general list I still stood fourth, but that failed to interest me, since I had reasoned things out to myself, and come to the conclusion that to try for first place was stupid—even "bad form:" that, in fact, it was better to pass neither very well nor very badly, as Woloda had done. This attitude I decided to maintain throughout the whole of my University career, notwithstanding that it was the first point on which my opinion had differed from that of my friend Dimitri.

Yet, to tell the truth, my thoughts were already turning towards a uniform, a "mortar-board," and the possession of a drozhki of my own, a room of my own, and, above all, freedom of my own. And certainly the prospect had its charm.

XIII. I BECOME GROWN-UP

When, on May 8th, I returned home from the final, the divinity, examination, I found my acquaintance, the foreman from Rozonoff's, awaiting me. He had called once before to fit me for my gown, as well as for a tunic of glossy black cloth (the lapels of which were, on that occasion, only sketched in chalk), but to-day he had come to bring me the clothes in their finished state, with their gilt buttons wrapped in tissue paper.

Donning the garments, and finding them splendid (notwithstanding that St. Jerome assured me that the back of the tunic wrinkled badly), I went downstairs with a complacent smile which I was powerless to banish from my face, and sought Woloda, trying the while to affect unconsciousness of the admiring looks of the servants, who came darting out of the hall and corridor to gaze upon me with ravished eyes. Gabriel, the butler, overtook me in the salle, and, after congratulating me with much empressement, handed me, according to instructions from my father, four bank-notes, as well as informed me that Papa had also given orders that, from that day forth, the groom Kuzma, the phaeton, and the bay horse Krassavchik were to be entirely at my disposal. I was so overjoyed at this not altogether expected good-fortune that I could no longer feign indifference in Gabriel's presence, but, flustered and panting, said the first thing which came into my head ("Krassavchik is a splendid trotter," I think it was). Then, catching sight of the various heads protruding from the doors of the hall and corridor, I felt that I could bear no more, and set off running at full speed across the salle, dressed as I was in the new tunic, with its shining gilt buttons. Just as I burst into Woloda's room, I heard behind me the voices of Dubkoff and Nechludoff, who had come to congratulate me, as well as to propose a dinner somewhere and the drinking of much champagne in honour of my matriculation. Dimitri informed me that, though he did not care for champagne, he would nevertheless join us that evening and drink my health, while Dubkoff remarked that I looked almost like a colonel, and Woloda omitted to congratulate me at all, merely saying in an acid way that he supposed we should now—i.e. in two days time—be off into the country. The truth was that Woloda, though pleased at my matriculation, did not altogether like my becoming as grown-up as himself. St. Jerome, who also joined us at this moment, said in a very pompous manner that his duties were now ended, and that, although he did not know whether they had been well done or ill, at least he had done his best, and must depart to-morrow to his Count's. In replying to their various remarks I could feel, in spite of myself, a pleased, agreeable, faintly self-sufficient smile playing over my countenance, as well as could remark that that smile, communicated itself to those to whom I was speaking.

So here was I without a tutor, yet with my own private drozhki, my name printed on the list of students, a sword and belt of my own, and a chance of an occasional salute from officials! In short, I was grownup and, I suppose, happy.

Finally, we arranged to go out and dine at five o'clock, but since Woloda presently went off to Dubkoff's, and Dimitri disappeared in his usual fashion (saying that there was something he MUST do before dinner), I was left with two whole hours still at my disposal. For a time I walked through the rooms of the house, and looked at myself in all the mirrors—firstly with the tunic buttoned, then with it unbuttoned, and lastly with only the top button fastened. Each time it looked splendid. Eventually, though anxious not to show any excess of delight, I found myself unable to refrain from crossing over to the coach-house and stables to gaze at Krassovchik, Kuzma, and the drozhki. Then I returned and once more began my tour of the rooms, where I looked at myself in all the mirrors as before, and counted my money over in my pocket—my face smiling happily the while. Yet not an hour had elapsed before I began to feel slightly ennuye—to feel a shade of regret that no one was present to see me in my splendid position. I began to long for life and movement, and so sent out orders for the drozhki to be got ready, since I had made up my mind to drive to the Kuznetski Bridge and make some purchases.

In this connection I recalled how, after matriculating, Woloda had gone and bought himself a lithograph of horses by Victor Adam and some pipes and tobacco: wherefore I felt that I too must do the same. Amid glances showered upon me from every side, and with the sunlight reflected from my buttons, cap-badge, and sword, I drove to the Kuznetski Bridge, where, halting at a Picture shop, I entered it with my eyes looking to every side. It was not precisely horses by Adam which I meant to buy, since I did not wish to be accused of too closely imitating Woloda; wherefore, out of shame for causing the obsequious shopmen such agitation as I appeared to do, I made a hasty selection, and pitched upon a water-colour of a woman's head which I saw displayed in the window—price twenty roubles. Yet no sooner had I paid the twenty roubles over the counter than my heart smote me for having put two such beautifully dressed shop-assistants to so much trouble for such a trifle. Moreover, I fancied that they were regarding me with some disdain. Accordingly, in my desire to show them what manner of man I was, I turned my attention to a silver trifle which I saw displayed in a show-case, and, recognising that it was a porte-crayon (price eighteen roubles), requested that it should forthwith be wrapped in paper for me. Next, the money paid, and the information acquired that splendid pipes and tobacco were to be obtained in an adjacent emporium, I bowed to the two shopmen politely, and issued into the street with the picture under my arm. At the shop next door (which had painted on its sign-board a negro smoking a cigar) I bought (likewise out of a desire to imitate no one) some Turkish tobacco, a Stamboul hookah, and two pipes. On coming out of the shop, I had just entered the drozhki when I caught sight of Semenoff, who was walking hurriedly along the pavement with his head bent down. Vexed that he should not have recognised me, I called out to him pretty loudly, "Hold on a minute!" and, whipping up the drozhki, soon overtook him.

"How do you do?" I said.

"My respects to you," he replied, but without stopping.

"Why are you not in your University uniform?" I next inquired.

At this he stopped short with a frown, and parted his white teeth as though the sun were hurting his eyes. The next moment, however, he threw a glance of studied indifference at my drozhki and uniform, and continued on his way.

From the Kuznetski Bridge, I drove to a confectioner's in Tverskaia

Street, and, much as I should have liked it to be supposed that it was the newspapers which most interested me, I had no choice but to begin falling upon tartlet after tartlet. In fact, for all my bashfulness before a gentleman who kept regarding me with some curiosity from behind a newspaper, I ate with great swiftness a tartlet of each of the eight different sorts which the confectioner kept.

On reaching home, I experienced a slight touch of stomach-ache, but paid no attention to it, and set to work to inspect my purchases. Of these, the picture so much displeased me that, instead of having it framed and hung in my room, as Woloda had done with his, I took pains to hide it behind a chest of drawers, where no one could see it. Likewise, though I also found the porte-crayon distasteful, I was able, as I laid it on my table, to comfort myself with the thought that it was at least a SILVER article—so much capital, as it were—and likely to be very useful to a student. As for the smoking things, I decided to put them into use at once, and try their capabilities.

Unsealing the four packages, and carefully filling the Stamboul pipe with some fine-cut, reddish-yellow Turkish tobacco, I applied a hot cinder to it, and, taking the mouthpiece between my first and second fingers (a position of the hand which greatly caught my fancy), started to inhale the smoke.

The smell of the tobacco seemed delightful, yet something burnt my mouth and caught me by the breath. Nevertheless, I hardened my heart, and continued to draw abundant fumes into my interior. Then I tried blowing rings and retaining the smoke. Soon the room became filled with blue vapours, while the pipe started to crackle and the tobacco to fly out in sparks. Presently, also, I began to feel a smarting in my mouth and a giddiness in my head. Accordingly, I was on the point of stopping and going to look at myself and my pipe in the mirror, when, to my surprise, I found myself staggering about. The room was whirling round and round, and as I peered into the mirror (which I reached only with some difficulty) I perceived that my face was as white as a sheet. Hardly had I thrown myself down upon a sofa when such nausea and faintness swept over me that, making up my mind that the pipe had proved my death, I expected every moment to expire. Terribly frightened, I tried to call out for some one to come and help me, and to send for the doctor.

However, this panic of mine did not last long, for I soon understood what the matter with me was, and remained lying on the sofa with a racking headache and my limbs relaxed as I stared dully at the stamp on the package of tobacco, the Pipe-tube coiled on the floor, and the odds and ends of tobacco and confectioner's tartlets which were littered about. "Truly," I thought to myself in my dejection and disillusionment, "I cannot be quite grown-up if I cannot smoke as other fellows do, and should be fated never to hold a chibouk between my first and second fingers, or to inhale and puff smoke through a flaxen moustache!"

When Dimitri called for me at five o'clock, he found me in this unpleasant predicament. After drinking a glass of water, however, I felt nearly recovered, and ready to go with him.

"So much for your trying to smoke!" said he as he gazed at the remnants of my debauch. "It is a silly thing to do, and waste of money as well. I long ago promised myself never to smoke. But come along; we have to call for Dubkoff."

XIV. HOW WOLODA AND DUBKOFF AMUSED THEMSELVES

THE moment that Dimitri entered my room I perceived from his face, manner of walking, and the signs which, in him, denoted ill-humour—a blinking of the eyes and a grim holding of his head to one side, as though to straighten his collar—that he was in the coldly-correct frame of mind which was his when he felt dissatisfied with himself. It was a frame of mind, too, which always produced a chilling effect upon my feelings towards him. Of late I had begun to observe and appraise my friend's character a little more, but our friendship had in no way suffered from that, since it was still too young and strong for me to be able to look upon Dimitri as anything but perfect, no matter in what light I regarded him. In him there were two personalities, both of which I thought beautiful. One, which I loved devotedly, was kind, mild, forgiving, gay, and conscious of being those various things. When he was in this frame of mind his whole exterior, the very tone of his voice, his every movement, appeared to say: "I am kind and good-natured, and rejoice in being so, and every one can see that I so rejoice." The other of his two personalities—one which I had only just begun to apprehend, and before the majesty of which I bowed in spirit—was that of a man who was cold, stern to himself and to others, proud, religious to the point of fanaticism, and pedantically moral. At the present moment he was, as I say, this second personality.

With that frankness which constituted a necessary condition of our relations I told him, as soon as we entered the drozhki, how much it depressed and hurt me to see him, on this my fete-day in a frame of mind so irksome and disagreeable to me.

"What has upset you so?" I asked him. "Will you not tell me?"

"My dear Nicolas," was his slow reply as he gave his head a nervous twitch to one side and blinked his eyes, "since I have given you my word never to conceal anything from you, you have no reason to suspect me of secretiveness. One cannot always be in exactly the same mood, and if I seem at all put out, that is all there is to say about it."

"What a marvellously open, honourable character his is!" I thought to myself, and dropped the subject.

We drove the rest of the way to Dubkoff's in silence. Dubkoff's flat was an unusually fine one—or, at all events, so it seemed to me. Everywhere were rugs, pictures, gardenias, striped hangings, photographs, and curved settees, while on the walls hung guns, pistols, pouches, and the mounted heads of wild beasts. It was the appearance of this apartment which made me aware whom, it was that Woloda had imitated in the scheme of his own sitting-room. We found Dubkoff and Woloda engaged in cards, while seated also at the table, and watching the game with close attention, was a gentleman whom I did not know, but who appeared to be of no great importance, judging by the modesty of his attitude. Dubkoff himself was in a silk dressing-gown and soft slippers, while Woloda—seated opposite him on a divan—was in his shirtsleeves, as well as (to judge by his flushed face and the impatient, cursory glance which he gave us for a second as he looked up from the cards) much taken up with the game. On seeing me, he reddened still more.

"Well, it is for you to deal," he remarked to Dubkoff. In an instant I divined that he did not altogether relish my becoming acquainted with the fact that he gambled. Yet his expression had nothing in it of confusion—only a look which seemed to me to say: "Yes, I play cards, and if you are surprised at that, it is only because you are so young. There is nothing wrong about it—it is a necessity at our age." Yes, I at once divined and understood that.

Instead of dealing, however, Dubkoff rose and shook hands with us; after which he bade us both be seated, and then offered us pipes, which we declined.

"Here is our DIPLOMAT, then—the hero of the day!" he said to me, "Good Lord! how you look like a colonel!"

"H-m!" I muttered in reply, though once more feeling a complacent smile overspread my countenance.

I stood in that awe of Dubkoff which a sixteen-year-old boy naturally feels for a twenty-seven-year-old man of whom his elders say that he is a very clever young man who can dance well and speak French, and who, though secretly despising one's youth, endeavours to conceal the fact. Yet, despite my respect for him, I somehow found it difficult and uncomfortable, throughout my acquaintanceship with him, to look him in the eyes, I have since remarked that there are three kinds of men whom I cannot face easily, namely those who are much better than myself, those who are much worse, and those between whom and myself there is a mutual determination not to mention some particular thing of which we are both aware. Dubkoff may have been a much better fellow than myself, or he may have been a much worse; but the point was that he lied very frequently without recognising the fact that I was aware of his doing so, yet had determined not to mention it.

"Let us play another round," said Woloda, hunching one shoulder after the manner of Papa, and reshuffling the cards.

"How persistent you are!" said Dubkoff. "We can play all we want to afterwards. Well, one more round, then."

During the play, I looked at their hands. Woloda's hands were large and red, whilst in the crook of the thumb and the way in which the other fingers curved themselves round the cards as he held them they so exactly resembled Papa's that now and then I could not help thinking that Woloda purposely held the cards thus so as to look the more like a grownup. Yet the next moment, looking at his face, I could see that he had not a thought in his mind beyond the game. Dubkoff's hands, on the contrary, were small, puffy, and inclined to clench themselves, as well as extremely neat and small-fingered. They were just the kind of hands which generally display rings, and which are most to be seen on persons who are both inclined to use them and fond of objets de vertu.

Woloda must have lost, for the gentleman who was watching the play remarked that Vladimir Petrovitch had terribly bad luck, while Dubkoff reached for a note book, wrote something in it, and then, showing Woloda what he had written, said:

"Is that right?"

"Yes," said Woloda, glancing with feigned carelessness at the note book. "Now let us go."

Woloda took Dubkoff, and I gave Dimitri a lift in my drozhki.

"What were they playing at?" I inquired of Dimitri.

"At piquet. It is a stupid game. In fact, all such games are stupid."

"And were they playing for much?"

"No, not very much, but more than they ought to."

"Do you ever play yourself?"

"No; I swore never to do so; but Dubkoff will play with any one he can get hold of."

"He ought not to do that," I remarked. "So Woloda does not play so well as he does?"

"Perhaps Dubkoff ought not to, as you say, yet there is nothing especially bad about it all. He likes playing, and plays well, but he is a good fellow all the same."

"I had no idea of this," I said.

"We must not think ill of him," concluded Dimitri, "since he is a simply splendid fellow. I like him very much, and always shall like him, in spite of his weakness."

For some reason or another the idea occurred to me that, just BECAUSE Dimitri stuck up so stoutly for Dubkoff, he neither liked nor respected him in reality, but was determined, out of stubbornness and a desire not to be accused of inconstancy, never to own to the fact. He was one of those people who love their friends their life long, not so much because those friends remain always dear to them, as because, having once—possibly mistakenly— liked a person, they look upon it as dishonourable to cease ever to do so.

XV. I AM FETED AT DINNER

Dubkoff and Woloda knew every one at the restaurant by name, and every one, from the waiters to the proprietor, paid them great respect. No time was lost in allotting us a private room, where a bottle of iced champagne-upon which I tried to look with as much indifference as I could—stood ready waiting for us, and where we were served with a most wonderful repast selected by Dubkoff from the French menu. The meal went off most gaily and agreeably, notwithstanding that Dubkoff, as usual, told us blood-curdling tales of doubtful veracity (among others, a tale of how his grandmother once shot dead three robbers who were attacking her—a recital at which I blushed, closed my eyes, and turned away from the narrator), and that Woloda reddened visibly whenever I opened my mouth to speak—which was the more uncalled for on his part, seeing that never once, so far as I can remember, did I say anything shameful. After we had been given champagne, every one congratulated me, and I drank "hands across" with Dimitri and Dubkoff, and wished them joy. Since, however, I did not know to whom the bottle of champagne belonged (it was explained to me later that it was common property), I considered that, in return, I ought to treat my friends out of the money which I had never ceased to finger in my pocket. Accordingly, I stealthily extracted a ten-rouble note, and, beckoning the waiter to my side, handed him the money, and told him in a whisper (yet not so softly but that every one could hear me, seeing that every one was staring at me in dead silence) to "bring, if you please, a half-bottle of champagne." At this Woloda reddened again, and began to fidget so violently, and to gaze upon myself and every one else with such a distracted air, that I felt sure I had somehow put my foot in it. However, the half-bottle came, and we drank it with great gusto. After that, things went on merrily. Dubkoff continued his unending fairy tales, while Woloda also told funny stories—and told them well, too—in a way I should never have credited him: so that our laughter rang long and loud. Their best efforts lay in imitation, and in variants of a certain well-known saw. "Have you ever been abroad?" one would say to the other, for instance. "No," the one interrogated would reply, "but my brother plays the fiddle." Such perfection had the pair attained in this species of comic absurdity that they could answer any question by its means, while they would also endeavour to unite two absolutely unconnected matters without a previous question having been asked at all, yet say everything with a perfectly serious face and produce a most comic effect. I too began to try to be funny, but as soon as ever I spoke they either looked at me askance or did not look at me until I had finished: so that my anecdotes fell flat. Yet, though Dubkoff always remarked, "Our DIPLOMAT is lying, brother," I felt so exhilarated with the champagne and the company of my elders that the remark scarcely touched me. Only Dimitri, though he drank level with the rest of us, continued in the same severe, serious frame of mind—a fact which put a certain check upon the general hilarity.

"Now, look here, gentlemen," said Dubkoff at last. "After dinner we ought to take the DIPLOMAT in hand. How would it be for him to go with us to see Auntie? There we could put him through his paces."

"Ah, but Nechludoff will not go there," objected Woloda.

"O unbearable, insupportable man of quiet habits that you are!" cried Dubkoff, turning to Dimitri. "Yet come with us, and you shall see what an excellent lady my dear Auntie is."

"I will neither go myself nor let him go," replied Dimitri.

"Let whom go? The DIPLOMAT? Why, you yourself saw how he brightened up at the very mention of Auntie."

"It is not so much that I WILL NOT LET HIM go," continued Dimitri, rising and beginning to pace the room without looking at me, "as that I neither wish him nor advise him to go. He is not a child now, and if he must go he can go alone—without you. Surely you are ashamed of this, Dubkoff?—ashamed of always wanting others to do all the wrong things that you yourself do?"

"But what is there so very wrong in my inviting you all to come and take a cup of tea with my Aunt?" said Dubkoff, with a wink at Woloda. "If you don't like us going, it is your affair; yet we are going all the same. Are you coming, Woloda?"

"Yes, yes," assented Woloda. "We can go there, and then return to my rooms and continue our piquet."

"Do you want to go with them or not?" said Dimitri, approaching me.

"No," I replied, at the same time making room for him to sit down beside me on the divan. "I did not wish to go in any case, and since you advise me not to, nothing on earth will make me go now. Yet," I added a moment later, "I cannot honestly say that I have NO desire to go. All I say is that I am glad I am not going."

"That is right," he said. "Live your own life, and do not dance to any one's piping. That is the better way."

This little tiff not only failed to mar our hilarity, but even increased it. Dimitri suddenly reverted to the kindly mood which I loved best—so great (as I afterwards remarked on more than one occasion) was the influence which the consciousness of having done a good deed exercised upon him. At the present moment the source of his satisfaction was the fact that he had stopped my expedition to "Auntie's." He grew extraordinarily gay, called for another bottle of champagne (which was against his rules), invited some one who was a perfect stranger into our room, plied him with wine, sang "Gaudeamus igitur," requested every one to join him in the chorus, and proposed that we should and rink at the Sokolniki. [Mews.]

"Let us enjoy ourselves to-night," he said with a laugh. "It is in honour of his matriculation that you now see me getting drunk for the first time in my life."

Yet somehow this merriment sat ill upon him. He was like some good-natured father or tutor who is pleased with his young charges, and lets himself go for their amusement, yet at the same time tries to show them that one can enjoy oneself decently and in an honourable manner. However, his unexpected gaiety had an infectious influence upon myself and my companions, and the more so because each of us had now drunk about half a bottle of champagne.

It was in this pleasing frame of mind that I went out into the main salon to smoke a cigarette which Dubkoff had given me. In rising I noticed that my head seemed to swim a little, and that my legs and arms retained their natural positions only when I bent my thoughts determinedly upon them. At other moments my legs would deviate from the straight line, and my arms describe strange gestures. I concentrated my whole attention upon the members in question, forced my hands first to raise themselves and button my tunic, and then to smooth my hair (though they ruffled my locks in doing so), and lastly commanded my legs to march me to the door—a function which they duly performed, though at one time with too much reluctance, and at another with too much ABANDON (the left leg, in particular, coming to a halt every moment on tiptoe). Some one called out to me, "Where are you going to? They will bring you a cigar-light directly," but I guessed the voice to be Woloda's, and, feeling satisfied, somehow, that I had succeeded in divining the fact, merely smiled airily in reply, and continued on my way.

XVI. THE QUARREL

In the main salon I perceived sitting at a small table a short, squat gentleman of the professional type. He had a red moustache, and was engaged in eating something or another, while by his side sat a tall, clean-shaven individual with whom he was carrying on a conversation in French. Somehow the aspect of these two persons displeased me; yet I decided, for all that, to light my cigarette at the candelabrum which was standing before them. Looking from side to side, to avoid meeting their gaze, I approached the table, and applied my cigarette to the flame. When it was fairly alight, I involuntarily threw a glance at the gentleman who was eating, and found his grey eyes fixed upon me with an expression of intense displeasure. Just as I was turning away his red moustache moved a little, and he said in French:

"I do not like people to smoke when I am dining, my good sir."

I murmured something inaudible.

"No, I do not like it at all," he went on sternly, and with a glance at his clean-shaven companion, as though inviting him to admire the way in which he was about to deal with me. "I do not like it, my good sir, nor do I like people who have the impudence to puff their smoke up one's very nose."

By this time I had gathered that it was myself he was scolding, and at first felt as though I had been altogether in the wrong.

"I did not mean to inconvenience you," I said.

"Well, if you did not suppose you were being impertinent, at least I did! You are a cad, young sir!" he shouted in reply.

"But what right have you to shout at me like that?" I exclaimed, feeling that it was now HE that was insulting ME, and growing angry accordingly.

"This much right," he replied, "that I never allow myself to be overlooked by any one, and that I always teach young fellows like yourself their manners. What is your name, young sir, and where do you live?"

At this I felt so hurt that my teeth chattered, and I felt as though I were choking. Yet all the while I was conscious of being in the wrong, and so, instead of offering any further rudeness to the offended one, humbly told him my name and address.

"And MY name, young sir," he returned, "is Kolpikoff, and I will trouble you to be more polite to me in future.—However, You will hear from me again" ("vous aurez de mes nouvelles"—the conversation had been carried on wholly in French), was his concluding remark.

To this I replied, "I shall be delighted," with an infusion of as much hauteur as I could muster into my tone. Then, turning on my heel, I returned with my cigarette—which had meanwhile gone out—to our own room.

I said nothing, either to my brother or my friends, about what had happened (and the more so because they were at that moment engaged in a dispute of their own), but sat down in a corner to think over the strange affair. The words, "You are a cad, young sir," vexed me more and more the longer that they sounded in my ears. My tipsiness was gone now, and, in considering my conduct during the dispute, the uncomfortable thought came over me that I had behaved like a coward.

"Yet what right had he to attack me?" I reflected. "Why did he not simply intimate to me that I was annoying him? After all, it may have been he that was in the wrong. Why, too, when he called me a young cad, did I not say to him, 'A cad, my good sir, is one who takes offence'? Or why did I not simply tell him to hold his tongue? That would have been the better course. Or why did I not challenge him to a duel? No, I did none of those things, but swallowed his insults like a wretched coward."

Still the words, "You are a cad, young sir," kept sounding in my ears with maddening iteration. "I cannot leave things as they are," I at length decided as I rose to my feet with the fixed intention of returning to the gentleman and saying something outrageous to him—perhaps, also, of breaking the candelabrum over his head if occasion offered. Yet, though I considered the advisability of this last measure with some pleasure, it was not without a good deal of trepidation that I re-entered the main salon. As luck would have it, M.

Kolpikoff was no longer there, but only a waiter engaged in clearing the table. For a moment I felt like telling the waiter the whole story, and explaining to him my innocence in the matter, but for some reason or another I thought better of it, and once more returned, in the same hazy condition of mind, to our own room.

"What has become of our DIPLOMAT?" Dubkoff was just saying. "Upon him now hang the fortunes of Europe."

"Oh, leave me alone," I said, turning moodily away. Then, as I paced the room, something made me begin to think that Dubkoff was not altogether a good fellow. "There is nothing very much to admire in his eternal jokes and his nickname of 'DIPLOMAT,'" I reflected. "All he thinks about is to win money from Woloda and to go and see his 'Auntie.' There is nothing very nice in all that. Besides, everything he says has a touch of blackguardism in it, and he is forever trying to make people laugh. In my opinion he is simply stupid when he is not absolutely a brute." I spent about five minutes in these reflections, and felt my enmity towards Dubkoff continually increasing. For his part, he took no notice of me, and that angered me the more. I actually felt vexed with Woloda and Dimitri because they went on talking to him.

"I tell you what, gentlemen: the DIPLOMAT ought to be christened," said Dubkoff suddenly, with a glance and a smile which seemed to me derisive, and even treacherous. "Yet, O Lord, what a poor specimen he is!"

"You yourself ought to be christened, and you yourself are a sorry specimen!" I retorted with an evil smile, and actually forgetting to address him as "thou." [In Russian as in French, the second person singular is the form of speech used between intimate friends.]

This reply evidently surprised Dubkoff, but he turned away good-humouredly, and went on talking to Woloda and Dimitri. I tried to edge myself into the conversation, but, since I felt that I could not keep it up, I soon returned to my corner, and remained there until we left.

When the bill had been paid and wraps were being put on, Dubkoff turned to Dimitri and said: "Whither are Orestes and Pedalion going now?

Home, I suppose, to talk about love. Well, let US go and see my dear Auntie. That will be far more entertaining than your sour company."

"How dare you speak like that, and laugh at us?" I burst out as I approached him with clenched fists. "How dare you laugh at feelings which you do not understand? I will not have you do it! Hold your tongue!" At this point I had to hold my own, for I did not know what to say next, and was, moreover, out of breath with excitement. At first Dubkoff was taken aback, but presently he tried to laugh it off, and to take it as a joke. Finally I was surprised to see him look crestfallen, and lower his eyes.

"I NEVER laugh at you or your feelings. It is merely my way of speaking," he said evasively.

"Indeed?" I cried; yet the next moment I felt ashamed of myself and sorry for him, since his flushed, downcast face had in it no other expression than one of genuine pain.

"What is the matter with you?" said Woloda and Dimitri simultaneously. "No one was trying to insult you."

"Yes, he DID try to insult me!" I replied.

"What an extraordinary fellow your brother is!" said Dubkoff to Woloda. At that moment he was passing out of the door, and could not have heard what I said. Possibly I should have flung myself after him and offered him further insult, had it not been that just at that moment the waiter who had witnessed my encounter with Kolpikoff handed me my greatcoat, and I at once quietened down—merely making such a pretence of having had a difference with Dimitri as was necessary to make my sudden appeasement appear nothing extraordinary. Next day, when I met Dubkoff at Woloda's, the quarrel was not raked up, yet he and I still addressed each other as "you," and found it harder than ever to look one another in the face.

The remembrance of my scene with Kolpikoff—who, by the way, never sent me "de ses nouvelles," either the following day or any day afterwards—remained for years a keen and unpleasant memory. Even so much as five years after it had happened I would begin fidgeting and muttering to myself whenever I remembered the unavenged insult, and was fain to comfort myself with the satisfaction of recollecting the sort of young fellow I had shown myself to be in my subsequent affair with Dubkoff. In fact, it was only later still that I began to regard the matter in another light, and both to recall with comic appreciation my passage of arms with Kolpikoff, and to regret the undeserved affront which I had offered my good friend Dubkoff.

When, at a later hour on the evening of the dinner, I told Dimitri of my affair with Kolpikoff, whose exterior I described in detail, he was astounded.

"That is the very man!" he cried. "Don't you know that this precious Kolpikoff is a known scamp and sharper, as well as, above all things, a coward, and that he was expelled from his regiment by his brother officers because, having had his face slapped, he would not fight? But how came you to let him get away?" he added, with a kindly smile and glance. "Surely he could not have said more to you than he did when he called you a cad?"

"No," I admitted with a blush.

"Well, it was not right, but there is no great harm done," said Dimitri consolingly.

Long afterwards, when thinking the matter over at leisure, I suddenly came to the conclusion that it was quite possible that Kolpikoff took the opportunity of vicariously wiping off upon me the slap in the face which he had once received, just as I myself took the opportunity of vicariously wiping off upon the innocent Dubkoff the epithet "cad" which Kolpikoff had just applied to me.

XVII. I GET READY TO PAY SOME CALLS

On awaking next morning my first thoughts were of the affair with Kolpikoff. Once again I muttered to myself and stamped about the room, but there was no help for it. To-day was the last day that I was to spend in Moscow, and it was to be spent, by Papa's orders, in my paying a round of calls which he had written out for me on a piece of paper—his first solicitude on our account being not so much for our morals or our education as for our due observance of the convenances. On the piece of paper was written in his swift, broken hand-writing: "(1) Prince Ivan Ivanovitch WITHOUT FAIL; (2) the Iwins WITHOUT FAIL; (3) Prince Michael; (4) the Princess Nechludoff and Madame Valakhina if you wish." Of course I was also to call upon my guardian, upon the rector, and upon the professors.

These last-mentioned calls, however, Dimitri advised me not to pay: saying that it was not only unnecessary to do so, but not the thing. However, there were the other visits to be got through. It was the first two on the list—those marked as to be paid "WITHOUT FAIL"—that most alarmed me. Prince Ivan Ivanovitch was a commander-in-chief, as well as old, wealthy, and a bachelor. Consequently, I foresaw that vis-a-vis conversation between him and myself—myself a sixteen-year-old student!—was not likely to be interesting. As for the Iwins, they too were rich—the father being a departmental official of high rank who had only on one occasion called at our house during my grandmother's time. Since her death, I had remarked that the younger Iwin had fought shy of us, and seemed to give himself airs. The elder of the pair, I had heard, had now finished his course in jurisprudence, and gone to hold a post in St. Petersburg, while his brother Sergius (the former object of my worship) was also in St. Petersburg, as a great fat cadet in the Corps of Pages.

When I was a young man, not only did I dislike intercourse with people who thought themselves above me, but such intercourse was, for me, an unbearable torture, owing partly to my constant dread of being snubbed, and partly to my straining every faculty of my intellect to prove to such people my independence. Yet, even if I failed to fulfil the latter part of my father's instructions, I felt that I must carry out the former. I paced my room and eyed my clothes ready disposed on chairs—the tunic, the sword, and the cap. Just as I was about to set forth, old Grap called to congratulate me, bringing with him Ilinka. Grap pere was a Russianised German and an intolerably effusive, sycophantic old man who was more often than not tipsy. As a rule, he visited us only when he wanted to ask for something, and although Papa sometimes entertained him in his study, old Grap never came to dinner with us. With his subserviency and begging propensities went such a faculty of good-humour and a power of making himself at home that every one looked upon his attachment to us as a great honour. For my part, however, I never liked him, and felt ashamed when he was speaking.

I was much put out by the arrival of these visitors, and made no effort to conceal the fact. Upon Ilinka I had been so used to look down, and he so used to recognise my right to do so, that it displeased me to think that he was now as much a matriculated student as myself. In some way he appeared to me to have made a POINT of attaining that equality. I greeted the pair coldly, and, without offering them any refreshment (since it went against the grain to do so, and I thought they could ask for anything, if they wanted it, without my first inviting them to state their requirements), gave orders for the drozhki to be got ready. Ilinka was a good-natured, extremely moral, and far from stupid young fellow; yet, for all that, what people call a person of moods. That is to say, for no apparent reason he was for ever in some PRONOUNCED frame of mind—now lachrymose, now frivolous, now touchy on the very smallest point. At the present moment he appeared to be in the last-named mood. He kept looking from his father to myself without speaking, except when directly addressed, at which times he smiled the self-deprecatory, forced smile under which he was accustomed to conceal his feelings, and more especially that feeling of shame for his father which he must have experienced in our house.

"So, Nicolas Petrovitch," the old man said to me, following me everywhere about the room as I went through the operation of dressing, while all the while his fat fingers kept turning over and over a silver snuff-box with which my grandmother had once presented me, "as soon as ever I heard from my son that you had passed your examinations so well (though of course your abilities are well-known to everyone), I at once came to congratulate you, my dear boy. Why, I have carried you on my shoulders before now, and God knows that I love you as though you were my own son. My Ilinka too has always been fond of you, and feels quite at home with you."

Meanwhile the said Ilinka remained sitting silently by the window, apparently absorbed in contemplation of my three-cornered cap, and every now and then angrily muttering something in an undertone.

"Now, I also wanted to ask you, Nicolas Petrovitch." His father went on, "whether my son did well in the examinations? He tells me that he is going to be in the same faculty as yourself, and that therefore you will be able to keep an eye on him, and advise him, and so on."

"Oh, yes, I suppose he passed well," I replied, with a glance at Ilinka, who, conscious of my gaze, reddened violently and ceased to move his lips about. "And might he spend the day with you?" was the father's next request, which he made with a deprecatory smile, as though he stood in actual awe of me, yet always keeping so close to me, wherever I moved, that the fumes of the drink and tobacco in which he had been indulging were constantly perceptible to my nostrils. I felt greatly vexed at his placing me in such a false position towards his son, as well as at his distracting my attention from what was, to me, a highly important operation—namely, the operation of dressing; while, over and above all, I was annoyed by the smell of liquor with which he followed me about. Accordingly, I said very coldly that I could not have the pleasure of Ilinka's company that day, since I should be out.

"Ah! I suppose you are going to see your sister?" put in Ilinka with a smile, but without looking at me. "Well, I too have business to attend to." At this I felt even more put out, as well as pricked with compunction; so, to soften my refusal a little, I hastened to say that the reason why I should not be at home that day was that I had to call upon the PRINCE Ivan Ivanovitch, the PRINCESS Kornakoff, and the Monsieur Iwin who held such an influential post, as well as, probably, to dine with the PRINCESS Nechludoff

351

(for I thought that, on learning what important folk I was in the habit of mixing with, the Graps would no longer think it worth while to pretend to me). However, just as they were leaving, I invited Ilinka to come and see me another day; but he only murmured something unintelligible, and it was plain that he meant never to set foot in the house again.

When they had departed, I set off on my round of calls. Woloda, whom I had asked that morning to come with me, in order that I might not feel quite so shy as when altogether alone, had declined on the ground that for two brothers to be seen driving in one drozhki would appear so horribly "proper."

XVIII. THE VALAKHIN FAMILY

Accordingly I set off alone. My first call on the route lay at the Valakhin mansion. It was now three years since I had seen Sonetchka, and my love for her had long become a thing of the past, yet there still lingered in my heart a sort of clear, touching recollection of our bygone childish affection. At intervals, also, during those three years, I had found myself recalling her memory with such force and vividness that I had actually shed tears, and imagined myself to be in love with her again, but those occasions had not lasted more than a few minutes at a time, and had been long in recurring.

I knew that Sonetchka and her mother had been abroad—that, in fact, they had been so for the last two years. Also, I had heard that they had been in a carriage accident, and that Sonetchka's face had been so badly cut with the broken glass that her beauty was marred. As I drove to their house, I kept recalling the old Sonetchka to my mind, and wondering what she would look like when I met her. Somehow I imagined that, after her two years' sojourn abroad, she would look very tall, with a beautiful waist, and, though sedate and imposing, extremely attractive. Somehow, also, my imagination refused to picture her with her face disfigured with scars, but, on the contrary, since I had read somewhere of a lover who remained true to his adored one in spite of her disfigurement with smallpox, strove to imagine that I was in love with Sonetchka, for the purpose of priding myself on holding to my troth in spite of her scars—Yet, as a matter of fact, I was not really in love with her during that drive, but having once stirred up in myself old MEMORIES of love, felt PREPARED to fall into that condition, and the more so because, of late, my conscience had often been pricking me for having discarded so many of my old flames.

The Valakhins lived in a neat little wooden mansion approached by a courtyard. I gained admittance by ringing a bell (then a rarity in Moscow), and was received by a mincing, smartly-attired page. He either could not or made no attempt to inform me whether there was any one at home, but, leaving me alone in the dark hall, ran off down a still darker corridor. For a long time I waited in solitude in this gloomy place, out of which, in addition to the front door and the corridor, there only opened a door which at the moment was closed. Rather surprised at the dismal appearance of the house, I came to the conclusion that the reason was that its inmates were still abroad. After five minutes, however, the door leading into the salon was opened by the page boy, who then conducted me into a neat, but not richly furnished, drawing-room, where presently I was joined by Sonetchka.

She was now seventeen years old, and very small and thin, as well as of an unhealthy pallor of face. No scars at all were visible, however, and the beautiful, prominent eyes and bright, cheerful smile were the same as I had known and loved in my childhood. I had not expected her to look at all like this, and therefore could not at once lavish upon her the sentiment which I had been preparing on the way. She gave me her hand in the English fashion (which was then as much a novelty as a door-bell), and, bestowing upon mine a frank squeeze, sat down on the sofa by my side.

"Ah! how glad I am to see you, my dear Nicolas!" she said as she looked me in the face with an expression of pleasure so sincere that in the words "my dear Nicolas" I caught the purely friendly rather than the patronising note. To my surprise she seemed to me simpler, kinder, and more sisterly after her foreign tour than she had been before it. True, I could now see that she had two small scars between her nose and temples, but her wonderful eyes and smile fitted in exactly with my recollections, and shone as of old.

"But how greatly you have changed!" she went on. "You are quite grown-up now. And I-I-well, what do you think of me?"

"I should never have known you," I replied, despite the fact that at the moment I was thinking that I should have known her anywhere and always.

"Why? Am I grown so ugly?" she inquired with a movement of her head.

"Oh, no, decidedly not!" I hastened to reply. "But you have grown taller and older. As for being uglier, why, you are even—

"Yes, yes; never mind. Do you remember our dances and games, and St.

354

Jerome, and Madame Dorat?" (As a matter of fact, I could not recollect any Madame Dorat, but saw that Sonetchka was being led away by the joy of her childish recollections, and mixing them up a little). "Ah! what a lovely time it was!" she went on—and once more there shone before me the same eyes and smile as I had always carried in my memory. While she had been speaking, I had been thinking over my position at the present moment, and had come to the conclusion that I was in love with her. The instant, however, that I arrived at that result my careless, happy mood vanished, a mist seemed to arise before me which concealed even her eyes and smile, and, blushing hotly, I became tongue-tied and ill-at-ease.

"But times are different now," she went on with a sigh and a little lifting of her eyebrows. "Everything seems worse than it used to be, and ourselves too. Is it not so, Nicolas?"

I could return her no answer, but sat silently looking at her.

"Where are those Iwins and Kornakoffs now? Do you remember them?" she continued, looking, I think, with some curiosity at my blushing, downcast countenance. "What splendid times we used to have!"

Still I could not answer her.

The next moment, I was relieved from this awkward position by the entry of old Madame Valakhin into the room. Rising, I bowed, and straightway recovered my faculty of speech. On the other hand, an extraordinary change now took place in Sonetchka. All her gaiety and bonhomie disappeared, her smile became quite a different one, and, except for the point of her shortness of stature, she became just the lady from abroad whom I had expected to find in her. Yet for this change there was no apparent reason, since her mother smiled every whit as pleasantly, and expressed in her every movement just the same benignity, as of old. Seating herself in her arm-chair, the old lady signed to me to come and sit beside her; after which she said something to her daughter in English, and Sonetchka left the room—a fact which still further helped to relieve me. Madame then inquired after my father and brother, and passed on to speak of her great bereavement—the loss of her husband. Presently, however, she seemed to become sensible of the fact that I was not helping much in the conversation, for she gave me a look as much as to say: "If, now, my dear boy, you were to get up, to take your leave, and to depart, it would be well." But a curious circumstance had overtaken me. While she had been speaking of her bereavement, I had recalled to myself, not only the fact that I was in love, but the probability that the mother knew of it: whereupon such a fit of bashfulness had come upon me that I felt powerless to put any member of my body to its legitimate use. I knew that if I were to rise and walk I should have to think where to plant each foot, what to do with my head, what with my hands, and so on. In a word, I foresaw that I should be very much as I had been on the night when I partook too freely of champagne, and therefore, since I felt uncertain of being able to manage myself if I DID rise, I ended by feeling UNABLE to rise. Meanwhile, I should say, Sonetchka had returned to the room with her work, and seated herself in a far corner—a corner whence, as I was nevertheless sensible, she could observe me. Madame must have felt some surprise as she gazed at my crimson face and noted my complete immobility, but I decided that it was better to continue sitting in that absurd position than to risk something unpleasant by getting up and walking. Thus I sat on and on, in the hope that some unforeseen chance would deliver me from my predicament. That unforeseen chance at length presented itself in the person of an unforeseen young man, who entered the room with an air of being one of the household, and bowed to me politely as he did so: whereupon Madame rose, excused herself to me for having to speak with her "homme d'affaires," and finally gave me a glance which said: "Well, if you DO mean to go on sitting there for ever, at least I can't drive you away." Accordingly, with a great effort I also rose, but, finding it impossible to do any leave-taking, moved away towards the door, followed by the pitying glances of mother and daughter. All at once I stumbled over a chair, although it was lying quite out of my route: the reason for my stumbling being that my whole attention was centred upon not tripping over the carpet. Driving through the fresh air, however—where at first I muttered and fidgeted about so much that Kuzma, my coachman, asked me what was the matter—I soon found this feeling pass away, and began to meditate quietly concerning my love for Sonetchka and her relations with her mother, which had appeared to me rather strange. When, afterwards, I told my father that mother and daughter had not seemed on the best of terms with one another, he said:

"Yes, Madame leads the poor girl an awful life with her meanness. Yet," added my father with a greater display of feeling than a man might naturally conceive for a mere relative, "she used to be such an original, dear, charming woman! I cannot think what has made her change so much. By the way, you didn't notice a secretary fellow about, did you? Fancy a Russian lady having an affaire with a secretary!"

"Yes, I saw him," I replied.

"And was he at least good-looking?"

"No, not at all."

"It is extraordinary!" concluded Papa, with a cough and an irritable hoist of his shoulder.

"Well, I am in love!" was my secret thought to myself as I drove along in my drozhki.

XIX. THE KORNAKOFFS

MY second call on the route lay at the Kornakoffs', who lived on the first floor of a large mansion facing the Arbat. The staircase of the building looked extremely neat and orderly, yet in no way luxurious—being lined only with drugget pinned down with highly-polished brass rods. Nowhere were there any flowers or mirrors to be seen. The salon, too, with its polished floor, which I traversed on my way to the drawing-room, was decorated in the same cold, severe, unostentatious style. Everything in it looked bright and solid, but not new, and pictures, flower-stands, and articles of bric-a-brac were wholly absent. In the drawing-room I found some of the young princesses seated, but seated with the sort of correct, "company" air about them which gave one the impression that they sat like that only when guests were expected.

"Mamma will be here presently," the eldest of them said to me as she seated herself by my side. For the next quarter of an hour, this young lady entertained me with such an easy flow of small-talk that the conversation never flagged a moment. Yet somehow she made so patent the fact that she was just entertaining me that I felt not altogether pleased. Amongst other things, she told me that their brother Stephen (whom they called Etienne, and who had been two years at the College of Cadets) had now received his commission. Whenever she spoke of him, and more particularly when she told me that he had flouted his mother's wishes by entering the Hussars, she assumed a nervous air, and immediately her sisters, sitting there in silence, also assumed a nervous air. When, again, she spoke of my grandmother's death, she assumed a MOURNFUL air, and immediately the others all did the same. Finally, when she recalled how I had once struck St. Jerome and been expelled from the room, she laughed and showed her bad teeth, and immediately all the other princesses laughed and showed their bad teeth too.

Next, the Princess-Mother herself entered—a little dried-up woman, with a wandering glance and a habit of always looking at somebody else when she was addressing one. Taking my hand, she raised her own to my lips for me to kiss it—which otherwise, not supposing it to be necessary, I should not have done.

"How pleased I am to see you!" she said with her usual clearness of articulation as she gazed at her daughters. "And how like your mother you look! Does he not, Lise?"

Lise assented, though I knew for a fact that I did not resemble my mother in the least.

"And what a grown-up you have become! My Etienne, you will remember, is your second cousin. No, not second cousin—what is it, Lise? My mother was Barbara Dimitrievna, daughter of Dimitri Nicolaevitch, and your grandmother was Natalia Nicolaevna."

"Then he is our THIRD cousin, Mamma," said the eldest girl.

"Oh, how you always confuse me!" was her mother's angry reply. "Not third cousin, but COUSIN GERMAN—that is your relationship to Etienne. He is an officer now. Did you know it? It is not well that he should have his own way too much. You young men need keeping in hand, or—! Well, you are not vexed because your old aunt tells you the plain truth? I always kept Etienne strictly in hand, for I found it necessary to do so."

"Yes, that is how our relationship stands," she went on. "Prince Ivan Ivanovitch is my uncle, and your late mother's uncle also. Consequently I must have been your mother's first cousin—no, second cousin. Yes, that is it. Tell me, have you been to call on Prince Ivan yet?"

I said no, but that I was just going to.

"Ah, is it possible?" she cried. "Why, you ought to have paid him the first call of all! Surely you know that he stands to you in the position of a father? He has no children of his own, and his only heirs are yourself and my children. You ought to pay him all possible deference, both because of his age, and because of his position in the world, and because of everything else. I know that you young fellows of the present day think nothing of relationships and are not fond of old men, yet do you listen to me, your old aunt, for I am fond of you, and was fond of your mother, and had a great—a very great-liking and respect for your grandmother. You must not fail to call upon him on any account."

I said that I would certainly go, and since my present call seemed to me to have lasted long enough, I rose, and was about to depart, but she restrained me.

"No, wait a minute," she cried. "Where is your father, Lise? Go and tell him to come here. He will be so glad to see you," she added, turning to me.

Two minutes later Prince Michael entered. He was a short, thick-set gentleman, very slovenly dressed and ill-shaven, yet wearing such an air of indifference that he looked almost a fool. He was not in the least glad to see me—at all events he did not intimate that he was; but the Princess (who appeared to stand in considerable awe of him) hastened to say:

"Is not Woldemar here" (she seemed to have forgotten my name) "exactly like his mother?" and she gave her husband a glance which forced him to guess what she wanted. Accordingly he approached me with his usual passionless, half-discontented expression, and held out to me an unshaven cheek to kiss.

"Why, you are not dressed yet, though you have to go out soon!" was the Princess's next remark to him in the angry tone which she habitually employed in conversation with her domestics. "It will only mean your offending some one again, and trying to set people against you."

"In a moment, in a moment, mother," said Prince Michael, and departed. I also made my bows and departed.

This was the first time I had heard of our being related to Prince Ivan Ivanovitch, and the news struck me unpleasantly.

XX. THE IWINS

As for the prospect of my call upon the Prince, it seemed even more unpleasant. However, the order of my route took me first to the Iwins, who lived in a large and splendid mansion in Tverskaia Street. It was not without some nervousness that I entered the great portico where a Swiss major-domo stood armed with his staff of office.

To my inquiry as to whether any one was at home he replied: "Whom do you wish to see, sir? The General's son is within."

"And the General himself?" I asked with forced assurance.

"I must report to him your business first. What may it be, sir?" said the major-domo as he rang a bell. Immediately the gaitered legs of a footman showed themselves on the staircase above; whereupon I was seized with such a fit of nervousness that I hastily bid the lacquey say nothing about my presence to the General, since I would first see his son. By the time I had reached the top of the long staircase, I seemed to have grown extremely small (metaphorically, I mean, not actually), and had very much the same feeling within me as had possessed my soul when my drozhki drew up to the great portico, namely, a feeling as though drozhki, horse, and coachman had all of them grown extremely small too. I found the General's son lying asleep on a sofa, with an open book before him. His tutor, Monsieur Frost, under whose care he still pursued his studies at home, had entered behind me with a sort of boyish tread, and now awoke his pupil. Iwin evinced no particular pleasure at seeing me, while I also seemed to notice that, while talking to me, he kept looking at my eyebrows. Although he was perfectly polite, I conceived that he was "entertaining" me much as the Princess Valakhin had done, and that he not only felt no particular liking for me, but even that he considered my acquaintance in no way necessary to one who possessed his own circle of friends. All this arose out of the idea that he was regarding my eyebrows. In short, his bearing towards me appeared to be (as I recognised with an awkward sensation) very much the same as my own towards Ilinka Grap. I began to feel irritated, and to interpret every fleeting glance which he cast at Monsieur Frost as a mute inquiry: "Why has this fellow come to see me?"

After some conversation he remarked that his father and mother were at home. Would I not like to visit them too?

"First I will go and dress myself," he added as he departed to another room, notwithstanding that he had seemed to be perfectly well dressed (in a new frockcoat and white waistcoat) in the present one. A few minutes later he reappeared in his University uniform, buttoned up to the chin, and we went downstairs together. The reception rooms through which we passed were lofty and of great size, and seemed to be richly furnished with marble and gilt ornaments, chintz-covered settees, and a number of mirrors. Presently Madame Iwin met us, and we went into a little room behind the drawing-room, where, welcoming me in very friendly fashion, she seated herself by my side, and began to inquire after my relations.

Closer acquaintance with Madame (whom I had seen only twice before, and that but for a moment on each occasion) impressed me favourably. She was tall, thin, and very pale, and looked as though she suffered from chronic depression and fatigue. Yet, though her smile was a sad one, it was very kind, and her large, mournful eyes, with a slight cast in their vision, added to the pathos and attractiveness of her expression. Her attitude, while not precisely that of a hunchback, made her whole form droop, while her every movement expressed languor. Likewise, though her speech was deliberate, the timbre of her voice, and the manner in which she lisped her r's and l's, were very pleasing to the ear. Finally, she did not "ENTERTAIN" me. Unfortunately, the answers which I returned to her questions concerning my relations seemed to afford her a painful interest, and to remind her of happier days: with the result that when, presently, her son left the room, she gazed at me in silence for a moment, and then burst into tears. As I sat there in mute bewilderment, I could not conceive what I had said to bring this about. At first I felt sorry for her as she sat there weeping with downcast eyes. Next I began to think to myself: "Ought I not to try and comfort her, and how ought that to be done?" Finally, I began to feel vexed with her for placing me in such an awkward position. "Surely my appearance is not so moving as all that?" I reflected. "Or is she merely acting like this to see what I shall do under the circumstances?"

"Yet it would not do for me to go," I continued to myself, "for that would look too much as though I were fleeing to escape her tears." Accordingly I began fidgeting about on my seat, in order to remind her of my presence.

"Oh, how foolish of me!" at length she said, as she gazed at me for a moment and tried to smile. "There are days when one weeps for no reason whatever." She felt about for her handkerchief, and then burst out weeping more violently than before.

"Oh dear! How silly of me to be for ever crying like this! Yet I was so fond of your mother! We were such friends! We-we—"

At this point she found her handkerchief, and, burying her face in it, went on crying. Once more I found myself in the same protracted dilemma. Though vexed, I felt sorry for her, since her tears appeared to be genuine— even though I also had an idea that it was not so much for my mother that she was weeping as for the fact that she was unhappy, and had known happier days. How it would all have ended I do not know, had not her son reappeared and said that his father desired to see her. Thereupon she rose, and was just about to leave the room, when the General himself entered. He was a small, grizzled, thick-set man, with bushy black eyebrows, a grey, close-cropped head, and a very stern, haughty expression of countenance.

I rose and bowed to him, but the General (who was wearing three stars on his green frockcoat) not only made no response to my salutation, but scarcely even looked at me; so that all at once I felt as though I were not a human being at all, but only some negligible object such as a settee or window; or, if I were a human being, as though I were quite indistinguishable from such a negligible object.

"Then you have not yet written to the Countess, my dear?" he said to his wife in French, and with an imperturbable, yet determined, expression on his countenance.

"Good-bye, Monsieur Irtenieff," Madame said to me, in her turn, as she made a proud gesture with her head and looked at my eyebrows just as her son had done. I bowed to her, and again to her husband, but my second salutation made no more impression upon him than if a window had just been opened or closed. Nevertheless the younger Iwin accompanied me to the door, and on the way told me that he was to go to St. Petersburg University, since his father had been appointed to a post in that city (and young Iwin named a very high office in the service).

"Well, his Papa may do whatsoever he likes," I muttered to myself as I climbed into the drozhki, "but at all events I will never set foot in that house again. His wife weeps and looks at me as though I were the embodiment of woe, while that old pig of a General does not even give me a bow. However, I will get even with him some day." How I meant to do that I do not know, but my words nevertheless came true.

Afterwards, I frequently found it necessary to remember the advice of my father when he said that I must cultivate the acquaintanceship of the Iwins, and not expect a man in the position of General Iwin to pay any attention to a boy like myself. But I had figured in that position long enough.

XXI. PRINCE IVAN IVANOVITCH

"Now for the last call—the visit to Nikitskaia Street," I said to Kuzma, and we started for Prince Ivan Ivanovitch's mansion.

Towards the end, a round of calls usually brings one a certain amount of self-assurance: consequently I was approaching the Prince's abode in quite a tranquil frame of mind, when suddenly I remembered the Princess Kornakoff's words that I was his heir, and at the same moment caught sight of two carriages waiting at the portico. Instantly, my former nervousness returned.

Both the old major-domo who opened the door to me, and the footman who took my coat, and the two male and three female visitors whom I found in the drawing-room, and, most of all, Prince Ivan Ivanovitch himself (whom I found clad in a "company" frockcoat and seated on a sofa) seemed to look at me as at an HEIR, and so to eye me with ill-will. Yet the Prince was very gracious and, after kissing me (that is to say, after pressing his cold, dry, flabby lips to my cheek for a second), asked me about my plans and pursuits, jested with me, inquired whether I still wrote verses of the kind which I used to indite in honour of my grandmother's birthdays, and invited me to dine with him that day. Nevertheless, in proportion as he grew the kinder, the more did I feel persuaded that his civility was only intended to conceal from me the fact that he disliked the idea of my being his heir. He had a custom (due to his false teeth, of which his mouth possessed a complete set) of raising his upper lip a little as he spoke, and producing a slight whistling sound from it; and whenever, on the present occasion, he did so it seemed to me that he was saying to himself: "A boy, a boy—I know it! And my heir, too—my heir!"

When we were children, we had been used to calling the Prince "dear Uncle;" but now, in my capacity of heir, I could not bring my tongue to the phrase, while to say "Your Highness," as did one of the other visitors, seemed derogatory to my self-esteem. Consequently, never once during that visit did I call him anything at all. The personage, however, who most disturbed me was the old Princess who shared with me the position of prospective inheritor, and who lived in the Prince's house. While seated beside her at dinner, I felt firmly persuaded that the reason why she would not speak to me was that she disliked me for being her co-heir, and that the Prince, for his part, paid no attention to our side of the table for the reason that the Princess and myself hoped to succeed him, and so were alike distasteful in his sight.

"You cannot think how I hated it all!" I said to Dimitrieff the same evening, in a desire to make a parade of disliking the notion of being an heir (somehow I thought it the thing to do). "You cannot think how I loathed the whole two hours that I spent there!—Yet he is a fine-looking old fellow, and was very kind to me," I added—wishing, among other things, to disabuse my friend of any possible idea that my loathing had arisen out of the fact that I had felt so small. "It is only the idea that people may be classing me with the Princess who lives with him, and who licks the dust off his boots. He is a wonderful old man, and good and considerate to everybody, but it is awful to see how he treats the Princess. Money is a detestable thing, and ruins all human relations.

"Do you know, I think it would be far the best thing for me to have an open explanation with the Prince," I went on; "to tell him that I respect him as a man, but think nothing of being his heir, and that I desire him to leave me nothing, since that is the only condition on which I can, in future, visit his house."

Instead of bursting out laughing when I said this, Dimitri pondered awhile in silence, and then answered:

"You are wrong. Either you ought to refrain from supposing that people may be classing you with this Princess of whom you speak, or, if you DO suppose such a thing, you ought to suppose further that people are thinking what you yourself know quite well—namely, that such thoughts are so utterly foreign to your nature that you despise them and would never make them a basis for action. Suppose, however, that people DO suppose you to suppose such a thing—Well, to sum up," he added, feeling that he was getting a little mixed in his pronouncements, "you had much better not suppose anything of the kind."

My friend was perfectly right, though it was not until long, long afterwards that experience of life taught me the evil that comes of thinking— still worse, of saying—much that seems very fine; taught me that there are certain thoughts which should always be kept to oneself, since brave words seldom go with brave deeds. I learnt then that the mere fact of giving utterance to a good intention often makes it difficult, nay, impossible, to carry that good intention into effect. Yet how is one to refrain from giving utterance to the brave, self-sufficient impulses of youth? Only long afterwards does one remember and regret them, even as one incontinently plucks a flower before its blooming, and subsequently finds it lying crushed and withered on the ground.

The very next morning I, who had just been telling my friend Dimitri that money corrupts all human relations, and had (as we have seen) squandered the whole of my cash on pictures and Turkish pipes, accepted a loan of twenty roubles which he suggested should pay for my travelling expenses into the country, and remained a long while thereafter in his debt!

XXII. INTIMATE CONVERSATION WITH MY FRIEND

THIS conversation of ours took place in a phaeton on the way to Kuntsevo. Dimitri had invited me in the morning to go with him to his mother's, and had called for me after luncheon; the idea being that I should spend the evening, and perhaps also pass the night, at the country-house where his family lived. Only when we had left the city and exchanged its grimy streets and the unbearably deafening clatter of its pavements for the open vista of fields and the subdued grinding of carriage-wheels on a dusty high road (while the sweet spring air and prospect enveloped us on every side) did I awake from the new impressions and sensations of freedom into which the past two days had plunged me. Dimitri was in his kind and sociable mood. That is to say, he was neither frowning nor blinking nervously nor straightening his neck in his collar. For my own part, I was congratulating myself on those noble sentiments which I have expressed above, in the belief that they had led him to overlook my shameful encounter with Kolpikoff, and to refrain from despising me for it. Thus we talked together on many an intimate subject which even a friend seldom mentions to a friend. He told me about his family whose acquaintance I had not yet made—about his mother, his aunt, and his sister, as also about her whom Woloda and Dubkoff believed to be his "flame," and always spoke of as "the lady with the chestnut locks." Of his mother he spoke with a certain cold and formal commendation, as though to forestall any further mention of her; his aunt he extolled enthusiastically, though with a touch of condescension in his tone; his sister he scarcely mentioned at all, as though averse to doing so in my presence; but on the subject of "the lady with the chestnut locks" (whose real name was Lubov Sergievna, and who was a grown-up young lady living on a family footing with the Nechludoffs) he discoursed with animation.

"Yes, she is a wonderful woman," he said with a conscious reddening of the face, yet looking me in the eyes with dogged temerity. "True, she is no longer young, and even rather elderly, as well as by no means good-looking; but as for loving a mere featherhead, a mere beauty—well, I never could understand that, for it is such a silly thing to do." (Dimitri said this as though he had just discovered a most novel and extraordinary truth.) "I am certain, too, that such a soul, such a heart and principles, as are hers are not to be found elsewhere in the world of the present day." (I do not know whence he had derived the habit of saying that few good things were discoverable in the world of the present day, but at all events he loved to repeat the expression, and it somehow suited him.)

"Only, I am afraid," he went on quietly, after thus annihilating all such men as were foolish enough to admire mere beauty, "I am afraid that you will not understand or realise her quickly. She is modest, even secretive, and by no means fond of exhibiting her beautiful and surprising qualities. Now, my mother—who, as you will see, is a noble, sensible woman—has known Lubov Sergievna, for many years; yet even to this day she does not properly understand her. Shall I tell you why I was out of temper last evening when you were questioning me? Well, you must know that the day before yesterday Lubov asked me to accompany her to Ivan Yakovlevitch's (you have heard of him, I suppose? the fellow who seems to be mad, but who, in reality, is a very remarkable man). Well, Lubov is extremely religious, and understands Ivan Yakovlevitch to the full. She often goes to see him, and converses with him, and gives him money for the poor—money which she has earned herself. She is a marvellous woman, as you will see. Well, I went with her to Ivan's, and felt very grateful to her for having afforded me the opportunity of exchanging a word with so remarkable a man; but my mother could not understand our action at all, and discerned in it only superstition. Consequently, last night she and I quarrelled for the first time in our lives. A very bitter one it was, too," he concluded, with a convulsive shrug of his shoulders, as though the mention of it recalled the feelings which he had then experienced.

"And what are your intentions about it all?" I inquired, to divert him from such a disagreeable recollection. "That is to say, how do you imagine it is going to turn out? Do you ever speak to her about the future, or about how your love or friendship are going to end?"

"Do you mean, do I intend to marry her eventually?" he inquired, in his turn, with a renewed blush, but turning himself round and looking me boldly in the face.

"Yes, certainly," I replied as I settled myself down. "We are both of us grown-up, as well as friends, so we may as well discuss our future life as we drive along. No one could very well overlook or overhear us now."

"Why should I NOT marry her?" he went on in response to my reassuring reply. "It is my aim—as it should be the aim of every honourable man—to be as good and as happy as possible; and with her, if she should still be willing when I have become more independent, I should be happier and better than with the greatest beauty in the world."

Absorbed in such conversation, we hardly noticed that we were approaching Kuntsevo, or that the sky was becoming overcast and beginning to threaten rain. On the right, the sun was slowly sinking behind the ancient trees of the Kuntsevo park—one half of its brilliant disc obscured with grey, subluminous cloud, and the other half sending forth spokes of flaming light which threw the old trees into striking relief as they stood there with their dense crowns of green showing against a blue patch of sky. The light and shimmer of that patch contrasted sharply with the heavy pink cloud which lay massed above a young birch-tree visible on the horizon before us, while, a little further to the right, the parti-coloured roofs of the Kuntsevo mansion could be seen projecting above a belt of trees and undergrowth—one side of them reflecting the glittering rays of the sun, and the other side harmonising with the more louring portion of the heavens. Below us, and to the left, showed the still blue of a pond where it lay surrounded with pale-green laburnums—its dull, concave-looking depths repeating the trees in more sombre shades of colour over the surface of a hillock. Beyond the water spread the black expanse of a ploughed field, with the straight line of a dark-green ridge by which it was bisected running far into the distance, and there joining the leaden, threatening horizon.

On either side of the soft road along which the phaeton was pursuing the even tenour of its way, bright-green, tangled, juicy belts of rye were sprouting here and there into stalk. Not a motion was perceptible in the air, only a sweet freshness, and everything looked extraordinarily clear and bright. Near the road I could see a little brown path winding its way among the dark-green, quarter-grown stems of rye, and somehow that path reminded me vividly of our village, and somehow (through some connection of thought) the idea of that village reminded me vividly of Sonetchka, and so of the fact that I was in love with her.

Notwithstanding my fondness for Dimitri and the pleasure which his frankness had afforded me, I now felt as though I desired to hear no more about his feelings and intentions with regard to Lubov Sergievna, but to talk unstintedly about my own love for Sonetchka, who seemed to me an object of affection of a far higher order. Yet for some reason or another I could not make up my mind to tell him straight out how splendid it would seem when I had married Sonetchka and we were living in the country—of how we should have little children who would crawl about the floor and call me Papa, and of how delighted I should be when he, Dimitri, brought his wife, Lubov Sergievna, to see us, wearing an expensive gown. Accordingly, instead of saying all that, I pointed to the setting sun, and merely remarked: "Look, Dimitri! How splendid!"

To this, however, Dimitri made no reply, since he was evidently dissatisfied at my answering his confession (which it had cost him much to make) by directing his attention to natural objects (to which he was, in general, indifferent). Upon him Nature had an effect altogether different to what she had upon myself, for she affected him rather by her industry than by her beauty—he loved her rather with his intellect than with his senses.

"I am absolutely happy," I went on, without noticing that he was altogether taken up with his own thoughts and oblivious of anything that I might be saying. "You will remember how told you about a girl with whom I used to be in love when was a little boy? Well, I saw her again only this morning, and am now infatuated with her." Then I told him—despite his continued expression of indifference—about my love, and about all my plans for my future connubial happiness. Strangely enough, no sooner had I related in detail the whole strength of my feelings than I instantly became conscious of its diminution.

The rain overtook us just as we were turning into the avenue of birch-trees which led to the house, but it did not really wet us. I only knew that it was raining by the fact that I felt a drop fall, first on my nose, and then on my hand, and heard something begin to patter upon the young, viscous leaves of the birch-trees as, drooping their curly branches overhead, they seemed to imbibe the pure, shining drops with an avidity which filled the whole avenue with scent. We descended from the carriage, so as to reach the house the quicker through the garden, but found ourselves confronted at the entrance-door by four ladies, two of whom were knitting, one reading a book, and the fourth walking to and fro with a little dog. Thereupon, Dimitri began to present me to his mother, sister, and aunt, as well as to Lubov Sergievna. For a moment they remained where they were, but almost instantly the rain became heavier.

"Let us go into the verandah; you can present him to us there," said the lady whom I took to be Dimitri's mother, and we all of us ascended the entrance-steps.

XXIII. THE NECHLUDOFFS

From the first, the member of this company who struck me the most was Lubov Sergievna, who, holding a lapdog in her arms and wearing stout laced boots, was the last of the four ladies to ascend the staircase, and twice stopped to gaze at me intently and then kiss her little dog. She was anything but good-looking, since she was red-haired, thin, short, and slightly crooked. What made her plain face all the plainer was the queer way in which her hair was parted to one side (it looked like the wigs which bald women contrive for themselves). However much I should have liked to applaud my friend, I could not find a single comely feature in her. Even her brown eyes, though expressive of good-humour, were small and dull—were, in fact, anything but pretty; while her hands (those most characteristic of features), were though neither large nor ill-shaped, coarse and red.

As soon as we reached the verandah, each of the ladies, except Dimitri's sister Varenika—who also had been regarding me attentively out of her large, dark-grey eyes—said a few words to me before resuming her occupation, while Varenika herself began to read aloud from a book which she held on her lap and steadied with her finger.

The Princess Maria Ivanovna was a tall, well-built woman of forty. To judge by the curls of half-grey hair which descended below her cap one might have taken her for more, but as soon as ever one observed the fresh, extraordinarily tender, and almost wrinkleless face, as well as, most of all, the lively, cheerful sparkle of the large eyes, one involuntarily took her for less. Her eyes were black and very frank, her lips thin and slightly severe, her nose regular and slightly inclined to the left, and her hands ringless, large, and almost like those of a man, but with finely tapering fingers. She wore a dark-blue dress fastened to the throat and sitting closely to her firm, still youthful waist—a waist which she evidently pinched. Lastly, she held herself very upright, and was knitting a garment of some kind. As soon as I stepped on to the verandah she took me by the hand, drew me to her as though wishing to scrutinise me more closely, and said, as she gazed at me with the same cold, candid glance as her son's, that she had long known me by report from Dimitri, and that therefore, in order to make my acquaintance thoroughly, she had invited me to stay these twenty-four hours in her house.

"Do just as you please here," she said, "and stand on no ceremony whatever with us, even as we shall stand on none with you. Pray walk, read, listen, or sleep as the mood may take you."

Sophia Ivanovna was an old maid and the Princess's younger sister, though she looked the elder of the two. She had that exceedingly overstuffed appearance which old maids always present who are short of stature but wear corsets. It seemed as though her healthiness had shifted upwards to the point of choking her, her short, fat hands would not meet below her projecting bust, and the line of her waist was scarcely visible at all.

Notwithstanding that the Princess Maria Ivanovna had black hair and eyes, while Sophia Ivanovna had white hair and large, vivacious, tranquilly blue eyes (a rare combination), there was a great likeness between the two sisters, for they had the same expression, nose, and lips. The only difference was that Sophia's nose and lips were a trifle coarser than Maria's, and that, when she smiled, those features inclined towards the right, whereas Maria's inclined towards the left. Sophia, to judge by her dress and coiffure, was still youthful at heart, and would never have displayed grey curls, even if she had possessed them. Yet at first her glance and bearing towards me seemed very proud, and made me nervous, whereas I at once felt at home with the Princess. Perhaps it was only Sophia's stoutness and a certain resemblance to portraits of Catherine the Great that gave her, in my eyes, a haughty aspect, but at all events I felt quite intimidated when she looked at me intently and said, "Friends of our friends are our friends also." I became reassured and changed my opinion about her only when, after saying those words, she opened her mouth and sighed deeply. It may be that she owed her habit of sighing after every few words—with a great distention of the mouth and a slight drooping of her large blue eyes—to her stoutness, yet it was none the less one which expressed so much good-humour that I at once lost all fear of her, and found her actually attractive. Her eyes were charming, her voice pleasant and musical, and even the flowing lines of her fullness seemed to my youthful vision not wholly lacking in beauty.

I had imagined that Lubov Sergievna, as my friend's friend, would at once say something friendly and familiar to me; yet, after gazing at me fixedly for a while, as though in doubt whether the remark she was about to make to me would not be too friendly, she at length asked me what faculty I was in. After that she stared at me as before, in evident hesitation as to whether or not to say something civil and familiar, until, remarking her perplexity, I besought her with a look to speak freely. Yet all she then said was, "They tell me the Universities pay very little attention to science now," and turned away to call her little dog.

All that evening she spoke only in disjointed fragments of this kind—fragments which had no connection either with the point or with one another; yet I had such faith in Dimitri, and he so often kept looking from her to me with an expression which mutely asked me, "Now, what do you think of that?" that, though I entirely failed to persuade myself that in Lubov Sergievna there was anything to speak of, I could not bear to express the thought, even to myself.

As for the last member of the family, Varenika, she was a well-developed girl of sixteen. The only good features in her were a pair of dark-grey eyes,—which, in their expression of gaiety mingled with quiet attention, greatly resembled those of her aunt—a long coil of flaxen hair, and extremely delicate, beautiful hands.

"I expect, Monsieur Nicolas, you find it wearisome to hear a story begun from the middle?" said Sophia Ivanovna with her good-natured sigh as she turned over some pieces of clothing which she was sewing. The reading aloud had ceased for the moment because Dimitri had left the room on some errand or another.

"Or perhaps you have read Rob Roy before?" she added.

At that period I thought it incumbent upon me, in virtue of my student's uniform, to reply in a very "clever and original" manner to every question put to me by people whom I did not know very well, and regarded such short, clear answers as "Yes," "No," "I like it," or "I do not care for it," as things to be ashamed of. Accordingly, looking down at my new and fashionably-cut trousers and the glittering buttons of my tunic, I replied that I had never read Rob Roy, but that it interested me greatly to hear it, since I preferred to read books from the middle rather than from the beginning.

"It is twice as interesting," I added with a self-satisfied smirk; "for then one can guess what has gone before as well as what is to come after."

The Princess smiled what I thought was a forced smile, but one which I discovered later to be her only one.

"Well, perhaps that is true," she said. "But tell me, Nicolas (you will not be offended if I drop the Monsieur)—tell me, are you going to be in town long? When do you go away?"

"I do not know quite. Perhaps to-morrow, or perhaps not for some while yet," I replied for some reason or another, though I knew perfectly well that in reality we were to go to-morrow.

"I wish you could stop longer, both for your own sake and for Dimitri's," she said in a meditative manner. "At your age friendship is a weak thing."

I felt that every one was looking at me, and waiting to see what I should say—though certainly Varenika made a pretence of looking at her aunt's work. I felt, in fact, as though I were being put through an examination, and that it behoved me to figure in it as well as possible.

"Yes, to ME Dimitri's friendship is most useful," I replied, "but to HIM mine cannot be of any use at all, since he is a thousand times better than I." (Dimitri could not hear what I said, or I should have feared his detecting the insincerity of my words.)

Again the Princess smiled her unnatural, yet characteristically natural, smile.

"Just listen to him!" she said. "But it is YOU who are the little monster of perfection."

376

"'Monster of perfection,'" I thought to myself. "That is splendid. I must make a note of it."

"Yet, to dismiss yourself, he has been extraordinarily clever in that quarter," she went on in a lower tone (which pleased me somehow) as she indicated Lubov Sergievna with her eyes, "since he has discovered in our poor little Auntie" (such was the pet name which they gave Lubov) "all sorts of perfections which I, who have known her and her little dog for twenty years, had never yet suspected. Varenika, go and tell them to bring me a glass of water," she added, letting her eyes wander again. Probably she had bethought her that it was too soon, or not entirely necessary, to let me into all the family secrets. "Yet no—let HIM go, for he has nothing to do, while you are reading. Pray go to the door, my friend," she said to me, "and walk about fifteen steps down the passage. Then halt and call out pretty loudly, 'Peter, bring Maria Ivanovna a glass of iced water'"—and she smiled her curious smile once more.

"I expect she wants to say something about me in my absence," I thought to myself as I left the room. "I expect she wants to remark that she can see very clearly that I am a very, very clever young man."

Hardly had I taken a dozen steps when I was overtaken by Sophia Ivanovna, who, though fat and short of breath, trod with surprising lightness and agility.

"Merci, mon cher," she said. "I will go and tell them myself."

XXIV. LOVE

SOPHIA IVANOVNA, as I afterwards came to know her, was one of those rare, young-old women who are born for family life, but to whom that happiness has been denied by fate. Consequently all that store of their love which should have been poured out upon a husband and children becomes pent up in their hearts, until they suddenly decide to let it overflow upon a few chosen individuals. Yet so inexhaustible is that store of old maids' love that, despite the number of individuals so selected, there still remains an abundant surplus of affection which they lavish upon all by whom they are surrounded—upon all, good or bad, whom they may chance to meet in their daily life.

Of love there are three kinds—love of beauty, the love which denies itself, and practical love.

Of the desire of a young man for a young woman, as well as of the reverse instance, I am not now speaking, for of such tendresses I am wary, seeing that I have been too unhappy in my life to have been able ever to see in such affection a single spark of truth, but rather a lying pretence in which sensuality, connubial relations, money, and the wish to bind hands or to unloose them have rendered feeling such a complex affair as to defy analysis. Rather am I speaking of that love for a human being which, according to the spiritual strength of its possessor, concentrates itself either upon a single individual, upon a few, or upon many—of love for a mother, a father, a brother, little children, a friend, a compatriot—of love, in short, for one's neighbour.

Love of beauty consists in a love of the sense of beauty and of its expression. People who thus love conceive the object of their affection to be desirable only in so far as it arouses in them that pleasurable sensation of which the consciousness and the expression soothes the senses. They change the object of their love frequently, since their principal aim consists in ensuring that the voluptuous feeling of their adoration shall be constantly titillated. To preserve in themselves this sensuous condition, they talk unceasingly, and in the most elegant terms, on the subject of the love which they feel, not only for its immediate object, but also for objects upon which it does not touch at all. This country of ours contains many such individuals—individuals of that well-known class who, cultivating "the beautiful," not only discourse of their cult to all and sundry, but speak of it pre-eminently in FRENCH. It may seem a strange and ridiculous thing to say, but I am convinced that among us we have had in the past, and still have, a large section of society—notably women—whose love for their friends, husbands, or children would expire to-morrow if they were debarred from dilating upon it in the tongue of France!

Love of the second kind—renunciatory love—consists in a yearning to undergo self-sacrifice for the object beloved, regardless of any consideration whether such self-sacrifice will benefit or injure the object in question. "There is no evil which I would not endure to show both the world and him or her whom I adore my devotion." There we have the formula of this kind of love. People who thus love never look for reciprocity of affection, since it is a finer thing to sacrifice yourself for one who does not comprehend you. Also, they are always painfully eager to exaggerate the merits of their sacrifice; usually constant in their love, for the reason that they would find it hard to forego the kudos of the deprivations which they endure for the object beloved; always ready to die, to prove to him or to her the entirety of their devotion; but sparing of such small daily proofs of their love as call for no special effort of self-immolation. They do not much care whether you eat well, sleep well, keep your spirits up, or enjoy good health, nor do they ever do anything to obtain for you those blessings if they have it in their power; but, should you be confronting a bullet, or have fallen into the water, or stand in danger of being burnt, or have had your heart broken in a love affair—well, for all these things they are prepared if the occasion should arise. Moreover, people addicted to love of such a self-sacrificing order are invariably proud of their love, exacting, jealous, distrustful, and—strange to tell—anxious that the object of their adoration should incur perils (so that they may save it from calamity, and console it thereafter) and even be vicious (so that they may purge it of its vice).

Suppose, now, that you are living in the country with a wife who loves you in this self-sacrificing manner. You may be healthy and contented, and have occupations which interest you, while, on the other hand, your wife may be too weak to superintend the household work (which, in consequence, will be left to the servants), or to look after the children (who, in consequence, will be left to the nurses), or to put her heart into any work whatsoever: and all because she loves nobody and nothing but yourself. She may be patently ill, yet she will say not a word to you about it, for fear of distressing you. She may be patently ennuyee, yet for your sake she will be prepared to be so for the rest of her life. She may be patently depressed because you stick so persistently to your occupations (whether sport, books, farming, state service, or anything else) and see clearly that they are doing you harm; yet, for all that, she will keep silence, and suffer it to be so. Yet, should you but fall sick—and, despite her own ailments and your prayers that she will not distress herself in vain, your loving wife will remain sitting inseparably by your bedside. Every moment you will feel her sympathetic gaze resting upon you and, as it were, saying: "There! I told you so, but it is all one to me, and I shall not leave you." In the morning you maybe a little better, and move into another room. The room, however, will be insufficiently warmed or set in order; the soup which alone you feel you could eat will not have been cooked; nor will any medicine have been sent for. Yet, though worn out with night watching, your loving wife will continue to regard you with an expression of sympathy, to walk about on tiptoe, and to whisper unaccustomed and obscure orders to the servants. You may wish to be read to—and your loving wife will tell you with a sigh that she feels sure you will be unable to hear her reading, and only grow angry at her awkwardness in doing it; wherefore you had better not be read to at all. You may wish to walk about the room—and she will tell you that it would be far better for you not to do so. You may wish to talk with some friends who have called—and she will tell you that talking is not good for you. At nightfall the fever may come upon you again, and you may wish to be left alone whereupon your loving wife, though wasted, pale, and full of yawns, will go on sitting in a chair opposite you, as dusk falls, until her very slightest movement, her very slightest sound, rouses you to feelings of anger and impatience. You may have a servant who has lived with you for twenty years, and to whom you are attached, and who would tend you well and to your satisfaction during the night, for the reason that he has been asleep all day and is, moreover, paid a salary for his services; yet your wife will not suffer him to wait upon you. No; everything she must do herself with her weak, unaccustomed fingers (of which you follow the movements with suppressed irritation as those pale members do their best to uncork a medicine bottle, to snuff a candle, to pour out physic, or to touch you in a squeamish sort of way). If you are an impatient, hasty sort of man, and beg of her to leave the room, you will hear by the vexed, distressed sounds which come from her that she is humbly sobbing and weeping behind the door, and whispering foolishness of some kind to the servant. Finally if you do not die, your loving wife—who has not slept during the whole three weeks of your illness (a fact of which she will constantly remind you)—will fall ill in her turn, waste away, suffer much, and become even more incapable of any useful pursuit than she was before; while by the time that you have regained your normal state of health she will express to you her self-sacrificing affection only by shedding around you a kind of benignant dullness which involuntarily communicates itself both to yourself and to every one else in your vicinity.

The third kind of love—practical love—consists of a yearning to satisfy every need, every desire, every caprice, nay, every vice, of the being beloved. People who love thus always love their life long, since, the more they love, the more they get to know the object beloved, and the easier they find the task of loving it—that is to say, of satisfying its desires. Their love seldom finds expression in words, but if it does so, it expresses itself neither with assurance nor beauty, but rather in a shamefaced, awkward manner, since people of this kind invariably have misgivings that they are loving unworthily. People of this kind love even the faults of their adored one, for the reason that those faults afford them the power of constantly satisfying new desires. They look for their affection to be returned, and even deceive themselves into believing that it is returned, and are happy accordingly: yet in the reverse case they will still continue to desire happiness for their beloved one, and try by every means in their power—whether moral or material, great or small—to provide it.

Such practical love it was—love for her nephew, for her niece, for her sister, for Lubov Sergievna, and even for myself, because I loved Dimitri—

381

that shone in the eyes, as well as in the every word and movement, of Sophia Ivanovna.

Only long afterwards did I learn to value her at her true worth. Yet even now the question occurred to me: "What has made Dimitri—who throughout has tried to understand love differently to other young fellows, and has always had before his eyes the gentle, loving Sophia Ivanovna—suddenly fall so deeply in love with the incomprehensible Lubov Sergievna, and declare that in his aunt he can only find good QUALITIES? Verily it is a true saying that 'a prophet hath no honour in his own country.' One of two things: either every man has in him more of bad than of good, or every man is more receptive to bad than to good. Lubov Sergievna he has not known for long, whereas his aunt's love he has known since the day of his birth."

XXV. I BECOME BETTER ACQUAINTED WITH THE NECHLUDOFFS

WHEN I returned to the verandah, I found that they were not talking of me at all, as I had anticipated. On the contrary, Varenika had laid aside the book, and was engaged in a heated dispute with Dimitri, who, for his part, was walking up and down the verandah, and frowningly adjusting his neck in his collar as he did so. The subject of the quarrel seemed to be Ivan Yakovlevitch and superstition, but it was too animated a difference for its underlying cause not to be something which concerned the family much more nearly. Although the Princess and Lubov Sergievna were sitting by in silence, they were following every word, and evidently tempted at times to take part in the dispute; yet always, just when they were about to speak, they checked themselves, and left the field clear for the two principles, Dimitri and Varenika. On my entry, the latter glanced at me with such an indifferent air that I could see she was wholly absorbed in the quarrel and did not care whether she spoke in my presence or not. The Princess too looked the same, and was clearly on Varenika's side, while Dimitri began, if anything, to raise his voice still more when I appeared, and Lubov Sergievna, for her part, observed to no one in particular: "Old people are quite right when they say, 'Si jeunesse savait, si vieillesse pouvait.'"

Nevertheless this quotation did not check the dispute, though it somehow gave me the impression that the side represented by the speaker and her friend was in the wrong. Although it was a little awkward for me to be present at a petty family difference, the fact that the true relations of the family revealed themselves during its progress, and that my presence did nothing to hinder that revelation, afforded me considerable gratification.

How often it happens that for years one sees a family cover themselves over with a conventional cloak of decorum, and preserve the real relations of its members a secret from every eye! How often, too, have I remarked that, the more impenetrable (and therefore the more decorous) is the cloak, the harsher are the relations which it conceals! Yet, once let some unexpected question—

often a most trivial one (the colour of a woman's hair, a visit, a man's horses, and so forth)—arise in that family circle, and without any visible cause there will also arise an ever-growing difference, until in time the cloak of decorum becomes unequal to confining the quarrel within due bounds, and, to the dismay of the disputants and the astonishment of the auditors, the real and ill-adjusted relations of the family are laid bare, and the cloak, now useless for concealment, is bandied from hand to hand among the contending factions until it serves only to remind one of the years during which it successfully deceived one's perceptions. Sometimes to strike one's head violently against a ceiling hurts one less than just to graze some spot which has been hurt and bruised before: and in almost every family there exists some such raw and tender spot. In the Nechludoff family that spot was Dimitri's extraordinary affection for Lubov Sergievna, which aroused in the mother and sister, if not a jealous feeling, at all events a sense of hurt family pride. This was the grave significance which underlay, for all those present, the seeming dispute about Ivan Yakovlevitch and superstition.

"In anything that other people deride and despise you invariably profess to see something extraordinarily good!" Varenika was saying in her clear voice, as she articulated each syllable with careful precision.

"Indeed?" retorted Dimitri with an impatient toss of his head. "Now, in the first place, only a most unthinking person could ever speak of DESPISING such a remarkable man as Ivan Yakovlevitch, while, in the second place, it is YOU who invariably profess to see nothing good in what confronts you."

Meanwhile Sophia Ivanovna kept looking anxiously at us as she turned first to her nephew, and then to her niece, and then to myself. Twice she opened her mouth as though to say what was in her mind and drew a deep sigh.

"Varia, PLEASE go on reading," she said at length, at the same time handing her niece the book, and patting her hand kindly. "I wish to know whether he ever found HER again" (as a matter of fact, the novel in question contained not a word about any one finding any one else). "And, Mitia dear," she added to her nephew, despite the glum looks which he was throwing at her for having interrupted the logical thread of his deductions, "you had better let me poultice your cheek, or your teeth will begin to ache again."

After that the reading was resumed. Yet the quarrel had in no way dispelled the calm atmosphere of family and intellectual harmony which enveloped this circle of ladies.

Clearly deriving its inspiration and character from the Princess Maria Ivanovna, it was a circle which, for me, had a wholly novel and attractive character of logicalness mingled with simplicity and refinement. That character I could discern in the daintiness, good taste, and solidity of everything about me, whether the handbell, the binding of the book, the settee, or the table. Likewise, I divined it in the upright, well-corseted pose of the Princess, in her pendant curls of grey hair, in the manner in which she had, at our first introduction, called me plain "Nicolas" and "he," in the occupations of the ladies (the reading and the sewing of garments), and in the unusual whiteness of their hands. Those hands, en passant, showed a family feature common to all—namely, the feature that the flesh of the palm on the outer side was rosy in colour, and divided by a sharp, straight line from the pure whiteness of the upper portion of the hand. Still more was the character of this feminine circle expressed in the manner in which the three ladies spoke Russian and French—spoke them, that is to say, with perfect articulation of syllables and pedantic accuracy of substantives and prepositions. All this, and more especially the fact that the ladies treated me as simply and as seriously as a real grown-up—telling me their opinions, and listening to my own (a thing to which I was so little accustomed that, for all my glittering buttons and blue facings, I was in constant fear of being told: "Surely you do not think that we are talking SERIOUSLY to you? Go away and learn something")—all this, I say, caused me to feel an entire absence of restraint in this society. I ventured at times to rise, to move about, and to talk boldly to each of the ladies except Varenika (whom I always felt it was unbecoming, or even forbidden, for me to address unless she first spoke to me).

As I listened to her clear, pleasant voice reading aloud, I kept glancing from her to the path of the flower-garden, where the rain-spots were making small dark circles in the sand, and thence to the lime-trees, upon the leaves of which the rain was pattering down in large detached drops shed from the pale, shimmering edge of the livid blue cloud which hung suspended over us. Then I would glance at her again, and then at the last purple rays of the setting sun where they were throwing the dense clusters of old, rain-washed birches into brilliant relief. Yet again my eyes would return to Varenika, and, each time that they did so, it struck me afresh that she was not nearly so plain as at first I had thought her.

"How I wish that I wasn't in love already!" I reflected, "or that Sonetchka was Varenika! How nice it would be if suddenly I could become a member of this family, and have the three ladies for my mother, aunt, and wife respectively!" All the time that these thoughts kept passing through my head I kept attentively regarding Varenika as she read, until somehow I felt as though I were magnetising her, and that presently she must look at me. Sure enough, at length she raised her head, threw me a glance, and, meeting my eyes, turned away.

"The rain does not seem to stop," she remarked.

Suddenly a new feeling came over me. I began to feel as though everything now happening to me was a repetition of some similar occurrence before—as though on some previous occasion a shower of rain had begun to fall, and the sun had set behind birch-trees, and I had been looking at her, and she had been reading aloud, and I had magnetised her, and she had looked up at me. Yes, all this I seemed to recall as though it had happened once before.

"Surely she is not—SHE?" was my thought. "Surely IT is not beginning?" However, I soon decided that Varenika was not the "SHE" referred to, and that "it" was not "beginning." "In the first place," I said to myself, "Varenika is not at all BEAUTIFUL. She is just an ordinary girl whose acquaintance I have made in the ordinary way, whereas she whom I shall meet somewhere and some day and in some not ordinary way will be anything but ordinary. This family pleases me so much only because hitherto I have never seen anybody. Such things will always be happening in the future, and I shall see many more such families during my life."

XXVI. I SHOW OFF

AT tea time the reading came to an end, and the ladies began to talk among themselves of persons and things unknown to me. This I conceived them to be doing on purpose to make me conscious (for all their kind demeanour) of the difference which years and position in the world had set between them and myself. In general discussions, however, in which I could take part I sought to atone for my late silence by exhibiting that extraordinary cleverness and originality to which I felt compelled by my University uniform. For instance, when the conversation turned upon country houses, I said that Prince Ivan Ivanovitch had a villa near Moscow which people came to see even from London and Paris, and that it contained balustrading which had cost 380,000 roubles. Likewise, I remarked that the Prince was a very near relation of mine, and that, when lunching with him the same day, he had invited me to go and spend the entire summer with him at that villa, but that I had declined, since I knew the villa well, and had stayed in it more than once, and that all those balustradings and bridges did not interest me, since I could not bear ornamental work, especially in the country, where I liked everything to be wholly countrified. After delivering myself of this extraordinary and complicated romance, I grew confused, and blushed so much that every one must have seen that I was lying. Both Varenika, who was handing me a cup of tea, and Sophia Ivanovna, who had been gazing at me throughout, turned their heads away, and began to talk of something else with an expression which I afterwards learnt that good-natured people assume when a very young man has told them a manifest string of lies—an expression which says, "Yes, we know he is lying, and why he is doing it, the poor young fellow!"

What I had said about Prince Ivan Ivanovitch having a country villa, I had related simply because I could find no other pretext for mentioning both my relationship to the Prince and the fact that I had been to luncheon with him that day; yet why I had said all I had about the balustrading costing 380,000 roubles, and about my having several times visited the Prince at that villa (I had never once been there—more especially since the Prince possessed no residences save in Moscow and Naples, as the Nechludoffs very well knew), I could not possibly tell you. Neither in childhood nor in adolescence nor in riper years did I ever remark in myself the vice of falsehood—on the contrary, I was, if anything, too outspoken and truthful. Yet, during this first stage of my manhood, I often found myself seized with a strange and unreasonable tendency to lie in the most desperate fashion. I say advisedly "in the most desperate fashion," for the reason that I lied in matters in which it was the easiest thing in the world to detect me. On the whole I think that a vain-glorious desire to appear different from what I was, combined with an impossible hope that the lie would never be found out, was the chief cause of this extraordinary impulse.

After tea, since the rain had stopped and the after-glow of sunset was calm and clear, the Princess proposed that we should go and stroll in the lower garden, and admire her favourite spots there. Following my rule to be always original, and conceiving that clever people like myself and the Princess must surely be above the banalities of politeness, I replied that I could not bear a walk with no object in view, and that, if I DID walk, I liked to walk alone. I had no idea that this speech was simply rude; all I thought was that, even as nothing could be more futile than empty compliments, so nothing could be more pleasing and original than a little frank brusquerie. However, though much pleased with my answer, I set out with the rest of the company.

The Princess's favourite spot of all was at the very bottom of the lower garden, where a little bridge spanned a narrow piece of swamp. The view there was very restricted, yet very intimate and pleasing. We are so accustomed to confound art with nature that, often enough, phenomena of nature which are never to be met with in pictures seem to us unreal, and give us the impression that nature is unnatural, or vice versa; whereas phenomena of nature which occur with too much frequency in pictures seem to us hackneyed, and views which are to be met with in real life, but which appear to us too penetrated with a single idea or a single sentiment, seem to us arabesques. The view from the Princess's favourite spot was as follows. On the further side of a small lake, over-grown with weeds round its edges, rose a steep ascent covered with bushes and with huge old trees of many shades of green, while, overhanging the lake at the foot of the ascent, stood an ancient birch tree which, though partly supported by stout roots implanted in the marshy bank of the lake, rested its crown upon a tall, straight poplar, and dangled its curved branches over the smooth surface of the pond—both branches and the surrounding greenery being reflected therein as in a mirror.

"How lovely!" said the Princess with a nod of her head, and addressing no one in particular.

"Yes, marvellous!" I replied in my desire to show that had an opinion of my own on every subject. "Yet somehow it all looks to me so terribly like a scheme of decoration."

The Princess went on gazing at the scene as though she had not heard me, and turning to her sister and Lubov Sergievna at intervals, in order to point out to them its details—especially a curved, pendent bough, with its reflection in the water, which particularly pleased her. Sophia Ivanovna observed to me that it was all very beautiful, and that she and her sister would sometimes spend hours together at this spot; yet it was clear that her remarks were meant merely to please the Princess. I have noticed that people who are gifted with the faculty of loving are seldom receptive to the beauties of nature. Lubov Sergievna also seemed enraptured, and asked (among other things), "How does that birch tree manage to support itself? Has it stood there long?" Yet the next moment she became absorbed in contemplation of her little dog Susetka, which, with its stumpy paws pattering to and fro upon the bridge in a mincing fashion, seemed to say by the expression of its face that this was the first time it had ever found itself out of doors. As for Dimitri, he fell to discoursing very logically to his mother on the subject of how no view can be beautiful of which the horizon is limited. Varenika alone said nothing. Glancing at her, I saw that she was leaning over the parapet of the bridge, her profile turned towards me, and gazing straight in front of her. Something seemed to be interesting her deeply, or even affecting her, since it was clear that she was oblivious to her surroundings, and thinking neither of herself nor of the fact that any one might be regarding her. In the expression of her large eyes there was nothing but wrapt attention and quiet, concentrated thought, while her whole attitude seemed so unconstrained and, for all her shortness, so dignified that once more some recollection or another touched me and once more I asked myself, "Is IT, then, beginning?" Yet again I assured myself that I was already in love with Sonetchka, and that Varenika was only an ordinary girl, the sister of my friend. Though she pleased me at that moment, I somehow felt a vague desire to show her, by word or deed, some small unfriendliness.

"I tell you what, Dimitri," I said to my friend as I moved nearer to Varenika, so that she might overhear what I was going to say, "it seems to me that, even if there had been no mosquitos here, there would have been nothing to commend this spot; whereas "—and here I slapped my cheek, and in very truth annihilated one of those insects—"it is simply awful."

"Then you do not care for nature?" said Varenika without turning her head.

"I think it a foolish, futile pursuit," I replied, well satisfied that I had said something to annoy her, as well as something original. Varenika only raised her eyebrows a little, with an expression of pity, and went on gazing in front of her as calmly as before.

I felt vexed with her. Yet, for all that, the rusty, paint-blistered parapet on which she was leaning, the way in which the dark waters of the pond reflected the drooping branch of the overhanging birch tree (it almost seemed to me as though branch and its reflection met), the rising odour of the swamp, the feeling of crushed mosquito on my cheek, and her absorbed look and statuesque pose—many times afterwards did these things recur with unexpected vividness to my recollection.

XXVII. DIMITRI

WHEN we returned to the house from our stroll, Varenika declined to sing as she usually did in the evenings, and I was conceited enough to attribute this to my doing, in the belief that its reason lay in what I had said on the bridge. The Nechludoffs never had supper, and went to bed early, while to-night, since Dimitri had the toothache (as Sophia Ivanovna had foretold), he departed with me to his room even earlier than usual. Feeling that I had done all that was required of me by my blue collar and gilt buttons, and that every one was very pleased with me, I was in a gratified, complacent mood, while Dimitri, on the other hand, was rendered by his quarrel with his sister and the toothache both taciturn and gloomy. He sat down at the table, got out a couple of notebooks—a diary and the copy-book in which it was his custom every evening to inscribe the tasks performed by or awaiting him—and, continually frowning and touching his cheek with his hand, continued writing for a while.

"Oh, DO leave me alone!" he cried to the maid whom Sophia Ivanovna sent to ask him whether his teeth were still hurting him, and whether he would not like to have a poultice made. Then, saying that my bed would soon be ready for me and that he would be back presently, he departed to Lubov Sergievna's room.

"What a pity that Varenika is not good-looking and, in general, Sonetchka!" I reflected when I found myself alone. "How nice it would be if, after I have left the University, I could go to her and offer her my hand! I would say to her, 'Princess, though no longer young, and therefore unable to love passionately, I will cherish you as a dear sister. And you,' I would continue to her mother, 'I greatly respect; and you, Sophia Ivanovna, I value highly. Therefore say to me, Varenika (since I ask you to be my wife), just the simple and direct word YES.' And she would give me her hand, and I should press it, and say, 'Mine is a love which depends not upon words, but upon deeds.' And suppose," next came into my head, "that Dimitri should suddenly fall in love with Lubotshka (as Lubotshka has already done with him), and should desire to marry her? Then either one or the other of us would have to resign all thought of marriage. Well, it would be splendid, for in that case I should act thus. As soon as I had noticed how things were, I should make no remark, but go to Dimitri and say, 'It is no use, my friend, for you and I to conceal our feelings from one another. You know that my love for your sister will terminate only with my life. Yet I know all; and though you have deprived me of all hope, and have rendered me an unhappy man, so that Nicolas Irtenieff will have to bewail his misery for the rest of his existence, yet do you take my sister,' and I should lay his hand in Lubotshka's. Then he would say to me, 'No, not for all the world!' and I should reply, 'Prince Nechludoff, it is in vain for you to attempt to outdo me in nobility. Not in the whole world does there exist a more magnanimous being than Nicolas Irtenieff.' Then I should salute him and depart. In tears Dimitri and Lubotshka would pursue me, and entreat me to accept their sacrifice, and I should consent to do so, and, perhaps, be happy ever afterwards—if only I were in love with Varenika." These fancies tickled my imagination so pleasantly that I felt as though I should like to communicate them to my friend; yet, despite our mutual vow of frankness, I also felt as though I had not the physical energy to do so.

Dimitri returned from Lubov Sergievna's room with some toothache capsules which she had given him, yet in even greater pain, and therefore in even greater depression, than before. Evidently no bedroom had yet been prepared for me, for presently the boy who acted as Dimitri's valet arrived to ask him where I was to sleep.

"Oh, go to the devil!" cried Dimitri, stamping his foot. "Vasika, Vasika, Vasika!" he went on, the instant that the boy had left the room, with a gradual raising of his voice at each repetition. "Vasika, lay me out a bed on the floor."

"No, let ME sleep on the floor," I objected.

"Well, it is all one. Lie anywhere you like," continued Dimitri in the same angry tone. "Vasika, why don't you go and do what I tell you?"

Evidently Vasika did not understand what was demanded of him, for he remained where he was.

"What is the matter with you? Go and lay the bed, Vasika, I tell you!" shouted Dimitri, suddenly bursting into a sort of frenzy; yet Vasika still did not understand, but, blushing hotly, stood motionless.

"So you are determined to drive me mad, are you?"—and leaping from his chair and rushing upon the boy, Dimitri struck him on the head with the whole weight of his fist, until the boy rushed headlong from the room. Halting in the doorway, Dimitri glanced at me, and the expression of fury and pain which had sat for a moment on his countenance suddenly gave place to such a boyish, kindly, affectionate, yet ashamed, expression that I felt sorry for him, and reconsidered my intention of leaving him to himself. He said nothing, but for a long time paced the room in silence, occasionally glancing at me with the same deprecatory expression as before. Then he took his notebook from the table, wrote something in it, took off his jacket and folded it carefully, and, stepping into the corner where the ikon hung, knelt down and began to say his prayers, with his large white hands folded upon his breast. So long did he pray that Vasika had time to bring a mattress and spread it, under my whispered directions, on the floor. Indeed, I had undressed and laid myself down upon the mattress before Dimitri had finished. As I contemplated his slightly rounded back and the soles of his feet (which somehow seemed to stick out in my direction in a sort of repentant fashion whenever he made his obeisances), I felt that I liked him more than ever, and debated within myself whether or not I should tell him all I had been fancying concerning our respective sisters. When he had finished his prayers, he lay down upon the bed near me, and, propping himself upon his elbow, looked at me in silence, with a kindly, yet abashed, expression. Evidently he found it difficult to do this, yet meant thus to punish himself. Then I smiled and returned his gaze, and he smiled back at me.

"Why do you not tell me that my conduct has been abominable?" he said. "You have been thinking so, have you not?"

"Yes," I replied; and although it was something quite different which had been in my mind, it now seemed to me that that was what I had been thinking. "Yes, it was not right of you, nor should I have expected it of you." It pleased me particularly at that moment to call him by the familiar second person singular. "But how are your teeth now?" I added.

"Oh, much better. Nicolinka, my friend," he went on, and so feelingly that it sounded as though tears were standing in his eyes, "I know and feel that I am bad, but God sees how I try to be better, and how I entreat Him to make me so. Yet what am I to do with such an unfortunate, horrible nature as mine? What am I to do with it? I try to keep myself in hand and to rule myself, but suddenly it becomes impossible for me to do so—at all events, impossible for me to do so unaided. I need the help and support of some one. Now, there is Lubov Sergievna; SHE understands me, and could help me in this, and I know by my notebook that I have greatly improved in this respect during the past year. Ah, my dear Nicolinka"—he spoke with the most unusual and unwonted tenderness, and in a tone which had grown calmer now that he had made his confession—"how much the influence of a woman like Lubov could do for me! Think how good it would be for me if I could have a friend like her to live with when I have become independent! With her I should be another man."

And upon that Dimitri began to unfold to me his plans for marriage, for a life in the country, and for continual self-discipline.

"Yes, I will live in the country," he said, "and you shall come to see me when you have married Sonetchka. Our children shall play together. All this may seem to you stupid and ridiculous, yet it may very well come to pass."

"Yes, it very well may" I replied with a smile, yet thinking how much nicer it would be if I married his sister.

"I tell you what," he went on presently; "you only imagine yourself to be in love with Sonetchka, whereas I can see that it is all rubbish, and that you do not really know what love means."

I did not protest, for, in truth, I almost agreed with him, and for a while we lay without speaking.

"Probably you have noticed that I have been in my old bad humour today, and have had a nasty quarrel with Varia?" he resumed. "I felt bad about it afterwards—more particularly since it occurred in your presence. Although she thinks wrongly on some subjects, she is a splendid girl and very good, as you will soon recognise."

His quick transition from mention of my love affairs to praise of his sister pleased me extremely, and made me blush, but I nevertheless said nothing more about his sister, and we went on talking of other things.

Thus we chattered until the cocks had crowed twice. In fact, the pale dawn was already looking in at the window when at last Dimitri lay down upon his bed and put out the candle.

"Well, now for sleep," he said.

"Yes," I replied, "but—"

"But what?"

"Now nice it is to be alive in the daylight!"

"Yes, it IS a splendid thing!" he replied in a voice which, even in the darkness, enabled me to see the expression of his cheerful, kindly eyes and boyish smile.

XXVIII. IN THE COUNTRY

Next day Woloda and myself departed in a post-chaise for the country. Turning over various Moscow recollections in my head as we drove along, I suddenly recalled Sonetchka Valakhin—though not until evening, and when we had already covered five stages of the road. "It is a strange thing," I thought, "that I should be in love, and yet have forgotten all about it. I must start and think about her," and straightway I proceeded to do so, but only in the way that one thinks when travelling—that is to say, disconnectedly, though vividly. Thus I brought myself to such a condition that, for the first two days after our arrival home, I somehow considered it incumbent upon me always to appear sad and moody in the presence of the household, and especially before Katenka, whom I looked upon as a great connoisseur in matters of this kind, and to whom I threw out a hint of the condition in which my heart was situated. Yet, for all my attempts at dissimulation and assiduous adoption of such signs of love sickness as I had occasionally observed in other people, I only succeeded for two days (and that at intervals, and mostly towards evening) in reminding myself of the fact that I was in love, and finally, when I had settled down into the new rut of country life and pursuits, I forgot about my affection for Sonetchka altogether.

We arrived at Petrovskoe in the night time, and I was then so soundly asleep that I saw nothing of the house as we approached it, nor yet of the avenue of birch trees, nor yet of the household—all of whom had long ago betaken themselves to bed and to slumber. Only old hunchbacked Foka—bare-footed, clad in some sort of a woman's wadded nightdress, and carrying a candlestick—opened the door to us. As soon as he saw who we were, he trembled all over with joy, kissed us on the shoulders, hurriedly put on his felt slippers, and started to dress himself properly. I passed in a semi-waking condition through the porch and up the steps, but in the hall the lock of the door, the bars and bolts, the crooked boards of the flooring, the chest, the ancient candelabrum (splashed all over with grease as of old), the shadows thrown by the crooked, chill, recently-lighted stump of candle, the perennially dusty, unopened window behind which I remembered sorrel to have grown—all was so familiar, so full of memories, so intimate of aspect, so, as it were, knit together by a single idea, that I suddenly became conscious of a tenderness for this quiet old house. Involuntarily I asked myself, "How have we, the house and I, managed to remain apart so long?" and, hurrying from spot to spot, ran to see if all the other rooms were still the same. Yes, everything was unchanged, except that everything had become smaller and lower, and I myself taller, heavier, and more filled out. Yet, even as I was, the old house received me back into its arms, and aroused in me with every board, every window, every step of the stairs, and every sound the shadows of forms, feelings, and events of the happy but irrevocable past. When we entered our old night nursery, all my childish fears lurked once more in the darkness of the corners and doorway. When we passed into the drawing-room, I could feel the old calm motherly love diffusing itself from every object in the apartment. In the breakfast-room, the noisy, careless merriment of childhood seemed merely to be waiting to wake to life again. In the divannaia (whither Foka first conducted us, and where he had prepared our beds) everything— mirror, screen, old wooden ikon, the lumps on the walls covered with white paper—seemed to speak of suffering and of death and of what would never come back to us again.

We got into bed, and Foka, bidding us good-night, retired.

"It was in this room that Mamma died, was it not?" said Woloda.

I made no reply, but pretended to be asleep. If I had said anything I should have burst into tears. On awaking next morning, I beheld Papa sitting on Woloda's bed in his dressing gown and slippers and smoking a cigar. Leaping up with a merry hoist of the shoulders, he came over to me, slapped me on the back with his great hand, and presented me his cheek to press my lips to.

"Well done, DIPLOMAT!" he said in his most kindly jesting tone as he looked at me with his small bright eyes. "Woloda tells me you have passed the examinations well for a youngster, and that is a splendid thing. Unless you start and play the fool, I shall have another fine little fellow in you.

Thanks, my dear boy. Well, we will have a grand time of it here now, and in the winter, perhaps, we shall move to St. Petersburg. I only wish the hunting was not over yet, or I could have given you some amusement in THAT way. Can you shoot, Woldemar? However, whether there is any game or not, I will take you out some day. Next winter, if God pleases, we will move to St. Petersburg, and you shall meet people, and make friends, for you are now my two young grown-ups. I have been telling Woldemar that you are just starting on your careers, whereas my day is ended. You are old enough now to walk by yourselves, but, whenever you wish to confide in me, pray do so, for I am no longer your nurse, but your friend. At least, I will be your friend and comrade and adviser as much as I can and more than that I cannot do. How does that fall in with your philosophy, eh, Koko? Well or ill, eh?"

Of course I said that it fell in with it entirely, and, indeed, I really thought so. That morning Papa had a particularly winning, bright, and happy expression on his face, and these new relations between us, as of equals and comrades, made me love him all the more.

"Now, tell me," he went on, "did you call upon all our kinsfolk and the Iwins? Did you see the old man, and what did he say to you? And did you go to Prince Ivan's?"

We continued talking so long that, before we were fully dressed, the sun had left the window of the divannaia, and Jakoff (the same old man who of yore had twirled his fingers behind his back and always repeated his words) had entered the room and reported to Papa that the carriage was ready.

"Where are you going to?" I asked Papa.

"Oh, I had forgotten all about it!" he replied, with a cough and the usual hoisting of his shoulder. "I promised to go and call upon Epifanova to-day. You remember Epifanova—'la belle Flamande'—don't you, who used to come and see your Mamma? They are nice people." And with a self-conscious shrug of his shoulders (so it appeared to me) Papa left the room.

During our conversation, Lubotshka had more than once come to the door and asked "Can I come in?" but Papa had always shouted to her that she could not do so, since we were not dressed yet.

"What rubbish!" she replied. "Why, I have seen you in your dressing-gown."

"Never mind; you cannot see your brothers without their inexpressibles," rejoined Papa. "If they each of them just go to the door, let that be enough for you. Now go. Even for them to SPEAK to you in such a neglige costume is unbecoming."

"How unbearable you are!" was Lubotshka's parting retort. "Well, at least hurry up and come down to the drawing-room, for Mimi wants to see them."

As soon as Papa had left the room, I hastened to array myself in my student's uniform, and to repair to the drawing-room.

Woloda, on the other hand, was in no hurry, but remained sitting on his bed and talking to Jakoff about the best places to find plover and snipe. As I have said, there was nothing in the world he so much feared as to be suspected of any affection for his father, brother, and sister; so that, to escape any expression of that feeling, he often fell into the other extreme, and affected a coldness which shocked people who did not comprehend its cause. In the hall, I collided with Papa, who was hurrying towards the carriage with short, rapid steps. He had a new and fashionable Moscow greatcoat on, and smelt of scent. On seeing me, he gave a cheerful nod, as much as to say, "Do you remark my splendour?" and once again I was struck with the happy expression of face which I had noted earlier in the morning.

The drawing-room looked the same lofty, bright room as of Yore, with its brown English piano, and its large open windows looking on to the green trees and yellowish-red paths of the garden. After kissing Mimi and Lubotshka, I was approaching Katenka for the same purpose when it suddenly struck me that it might be improper for me to salute her in that fashion. Accordingly I halted, silent and blushing. Katenka, for her part, was quite at her ease as she held out a white hand to me and congratulated me on my passing into the University. The same thing took place when Woloda entered the drawing-room and met Katenka. Indeed, it was something of a problem how, after being brought up together and seeing one another daily, we ought now, after this first separation, to meet again. Katenka had grown better-looking than any of us, yet Woloda seemed not at all confused as, with a slight bow to her, he crossed over to Lubotshka, made a jesting remark to her, and then departed somewhere on some solitary expedition.

XXIX. RELATIONS BETWEEN THE GIRLS AND OURSELVES

OF the girls Woloda took the strange view that, although he wished that they should have enough to eat, should sleep well, be well dressed, and avoid making such mistakes in French as would shame him before strangers, he would never admit that they could think or feel like human beings, still less that they could converse with him sensibly about anything. Whenever they addressed to him a serious question (a thing, by the way, which he always tried to avoid), such as asking his opinion on a novel or inquiring about his doings at the University, he invariably pulled a grimace, and either turned away without speaking or answered with some nonsensical French phrase— "Comme c'est tres jolie!" or the like. Or again, feigning to look serious and stolidly wise, he would say something absolutely meaningless and bearing no relation whatever to the question asked him, or else suddenly exclaim, with a look of pretended unconsciousness, the word bulku or poyechali or kapustu, [Respectively, "roll of butter," "away," and "cabbage."] or something of the kind; and when, afterwards, I happened to repeat these words to him as having been told me by Lubotshka or Katenka, he would always remark:

"Hm! So you actually care about talking to them? I can see you are a duffer still"—and one needed to see and near him to appreciate the profound, immutable contempt which echoed in this remark. He had been grown-up now two years, and was in love with every good-looking woman that he met; yet, despite the fact that he came in daily contact with Katenka (who during those two years had been wearing long dresses, and was growing prettier every day), the possibility of his falling in love with her never seemed to enter his head. Whether this proceeded from the fact that the prosaic recollections of childhood were still too fresh in his memory, or whether from the aversion which very young people feel for everything domestic, or whether from the common human weakness which, at a first encounter with anything fair and pretty, leads a man to say to himself, "Ah! I shall meet much more of the same kind during my life," but at all events Woloda had never yet looked upon Katenka with a man's eyes.

All that summer Woloda appeared to find things very wearisome—a fact which arose out of that contempt for us all which, as I have said, he made no effort to conceal. His expression of face seemed to be constantly saying, "Phew! how it bores me to have no one to speak to!" The first thing in the morning he would go out shooting, or sit reading a book in his room, and not dress until luncheon time. Indeed, if Papa was not at home, he would take his book into that meal, and go on reading it without addressing so much as a single word to any one of us, who felt, somehow, guilty in his presence. In the evening, too, he would stretch himself on a settee in the drawing-room, and either go to sleep, propped on his elbow, or tell us farcical stories—sometimes stories so improper as to make Mimi grow angry and blush, and ourselves die with laughter. At other times he would not condescend to address a single serious word to any member of the family except Papa or (occasionally) myself. Involuntarily I offended against his view of girls, seeing that I was not so afraid of seeming affectionate as he, and, moreover, had not such a profound and confirmed contempt for young women. Yet several times that summer, when driven by lack of amusement to try and engage Lubotshka and Katenka in conversation, I always encountered in them such an absence of any capacity for logical thinking, and such an ignorance of the simplest, most ordinary matters (as, for instance, the nature of money, the subjects studied at universities, the effect of war, and so forth), as well as such indifference to my explanations of such matters, that these attempts of mine only ended in confirming my unfavourable opinion of feminine ability.

I remember one evening when Lubotshka kept repeating some unbearably tedious passage on the piano about a hundred times in succession, while Woloda, who was dozing on a settee in the drawing-room, kept addressing no one in particular as he muttered, "Lord! how she murders it! WHAT a musician! WHAT a Beethoven!" (he always pronounced the composer's name with especial irony). "Wrong again! Now—a second time! That's it!" and so on. Meanwhile Katenka and I were sitting by the tea-table, and somehow she began to talk about her favourite subject—love. I was in the right frame of mind to philosophise, and began by loftily defining love as the wish to acquire in another what one does not possess in oneself. To this Katenka retorted that, on the contrary, love is not love at all if a girl desires to marry a man for his money alone, but that, in her opinion, riches were a vain thing, and true love only the affection which can stand the test of separation (this I took to be a hint concerning her love for Dubkoff). At this point Woloda, who must have been listening all the time, raised himself on his elbow, and cried out some rubbish or another; and I felt that he was right.

Apart from the general faculties (more or less developed in different persons) of intellect, sensibility, and artistic feeling, there also exists (more or less developed in different circles of society, and especially in families) a private or individual faculty which I may call APPREHENSION. The essence of this faculty lies in sympathetic appreciation of proportion, and in identical understanding of things. Two individuals who possess this faculty and belong to the same social circle or the same family apprehend an expression of feeling precisely to the same point, namely, the point beyond which such expression becomes mere phrasing. Thus they apprehend precisely where commendation ends and irony begins, where attraction ends and pretence begins, in a manner which would be impossible for persons possessed of a different order of apprehension. Persons possessed of identical apprehension view objects in an identically ludicrous, beautiful, or repellent light; and in order to facilitate such identical apprehension between members of the same social circle or family, they usually establish a language, turns of speech, or terms to define such shades of apprehension as exist for them alone. In our particular family such apprehension was common to Papa, Woloda, and myself, and was developed to the highest pitch, Dubkoff also approximated to our coterie in apprehension, but Dimitri, though infinitely more intellectual than Dubkoff, was grosser in this respect. With no one, however, did I bring this faculty to such a point as with Woloda, who had grown up with me under identical conditions. Papa stood a long way from us, and much that was to us as clear as "two and two make four" was to him incomprehensible. For instance, I and Woloda managed to establish between ourselves the following terms, with meanings to correspond. Izium [Raisins.] meant a desire to boast of one's money; shishka [Bump or swelling.] (on pronouncing which one had to join one's fingers together, and to put a particular emphasis upon the two sh's in the word) meant anything fresh, healthy, and comely, but not elegant; a substantive used in the plural meant an undue partiality for the object which it denoted; and so forth, and so forth. At the same time, the meaning depended considerably upon the expression of the face and the context of the conversation; so that, no matter what new expression one of us might invent to define a shade of feeling the other could immediately understand it by a hint alone. The girls did not share this faculty of apprehension, and herein lay the chief cause of our moral estrangement, and of the contempt which we felt for them.

It may be that they too had their "apprehension," but it so little ran with ours that, where we already perceived the "phrasing," they still saw only the feeling—our irony was for them truth, and so on. At that time I had not yet learnt to understand that they were in no way to blame for this, and that absence of such apprehension in no way prevented them from being good and clever girls. Accordingly I looked down upon them. Moreover, having once lit upon my precious idea of "frankness," and being bent upon applying it to the full in myself, I thought the quiet, confiding nature of Lubotshka guilty of secretiveness and dissimulation simply because she saw no necessity for digging up and examining all her thoughts and instincts. For instance, the fact that she always signed the sign of the cross over Papa before going to bed, that she and Katenka invariably wept in church when attending requiem masses for Mamma, and that Katenka sighed and rolled her eyes about when playing the piano—all these things seemed to me sheer make-believe, and I asked myself: "At what period did they learn to pretend like grown-up people, and how can they bring themselves to do it?"

XXX. HOW I EMPLOYED MY TIME

Nevertheless, the fact that that summer I developed a passion for music caused me to become better friends with the ladies of our household than I had been for years. In the spring, a young fellow came to see us, armed with a letter of introduction, who, as soon as ever he entered the drawing-room, fixed his eyes upon the piano, and kept gradually edging his chair closer to it as he talked to Mimi and Katenka. After discoursing awhile of the weather and the amenities of country life, he skilfully directed the conversation to piano-tuners, music, and pianos generally, and ended by saying that he himself played—and in truth he did sit down and perform three waltzes, with Mimi, Lubotshka, and Katenka grouped about the instrument, and watching him as he did so. He never came to see us again, but his playing, and his attitude when at the piano, and the way in which he kept shaking his long hair, and, most of all, the manner in which he was able to execute octaves with his left hand as he first of all played them rapidly with his thumb and little finger, and then slowly closed those members, and then played the octaves afresh, made a great impression upon me. This graceful gesture of his, together with his easy pose and his shaking of hair and successful winning of the ladies' applause by his talent, ended by firing me to take up the piano. Convinced that I possessed both talent and a passion for music, I set myself to learn, and, in doing so, acted just as millions of the male—still more, of the female—sex have done who try to teach themselves without a skilled instructor, without any real turn for the art, or without the smallest understanding either of what the art can give or of what ought to be done to obtain that gift. For me music (or rather, piano-playing) was simply a means of winning the ladies' good graces through their sensibility. With the help of Katenka I first learnt the notes (incidentally breaking several of them with my clumsy fingers), and then—that is to say, after two months of hard work, supplemented by ceaseless twiddling of my rebellious fingers on my knees after luncheon, and on the pillow when in bed—went on to "pieces," which I played (so Katenka assured me) with "soul" ("avec ame"), but altogether regardless of time.

My range of pieces was the usual one—waltzes, galops, "romances," "arrangements," etcetera; all of them of the class of delightful compositions of which any one with a little healthy taste could point out a selection among the better class works contained in any volume of music and say, "These are what you ought NOT to play, seeing that anything worse, less tasteful, and more silly has never yet been included in any collection of music,"—but which (probably for that very reason) are to be found on the piano of every Russian lady. True, we also possessed an unfortunate volume which contained Beethoven's "Sonate Pathetique" and the C minor Sonata (a volume lamed for life by the ladies—more especially by Lubotshka, who used to discourse music from it in memory of Mamma), as well as certain other good pieces which her teacher in Moscow had given her; but among that collection there were likewise compositions of the teacher's own, in the shape of clumsy marches and galops—and these too Lubotshka used to play! Katenka and I cared nothing for serious works, but preferred, above all things, "Le Fou" and "The Nightingale"—the latter of which Katenka would play until her fingers almost became invisible, and which I too was beginning to execute with much vigour and some continuity. I had adopted the gestures of the young man of whom I have spoken, and frequently regretted that there were no strangers present to see me play. Soon, however, I began to realise that Liszt and Kalkbrenner were beyond me, and that I should never overtake Katenka. Accordingly, imagining that classical music was easier (as well as, partly, for the sake of originality), I suddenly came to the conclusion that I loved abstruse German music. I began to go into raptures whenever Lubotshka played the "Sonate Pathetique," and although (if the truth be told) that work had for years driven me to the verge of distraction, I set myself to play Beethoven, and to talk of him as "Beethoven." Yet through all this chopping and changing and pretence (as I now conceive) there may have run in me a certain vein of talent, since music sometimes affected me even to tears, and things which particularly pleased me I could strum on the piano afterwards (in a certain fashion) without the score; so that, had any one taught me at that period to look upon music as an end, a grace, in itself, and not merely as a means for pleasing womenfolk with the velocity and pseudo-sentiment of one's playing, I might possibly have become a passable musician.

The reading of French novels (of which Woloda had brought a large store with him from Moscow) was another of my amusements that summer. At that period Monte Cristo and Taine's works had just appeared, while I also revelled in stories by Sue, Dumas, and Paul de Kock. Even their most unnatural personages and events were for me as real as actuality, and not only was I incapable of suspecting an author of lying, but, in my eyes, there existed no author at all. That is to say, the various personages and events of a book paraded themselves before me on the printed page as personages and events that were alive and real; and although I had never in my life met such characters as I there read about, I never for a second doubted that I should one day do so. I discovered in myself all the passions described in every novel, as well as a likeness to all the characters—heroes and villains impartially— who figured therein, just as a suspicious man finds in himself the signs of every possible disease when reading a book on medicine. I took pleasure both in the cunning designs, the glowing sentiments, the tumultuous events, and the character-drawing of these works. A good man was of the goodness, a bad man of the badness, possible only to the imagination of early youth. Likewise I found great pleasure in the fact that it was all written in French, and that I could lay to heart the fine words which the fine heroes spoke, and recall them for use some day when engaged in some noble deed. What quantities of French phrases I culled from those books for Kolpikoff's benefit if I should ever meet him again, as well as for HERS, when at length I should find her and reveal to her my love! For them both I prepared speeches which should overcome them as soon as spoken! Upon novels, too, I founded new ideals of the moral qualities which I wished to attain. First of all, I wished to be NOBLE in all my deeds and conduct (I use the French word noble instead of the Russian word blagorodni for the reason that the former has a different meaning to the latter—as the Germans well understood when they adopted noble as nobel and differentiated it from ehrlich); next, to be strenuous; and lastly, to be what I was already inclined to be, namely, comme il faut. I even tried to approximate my appearance and bearing to that of the heroes who possessed these qualities. In particular I remember how in one of the hundred or so novels which I read that summer there was a very strenuous hero with heavy eyebrows, and that I so greatly wished to resemble him (I felt that I did so already from a moral point of view) that one day, when looking at my eyebrows in the glass, I conceived the idea of clipping them, in order to make them grow bushier. Unfortunately, after I had started to do so, I happened to clip one spot rather shorter than the rest, and so had to level down the rest to it-with the result that, to my horror, I beheld myself eyebrow-less, and anything but presentable. However, I comforted myself with the reflection that my eyebrows would soon sprout again as bushy as my hero's, and was only perplexed to think how I could explain the circumstance to the household when they next perceived my eyebrow-less condition. Accordingly I borrowed some gunpowder from Woloda, rubbed it on my temples, and set it alight. The powder did not fire properly, but I succeeded in singeing myself sufficiently to avert all suspicion of my pranks. And, indeed, afterwards, when I had forgotten all about my hero, my eyebrows grew again, and much thicker than they had been before.

XXXI. "COMME IL FAUT"

SEVERAL times in the course of this narrative I have hinted at an idea corresponding to the above French heading, and now feel it incumbent upon me to devote a whole chapter to that idea, which was one of the most ruinous, lying notions which ever became engrafted upon my life by my upbringing and social milieu.

The human race may be divided into several categories—rich and poor, good and bad, military and civilian, clever and stupid, and so forth, and so forth. Yet each man has his own favourite, fundamental system of division which he unconsciously uses to class each new person with whom he meets. At the time of which I am speaking, my own favourite, fundamental system of division in this respect was into people "comme il faut" and people "comme il ne faut pas"—the latter subdivided, again, into people merely not "comme il faut" and the lower orders. People "comme il faut" I respected, and looked upon as worthy to consort with me as my equals; the second of the above categories I pretended merely to despise, but in reality hated, and nourished towards them a kind of feeling of offended personality; while the third category had no existence at all, so far as I was concerned, since my contempt for them was too complete. This "comme il faut"-ness of mine lay, first and foremost, in proficiency in French, especially conversational French. A person who spoke that language badly at once aroused in me a feeling of dislike. "Why do you try to talk as we do when you haven't a notion how to do it?" I would seem to ask him with my most venomous and quizzing smile. The second condition of "comme il faut"-ness was long nails that were well kept and clean; the third, ability to bow, dance, and converse; the fourth—and a very important one—indifference to everything, and a constant air of refined, supercilious ennui. Moreover, there were certain general signs which, I considered, enabled me to tell, without actually speaking to a man, the class to which he belonged. Chief among these signs (the others being the fittings of his rooms, his gloves, his handwriting, his turn-out, and so forth) were his feet. The relation of boots to trousers was sufficient to determine, in my eyes, the social status of a man. Heelless boots with angular toes, wedded to narrow, unstrapped trouser-ends—these denoted the vulgarian. Boots with narrow, round toes and heels, accompanied either by tight trousers strapped under the instep and fitting close to the leg or by wide trousers similarly strapped, but projecting in a peak over the toe—these meant the man of mauvais genre; and so on, and so on.

It was a curious thing that I who lacked all ability to become "comme il faut," should have assimilated the idea so completely as I did. Possibly it was the fact that it had cost me such enormous labour to acquire that brought about its strenuous development in my mind. I hardly like to think how much of the best and most valuable time of my first sixteen years of existence I wasted upon its acquisition. Yet every one whom I imitated—Woloda, Dubkoff, and the majority of my acquaintances—seemed to acquire it easily. I watched them with envy, and silently toiled to become proficient in French, to bow gracefully and without looking at the person whom I was saluting, to gain dexterity in small-talk and dancing, to cultivate indifference and ennui, and to keep my fingernails well trimmed (though I frequently cut my finger-ends with the scissors in so doing). And all the time I felt that so much remained to be done if I was ever to attain my end! A room, a writing-table, an equipage I still found it impossible to arrange "comme il faut," however much I fought down my aversion to practical matters in my desire to become proficient. Yet everything seemed to arrange itself properly with other people, just as though things could never have been otherwise! Once I remember asking Dubkoff, after much zealous and careful labouring at my finger-nails (his own were extraordinarily good), whether his nails had always been as now, or whether he had done anything to make them so: to which he replied that never within his recollection had he done anything to them, and that he could not imagine a gentleman's nails possibly being different. This answer incensed me greatly, for I had not yet learnt that one of the chief conditions of "comme il faut"-ness was to hold one's tongue about the labour by which it had been acquired. "Comme il faut"-ness I looked upon as not only a great merit, a splendid accomplishment, an embodiment of all the perfection which must strive to attain, but as the one indispensable condition without which there could never be happiness, nor glory, nor any good whatsoever in this world. Even the greatest artist or savant or benefactor of the human race would at that time have won from me no respect if he had not also been "comme il faut." A man possessed of "comme il faut"-ness stood higher than, and beyond all possible equality with, such people, and might well leave it to them to paint pictures, to compose music, to write books, or to do good. Possibly he might commend them for so doing (since why should not merit be commended where-ever it be found?), but he could never stand ON A LEVEL with them, seeing that he was "comme il faut" and they were not—a quite final and sufficient reason. In fact, I actually believe that, had we possessed a brother or a father or a mother who had not been "comme il faut," I should have declared it to be a great misfortune for us, and announced that between myself and them there could never be anything in common. Yet neither waste of the golden hours which I consumed in constantly endeavouring to observe the many arduous, unattainable conditions of "comme il faut"-ness (to the exclusion of any more serious pursuit), nor dislike of and contempt for nine-tenths of the human race, nor disregard of all the beauty that lay outside the narrow circle of "comme il faut"-ness comprised the whole of the evil which the idea wrought in me. The chief evil of all lay in the notion acquired that a man need not strive to become a tchinovnik, [Official.] a coachbuilder, a soldier, a savant, or anything useful, so long only as he was "comme il faut "—that by attaining the latter quality he had done all that was demanded of him, and was even superior to most people.

Usually, at a given period in youth, and after many errors and excesses, every man recognises the necessity of his taking an active part in social life, and chooses some branch of labour to which to devote himself. Only with the "comme il faut" man does this rarely happen. I have known, and know, very, very many people—old, proud, self-satisfied, and opinionated—who to the question (if it should ever present itself to them in their world) "Who have you been, and what have you ever done?" would be unable to reply otherwise than by saying,

"Je fus un homme tres comme il faut,"

Such a fate was awaiting myself.

XXXII. YOUTH

Despite the confusion of ideas raging in my head, I was at least young, innocent, and free that summer—consequently almost happy.

Sometimes I would rise quite early in the morning, for I slept on the open verandah, and the bright, horizontal beams of the morning sun would wake me up. Dressing myself quickly, I would tuck a towel and a French novel under my arm, and go off to bathe in the river in the shade of a birch tree which stood half a verst from the house. Next, I would stretch myself on the grass and read—raising my eyes from time to time to look at the surface of the river where it showed blue in the shade of the trees, at the ripples caused by the first morning breeze, at the yellowing field of rye on the further bank, and at the bright-red sheen of the sunlight as it struck lower and lower down the white trunks of the birch-trees which, ranged in ranks one behind the other, gradually receded into the remote distance of the home park. At such moments I would feel joyously conscious of having within me the same young, fresh force of life as nature was everywhere exuding around me. When, however, the sky was overcast with grey clouds of morning and I felt chilly after bathing, I would often start to walk at random through the fields and woods, and joyously trail my wet boots in the fresh dew. All the while my head would be filled with vivid dreams concerning the heroes of my last-read novel, and I would keep picturing to myself some leader of an army or some statesman or marvellously strong man or devoted lover or another, and looking round me in, a nervous expectation that I should suddenly descry HER somewhere near me, in a meadow or behind a tree. Yet, whenever these rambles led me near peasants engaged at their work, all my ignoring of the existence of the "common people" did not prevent me from experiencing an involuntary, overpowering sensation of awkwardness; so that I always tried to avoid their seeing me. When the heat of the day had increased, it was not infrequently my habit—if the ladies did not come out of doors for their morning tea—to go rambling through the orchard and kitchen-garden, and to pluck ripe fruit there. Indeed, this was an occupation which furnished me with one of my greatest pleasures. Let any one go into an orchard, and dive into the midst of a tall, thick, sprouting raspberry-bed. Above will be seen the clear, glowing sky, and, all around, the pale-green, prickly stems of raspberry-trees where they grow mingled together in a tangle of profusion. At one's feet springs the dark-green nettle, with its slender crown of flowers, while the broad-leaved burdock, with its bright-pink, prickly blossoms, overtops the raspberries (and even one's head) with its luxuriant masses, until, with the nettle, it almost meets the pendent, pale-green branches of the old apple-trees where apples, round and lustrous as bone, but as yet unripe, are mellowing in the heat of the sun. Below, again, are seen young raspberry-shoots, twining themselves around the partially withered, leafless parent plant, and stretching their tendrils towards the sunlight, with green, needle-shaped blades of grass and young, dew-coated pods peering through last year's leaves, and growing juicily green in the perennial shade, as though they care nothing for the bright sunshine which is playing on the leaves of the apple-trees above them. In this density there is always moisture—always a smell of confined, perpetual shade, of cobwebs, fallen apples (turning black where they roll on the mouldy sod), raspberries, and earwigs of the kind which impel one to reach hastily for more fruit when one has inadvertently swallowed a member of that insect tribe with the last berry. At every step one's movements keep flushing the sparrows which always make their home in these depths, and one hears their fussy chirping and the beating of their tiny, fluttering wings against the stalks, and catches the low buzzing of a bumble bee somewhere, and the sound of the gardener's footsteps (it is half-daft Akim) on the path as he hums his eternal sing-song to himself. Then one mutters under one's breath, "No! Neither he nor any one else shall find me here!" yet still one goes on stripping juicy berries from their conical white pilasters, and cramming them into one's mouth. At length, one's legs soaked to the knees as one repeats, over and over again, some rubbish which keeps running in one's head, and one's hands and nether limbs (despite the protection of one's wet trousers) thoroughly stung with the nettles, one comes to the conclusion that the sun's rays are beating too straight upon one's head for eating to be any longer desirable, and, sinking down into the tangle of greenery, one remains there—looking and listening, and continuing in mechanical fashion to strip off one or two of

413

the finer berries and swallow them.

At eleven o'clock—that is to say, when the ladies had taken their morning tea and settled down to their occupations—I would repair to the drawing-room. Near the first window, with its unbleached linen blind lowered to exclude the sunshine, but through the chink of which the sun kept throwing brilliant circles of light which hurt the eye to look at them, there would be standing a screen, with flies quietly parading the whiteness of its covering. Behind it would be seated Mimi, shaking her head in an irritable manner, and constantly shifting from spot to spot to avoid the sunshine as at intervals it darted her from somewhere and laid a streak of flame upon her hand or face. Through the other three windows the sun would be throwing three squares of light, crossed with the shadows of the window-frames, and where one of these patches marked the unstained floor of the room there would be lying, in accordance with invariable custom, Milka, with her ears pricked as she watched the flies promenading the lighted space. Seated on a settee, Katenka would be knitting or reading aloud as from time to time she gave her white sleeves (looking almost transparent in the sunshine) an impatient shake, or tossed her head with a frown to drive away some fly which had settled upon her thick auburn hair and was now buzzing in its tangles. Lubotshka would either be walking up and down the room (her hands clasped behind her) until the moment should arrive when a movement would be made towards the garden, or playing some piece of which every note had long been familiar to me. For my own part, I would sit down somewhere, and listen to the music or the reading until such time as I myself should have an opportunity of performing on the piano. After luncheon I would condescend to take the girls out riding (since to go for a mere walk at that hour seemed to me unsuitable to my years and position in the world), and these excursions of ours—in which I often took my companions through unaccustomed spots and dells— were very pleasant. Indeed, on some of these occasions I grew quite boyish, and the girls would praise my riding and daring, and pretend that I was their protector. In the evening, if we had no guests with us, tea (served in the dim verandah), would be followed by a walk round the homestead with Papa, and then I would stretch myself on my usual settee, and read and ponder as of old, as I listened to Katenka or Lubotshka playing. At other times, if

I was alone in the drawing-room and Lubotshka was performing some old-time air, I would find myself laying my book down, and gazing through the open doorway on to the balcony at the pendent, sinuous branches of the tall birch-trees where they stood overshadowed by the coming night, and at the clear sky where, if one looked at it intently enough, misty, yellowish spots would appear suddenly, and then disappear again. Next, as I listened to the sounds of the music wafted from the salon, and to the creaking of gates and the voices of the peasant women when the cattle returned to the village, I would suddenly bethink me of Natalia Savishna and of Mamma and of Karl Ivanitch, and become momentarily sad. But in those days my spirit was so full of life and hope that such reminiscences only touched me in passing, and soon fled away again.

After supper and (sometimes) a night stroll with some one in the garden (for I was afraid to walk down the dark avenues by myself), I would repair to my solitary sleeping-place on the verandah—a proceeding which, despite the countless mosquitos which always devoured me, afforded me the greatest pleasure. If the moon was full, I frequently spent whole nights sitting up on my mattress, looking at the light and shade, listening to the sounds or stillness, dreaming of one matter and another (but more particularly of the poetic, voluptuous happiness which, in those days, I believed was to prove the acme of my felicity) and lamenting that until now it had only been given to me to IMAGINE things. No sooner had every one dispersed, and I had seen lights pass from the drawing-room to the upper chambers (whence female voices would presently be heard, and the noise of windows opening and shutting), than I would depart to the verandah, and walk up and down there as I listened attentively to the sounds from the slumbering mansion. To this day, whenever I feel any expectation (no matter how small and baseless) of realising a fraction of some happiness of which I may be dreaming, I somehow invariably fail to picture to myself what the imagined happiness is going to be like.

At the least sound of bare footsteps, or of a cough, or of a snore, or of the rattling of a window, or of the rustling of a dress, I would leap from my mattress, and stand furtively gazing and listening, thrown, without any visible cause, into extreme agitation. But the lights would disappear from the upper rooms, the sounds of footsteps and talking give place to snores, the watchman begin his nightly tapping with his stick, the garden grow brighter and more mysterious as the streaks of light vanished from the windows, the last candle pass from the pantry to the hall (throwing a glimmer into the dewy garden as it did so), and the stooping figure of Foka (decked in a nightcap, and carrying the candle) become visible to my eyes as he went to his bed. Often I would find a great and fearful pleasure in stealing over the grass, in the black shadow of the house, until I had reached the hall window, where I would stand listening with bated breath to the snoring of the boy, to Foka's gruntings (in the belief that no one heard him), and to the sound of his senile voice as he drawled out the evening prayers. At length even his candle would be extinguished, and the window slammed down, so that I would find myself utterly alone; whereupon, glancing nervously from side to side, lest haply I should see the white woman standing near a flower-bed or by my couch, I would run at full speed back to the verandah. Then, and only then, I would lie down with my face to the garden, and, covering myself over, so far as possible, from the mosquitos and bats, fall to gazing in front of me as I listened to the sounds of the night and dreamed of love and happiness.

At such times everything would take on for me a different meaning. The look of the old birch trees, with the one side of their curling branches showing bright against the moonlit sky, and the other darkening the bushes and carriage-drive with their black shadows; the calm, rich glitter of the pond, ever swelling like a sound; the moonlit sparkle of the dewdrops on the flowers in front of the verandah; the graceful shadows of those flowers where they lay thrown upon the grey stonework; the cry of a quail on the far side of the pond; the voice of some one walking on the high road; the quiet, scarcely audible scrunching of two old birch trees against one another; the humming of a mosquito at my car under the coverlet; the fall of an apple as it caught against a branch and rustled among the dry leaves; the leapings of frogs as they approached almost to the verandah-steps and sat with the moon shining mysteriously on their green backs—all these things took on for me a strange significance—a significance of exceeding beauty and of infinite love. Before me would rise SHE, with long black tresses and a high

416

bust, but always mournful in her fairness, with bare hands and voluptuous arms. She loved me, and for one moment of her love I would sacrifice my whole life!—But the moon would go on rising higher and higher, and shining brighter and brighter, in the heavens; the rich sparkle of the pond would swell like a sound, and become ever more and more brilliant, while the shadows would grow blacker and blacker, and the sheen of the moon more and more transparent: until, as I looked at and listened to all this, something would say to me that SHE with the bare hands and voluptuous arms did not represent ALL happiness, that love for her did not represent ALL good; so that, the more I gazed at the full, high-riding moon, the higher would true beauty and goodness appear to me to lie, and the purer and purer they would seem—the nearer and nearer to Him who is the source of all beauty and all goodness. And tears of a sort of unsatisfied, yet tumultuous, joy would fill my eyes.

Always, too, I was alone; yet always, too, it seemed to me that, although great, mysterious Nature could draw the shining disc of the moon to herself, and somehow hold in some high, indefinite place the pale-blue sky, and be everywhere around me, and fill of herself the infinity of space, while I was but a lowly worm, already defiled with the poor, petty passions of humanity—always it seemed to me that, nevertheless, both Nature and the moon and I were one.

XXXIII. OUR NEIGHBOURS

ON the first day after our arrival, I had been greatly astonished that Papa should speak of our neighbours, the Epifanovs, as "nice people," and still more so that he should go to call upon them. The fact was that we had long been at law over some land with this family. When a child, I had more than once heard Papa raging over the litigation, abusing the Epifanovs, and warning people (so I understood him) against them. Likewise, I had heard Jakoff speak of them as "our enemies" and "black people" and could remember Mamma requesting that their names should never be mentioned in her presence, nor, indeed, in the house at all.

From these data I, as a child, had arrived at the clear and assured conviction that the Epifanovs were foemen of ours who would at any time stab or strangle both Papa and his sons if they should ever come across them, as well as that they were "black people", in the literal sense of the term. Consequently, when, in the year that Mamma died, I chanced to catch sight of Avdotia ("La Belle Flamande") on the occasion of a visit which she paid to my mother, I found it hard to believe that she did not come of a family of negroes. All the same, I had the lowest possible opinion of the family, and, for all that we saw much of them that summer, continued to be strongly prejudiced against them. As a matter of fact, their household only consisted of the mother (a widow of fifty, but a very well-preserved, cheery old woman), a beautiful daughter named Avdotia, and a son, Peter, who was a stammerer, unmarried, and of very serious disposition.

For the last twenty years before her husband's death, Madame Epifanov had lived apart from him—sometimes in St. Petersburg, where she had relatives, but more frequently at her village of Mitishtchi, which stood some three versts from ours. Yet the neighbourhood had taken to circulating such horrible tales concerning her mode of life that Messalina was, by comparison, a blameless child: which was why my mother had requested her name never to be mentioned. As a matter of fact, not one-tenth part of the most cruel of all gossip—the gossip of country-houses—is worthy of credence; and although, when I first made Madame's acquaintance, she had living with her in the house a clerk named Mitusha, who had been promoted from a serf, and who, curled, pomaded, and dressed in a frockcoat of Circassian pattern, always stood behind his mistress's chair at luncheon, while from time to time she invited her guests to admire his handsome eyes and mouth, there was nothing for gossip to take hold of. I believe, too, that since the time—ten years earlier—when she had recalled her dutiful son Peter from the service, she had wholly changed her mode of living. It seems her property had never been a large one—merely a hundred souls or so—[This refers, of course, to the days of serfdom.]and that during her previous life of gaiety she had spent a great deal. Consequently, when, some ten years ago, those portions of the property which had been mortgaged and re-mortgaged had been foreclosed upon and compulsorily sold by auction, she had come to the conclusion that all these unpleasant details of distress upon and valuation of her property had been due not so much to failure to pay the interest as to the fact that she was a woman: wherefore she had written to her son (then serving with his regiment) to come and save his mother from her embarrassments, and he, like a dutiful son—conceiving that his first duty was to comfort his mother in her old age—had straightway resigned his commission (for all that he had been doing well in his profession, and was hoping soon to become independent), and had come to join her in the country.

Despite his plain face, uncouth demeanour, and fault of stuttering, Peter was a man of unswerving principles and of the most extraordinary good sense. Somehow—by small borrowings, sundry strokes of business, petitions for grace, and promises to repay—he contrived to carry on the property, and, making himself overseer, donned his father's greatcoat (still preserved in a drawer), dispensed with horses and carriages, discouraged guests from calling at Mitishtchi, fashioned his own sleighs, increased his arable land and curtailed that of the serfs, felled his own timber, sold his produce in person, and saw to matters generally. Indeed, he swore, and kept his oath, that, until all outstanding debts were paid, he would never wear any clothes than his father's greatcoat and a corduroy jacket which he had made for himself, nor yet ride in aught but a country waggon, drawn by peasants' horses. This stoical

419

mode of life he sought to apply also to his family, so far as the sympathetic respect which he conceived to be his mother's due would allow of; so that, although, in the drawing-room, he would show her only stuttering servility, and fulfil all her wishes, and blame any one who did not do precisely as she bid them, in his study or his office he would overhaul the cook if she had served up so much as a duck without his orders, or any one responsible for sending a serf (even though at Madame's own bidding) to inquire after a neighbour's health or for despatching the peasant girls into the wood to gather wild raspberries instead of setting them to weed the kitchen-garden.

Within four years every debt had been repaid, and Peter had gone to Moscow and returned thence in a new jacket and tarantass. [A two-wheeled carriage.] Yet, despite this flourishing position of affairs, he still preserved the stoical tendencies in which, to tell the truth, he took a certain vague pride before his family and strangers, since he would frequently say with a stutter: "Any one who REALLY wishes to see me will be glad to see me even in my dressing-gown, and to eat nothing but shtchi [Cabbage-soup.] and kasha [Buckwheat gruel.] at my table." "That is what I eat myself," he would add. In his every word and movement spoke pride based upon a consciousness of having sacrificed himself for his mother and redeemed the property, as well as contempt for any one who had not done something of the same kind.

The mother and daughter were altogether different characters from Peter, as well as altogether different from one another. The former was one of the most agreeable, uniformly good-tempered, and cheerful women whom one could possibly meet. Anything attractive and genuinely happy delighted her. Even the faculty of being pleased with the sight of young people enjoying themselves (it is only in the best-natured of elderly folk that one meets with that TRAIT) she possessed to the full. On the other hand, her daughter was of a grave turn of mind. Rather, she was of that peculiarly careless, absent-minded, gratuitously distant bearing which commonly distinguishes unmarried beauties. Whenever she tried to be gay, her gaiety somehow seemed to be unnatural to her, so that she always appeared to be laughing either at herself or at the persons to whom she was speaking or at the world in general—a thing which, possibly, she had no real intention of doing. Often I asked myself in astonishment what she could mean when she said something like, "Yes, I know how terribly good-looking I am," or, "Of course every one is in love with me," and so forth. Her mother was a person always busy, since she had a passion for housekeeping, gardening, flowers, canaries, and pretty trinkets. Her rooms and garden, it is true, were small and poorly fitted-up, yet everything in them was so neat and methodical, and bore such a general air of that gentle gaiety which one hears expressed in a waltz or polka, that the word "toy" by which guests often expressed their praise of it all exactly suited her surroundings. She herself was a "toy"—being petite, slender, fresh-coloured, small, and pretty-handed, and invariably gay and well-dressed. The only fault in her was that a slight over-prominence of the dark-blue veins on her little hands rather marred the general effect of her appearance. On the other hand, her daughter scarcely ever did anything at all. Not only had she no love for trifling with flowers and trinkets, but she neglected her personal exterior, and only troubled to dress herself well when guests happened to call. Yet, on returning to the room in society costume, she always looked extremely handsome—save for that cold, uniform expression of eyes and smile which is common to all beauties. In fact, her strictly regular, beautiful face and symmetrical figure always seemed to be saying to you, "Yes, you may look at me."

At the same time, for all the mother's liveliness of disposition and the daughter's air of indifference and abstraction, something told one that the former was incapable of feeling affection for anything that was not pretty and gay, but that Avdotia, on the contrary, was one of those natures which, once they love, are willing to sacrifice their whole life for the man they adore.

XXXIV. MY FATHER'S SECOND MARRIAGE

MY father was forty-eight when he took as his second wife Avdotia Vassilievna Epifanov.

I suspect that when, that spring, he had departed for the country with the girls, he had been in that communicatively happy, sociable mood in which gamblers usually find themselves who have retired from play after winning large stakes. He had felt that he still had a fortune left to him which, so long as he did not squander it on gaming, might be used for our advancement in life. Moreover, it was springtime, he was unexpectedly well supplied with ready money, he was alone, and he had nothing to do. As he conversed with Jakoff on various matters, and remembered both the interminable suit with the Epifanovs and Avdotia's beauty (it was a long while since he had seen her), I can imagine him saying: "How do you think we ought to act in this suit, Jakoff? My idea is simply to let the cursed land go. Eh? What do you think about it?" I can imagine, too, how, thus interrogated, Jakoff twirled his fingers behind his back in a deprecatory sort of way, and proceeded to argue that it all the same, "Peter Alexandritch, we are in the right." Nevertheless, I further conjecture, Papa ordered the dogcart to be got ready, put on his fashionable olive-coloured driving-coat, brushed up the remnants of his hair, sprinkled his clothes with scent, and, greatly pleased to think that he was acting a la seignior (as well as, even more, revelling in the prospect of soon seeing a pretty woman), drove off to visit his neighbours.

I can imagine, too, that when the flustered housemaid ran to inform Peter Vassilievitch that Monsieur Irtenieff himself had called, Peter answered angrily, "Well, what has he come for?" and, stepping softly about the house, first went into his study to put on his old soiled jacket, and then sent down word to the cook that on no account whatever—no, not even if she were ordered to do so by the mistress herself—was she to add anything to luncheon.

Since, later, I often saw Papa with Peter, I can form a very good idea of this first interview between them. I can imagine that, despite Papa's proposal to end the suit in a peaceful manner, Peter was morose and resentful at the thought of having sacrificed his career to his mother, and at Papa having done nothing of the kind—a by no means surprising circumstance, Peter probably said to himself. Next, I can see Papa taking no notice of this ill-humour, but cracking quips and jests, while Peter gradually found himself forced to treat him as a humorist with whom he felt offended one moment and inclined to be reconciled the next. Indeed, with his instinct for making fun of everything, Papa often used to address Peter as "Colonel;" and though I can remember Peter once replying, with an unusually violent stutter and his face scarlet with indignation, that he had never been a c-c-colonel, but only a l-l-lieutenant, Papa called him "Colonel" again before another five minutes were out.

Lubotshka told me that, up to the time of Woloda's and my arrival from Moscow, there had been daily meetings with the Epifanovs, and that things had been very lively, since Papa, who had a genius for arranging, everything with a touch of originality and wit, as well as in a simple and refined manner, had devised shooting and fishing parties and fireworks for the Epifanovs' benefit. All these festivities—so said Lubotshka—would have gone off splendidly but for the intolerable Peter, who had spoilt everything by his puffing and stuttering. After our coming, however, the Epifanovs only visited us twice, and we went once to their house, while after St. Peter's Day (on which, it being Papa's nameday, the Epifanovs called upon us in common with a crowd of other guests) our relations with that family came entirely to an end, and, in future, only Papa went to see them.

During the brief period when I had opportunities of seeing Papa and Dunetchka (as her mother called Avdotia) together, this is what I remarked about them. Papa remained unceasingly in the same buoyant mood as had so greatly struck me on the day after our arrival. So gay and youthful and full of life and happy did he seem that the beams of his felicity extended themselves to all around him, and involuntarily communicated to them a similar frame of mind. He never stirred from Avdotia's side so long as she was in the room, but either kept on plying her with sugary-sweet compliments which made me feel ashamed for him or, with his gaze fixed upon her with an air at once passionate and complacent, sat hitching his shoulder and coughing as from

423

time to time he smiled and whispered something in her ear. Yet throughout he wore the same expression of raillery as was peculiar to him even in the most serious matters.

As a rule, Avdotia herself seemed to catch the infection of the happiness which sparkled at this period in Papa's large blue eyes; yet there were moments also when she would be seized with such a fit of shyness that I, who knew the feeling well, was full of sympathy and compassion as I regarded her embarrassment. At moments of this kind she seemed to be afraid of every glance and every movement—to be supposing that every one was looking at her, every one thinking of no one but her, and that unfavourably. She would glance timidly from one person to another, the colour coming and going in her cheeks, and then begin to talk loudly and defiantly, but, for the most part, nonsense; until presently, realising this, and supposing that Papa and every one else had heard her, she would blush more painfully than ever. Yet Papa never noticed her nonsense, for he was too much taken up with coughing and with gazing at her with his look of happy, triumphant devotion. I noticed, too, that, although these fits of shyness attacked Avdotia, without any visible cause, they not infrequently ensued upon Papa's mention of one or another young and beautiful woman. Frequent transitions from depression to that strange, awkward gaiety of hers to which I have referred before the repetition of favourite words and turns of speech of Papa's; the continuation of discussions with others which Papa had already begun—all these things, if my father had not been the principal actor in the matter and I had been a little older, would have explained to me the relations subsisting between him and Avdotia. At the time, however, I never surmised them—no, not even when Papa received from her brother Peter a letter which so upset him that not again until the end of August did he go to call upon the Epifanovs'. Then, however, he began his visits once more, and ended by informing us, on the day before Woloda and I were to return to Moscow, that he was about to take Avdotia Vassilievna Epifanov to be his wife.

XXXV. HOW WE RECEIVED THE NEWS

Yet, even on the eve of the official announcement, every one had learnt of the matter, and was discussing it. Mimi never left her room that day, and wept copiously. Katenka kept her company, and only came out for luncheon, with a grieved expression on her face which was manifestly borrowed from her mother. Lubotshka, on the contrary, was very cheerful, and told us after luncheon that she knew of a splendid secret which she was going to tell no one.

"There is nothing so splendid about your secret," said Woloda, who did not in the least share her satisfaction. "If you were capable of any serious thought at all, you would understand that it is a very bad lookout for us."

Lubotshka stared at him in amazement, and said no more. After the meal was over, Woloda made a feint of taking me by the arm, and then, fearing that this would seem too much like "affection," nudged me gently by the elbow, and beckoned me towards the salon.

"You know, I suppose, what the secret is of which Lubotshka was speaking?" he said when he was sure that we were alone. It was seldom that he and I spoke together in confidence: with the result that, whenever it came about, we felt a kind of awkwardness in one another's presence, and "boys began to jump about" in our eyes, as Woloda expressed it. On the present occasion, however, he answered the excitement in my eyes with a grave, fixed look which said: "You need not be surprised, for we are brothers, and we have to consider an important family matter." I understood him, and he went on:

"You know, I suppose, that Papa is going to marry Avdotia Epifanov?"

I nodded, for I had already heard so. "Well, it is not a good thing," continued Woloda.

"Why so?"

"Why?" he repeated irritably. "Because it will be so pleasant, won't it, to have this stuttering 'colonel' and all his family for relations! Certainly she seems nice enough, as yet; but who knows what she will turn out to be later? It won't matter much to you or myself, but Lubotshka will soon be making her debut, and it will hardly be nice for her to have such a 'belle mere' as this—a woman who speaks French badly, and has no manners to teach her."

Although it seemed odd to hear Woloda criticising Papa's choice so coolly, I felt that he was right.

"Why is he marrying her?" I asked.

"Oh, it is a hole-and-corner business, and God only knows why," he answered. "All I know is that her brother, Peter, tried to make conditions about the marriage, and that, although at first Papa would not hear of them, he afterwards took some fancy or knight-errantry or another into his head. But, as I say, it is a hole-and-corner business. I am only just beginning to understand my father "—the fact that Woloda called Papa "my father" instead of "Papa" somehow hurt me—"and though I can see that he is kind and clever, he is irresponsible and frivolous to a degree that—Well, the whole thing is astonishing. He cannot so much as look upon a woman calmly. You yourself know how he falls in love with every one that he meets. You know it, and so does Mimi."

"What do you mean?" I said.

"What I say. Not long ago I learnt that he used to be in love with Mimi herself when he was a young man, and that he used to send her poetry, and that there really was something between them. Mimi is heart-sore about it to this day"—and Woloda burst out laughing.

"Impossible!" I cried in astonishment.

"But the principal thing at this moment," went on Woloda, becoming serious again, and relapsing into French, "is to think how delighted all our relations will be with this marriage! Why, she will probably have children!"

Woloda's prudence and forethought struck me so forcibly that I had no answer to make. Just at this moment Lubotshka approached us.

"So you know?" she said with a joyful face.

"Yes," said Woloda. "Still, I am surprised at you, Lubotshka. You are no longer a baby in long clothes. Why should you be so pleased because Papa is going to marry a piece of trash?"

At this Lubotshka's face fell, and she became serious.

"Oh, Woloda!" she exclaimed. "Why 'a piece of trash' indeed? How can you dare to speak of Avdotia like that? If Papa is going to marry her she cannot be 'trash.'"

"No, not trash, so to speak, but—"

"No 'buts' at all!" interrupted Lubotshka, flaring up. "You have never heard me call the girl whom you are in love with 'trash!' How, then, can you speak so of Papa and a respectable woman? Although you are my elder brother, I won't allow you to speak like that! You ought not to!"

"Mayn't I even express an opinion about—"

"No, you mayn't!" repeated Lubotshka. "No one ought to criticise such a father as ours. Mimi has the right to, but not you, however much you may be the eldest brother."

"Oh you don't understand anything," said Woloda contemptuously. "Try and do so. How can it be a good thing that a 'Dunetchka' of an Epifanov should take the place of our dead Mamma?"

For a moment Lubotshka was silent. Then the tears suddenly came into her eyes.

"I knew that you were conceited, but I never thought that you could be cruel," she said, and left us.

"Pshaw!" said Woloda, pulling a serio-comic face and make-believe, stupid eyes. "That's what comes of arguing with them." Evidently he felt that he was at fault in having so far forgot himself as to descend to discuss matters at all with Lubotshka.

Next day the weather was bad, and neither Papa nor the ladies had come

427

down to morning tea when I entered the drawing-room. There had been cold rain in the night, and remnants of the clouds from which it had descended were still scudding across the sky, with the sun's luminous disc (not yet risen to any great height) showing faintly through them. It was a windy, damp, grey morning. The door into the garden was standing open, and pools left by the night's rain were drying on the damp-blackened flags of the terrace. The open door was swinging on its iron hinges in the wind, and all the paths looked wet and muddy. The old birch trees with their naked white branches, the bushes, the turf, the nettles, the currant-trees, the elders with the pale side of their leaves turned upwards—all were dashing themselves about, and looking as though they were trying to wrench themselves free from their roots. From the avenue of lime-trees showers of round, yellow leaves were flying through the air in tossing, eddying circles, and strewing the wet road and soaked aftermath of the hayfield with a clammy carpet. At the moment, my thoughts were wholly taken up with my father's approaching marriage and with the point of view from which Woloda regarded it. The future seemed to me to bode no good for any of us. I felt distressed to think that a woman who was not only a stranger but young should be going to associate with us in so many relations of life, without having any right to do so—nay, that this young woman was going to usurp the place of our dead mother. I felt depressed, and kept thinking more and more that my father was to blame in the matter. Presently I heard his voice and Woloda's speaking together in the pantry, and, not wishing to meet Papa just then, had just left the room when I was pursued by Lubotshka, who said that Papa wanted to see me.

He was standing in the drawing-room, with his hand resting on the piano, and was gazing in my direction with an air at once grave and impatient. His face no longer wore the youthful, gay expression which had struck me for so long, but, on the contrary, looked sad. Woloda was walking about the room with a pipe in his hand. I approached my father, and bade him good morning.

"Well, my children," he said firmly, with a lift of his head and in the peculiarly hurried manner of one who wishes to announce something obviously unwelcome, but no longer admitting of reconsideration, "you know, I suppose, that I am going to marry Avdotia Epifanov." He paused a moment. "Hitherto I had had no desire for any one to succeed your mother, but"—and again he paused—"it-it is evidently my fate. Dunetchka is an excellent, kind girl, and no longer in her first youth. I hope, therefore, my children, that you will like her, and she, I know, will be sincerely fond of you, for she is a good woman. And now," he went on, addressing himself more particularly to Woloda and myself, and having the appearance of speaking hurriedly in order to prevent us from interrupting him, "it is time for you to depart, while I myself am going to stay here until the New Year, and then to follow you to Moscow with"—again he hesitated a moment—"my wife and Lubotshka." It hurt me to see my father standing as though abashed and at fault before us, so I moved a little nearer him, but Woloda only went on walking about the room with his head down, and smoking.

"So, my children, that is what your old father has planned to do," concluded Papa—reddening, coughing, and offering Woloda and myself his hands. Tears were in his eyes as he said this, and I noticed, too, that the hand which he was holding out to Woloda (who at that moment chanced to be at the other end of the room) was shaking slightly. The sight of that shaking hand gave me an unpleasant shock, for I remembered that Papa had served in 1812, and had been, as every one knew, a brave officer. Seizing the great veiny hand, I covered it with kisses, and he squeezed mine hard in return. Then, with a sob amid his tears, he suddenly threw his arms around Lubotshka's dark head, and kissed her again and again on the eyes. Woloda pretended that he had dropped his pipe, and, bending down, wiped his eyes furtively with the back of his hand. Then, endeavouring to escape notice, he left the room.

XXXVI. THE UNIVERSITY

THE wedding was to take place in two weeks' time, but, as our lectures had begun already, Woloda and myself were forced to return to Moscow at the beginning of September. The Nechludoffs had also returned from the country, and Dimitri (with whom, on parting, I had made an agreement that we should correspond frequently with the result, of course, that we had never once written to one another) came to see us immediately after our arrival, and arranged to escort me to my first lecture on the morrow.

It was a beautiful sunny day. No sooner had I entered the auditorium than I felt my personality entirely disappear amid the swarm of light-hearted youths who were seething tumultuously through every doorway and corridor under the influence of the sunlight pouring through the great windows. I found the sense of being a member of this huge community very pleasing, yet there were few among the throng whom I knew, and that only on terms of a nod and a "How do you do, Irtenieff?"

All around me men were shaking hands and chatting together—from every side came expressions of friendship, laughter, jests, and badinage. Everywhere I could feel the tie which bound this youthful society in one, and everywhere, too, I could feel that it left me out. Yet this impression lasted for a moment only, and was succeeded, together with the vexation which it had caused, by the idea that it was best that I should not belong to that society, but keep to my own circle of gentlemen; wherefore I proceeded to seat myself upon the third bench, with, as neighbours, Count B., Baron Z., the Prince R., Iwin, and some other young men of the same class with none of whom, however, was acquainted save with Iwin and Count B. Yet the look which these young gentlemen threw at me at once made me feel that I was not of their set, and I turned to observe what was going on around me. Semenoff, with grey, matted hair, white teeth, and tunic flying open, was seated a little distance off, and leaning forward on his elbows as he nibbled a pen, while the gymnasium student who had come out first in the examinations had established himself on the front bench, and, with a black stock coming halfway up his cheek, was toying with the silver watch-chain which adorned his satin waistcoat. On a bench in a raised part of the hall I could descry Ikonin (evidently he had contrived to enter the University somehow!), and hear him fussily proclaiming, in all the glory of blue piped trousers which completely hid his boots, that he was now seated on Parnassus. Ilinka—who had surprised me by giving me a bow not only cold, but supercilious, as though to remind me that here we were all equals—was just in front of me, with his legs resting in free and easy style on another bench (a hit, somehow I thought, at myself), and conversing with a student as he threw occasional glances in my direction. Iwin's set by my side were talking in French, yet every word which I overheard of their conversation seemed to me both stupid and incorrect ("Ce n'est pas francais," I thought to myself), while all the attitudes, utterances, and doings of Semenoff, Ilinka, and the rest struck me as uniformly coarse, ungentlemanly, and "comme il ne faut pas."

Thus, attached to no particular set, I felt isolated and unable to make friends, and so grew resentful. One of the students on the bench in front of me kept biting his nails, which were raw to the quick already, and this so disgusted me that I edged away from him. In short, I remember finding my first day a most depressing affair.

When the professor entered, and there was a general stir and a cessation of chatter, I remember throwing a scornful glance at him, as also that he began his discourse with a sentence which I thought devoid of meaning. I had expected the lecture to be, from first to last, so clever that not a word ought to be taken from or added to it. Disappointed in this, I at once proceeded to draw beneath the heading "First Lecture" with which I had adorned my beautifully-bound notebook no less than eighteen faces in profile, joined together in a sort of chaplet, and only occasionally moved my hand along the page in order to give the professor (who, I felt sure, must be greatly interested in me) the impression that I was writing something. In fact, at this very first lecture I came to the decision which I maintained to the end of my course, namely, that it was unnecessary, and even stupid, to take down every word said by every professor.

At subsequent lectures, however, I did not feel my isolation so strongly, since I made several acquaintances and got into the way of shaking hands and entering into conversation. Yet for some reason or another no real intimacy ever sprang up between us, and I often found myself depressed and only feigning cheerfulness. With the set which comprised Iwin and "the aristocrats," as they were generally known, I could not make any headway at all, for, as I now remember, I was always shy and churlish to them, and nodded to them only when they nodded to me; so that they had little inducement to desire my acquaintance. With most of the other students, however, this arose from quite a different cause. As soon as ever I discerned friendliness on the part of a comrade, I at once gave him to understand that I went to luncheon with Prince Ivan Ivanovitch and kept my own drozhki. All this I said merely to show myself in the most favourable light in his eyes, and to induce him to like me all the more; yet almost invariably the only result of my communicating to him the intelligence concerning the drozhki and my relationship to Prince Ivan Ivanovitch was that, to my astonishment, he at once adopted a cold and haughty bearing towards me.

Among us we had a Crown student named Operoff—a very modest, industrious, and clever young fellow, who always offered one his hand like a slab of wood (that is to say, without closing his fingers or making the slightest movement with them); with the result that his comrades often did the same to him in jest, and called it the "deal board" way of shaking hands. He and I nearly always sat next to one another, and discussed matters generally. In particular he pleased me with the freedom with which he would criticise the professors as he pointed out to me with great clearness and acumen the merits or demerits of their respective ways of teaching and made occasional fun of them. Such remarks I found exceedingly striking and diverting when uttered in his quiet, mincing voice. Nevertheless he never let a lecture pass without taking careful notes of it in his fine handwriting, and eventually we decided to join forces, and to do our preparation together. Things had progressed to the point of his always looking pleased when I took my usual seat beside him when, unfortunately, I one day found it necessary to inform him that, before her death, my mother had besought my father never to allow us to enter for a government scholarship, as well as that I myself considered Crown students, no matter how clever, to be-"well, they are not GENTLEMEN," I concluded, though beginning to flounder a little and grow red. At the moment Operoff said nothing, but at subsequent lectures he ceased to greet me or to offer me his board-like hand, and never attempted to talk to me, but, as soon as ever I sat down, he would lean his head upon his arm, and purport to be absorbed in his notebooks. I was surprised at this sudden coolness, but looked upon it as infra dig, "pour un jeune homme de bonne maison" to curry favour with a mere Crown student of an Operoff, and so left him severely alone—though I confess that his aloofness hurt my feelings. On one occasion I arrived before him, and, since the lecture was to be delivered by a popular professor whom students came to hear who did not usually attend such functions, I found almost every seat occupied. Accordingly I secured Operoff's place for myself by spreading my notebooks on the desk before it; after which I left the room again for a moment. When I returned I perceived that my paraphernalia had been relegated to the bench behind, and the place taken by Operoff himself. I remarked to him that I had already secured it by placing my notebooks there.

"I know nothing about that," he replied sharply, yet without looking up at me.

"I tell you I placed my notebooks there," I repeated, purposely trying to bluster, in the hope of intimidating him. "Every one saw me do it," I added, including the students near me in my glance. Several of them looked at me with curiosity, yet none of them spoke.

"Seats cannot be booked here," said Operoff. "Whoever first sits down in a place keeps it," and, settling himself angrily where he was, he flashed at me a glance of defiance.

"Well, that only means that you are a cad," I said.

I have an idea that he murmured something about my being "a stupid young idiot," but I decided not to hear it. What would be the use, I asked myself, of my hearing it? That we should brawl like a couple of manants over less than nothing? (I was very fond of the word manants, and often used it for meeting awkward junctures.) Perhaps I should have said something more had not, at that moment, a door slammed and the professor (dressed in a blue frockcoat, and shuffling his feet as he walked) ascended the rostrum.

Nevertheless, when the examination was about to come on, and I had need of some one's notebooks, Operoff remembered his promise to lend me his, and we did our preparation together.

XXXVII. AFFAIRS OF THE HEART

Affaires du coeur exercised me greatly that winter. In fact, I fell in love three times. The first time, I became passionately enamoured of a buxom lady whom I used to see riding at Freitag's riding-school; with the result that every day when she was taking a lesson there (that is to say, every Tuesday and Friday) I used to go to gaze at her, but always in such a state of trepidation lest I should be seen that I stood a long way off, and bolted directly I thought her likely to approach the spot where I was standing. Likewise, I used to turn round so precipitately whenever she appeared to be glancing in my direction that I never saw her face well, and to this day do not know whether she was really beautiful or not.

Dubkoff, who was acquainted with her, surprised me one day in the riding-school, where I was lurking concealed behind the lady's grooms and the fur wraps which they were holding, and, having heard from Dimitri of my infatuation, frightened me so terribly by proposing to introduce me to the Amazon that I fled incontinently from the school, and was prevented by the mere thought that possibly he had told her about me from ever entering the place again, or even from hiding behind her grooms, lest I should encounter her.

Whenever I fell in love with ladies whom I did not know, and especially married women, I experienced a shyness a thousand times greater than I had ever felt with Sonetchka. I dreaded beyond measure that my divinity should learn of my passion, or even of my existence, since I felt sure that, once she had done so, she would be so terribly offended that I should never be forgiven for my presumption. And indeed, if the Amazon referred to above had ever come to know how I used to stand behind the grooms and dream of seizing her and carrying her off to some country spot—if she had ever come to know how I should have lived with her there, and how I should have treated her, it is probable that she would have had very good cause for indignation! But I always felt that, once I got to know her, she would straightway divine these thoughts, and consider herself insulted by my acquaintance.

As my second affaire du coeur, I, (for the third time) fell in love with Sonetchka when I saw her at her sister's. My second passion for her had long since come to an end, but I became enamoured of her this third time through Lubotshka sending me a copy-book in which Sonetchka had copied some extracts from Lermontoff's The Demon, with certain of the more subtly amorous passages underlined in red ink and marked with pressed flowers. Remembering how Woloda had been wont to kiss his inamorata's purse last year, I essayed to do the same thing now; and really, when alone in my room in the evenings and engaged in dreaming as I looked at a flower or occasionally pressed it to my lips, I would feel a certain pleasantly lachrymose mood steal over me, and remain genuinely in love (or suppose myself to be so) for at least several days.

Finally, my third affaire du coeur that winter was connected with the lady with whom Woloda was in love, and who used occasionally to visit at our house. Yet, in this damsel, as I now remember, there was not a single beautiful feature to be found—or, at all events, none of those which usually pleased me. She was the daughter of a well-known Moscow lady of light and leading, and, petite and slender, wore long flaxen curls after the English fashion, and could boast of a transparent profile. Every one said that she was even cleverer and more learned than her mother, but I was never in a position to judge of that, since, overcome with craven bashfulness at the mere thought of her intellect and accomplishments, I never spoke to her alone but once, and then with unaccountable trepidation. Woloda's enthusiasm, however (for the presence of an audience never prevented him from giving vent to his rapture), communicated itself to me so strongly that I also became enamoured of the lady. Yet, conscious that he would not be pleased to know that two brothers were in love with the same girl, I never told him of my condition. On the contrary, I took special delight in the thought that our mutual love for her was so pure that, though its object was, in both cases, the same charming being, we remained friends and ready, if ever the occasion should arise, to sacrifice ourselves for one another. Yet I have an idea that, as regards self-sacrifice, he did not quite share my views, for he was so passionately in love with the lady that once he was for giving a member of the diplomatic corps, who was said to be going to marry her, a slap in the face and a challenge to a duel; but, for my part, I would gladly have sacrificed my feelings for his sake, seeing that the fact that the only remark I had ever addressed to her had been on the subject of the dignity of classical music, and that my passion, for all my efforts to keep it alive, expired the following week, would have rendered it the more easy for me to do so.

XXXVIII. THE WORLD

As regards those worldly delights to which I had intended, on entering the University, to surrender myself in imitation of my brother, I underwent a complete disillusionment that winter. Woloda danced a great deal, and Papa also went to balls with his young wife, but I appeared to be thought either too young or unfitted for such delights, and no one invited me to the houses where balls were being given. Yet, in spite of my vow of frankness with Dimitri, I never told him (nor any one else) how much I should have liked to go to those dances, and how I felt hurt at being forgotten and (apparently) taken for the philosopher that I pretended to be.

Nevertheless, a reception was to be given that winter at the Princess Kornakoff's, and to it she sent us personal invitations—to myself among the rest! Consequently, I was to attend my first ball. Before starting, Woloda came into my room to see how I was dressing myself—an act on his part which greatly surprised me and took me aback. In my opinion (it must be understood) solicitude about one's dress was a shameful thing, and should be kept under, but he seemed to think it a thing so natural and necessary that he said outright that he was afraid I should be put out of countenance on that score. Accordingly, he bid me don my patent leather boots, and was horrified to find that I wanted to put on gloves of peau de chamois. Next, he adjusted my watch-chain in a particular manner, and carried me off to a hairdresser's near the Kuznetski Bridge to have my locks coiffured. That done, he withdrew to a little distance and surveyed me.

"Yes, he looks right enough now," said he to the hairdresser. "Only—couldn't you smooth those tufts of his in front a little?" Yet, for all that Monsieur Charles treated my forelocks with one essence and another, they persisted in rising up again when ever I put on my hat. In fact, my curled and tonsured figure seemed to me to look far worse than it had done before. My only hope of salvation lay in an affectation of untidiness. Only in that guise would my exterior resemble anything at all. Woloda, apparently, was of the same opinion, for he begged me to undo the curls, and when I had done so and still looked unpresentable, he ceased to regard me at all, but throughout the drive to the Kornakoffs remained silent and depressed.

Nevertheless, I entered the Kornakoffs' mansion boldly enough, and it was only when the Princess had invited me to dance, and I, for some reason or another (though I had driven there with no other thought in my head than to dance well), had replied that I never indulged in that pastime, that I began to blush, and, left solitary among a crowd of strangers, became plunged in my usual insuperable and ever-growing shyness. In fact, I remained silent on that spot almost the whole evening!

Nevertheless, while a waltz was in progress, one of the young princesses came to me and asked me, with the sort of official kindness common to all her family, why I was not dancing. I can remember blushing hotly at the question, but at the same time feeling—for all my efforts to prevent it—a self-satisfied smile steal over my face as I began talking, in the most inflated and long-winded French, such rubbish as even now, after dozens of years, it shames me to recall. It must have been the effect of the music, which, while exciting my nervous sensibility, drowned (as I supposed) the less intelligible portion of my utterances. Anyhow, I went on speaking of the exalted company present, and of the futility of men and women, until I had got myself into such a tangle that I was forced to stop short in the middle of a word of a sentence which I found myself powerless to conclude.

Even the worldly-minded young Princess was shocked by my conduct, and gazed at me in reproach; whereat I burst out laughing. At this critical moment, Woloda, who had remarked that I was conversing with great animation, and probably was curious to know what excuses I was making for not dancing, approached us with Dubkoff. Seeing, however, my smiling face and the Princess's frightened mien, as well as overhearing the appalling rubbish with which I concluded my speech, he turned red in the face, and wheeled round again. The Princess also rose and left me. I continued to smile, but in such a state of agony from the consciousness of my stupidity that I felt ready to sink into the floor. Likewise I felt that, come what might, I must move about and say something, in order to effect a change in my position.

Accordingly I approached Dubkoff, and asked him if he had danced many waltzes with her that night. This I feigned to say in a gay and jesting manner, yet in reality I was imploring help of the very Dubkoff to whom I had cried "Hold your tongue!" on the night of the matriculation dinner. By way of answer, he made as though he had not heard me, and turned away. Next, I approached Woloda, and said with an effort and in a similar tone of assumed gaiety: "Hullo, Woloda! Are you played out yet?" He merely looked at me as much as to say, "You wouldn't speak to me like that if we were alone," and left me without a word, in the evident fear that I might continue to attach myself to his person.

"My God! Even my own brother deserts me!" I thought to myself.

Yet somehow I had not the courage to depart, but remained standing where I was until the very end of the evening. At length, when every one was leaving the room and crowding into the hall, and a footman slipped my greatcoat on to my shoulders in such a way as to tilt up my cap, I gave a dreary, half-lachrymose smile, and remarked to no one in particular: "Comme c'est gracieux!"

XXXIX. THE STUDENTS' FEAST

NOTWITHSTANDING that, as yet, Dimitri's influence had kept me from indulging in those customary students' festivities known as kutezhi or "wines," that winter saw me participate in such a function, and carry away with me a not over-pleasant impression of it. This is how it came about.

At a lecture soon after the New Year, Baron Z.—a tall, light-haired young fellow of very serious demeanour and regular features—invited us all to spend a sociable evening with him. By "us all", I mean all the men more or less "comme il faut", of our course, and exclusive of Grap, Semenoff, Operoff, and commoners of that sort. Woloda smiled contemptuously when he heard that I was going to a "wine" of first course men, but I looked to derive great and unusual pleasure from this, to me, novel method of passing the time. Accordingly, punctually at the appointed hour of eight I presented myself at the Baron's.

Our host, in an open tunic and white waistcoat, received his guests in the brilliantly lighted salon and drawing-room of the small mansion where his parents lived—they having given up their reception rooms to him for the evening for purposes of this party. In the corridor could be seen the heads and skirts of inquisitive domestics, while in the dining-room I caught a glimpse of a dress which I imagined to belong to the Baroness herself. The guests numbered a score, and were all of them students except Herr Frost (in attendance upon Iwin) and a tall, red-faced gentleman who was superintending the feast and who was introduced to every one as a relative of the Baron's and a former student of the University of Dorpat. At first, the excessive brilliancy and formal appointments of the reception-rooms had such a chilling effect upon this youthful company that every one involuntarily hugged the walls, except a few bolder spirits and the ex-Dorpat student, who, with his waistcoat already unbuttoned, seemed to be in every room, and in every corner of every room, at once, and filled the whole place with his resonant, agreeable, never-ceasing tenor voice. The remainder of the guests preferred either to remain silent or to talk in discreet tones of professors, faculties, examinations, and other serious and interesting matters. Yet every one, without exception, kept watching the door of the dining-room, and, while trying to conceal the fact, wearing an expression which said: "Come! It is time to begin." I too felt that it was time to begin, and awaited the beginning with pleasurable impatience.

After footmen had handed round tea among the guests, the Dorpat student asked Frost in Russian:

"Can you make punch, Frost?"

"Oh ja!" replied Frost with a joyful flourish of his heels, and the other went on:

"Then do you set about it" (they addressed each other in the second person singular, as former comrades at Dorpat). Frost accordingly departed to the dining-room, with great strides of his bowed, muscular legs, and, after some walking backwards and forwards, deposited upon the drawing-room table a large punchbowl, accompanied by a ten-pound sugar loaf supported on three students' swords placed crosswise. Meanwhile, the Baron had been going round among his guests as they sat regarding the punch-bowl, and addressing them, with a face of immutable gravity, in the formula: "I beg of you all to drink of this loving-cup in student fashion, that there may be good-fellowship among the members of our course. Unbutton your waistcoats, or take them off altogether, as you please." Already the Dorpat student had divested himself of his tunic and rolled up his white shirt-sleeves above his elbows, and now, planting his feet firmly apart, he proceeded to set fire to the rum in the punch-bowl.

"Gentlemen, put out the candles!" he cried with a sudden shout so loud and insistent that we seemed all of us to be shouting at once. However, we still went on silently regarding the punch-bowl and the white shirt of the Dorpat student, with a feeling that a moment of great solemnity was approaching.

"Put out the lights, Frost, I tell you!" the Dorpat student shouted again. Evidently the punch was now sufficiently burnt. Accordingly every one helped to extinguish the candles, until the room was in total darkness save for a spot where the white shirts and hands of the three students supporting the sugarloaf on their crossed swords were lit up by the lurid flames from the bowl. Yet the Dorpat student's tenor voice was not the only one to be heard, for in different quarters of the room resounded chattering and laughter. Many had taken off their tunics (especially students whose garments were of fine cloth and perfectly new), and I now did the same, with a consciousness that "IT" was "beginning." There had been no great festivity as yet, but I felt assured that things would go splendidly when once we had begun drinking tumblers of the potion that was now in course of preparation.

At length, the punch was ready, and the Dorpat student, with much bespattering of the table as he did so, ladled the liquor into tumblers, and cried: "Now, gentlemen, please!" When we had each of us taken a sticky tumbler of the stuff into our hands, the Dorpat student and Frost sang a German song in which the word "Hoch!" kept occurring again and again, while we joined, in haphazard fashion, in the chorus. Next we clinked glasses together, shouted something in praise of punch, crossed hands, and took our first drink of the sweet, strong mixture. After that there was no further waiting; the "wine" was in full swing. The first glassful consumed, a second was poured out. Yet, for all that I began to feel a throbbing in my temples, and that the flames seemed to be turning purple, and that every one around me was laughing and shouting, things seemed lacking in real gaiety, and I somehow felt that, as a matter of fact, we were all of us finding the affair rather dull, and only PRETENDING to be enjoying it. The Dorpat student may have been an exception, for he continued to grow more and more red in the face and more and more ubiquitous as he filled up empty glasses and stained the table with fresh spots of the sweet, sticky stuff. The precise sequence of events I cannot remember, but I can recall feeling strongly attracted towards Frost and the Dorpat student that evening, learning their German song by heart, and kissing them each on their sticky-sweet lips; also that that same evening I conceived a violent hatred against the Dorpat student, and was for pushing him from his chair, but thought better of it; also that, besides feeling the same spirit of independence towards the rest of the company as I had felt on the night of the matriculation dinner, my head ached and swam so badly that I thought each moment would be my last; also that, for some reason or another, we all of us sat down on the floor and imitated the movements of rowers in a boat as we sang in chorus, "Down our mother stream the Volga;" also that I conceived this procedure on our part to be uncalled for; also that, as I lay prone upon the floor, I crossed my legs and began wriggling about like a tsigane; [Gipsy dancer.] also that I ricked some one's neck, and came to the conclusion that I should never have done such a thing if I had not been drunk; also that we had some supper and another kind of liquor, and that I then went to the door to get some fresh air; also that my head seemed suddenly to grow chill, and that I noticed, as I drove away, that the scat of the vehicle was so sharply aslant and slippery that for me to retain my position behind Kuzma was impossible; also that he seemed to have turned all flabby, and to be waving about like a dish clout. But what I remember best is that throughout the whole of that evening I never ceased to feel that I was acting with excessive stupidity in pretending to be enjoying myself, to like drinking a great deal, and to be in no way drunk, as well as that every one else present was acting with equal stupidity in pretending those same things. All the time I had a feeling that each one of my companions was finding the festivities as distasteful as I was myself; but, in the belief that he was the only one doing so, felt himself bound to pretend that he was very merry, in order not to mar the general hilarity. Also, strange to state, I felt that I ought to keep up this pretence for the sole reason that into a punch-bowl there had been poured three bottles of champagne at nine roubles the bottle and ten bottles of rum at four—making seventy roubles in all, exclusive of the supper. So convinced of my folly did I feel that, when, at next day's lecture, those of my comrades who had been at Baron Z.'s party seemed not only in no way ashamed to remember what they had done, but even talked about it so that other students might hear of their doings, I felt greatly astonished. They all declared that it had been a splendid "wine," that Dorpat students were just the fellows for that kind of thing, and that there had been consumed at it no less than forty bottles of rum among twenty guests, some of whom had dropped senseless under the table! That they should care to talk about such things seemed strange enough, but that they should care to lie about them seemed absolutely unintelligible.

XL. MY FRIENDSHIP WITH THE NECHLUDOFFS

That winter, too, I saw a great deal both of Dimitri who often looked us up, and of his family, with whom I was beginning to stand on intimate terms.

The Nechludoffs (that is to say, mother, aunt, and daughter) always spent their evenings at home, at which time the Princess liked young men to visit her—at all events young men of the kind whom she described as able to spend an evening without playing cards or dancing. Yet such young fellows must have been few and far between, for, although I went to the Nechludoffs almost every evening, I seldom found other guests present. Thus, I came to know the members of this family and their several dispositions well enough to be able to form clear ideas as to their mutual relations, and to be quite at home amid the rooms and furniture of their house. Indeed, so long as no other guests were present, I felt entirely at my ease. True, at first I used to feel a little uncomfortable when left alone in the room with Varenika, for I could not rid myself of the idea that, though far from pretty, she wished me to fall in love with her; but in time this nervousness of mine began to lessen, since she always looked so natural, and talked to me so exactly as though she were conversing with her brother or Lubov Sergievna, that I came to look upon her simply as a person to whom it was in no way dangerous or wrong to show that I took pleasure in her company. Throughout the whole of our acquaintance she appeared to me merely a plain, though not positively ugly, girl, concerning whom one would never ask oneself the question,

"Am I, or am I not, in love with her?" Sometimes I would talk to her direct, but more often I did so through Dimitri or Lubov Sergievna; and it was the latter method which afforded me the most pleasure. I derived considerable gratification from discoursing when she was there, from hearing her sing, and, in general, from knowing that she was in the same room as myself; but it was seldom now that any thoughts of what our future relations might ever be, or that any dreams of self-sacrifice for my friend if he should ever fall in love with my sister, came into my head. If any such ideas or fancies occurred to me, I felt satisfied with the present, and drove away all thoughts about the future.

Yet, in spite of this intimacy, I continued to look upon it as my bounden duty to keep the Nechludoffs in general, and Varenika in particular, in ignorance of my true feelings and tastes, and strove always to appear altogether another young man than what I really was—to appear, indeed, such a young man as could never possibly have existed. I affected to be "soulful" and would go off into raptures and exclamations and impassioned gestures whenever I wished it to be thought that anything pleased me, while, on the other hand, I tried always to seem indifferent towards any unusual circumstance which I myself perceived or which I had had pointed out to me. I aimed always at figuring both as a sarcastic cynic divorced from every sacred tie and as a shrewd observer, as well as at being accounted logical in all my conduct, precise and methodical in all my ways of life, and at the same time contemptuous of all materiality. I may safely say that I was far better in reality than the strange being into whom I attempted to convert myself; yet, whatever I was or was not, the Nechludoffs were unfailingly kind to me, and (happily for myself) took no notice (as it now appears) of my play-acting. Only Lubov Sergievna, who, I believe, really believed me to be a great egoist, atheist, and cynic, had no love for me, but frequently disputed what I said, flew into tempers, and left me petrified with her disjointed, irrelevant utterances. Yet Dimitri held always to the same strange, something more than friendly, relations with her, and used to say not only that she was misunderstood by every one, but that she did him a world of good. This, however, did not prevent the rest of his family from finding fault with his infatuation.

Once, when talking to me about this incomprehensible attachment, Varenika explained the matter thus: "You see, Dimitri is a selfish person. He is very proud, and, for all his intellect, very fond of praise, and of surprising people, and of always being FIRST, while little Auntie" (the general nickname for Lubov Sergievna) "is innocent enough to admire him, and at the same time devoid of the tact to conceal her admiration. Consequently she flatters his vanity—not out of pretence, but sincerely."

This dictum I laid to heart, and, when thinking it over afterwards, could not but come to the conclusion that Varenika was very sensible; wherefore I was glad to award her promotion thenceforth in my regard. Yet, though I was always glad enough to assign her any credit which might arise from my discovering in her character any signs of good sense or other moral qualities, I did so with strict moderation, and never ran to any extreme pitch of enthusiasm in the process. Thus, when Sophia Ivanovna (who was never weary of discussing her niece) related to me how, four years ago, Varenika had suddenly given away all her clothes to some peasant children without first asking permission to do so, so that the garments had subsequently to be recovered, I did not at once accept the fact as entitling Varenika to elevation in my opinion, but went on giving her good advice about the unpracticalness of such views on property.

When other guests were present at the Nechludoffs (among them, sometimes, Woloda and Dubkoff) I used to withdraw myself to a remote plane, and, with the complacency and quiet consciousness of strength of an habitue of the house, listen to what others were saying without putting in a remark myself. Yet everything that these others said seemed to me so immeasurably stupid that I used to feel inwardly amazed that such a clever, logical woman as the Princess, with her equally logical family, could listen to and answer such rubbish. Had it, however, entered into my head to compare what, others said with what I myself said when there alone, I should probably have ceased to feel surprise. Still less should I have continued to feel surprise had I not believed that the women of our own household—Avdotia, Lubotshka, and Katenka—were superior to the rest of their sex, for in that case I should have remembered the kind of things over which Avdotia and Katenka would laugh and jest with Dubkoff from one end of an evening to the other. I should have remembered that seldom did an evening pass but Dubkoff would first have, an argument about something, and then read in a sententious voice either some verses beginning "Au banquet de la vie, infortune convive" or extracts from The Demon. In short, I should have remembered what nonsense they used to chatter for hours at a time.

It need hardly be said that, when guests were present, Varenika paid less attention to me than when we were alone, as well as that I was deprived of the reading and music which I so greatly loved to hear. When talking to guests, she lost, in my eyes, her principal charm—that of quiet seriousness and simplicity. I remember how strange it used to seem to me to hear her discoursing on theatres and the weather to my brother Woloda! I knew that of all things in the world he most despised and shunned banality, and that Varenika herself used to make fun of forced conversations on the weather and similar matters. Why, then, when meeting in society, did they both of them talk such intolerable nothings, and, as it were, shame one another? After talks of this kind I used to feel silently resentful against Woloda, as well as next day to rally Varenika on her overnight guests. Yet one result of it was that I derived all the greater pleasure from being one of the Nechludoffs' family circle. Also, for some reason or another I began to prefer meeting Dimitri in his mother's drawing-room to being with him alone.

XLI. MY FRIENDSHIP WITH THE NECHLUDOFFS

At this period, indeed, my friendship with Dimitri hung by a hair. I had been criticising him too long not to have discovered faults in his character, for it is only in first youth that we love passionately and therefore love only perfect people. As soon as the mists engendered by love of this kind begin to dissolve, and to be penetrated by the clear beams of reason, we see the object of our adoration in his true shape, and with all his virtues and failings exposed. Some of those failings strike us with the exaggerated force of the unexpected, and combine with the instinct for novelty and the hope that perfection may yet be found in a fellow-man to induce us not only to feel coldness, but even aversion, towards the late object of our adoration. Consequently, desiring it no longer, we usually cast it from us, and pass onwards to seek fresh perfection. For the circumstance that that was not what occurred with respect to my own relation to Dimitri, I was indebted to his stubborn, punctilious, and more critical than impulsive attachment to myself—a tie which I felt ashamed to break. Moreover, our strange vow of frankness bound us together. We were afraid that, if we parted, we should leave in one another's power all the incriminatory moral secrets of which we had made mutual confession. At the same time, our rule of frankness had long ceased to be faithfully observed, but, on the contrary, proved a frequent cause of constraint, and brought about strange relations between us.

Almost every time that winter that I went upstairs to Dimitri's room, I used to find there a University friend of his named Bezobiedoff, with whom he appeared to be very much taken up. Bezobiedoff was a small, slight fellow, with a face pitted over with smallpox, freckled, effeminate hands, and a huge flaxen moustache much in need of the comb. He was invariably dirty, shabby, uncouth, and uninteresting. To me, Dimitri's relations with him were as unintelligible as his relations with Lubov Sergievna, and the only reason he could have had for choosing such a man for his associate was that in the whole University there was no worse-looking student than Bezobiedoff. Yet that alone would have been sufficient to make Dimitri extend him his friendship, and, as a matter of fact, in all his intercourse with this fellow he seemed to be saying proudly: "I care nothing who a man may be. In my eyes every one is equal. I like him, and therefore he is a desirable acquaintance." Nevertheless I could not imagine how he could bring himself to do it, nor how the wretched Bezobiedoff ever contrived to maintain his awkward position. To me the friendship seemed a most distasteful one.

One night, I went up to Dimitri's room to try and get him to come down for an evening's talk in his mother's drawing-room, where we could also listen to Varenika's reading and singing, but Bezobiedoff had forestalled me there, and Dimitri answered me curtly that he could not come down, since, as I could see for myself, he had a visitor with him.

"Besides," he added, "what is the fun of sitting there? We had much better stay HERE and talk."

I scarcely relished the prospect of spending a couple of hours in Bezobiedoff's company, yet could not make up my mind to go down alone; wherefore, cursing my friend's vagaries, I seated myself in a rocking-chair, and began rocking myself silently to and fro. I felt vexed with them both for depriving me of the pleasures of the drawing-room, and my only hope as I listened irritably to their conversation was that Bezobiedoff would soon take his departure. "A nice guest indeed to be sitting with!" I thought to myself when a footman brought in tea and Dimitri had five times to beg Bezobiedoff to have a cup, for the reason that the bashful guest thought it incumbent upon him always to refuse it at first and to say, "No, help yourself." I could see that Dimitri had to put some restraint upon himself as he resumed the conversation. He tried to inveigle me also into it, but I remained glum and silent.

"I do not mean to let my face give any one the suspicion that I am bored" was my mental remark to Dimitri as I sat quietly rocking myself to and fro with measured beat. Yet, as the moments passed, I found myself—not without a certain satisfaction—growing more and more inwardly hostile to my friend. "What a fool he is!" I reflected. "He might be spending the evening agreeably with his charming family, yet he goes on sitting with this brute!—

will go on doing so, too, until it is too late to go down to the drawing-room!" Here I glanced at him over the back of my chair, and thought the general look of his attitude and appearance so offensive and repellant that at the moment I could gladly have offered him some insult, even a most serious one.

At last Bezobiedoff rose, but Dimitri could not easily let such a delightful friend depart, and asked him to stay the night. Fortunately, Bezobiedoff declined the invitation, and departed. Having seen him off, Dimitri returned, and, smiling a faintly complacent smile as he did so, and rubbing his hands together (in all probability partly because he had sustained his character for eccentricity, and partly because he had got rid of a bore), started to pace the room, with an occasional glance at myself. I felt more offended with him than ever. "How can he go on walking about the room and grinning like that?" was my inward reflection.

"What are you so angry about?" he asked me suddenly as he halted in front of my chair.

"I am not in the least angry," I replied (as people always do answer under such circumstances). "I am merely vexed that you should play-act to me, and to Bezobiedoff, and to yourself."

"What rubbish!" he retorted. "I never play-act to any one."

"I have in mind our rule of frankness," I replied, "when I tell you that I am certain you cannot bear this Bezobiedoff any more than I can. He is an absolute cad, yet for some inexplicable reason or another it pleases you to masquerade before him."

"Not at all! To begin with, he is a splendid fellow, and—"

"But I tell you it IS so. I also tell you that your friendship for Lubov Sergievna is founded on the same basis, namely, that she thinks you a god."

"And I tell you once more that it is not so."

"Oh, I know it for myself," I retorted with the heat of suppressed anger, and designing to disarm him with my frankness. "I have told you before, and I repeat it now, that you always seem to like people who say pleasant things to you, but that, as soon as ever I come to examine your friendship, I invariably find that there exists no real attachment between you."

"Oh, but you are wrong," said Dimitri with an angry straightening of the neck in his collar. "When I like people, neither their praise nor their blame can make any difference to my opinion of them."

"Well, dreadful though it may seem to you, I confess that I myself often used to hate my father when he abused me, and to wish that he was dead. In the same way, you—"

"Speak for yourself. I am very sorry that you could ever have been so—"

"No, no!" I cried as I leapt from my chair and faced him with the courage of exasperation. "It is for YOURSELF that you ought to feel sorry—sorry because you never told me a word about this fellow. You know that was not honourable of you. Nevertheless, I will tell YOU what I think of you," and, burning to wound him even more than he had wounded me, I set out to prove to him that he was incapable of feeling any real affection for anybody, and that I had the best of grounds (as in very truth I believed I had) for reproaching him. I took great pleasure in telling him all this, but at the same time forgot that the only conceivable purpose of my doing so—to force him to confess to the faults of which I had accused him—could not possibly be attained at the present moment, when he was in a rage. Had he, on the other hand, been in a condition to argue calmly, I should probably never have said what I did.

The dispute was verging upon an open quarrel when Dimitri suddenly became silent, and left the room. I pursued him, and continued what I was saying, but he did not answer. I knew that his failings included a hasty temper, and that he was now fighting it down; wherefore I cursed his good resolutions the more in my heart.

This, then, was what our rule of frankness had brought us to—the rule that we should "tell one another everything in our minds, and never discuss one another with a third person!" Many a time we had exaggerated frankness to the pitch of making mutual confession of the most shameless thoughts, and of shaming ourselves by voicing to one another proposals or schemes for attaining our desires; yet those confessions had not only failed to draw closer the tie which united us, but had dissipated sympathy and thrust us further apart, until now pride would not allow him to expose his feelings even in the smallest detail, and we employed in our quarrel the very weapons which we had formerly surrendered to one another—the weapons which could strike the shrewdest blows!

XLII. OUR STEPMOTHER

Notwithstanding that Papa had not meant to return to Moscow before the New Year, he arrived in October, when there was still good riding to hounds to be had in the country. He alleged as his reason for changing his mind that his suit was shortly to come on before the Senate, but Mimi averred that Avdotia had found herself so ennuyee in the country, and had so often talked about Moscow and pretended to be unwell, that Papa had decided to accede to her wishes. "You see, she never really loved him—she and her love only kept buzzing about his ears because she wanted to marry a rich man," added Mimi with a pensive sigh which said: "To think what a certain other person could have done for him if only he had valued her!"

Yet that "certain other person" was unjust to Avdotia, seeing that the latter's affection for Papa—the passionate, devoted love of self-abandonment—revealed itself in her every look and word and movement. At the same time, that love in no way hindered her, not only from being averse to parting with her adored husband, but also from desiring to visit Madame Annette's and order there a lovely cap, a hat trimmed with a magnificent blue ostrich feather, and a blue Venetian velvet bodice which was to expose to the public gaze the snowy, well shaped breast and arms which no one had yet gazed upon except her husband and maids. Of course Katenka sided with her mother and, in general, there became established between Avdotia and ourselves, from the day of her arrival, the most extraordinary and burlesque order of relations. As soon as she stepped from the carriage, Woloda assumed an air of great seriousness and ceremony, and, advancing towards her with much bowing and scraping, said in the tone of one who is presenting something for acceptance:

"I have the honour to greet the arrival of our dear Mamma, and to kiss her hand."

"Ah, my dear son!" she replied with her beautiful, unvarying smile.

"And do not forget the younger son," I said as I also approached her hand, with an involuntary imitation of Woloda's voice and expression.

Had our stepmother and ourselves been certain of any mutual affection, that expression might have signified contempt for any outward manifestation of our love. Had we been ill-disposed towards one another, it might have denoted irony, or contempt for pretence, or a desire to conceal from Papa (standing by the while) our real relations, as well as many other thoughts and sentiments. But, as a matter of fact, that expression (which well consorted with Avdotia's own spirit) simply signified nothing at all—simply concealed the absence of any definite relations between us. In later life I often had occasion to remark, in the case of other families whose members anticipated among themselves relations not altogether harmonious, the sort of provisional, burlesque relations which they formed for daily use; and it was just such relations as those which now became established between ourselves and our stepmother. We scarcely ever strayed beyond them, but were polite to her, conversed with her in French, bowed and scraped before her, and called her "chere Maman"—a term to which she always responded in a tone of similar lightness and with her beautiful, unchanging smile. Only the lachrymose Lubotshka, with her goose feet and artless prattle, really liked our stepmother, or tried, in her naive and frequently awkward way, to bring her and ourselves together: wherefore the only person in the world for whom, besides Papa, Avdotia had a spark of affection was Lubotshka. Indeed, Avdotia always treated her with a kind of grave admiration and timid deference which greatly surprised me.

From the first Avdotia was very fond of calling herself our stepmother and hinting that, since children and servants usually adopt an unjust and hostile attitude towards a woman thus situated, her own position was likely to prove a difficult one. Yet, though she foresaw all the unpleasantness of her predicament, she did nothing to escape from it by (for instance) conciliating this one, giving presents to that other one, and forbearing to grumble—the last a precaution which it would have been easy for her to take, seeing that by nature she was in no way exacting, as well as very good-tempered. Yet, not only did she do none of these things, but her expectation of difficulties led her to adopt the defensive before she had been attacked. That is to say, supposing that the entire household was designing to show her every kind of insult and annoyance, she would see plots where no plots were, and consider that her most dignified course was to suffer in silence—an attitude of passivity as regards winning AFfection which of course led to DISaffection. Moreover, she was so totally lacking in that faculty of "apprehension" to which I have already referred as being highly developed in our household, and all her customs were so utterly opposed to those which had long been rooted in our establishment, that those two facts alone were bound to go against her. From the first, her mode of life in our tidy, methodical household was that of a person only just arrived there. Sometimes she went to bed late, sometimes early; sometimes she appeared at luncheon, sometimes she did not; sometimes she took supper, sometimes she dispensed with it. When we had no guests with us she more often than not walked about the house in a semi-nude condition, and was not ashamed to appear before us—even before the servants—in a white chemise, with only a shawl thrown over her bare shoulders. At first this Bohemianism pleased me, but before very long it led to my losing the last shred of respect which I felt for her. What struck me as even more strange was the fact that, according as we had or had not guests, she was two different women. The one (the woman figuring in society) was a young and healthy, but rather cold, beauty, a person richly dressed, neither stupid nor clever, and unfailingly cheerful. The other woman (the one in evidence when no guests were present) was considerably past her first youth, languid, depressed, slovenly, and ennuyee, though affectionate. Frequently, as I looked at her when, smiling, rosy with the winter air, and happy in the consciousness of her beauty, she came in from a round of calls and, taking off her hat, went to look at herself in a mirror; or when, rustling in her rich, decollete ball dress, and at once shy and proud before the servants, she was passing to her carriage; or when, at one of our small receptions at home, she was sitting dressed in a high silken dress finished with some sort of fine lace about her soft neck, and flashing her unvarying, but lovely, smile around her—as I looked at her at such times I could not help wondering what would have been said by persons who had been ravished to behold her thus if they could have seen her as I often saw her, namely, when, waiting in the lonely midnight hours for her husband to return from his club, she would walk like a shadow from room to room, with her hair dishevelled and her form clad in a sort of dressing-jacket. Presently, she would sit down to the piano and, her brows all puckered with the effort, play over the only waltz that she knew; after which she would pick up a novel, read a few pages somewhere in the middle of it, and throw it aside. Next, repairing in person to the dining-room, so as not to disturb the servants, she would get herself a cucumber and some cold veal, and eat it standing by the window-sill—then once more resume her weary, aimless, gloomy wandering from room to room. But what, above all other things, caused estrangement between us was that lack of understanding which expressed itself chiefly in the peculiar air of indulgent attention with which she would listen when any one was speaking to her concerning matters of which she had no knowledge. It was not her fault that she acquired the unconscious habit of bending her head down and smiling slightly with her lips only when she found it necessary to converse on topics which did not interest her (which meant any topic except herself and her husband); yet that smile and that inclination of the head, when incessantly repeated, could become unbearably wearisome. Also, her peculiar gaiety—which always sounded as though she were laughing at herself, at you, and at the world in general—was gauche and anything but infectious, while her sympathy was too evidently forced. Lastly, she knew no reticence with regard to her ceaseless rapturising to all and sundry concerning her love for Papa. Although she only spoke the truth when she said that her whole life was bound up with him, and although she proved it her life long, we considered such unrestrained, continual insistence upon her affection for him bad form, and felt more ashamed for her when she was descanting thus before strangers even than we did when she was perpetrating bad blunders in French. Yet, although, as I have said, she loved her husband more than anything else in the world, and he too had a great affection for her (or at all events he had at first, and when he saw that others besides himself admired her beauty), it seemed almost as though she purposely did everything most likely to displease him—simply to prove to him the strength of her love, her readiness to sacrifice herself for his sake, and the fact that her one aim in life was to win his affection! She was fond of display, and my father too liked to see her as a beauty who excited wonder and admiration; yet she sacrificed her weakness for fine clothes to her love for him, and grew more and more accustomed to remain at home in a plain grey blouse. Again, Papa considered freedom and equality to be indispensable conditions of family life, and hoped that his favourite Lubotshka and his kind-hearted young wife would become sincere friends; yet once again Avdotia sacrificed herself by considering it incumbent upon her to pay the "real mistress of the house," as she called Lubotshka, an amount of deference which only shocked and annoyed my father. Likewise, he played cards a great deal that winter, and lost considerable sums towards the end of it, wherefore, unwilling, as usual, to let his gambling affairs intrude upon his family life, he began to preserve complete secrecy concerning his play; yet Avdotia, though often ailing, as well as, towards the end of the winter, enceinte, considered herself bound always to sit up (in a grey blouse, and with her hair dishevelled) for my father when, at, say, four or five o'clock in the morning, he returned home from the club ashamed, depleted in pocket, and weary. She would ask him absent-mindedly whether he had been fortunate in play, and listen with indulgent attention, little nods of her head, and a faint smile upon her face as he told her of his doings at the club and begged her, for about the hundredth time, never to sit up for him again. Yet, though Papa's winnings or losings (upon which his substance practically depended) in no way interested her, she was always the first to meet him when he returned home in the small hours of the morning. This she was incited to do, not only by the strength of her devotion, but by a certain secret jealousy from which she suffered. No one in the world could persuade her that it was REALLY from his club, and not from a mistress's, that Papa came home so late. She would try to read love secrets in his face, and, discerning none there, would sigh with a sort of enjoyment of her grief, and give herself up once more to the contemplation of her unhappiness.

As the result of these and many other constant sacrifices which occurred in Papa's relations with his wife during the latter months of that winter (a time when he lost much, and was therefore out of spirits), there gradually grew up between the two an intermittent feeling of tacit hostility—of restrained aversion to the object of devotion of the kind which expresses itself in an unconscious eagerness to show the object in question every possible species of petty annoyance.

XLIII. NEW COMRADES

The winter had passed imperceptibly and the thaw begun when the list of examinations was posted at the University, and I suddenly remembered that I had to return answers to questions in eighteen subjects on which I had heard lectures delivered, but with regard to some of which I had taken no notes and made no preparation whatever. It seems strange that the question "How am I going to pass?" should never have entered my head, but the truth is that all that winter I had been in such a state of haze through the delights of being both grown-up and "comme il faut" that, whenever the question of the examinations had occurred to me, I had mentally compared myself with my comrades, and thought to myself, "They are certain to pass, and as most of them are not 'comme il faut,' and I am therefore their personal superior, I too am bound to come out all right." In fact, the only reason why I attended lectures at all was that I might become an habitue of the University, and obtain Papa's leave to go in and out of the house. Moreover, I had many acquaintances now, and often enjoyed myself vastly at the University. I loved the racket, talking, and laughter in the auditorium, the opportunities for sitting on a back bench, and letting the measured voice of the professor lure one into dreams as one contemplated one's comrades, the occasional runnings across the way for a snack and a glass of vodka (sweetened by the fearful joy of knowing that one might be hauled before the professor for so doing), the stealthy closing of the door as one returned to the auditorium, and the participation in "course versus course" scuffles in the corridors. All this was very enjoyable.

By the time, however, that every one had begun to put in a better attendance at lectures, and the professor of physics had completed his course and taken his leave of us until the examinations came on, and the students were busy collecting their notebooks and arranging to do their preparation in parties, it struck me that I also had better prepare for the ordeal. Operoff, with whom I still continued on bowing, but otherwise most frigid, terms, suddenly offered not only to lend me his notebooks, but to let me do my preparation with himself and some other students. I thanked him, and accepted the invitation—hoping by that conferment of honour completely to dissipate our old misunderstanding; but at the same time I requested that the gatherings should always be held at my home, since my quarters were so splendid! To this the students replied that they meant to take turn and turn about—sometimes to meet at one fellow's place, sometimes at another's, as might be most convenient.

The first of our reunions was held at Zuchin's, who had a small partition-room in a large building on the Trubni Boulevard. The opening night I arrived late, and entered when the reading aloud had already begun. The little apartment was thick with tobacco-smoke, while on the table stood a bottle of vodka, a decanter, some bread, some salt, and a shin-bone of mutton. Without rising, Zuchin asked me to have some vodka and to doff my tunic.

"I expect you are not accustomed to such entertainment," he added.

Every one was wearing a dirty cotton shirt and a dickey. Endeavouring not to show my contempt for the company, I took off my tunic, and lay down in a sociable manner on the sofa. Zuchin went on reading aloud and correcting himself with the help of notebooks, while the others occasionally stopped him to ask a question, which he always answered with ability, correctness, and precision. I listened for a time with the rest, but, not understanding much of it, since I had not been present at what had been read before, soon interpolated a question.

"Hullo, old fellow! It will be no good for you to listen if you do not know the subject," said Zuchin. "I will lend you my notebooks, and then you can read it up by to-morrow, and I will explain it to you."

I felt rather ashamed of my ignorance. Also, I felt the truth of what he said; so I gave up listening, and amused myself by observing my new comrades. According to my classification of humanity, into persons "comme il faut" and persons not "comme il faut," they evidently belonged to the latter category, and so aroused in me not only a feeling of contempt, but also a certain sensation of personal hostility, for the reason that, though not "comme il faut," they accounted me their equal, and actually patronised me in a sort of good-humoured fashion. What in particular excited in me this feeling was their feet, their dirty nails and fingers, a particularly long talon on Operoff's obtrusive little finger, their red shirts, their dickeys, the chaff which they good-naturedly threw at one another, the dirty room, a habit which Zuchin had of continually snuffling and pressing a finger to his nose, and, above all, their manner of speaking—that is to say, their use and intonation of words. For instance, they said "flat" for fool, "just the ticket" for exactly, "grandly" for splendidly, and so on—all of which seemed to me either bookish or disagreeably vulgar. Still more was my "comme il faut" refinement disturbed by the accents which they put upon certain Russian—and, still more, upon foreign—words. Thus they said dieYATelnost for DIEyatelnost, NARochno for naROChno, v'KAMinie for v'kaMINie, SHAKespeare for ShakesPEARe, and so forth.

Yet, for all their insuperably repellent exterior, I could detect something good in these fellows, and envied them the cheerful good-fellowship which united them in one. Consequently, I began to feel attracted towards them, and made up my mind that, come what might, I would become of their number. The kind and honourable Operoff I knew already, and now the brusque, but exceptionally clever, Zuchin (who evidently took the lead in this circle) began to please me greatly. He was a dark, thick-set little fellow, with a perennially glistening, polished face, but one that was extremely lively, intellectual, and independent in its expression. That expression it derived from a low, but prominent, forehead, deep black eyes, short, bristly hair, and a thick, dark beard which looked as though it stood in constant need of trimming. Although, too, he seemed to think nothing of himself (a trail which always pleased me in people), it was clear that he never let his brain rest. He had one of those expressive faces which, a few hours after you have seen them for the first time, change suddenly and entirely to your view. Such a change took place, in my eyes, with regard to Zuchin's face towards the end of that evening. Suddenly, I seemed to see new wrinkles appear upon its surface, its eyes grow deeper, its smile become a different one, and the whole face assume such an altered aspect that I scarcely recognised it.

When the reading was ended, Zuchin, the other students, and myself

461

manifested our desire to be "comrades all" by drinking vodka until little remained in the bottle. Thereupon Zuchin asked if any one had a quarter-rouble to spare, so that he could send the old woman who looked after him to buy some more; yet, on my offering to provide the money, he made as though he had not heard me, and turned to Operoff, who pulled out a purse sewn with bugles, and handed him the sum required.

"And mind you don't get drunk," added the giver, who himself had not partaken of the vodka.

"By heavens!" answered Zuchin as he sucked the marrow out of a mutton bone (I remember thinking that it must be because he ate marrow that he was so clever). "By heavens!" he went on with a slight smile (and his smile was of the kind that one involuntarily noticed, and somehow felt grateful for), "even if I did get drunk, there would be no great harm done. I wonder which of us two could look after himself the better—you or I? Anyway I am willing to make the experiment," and he slapped his forehead with mock boastfulness. "But what a pity it is that Semenoff has disappeared! He has gone and completely hidden himself somewhere."

Sure enough, the grey-haired Semenoff who had comforted me so much at my first examination by being worse dressed than myself, and who, after passing the second examination, had attended his lectures regularly during the first month, had disappeared thereafter from view, and never been seen at the University throughout the latter part of the course.

"Where is he?" asked some one.

"I do not know" replied Zuchin. "He has escaped my eye altogether. Yet what fun I used to have with him! What fire there was in the man! and what an intellect! I should be indeed sorry if he has come to grief—and come to grief he probably has, for he was no mere boy to take his University course in instalments."

After a little further conversation, and agreeing to meet again the next night at Zuchin's, since his abode was the most central point for us all, we began to disperse. As, one by one, we left the room, my conscience started pricking me because every one seemed to be going home on foot, whereas I had my drozhki. Accordingly, with some hesitation I offered Operoff a lift. Zuchin came to the door with us, and, after borrowing a rouble of Operoff, went off to make a night of it with some friends. As we drove along, Operoff told me a good deal about Zuchin's character and mode of life, and on reaching home it was long before I could get to sleep for thinking of the new acquaintances I had made. For many an hour, as I lay awake, I kept wavering between the respect which their knowledge, simplicity, and sense of honour, as well as the poetry of their youth and courage, excited in my regard, and the distaste which I felt for their outward man. In spite of my desire to do so, it was at that time literally impossible for me to associate with them, since our ideas were too wholly at variance. For me, life's meaning and charm contained an infinitude of shades of which they had not an inkling, and vice versa. The greatest obstacles of all, however, to our better acquaintance I felt to be the twenty roubles' worth of cloth in my tunic, my drozhki, and my white linen shirt; and they appeared to me most important obstacles, since they made me feel as though I had unwittingly insulted these comrades by displaying such tokens of my wealth. I felt guilty in their eyes, and as though, whether I accepted or rejected their acquittal and took a line of my own, I could never enter into equal and unaffected relations with them. Yet to such an extent did the stirring poetry of the courage which I could detect in Zuchin (in particular) overshadow the coarse, vicious side of his nature that the latter made no unpleasant impression upon me.

For a couple of weeks I visited Zuchin's almost every night for purposes of work. Yet I did very little there, since, as I have said, I had lost ground at the start, and, not having sufficient grit in me to catch up my companions by solitary study, was forced merely to PRETEND that I was listening to and taking in all they were reading. I have an idea, too, that they divined my pretence, since I often noticed that they passed over points which they themselves knew without first inquiring of me whether I did the same. Yet, day by day, I was coming to regard the vulgarity of this circle with more indulgence, to feel increasingly drawn towards its way of life, and to find in it much that was poetical. Only my word of honour to Dimitri that I would never indulge in dissipation with these new comrades kept me from deciding also to share their diversions.

Once, I thought I would make a display of my knowledge of literature, particularly French literature, and so led the conversation to that theme. Judge, then, of my surprise when I discovered that not only had my companions been reading the foreign passages in Russian, but that they had studied far more foreign works than I had, and knew and could appraise English, and even Spanish, writers of whom I had never so much as heard! Likewise, Pushkin and Zhukovski represented to them LITERATURE, and not, as to myself, certain books in yellow covers which I had once read and studied when a child. For Dumas and Sue they had an almost equal contempt, and, in general, were competent to form much better and clearer judgments on literary matters than I was, for all that I refused to recognise the fact. In knowledge of music, too, I could not beat them, and was astonished to find that Operoff played the violin, and another student the cello and piano, while both of them were members of the University orchestra, and possessed a wide knowledge of and appreciation of good music. In short, with the exception of the French and German languages, my companions were better posted at every point than I was, yet not the least proud of the fact. True, I might have plumed myself on my position as a man of the world, but Woloda excelled me even in that. Wherein, then, lay the height from which I presumed to look down upon these comrades? In my acquaintanceship with Prince Ivan Ivanovitch? In my ability to speak French? In my drozhki? In my linen shirt? In my finger-nails? "Surely these things are all rubbish," was the thought which would come flitting through my head under the influence of the envy which the good-fellowship and kindly, youthful gaiety displayed around me excited in my breast. Every one addressed his interlocutor in the second person singular. True, the familiarity of this address almost approximated to rudeness, yet even the boorish exterior of the speaker could not conceal a constant endeavour never to hurt another one's feelings. The terms "brute" or "swine," when used in this good-natured fashion, only convulsed me, and gave me cause for inward merriment. In no way did they offend the person addressed, or prevent the company at large from remaining on the most sincere and friendly footing. In all their intercourse these youths were delicate and forbearing in a way that only very poor and very young men can be. However much I might detect in Zuchin's character and amusements an element of coarseness and profligacy, I could also detect the fact that his drinking-bouts were of a very different order to the puerility with burnt rum and champagne in which I had participated at Baron Z.'s.

XLIV. ZUCHIN AND SEMENOFF

Although I do not know what class of society Zuchin belonged to, I know that, without the help either of means or social position, he had matriculated from the Seventh Gymnasium. At that time he was eighteen—though he looked much older—and very clever, especially in his powers of assimilation. To him it was easier to survey the whole of some complicated subject, to foresee its various parts and deductions, than to use that knowledge, when gained, for reasoning out the exact laws to which those deductions were due. He knew that he was clever, and of the fact he was proud; yet from that very pride arose the circumstance that he treated every one with unvarying simplicity and good-nature. Moreover, his experience of life must have been considerable, for already he had squandered much love, friendship, activity, and money. Though poor and moving only in the lower ranks of society, there was nothing which he had ever attempted for which he did not thenceforth feel the contempt, the indifference, or the utter disregard which were bound to result from his attaining his goal too easily. In fact, the very ardour with which he applied himself to a new pursuit seemed to be due to his contempt for what he had already attained, since his abilities always led him to success, and therefore to a certain right to despise it. With the sciences it was the same. Though little interested in them, and taking no notes, he knew mathematics thoroughly, and was uttering no vain boast when he said that he could beat the professor himself. Much of what he heard said in lectures he thought rubbish, yet with his peculiar habit of unconsciously practical roguishness he feigned to subscribe to all that the professors thought important, and every professor adored him. True, he was outspoken to the authorities, but they none the less respected him. Besides disliking and despising the sciences, he despised all who laboured to attain what he himself had mastered so easily, since the sciences, as he understood them, did not occupy one-tenth part of his powers. In fact, life, as he saw it from the student's standpoint, contained nothing to which he could devote himself wholly, and his impetuous, active nature (as he himself often said) demanded life complete: wherefore he frequented the drinking-bout in so far as he could afford it, and surrendered himself to dissipation chiefly out of a desire to get as far away from himself as possible. Consequently, just as the examinations were approaching, Operoff's prophecy to me came true, for Zuchin wasted two whole weeks in this fashion, and we had to do the latter part of our preparation at another student's. Yet at the first examination he reappeared with pale, haggard face and tremulous hands, and passed brilliantly into the second course!

The company of roisterers of which Zuchin had been the leader since its formation at the beginning of the term consisted of eight students, among whom, at first, had been numbered Ikonin and Semenoff; but the former had left under the strain of the continuous revelry in which the band had indulged in the early part of the term, and the latter seceded later for reasons which were never wholly explained. In its early days this band had been looked upon with awe by all the fellows of our course, and had had its exploits much discussed. Of these exploits the leading heroes had been Zuchin and, towards the end of the term, Semenoff, but the latter had come to be generally shunned, and to cause disturbances on the rare occasions when he attended a lecture. Just before the examinations began, he rounded off his drinking exploits in a most energetic and original fashion, as I myself had occasion to witness (through my acquaintanceship with Zuchin). This is how it was. One evening we had just assembled at Zuchin's, and Operoff, reinforcing a candlestick with a candle stuck in a bottle, had just plunged his nose into his notebooks and begun to read aloud in his thin voice from his neatly-written notes on physics, when the landlady entered the room, and informed Zuchin that some one had brought a note for him... [The remainder of this chapter is omitted in the original.]

XLV. I COME TO GRIEF

At length the first examination—on differentials and integrals—drew near, but I continued in a vague state which precluded me from forming any clear idea of what was awaiting me. Every evening, after consorting with Zuchin and the rest, the thought would occur to me that there was something in my convictions which I must change—something wrong and mistaken; yet every morning the daylight would find me again satisfied to be "comme il faut," and desirous of no change whatsoever.

Such was the frame of mind in which I attended for the first examination. I seated myself on the bench where the princes, counts, and barons always sat, and began talking to them in French, with the not unnatural result that I never gave another thought to the answers which I was shortly to return to questions in a subject of which I knew nothing. I gazed supinely at other students as they went up to be examined, and even allowed myself to chaff some of them.

"Well, Grap," I said to Ilinka (who, from our first entry into the University, had shaken off my influence, had ceased to smile when I spoke to him, and always remained ill-disposed towards me), "have you survived the ordeal?"

"Yes," retorted Ilinka. "Let us see if YOU can do so."

I smiled contemptuously at the answer, notwithstanding that the doubt which he had expressed had given me a momentary shock. Once again, however, indifference overlaid that feeling, and I remained so entirely absent-minded and supine that, the very moment after I had been examined (a mere formality for me, as it turned out) I was making a dinner appointment with Baron Z. When called out with Ikonin, I smoothed the creases in my uniform, and walked up to the examiner's table with perfect sang froid.

True, a slight shiver of apprehension ran down my back when the young professor—the same one as had examined me for my matriculation—looked me straight in the face as I reached across to the envelope containing the tickets. Ikonin, though taking a ticket with the same plunge of his whole body as he had done at the previous examinations, did at least return some sort of an answer this time, though a poor one. I, on the contrary, did just as he had done on the two previous occasions, or even worse, since I took a second ticket, yet for a second time returned no answer. The professor looked me compassionately in the face, and said in a quiet, but determined, voice:

"You will not pass into the second course, Monsieur Irtenieff. You had better not complete the examinations. The faculty must be weeded out. The same with you, Monsieur Ikonin."

Ikonin implored leave to finish the examinations, as a great favour, but the professor replied that he (Ikonin) was not likely to do in two days what he had not succeeded in doing in a year, and that he had not the smallest chance of passing. Ikonin renewed his humble, piteous appeals, but the professor was inexorable.

"You can go, gentlemen," he remarked in the same quiet, resolute voice.

I was only too glad to do so, for I felt ashamed of seeming, by my silent presence, to be joining in Ikonin's humiliating prayers for grace. I have no recollection of how I threaded my way through the students in the hall, nor of what I replied to their questions, nor of how I passed into the vestibule and departed home. I was offended, humiliated, and genuinely unhappy.

For three days I never left my room, and saw no one, but found relief in copious tears. I should have sought a pistol to shoot myself if I had had the necessary determination for the deed. I thought that Ilinka Grap would spit in my face when he next met me, and that he would have the right to do so; that Operoff would rejoice at my misfortune, and tell every one of it; that Kolpikoff had justly shamed me that night at the restaurant; that my stupid speeches to Princess Kornikoff had had their fitting result; and so on, and so on. All the moments in my life which had been for me most difficult and painful recurred to my mind. I tried to blame some one for my calamity, and thought that some one must have done it on purpose—must have conspired a whole intrigue against me. Next, I murmured against the professors, against my comrades, Woloda, Dimitri, and Papa (the last for having sent me to the University at all). Finally, I railed at Providence for ever having let me see such ignominy. Believing myself ruined for ever in the eyes of all who knew me, I besought Papa to let me go into the hussars or to the Caucasus. Naturally, Papa was anything but pleased at what had happened; yet, on seeing my passionate grief, he comforted me by saying that, though it was a bad business, it might yet be mended by my transferring to another faculty. Woloda, who also saw nothing very terrible in my misfortune, added that at least I should not be put out of countenance in a new faculty, since I should have new comrades there. As for the ladies of the household, they neither knew nor cared what either an examination or a plucking meant, and condoled with me only because they saw me in such distress. Dimitri came to see me every day, and was very kind and consolatory throughout; but for that very reason he seemed to me to have grown colder than before. It always hurt me and made me feel uncomfortable when he came up to my room and seated himself in silence beside me, much as a doctor might scat himself by the bedside of an awkward patient. Sophia Ivanovna and Varenika sent me books for which I had expressed a wish, as also an invitation to go and see them, but in that very thoughtfulness of theirs I saw only proud, humiliating condescension to one who had fallen beyond forgiveness. Although, in three days' time, I grew calmer, it was not until we departed for the country that I left the house, but spent the time in nursing my grief and wandering, fearful of all the household, through the various rooms.

One evening, as I was sitting deep in thought and listening to Avdotia playing her waltz, I suddenly leapt to my feet, ran upstairs, got out the copy-book whereon I had once inscribed "Rules of My Life," opened it, and experienced my first moment of repentance and moral resolution. True, I burst into tears once more, but they were no longer tears of despair. Pulling myself together, I set about writing out a fresh set of rules, in the assured conviction that never again would I do a wrong action, waste a single moment on frivolity, or alter the rules which I now decided to frame.

How long that moral impulse lasted, what it consisted of, and what new principles I devised for my moral growth I will relate when speaking of the ensuing and happier portion of my early manhood.

About Author

In the 1870s Tolstoy experienced a profound moral crisis, followed by what he regarded as an equally profound spiritual awakening, as outlined in his non-fiction work A Confession (1882). His literal interpretation of the ethical teachings of Jesus, centering on the Sermon on the Mount, caused him to become a fervent Christian anarchist and pacifist. Tolstoy's ideas on nonviolent resistance, expressed in such works as The Kingdom of God Is Within You (1894), were to have a profound impact on such pivotal 20th-century figures as Mahatma Gandhi and Martin Luther King Jr. Tolstoy also became a dedicated advocate of Georgism, the economic philosophy of Henry George, which he incorporated into his writing, particularly Resurrection (1899).

Origins

The Tolstoys were a well-known family of old Russian nobility who traced their ancestry to a mythical nobleman named Indris described by Pyotr Tolstoy as arriving "from Nemec, from the lands of Caesar" to Chernigov in 1353 along with his two sons Litvinos (or Litvonis) and Zimonten (or Zigmont) and a druzhina of 3000 people. While the word "Nemec" has been long used to describe Germans only, at that time it was applied to any foreigner who didn't speak Russian (from the word nemoy meaning mute). Indris was then converted to Eastern Orthodoxy under the name of Leonty and his sons – as Konstantin and Feodor, respectively. Konstantin's grandson Andrei Kharitonovich was nicknamed Tolstiy (translated as fat) by Vasily II of Moscow after he moved from Chernigov to Moscow.

Because of the pagan names and the fact that Chernigov at the time was ruled by Demetrius I Starshy some researches concluded that they were Lithuanians who arrived from the Grand Duchy of Lithuania, then part of the State of the Teutonic Order. At the same time, no mention of Indris was ever found in the 14th – 16th-century documents, while the Chernigov Chronicles used by Pyotr Tolstoy as a reference were lost. The first documented members of the Tolstoy family also lived during the 17th century, thus Pyotr

Tolstoy himself is generally considered the founder of the noble house, being granted the title of count by Peter the Great.

Life and career

Tolstoy was born at Yasnaya Polyana, a family estate 12 kilometres (7.5 mi) southwest of Tula, Russia, and 200 kilometers (120 mi) south of Moscow. He was the fourth of five children of Count Nikolai Ilyich Tolstoy (1794–1837), a veteran of the Patriotic War of 1812, and Countess Mariya Tolstaya (née Volkonskaya; 1790–1830). After his mother died when he was two and his father when he was nine, Tolstoy and his siblings were brought up by relatives. In 1844, he began studying law and oriental languages at Kazan University, where teachers described him as "both unable and unwilling to learn." Tolstoy left the university in the middle of his studies, returned to Yasnaya Polyana and then spent much of his time in Moscow, Tula and Saint Petersburg, leading a lax and leisurely lifestyle. He began writing during this period, including his first novel Childhood, a fictitious account of his own youth, which was published in 1852. In 1851, after running up heavy gambling debts, he went with his older brother to the Caucasus and joined the army. Tolstoy served as a young artillery officer during the Crimean War and was in Sevastopol during the 11-month-long siege of Sevastopol in 1854–55, including the Battle of the Chernaya. During the war he was recognised for his bravery and courage and promoted to lieutenant. He was appalled by the number of deaths involved in warfare, and left the army after the end of the Crimean War.

His conversion from a dissolute and privileged society author to the non-violent and spiritual anarchist of his latter days was brought about by his experience in the army as well as two trips around Europe in 1857 and 1860–61. Others who followed the same path were Alexander Herzen, Mikhail Bakunin and Peter Kropotkin. During his 1857 visit, Tolstoy witnessed a public execution in Paris, a traumatic experience that would mark the rest of his life. Writing in a letter to his friend Vasily Botkin: "The truth is that the State is a conspiracy designed not only to exploit, but above all to corrupt its citizens ... Henceforth, I shall never serve any government anywhere." Tolstoy's concept of non-violence or Ahimsa was bolstered when he read a

German version of the Tirukkural. He later instilled the concept in Mahatma Gandhi through his A Letter to a Hindu when young Gandhi corresponded with him seeking his advice.

His European trip in 1860–61 shaped both his political and literary development when he met Victor Hugo, whose literary talents Tolstoy praised after reading Hugo's newly finished Les Misérables. The similar evocation of battle scenes in Hugo's novel and Tolstoy's War and Peace indicates this influence. Tolstoy's political philosophy was also influenced by a March 1861 visit to French anarchist Pierre-Joseph Proudhon, then living in exile under an assumed name in Brussels. Apart from reviewing Proudhon's forthcoming publication, La Guerre et la Paix (War and Peace in French), whose title Tolstoy would borrow for his masterpiece, the two men discussed education, as Tolstoy wrote in his educational notebooks: "If I recount this conversation with Proudhon, it is to show that, in my personal experience, he was the only man who understood the significance of education and of the printing press in our time."

Fired by enthusiasm, Tolstoy returned to Yasnaya Polyana and founded 13 schools for the children of Russia's peasants, who had just been emancipated from serfdom in 1861. Tolstoy described the school's principles in his 1862 essay "The School at Yasnaya Polyana". Tolstoy's educational experiments were short-lived, partly due to harassment by the Tsarist secret police. However, as a direct forerunner to A.S. Neill's Summerhill School, the school at Yasnaya Polyana can justifiably be claimed the first example of a coherent theory of democratic education.

Towards the end of his career, Tolstoy was selected to receive the first Nobel Prize in Literature in 1901, but turned down the honor in October of the same year, worrying that the prize money would bring unwanted complications to his life.

Personal life

The death of his brother Nikolay in 1860 had an impact on Tolstoy, and led him to a desire to marry. On 23 September 1862, Tolstoy married Sophia Andreevna Behrs, who was 16 years his junior and the daughter of a court physician. She was called Sonya, the Russian diminutive of Sofia, by her family and friends. They had 13 children, eight of whom survived childhood:

Count Sergei Lvovich Tolstoy (1863–1947), composer and ethnomusicologist

Countess Tatyana Lvovna Tolstaya (1864–1950), wife of Mikhail Sergeevich Sukhotin

Count Ilya Lvovich Tolstoy (1866–1933), writer

Count Lev Lvovich Tolstoy (1869–1945), writer and sculptor

Countess Maria Lvovna Tolstaya (1871–1906), wife of Nikolai Leonidovich Obolensky

Count Peter Lvovich Tolstoy (1872–1873), died in infancy

Count Nikolai Lvovich Tolstoy (1874–1875), died in infancy

Countess Varvara Lvovna Tolstaya (1875–1875), died in infancy

Count Andrei Lvovich Tolstoy (1877–1916), served in the Russo-Japanese War

Count Michael Lvovich Tolstoy (1879–1944)

Count Alexei Lvovich Tolstoy (1881–1886)

Countess Alexandra Lvovna Tolstaya (1884–1979)

Count Ivan Lvovich Tolstoy (1888–1895)

The marriage was marked from the outset by sexual passion and emotional insensitivity when Tolstoy, on the eve of their marriage, gave her his diaries detailing his extensive sexual past and the fact that one of the serfs on his estate had borne him a son. Even so, their early married life was happy and allowed Tolstoy much freedom and the support system to compose War and Peace and Anna Karenina with Sonya acting as his secretary, editor, and financial manager. Sonya was copying and handwriting his epic works time after time. Tolstoy would continue editing War and Peace and had to have clean final drafts to be delivered to the publisher.

However, their later life together has been described by A.N. Wilson as one of the unhappiest in literary history. Tolstoy's relationship with his wife deteriorated as his beliefs became increasingly radical. This saw him seeking to reject his inherited and earned wealth, including the renunciation of the copyrights on his earlier works.

Some of the members of the Tolstoy family left Russia in the aftermath of the 1905 Russian Revolution and the subsequent establishment of the Soviet Union, and many of Leo Tolstoy's relatives and descendants today live in Sweden, Germany, the United Kingdom, France and the United States. Among them are Swedish jazz singer Viktoria Tolstoy and the Swedish landowner Christopher Paus, whose family owns the major estate Herresta outside Stockholm.

One of his great-great-grandsons, Vladimir Tolstoy (born 1962), is a director of the Yasnaya Polyana museum since 1994 and an adviser to the President of Russia on cultural affairs since 2012. Ilya Tolstoy's great-grandson, Pyotr Tolstoy, is a well-known Russian journalist and TV presenter as well as a State Duma deputy since 2016. His cousin Fyokla Tolstaya (born Anna Tolstaya in 1971), daughter of the acclaimed Soviet Slavist Nikita Tolstoy (ru) (1923–1996), is also a Russian journalist, TV and radio host.

Novels and fictional works

Tolstoy is considered one of the giants of Russian literature; his works include the novels War and Peace and Anna Karenina and novellas such as Hadji Murad and The Death of Ivan Ilyich.

Tolstoy's earliest works, the autobiographical novels Childhood, Boyhood, and Youth (1852–1856), tell of a rich landowner's son and his slow realization of the chasm between himself and his peasants. Though he later rejected them as sentimental, a great deal of Tolstoy's own life is revealed. They retain their relevance as accounts of the universal story of growing up.

Tolstoy served as a second lieutenant in an artillery regiment during the Crimean War, recounted in his Sevastopol Sketches. His experiences in battle helped stir his subsequent pacifism and gave him material for realistic depiction of the horrors of war in his later work.

His fiction consistently attempts to convey realistically the Russian society in which he lived. The Cossacks (1863) describes the Cossack life and people through a story of a Russian aristocrat in love with a Cossack girl. Anna Karenina (1877) tells parallel stories of an adulterous woman trapped by the conventions and falsities of society and of a philosophical landowner (much like Tolstoy), who works alongside the peasants in the fields and seeks to reform their lives. Tolstoy not only drew from his own life experiences but also created characters in his own image, such as Pierre Bezukhov and Prince Andrei in War and Peace, Levin in Anna Karenina and to some extent, Prince Nekhlyudov in Resurrection.

War and Peace is generally thought to be one of the greatest novels ever written, remarkable for its dramatic breadth and unity. Its vast canvas includes 580 characters, many historical with others fictional. The story moves from family life to the headquarters of Napoleon, from the court of Alexander I of Russia to the battlefields of Austerlitz and Borodino. Tolstoy's original idea for the novel was to investigate the causes of the Decembrist revolt, to which it refers only in the last chapters, from which can be deduced that Andrei Bolkonsky's son will become one of the Decembrists. The novel explores Tolstoy's theory of history, and in particular the insignificance of individuals such as Napoleon and Alexander. Somewhat surprisingly, Tolstoy did not consider War and Peace to be a novel (nor did he consider many of the great Russian fictions written at that time to be novels). This view becomes less surprising if one considers that Tolstoy was a novelist of the realist school who considered the novel to be a framework for the examination of social and political issues in nineteenth-century life. War and Peace (which is to Tolstoy really an epic in prose) therefore did not qualify. Tolstoy thought that Anna Karenina was his first true novel.

After Anna Karenina, Tolstoy concentrated on Christian themes, and his later novels such as The Death of Ivan Ilyich (1886) and What Is to Be Done? develop a radical anarcho-pacifist Christian philosophy which led to his excommunication from the Russian Orthodox Church in 1901. For all the praise showered on Anna Karenina and War and Peace, Tolstoy rejected the two works later in his life as something not as true of reality.

In his novel Resurrection, Tolstoy attempts to expose the injustice of man-made laws and the hypocrisy of institutionalized church. Tolstoy also explores and explains the economic philosophy of Georgism, of which he had become a very strong advocate towards the end of his life.

Tolstoy also tried himself in poetry with several soldier songs written during his military service and fairy tales in verse such as Volga-bogatyr and Oaf stylized as national folk songs. They were written between 1871 and 1874 for his Russian Book for Reading, a collection of short stories in four volumes (total of 629 stories in various genres) published along with the New Azbuka textbook and addressed to schoolchildren. Nevertheless, he was skeptical about poetry as a genre. As he famously said, "Writing poetry is like ploughing and dancing at the same time". According to Valentin Bulgakov, he criticised poets, including Alexander Pushkin, for their "false" epithets used "simply to make it rhyme".

Critical appraisal by other authors

Tolstoy's contemporaries paid him lofty tributes. Fyodor Dostoyevsky, who died thirty years before Tolstoy's death, thought him the greatest of all living novelists. Gustave Flaubert, on reading a translation of War and Peace, exclaimed, "What an artist and what a psychologist!" Anton Chekhov, who often visited Tolstoy at his country estate, wrote, "When literature possesses a Tolstoy, it is easy and pleasant to be a writer; even when you know you have achieved nothing yourself and are still achieving nothing, this is not as terrible as it might otherwise be, because Tolstoy achieves for everyone. What he does serves to justify all the hopes and aspirations invested in literature." The 19th-century British poet and critic Matthew Arnold opined that "A novel by Tolstoy is not a work of art but a piece of life."

Later novelists continued to appreciate Tolstoy's art, but sometimes also expressed criticism. Arthur Conan Doyle wrote "I am attracted by his earnestness and by his power of detail, but I am repelled by his looseness of construction and by his unreasonable and impracticable mysticism." Virginia

Woolf declared him "the greatest of all novelists." James Joyce noted that "He is never dull, never stupid, never tired, never pedantic, never theatrical!" Thomas Mann wrote of Tolstoy's seemingly guileless artistry: "Seldom did art work so much like nature." Vladimir Nabokov heaped superlatives upon The Death of Ivan Ilyich and Anna Karenina; he questioned, however, the reputation of War and Peace, and sharply criticized Resurrection and The Kreutzer Sonata.

Religious and political beliefs

After reading Schopenhauer's The World as Will and Representation, Tolstoy gradually became converted to the ascetic morality upheld in that work as the proper spiritual path for the upper classes: "Do you know what this summer has meant for me? Constant raptures over Schopenhauer and a whole series of spiritual delights which I've never experienced before. ... no student has ever studied so much on his course, and learned so much, as I have this summer"

In Chapter VI of A Confession, Tolstoy quoted the final paragraph of Schopenhauer's work. It explained how the nothingness that results from complete denial of self is only a relative nothingness, and is not to be feared. The novelist was struck by the description of Christian, Buddhist, and Hindu ascetic renunciation as being the path to holiness. After reading passages such as the following, which abound in Schopenhauer's ethical chapters, the Russian nobleman chose poverty and formal denial of the will:

But this very necessity of involuntary suffering (by poor people) for eternal salvation is also expressed by that utterance of the Savior (Matthew 19:24): "It is easier for a camel to go through the eye of a needle, than for a rich man to enter into the kingdom of God." Therefore, those who were greatly in earnest about their eternal salvation, chose voluntary poverty when fate had denied this to them and they had been born in wealth. Thus Buddha Sakyamuni was born a prince, but voluntarily took to the mendicant's staff; and Francis of Assisi, the founder of the mendicant orders who, as a youngster at a ball, where the daughters of all the notabilities were sitting together, was asked: "Now Francis, will you not soon make your choice from these beauties?"

and who replied: "I have made a far more beautiful choice!" "Whom?" "La povertà (poverty)": whereupon he abandoned every thing shortly afterwards and wandered through the land as a mendicant.

In 1884, Tolstoy wrote a book called What I Believe, in which he openly confessed his Christian beliefs. He affirmed his belief in Jesus Christ's teachings and was particularly influenced by the Sermon on the Mount, and the injunction to turn the other cheek, which he understood as a "commandment of non-resistance to evil by force" and a doctrine of pacifism and nonviolence. In his work The Kingdom of God Is Within You, he explains that he considered mistaken the Church's doctrine because they had made a "perversion" of Christ's teachings. Tolstoy also received letters from American Quakers who introduced him to the non-violence writings of Quaker Christians such as George Fox, William Penn and Jonathan Dymond. Tolstoy believed being a Christian required him to be a pacifist; the consequences of being a pacifist, and the apparently inevitable waging of war by government, are the reason why he is considered a philosophical anarchist.

Later, various versions of "Tolstoy's Bible" would be published, indicating the passages Tolstoy most relied on, specifically, the reported words of Jesus himself.

Tolstoy believed that a true Christian could find lasting happiness by striving for inner self-perfection through following the Great Commandment of loving one's neighbor and God rather than looking outward to the Church or state for guidance. His belief in nonresistance when faced by conflict is another distinct attribute of his philosophy based on Christ's teachings. By directly influencing Mahatma Gandhi with this idea through his work The Kingdom of God Is Within You (full text of English translation available on Wikisource), Tolstoy's profound influence on the nonviolent resistance movement reverberates to this day. He believed that the aristocracy were a burden on the poor, and that the only solution to how we live together is through anarchism.

He also opposed private property in land ownership and the institution of marriage and valued the ideals of chastity and sexual abstinence (discussed in Father Sergius and his preface to The Kreutzer Sonata), ideals also held by the young Gandhi. Tolstoy's later work derives a passion and verve from the depth of his austere moral views. The sequence of the temptation of Sergius in Father Sergius, for example, is among his later triumphs. Gorky relates how Tolstoy once read this passage before himself and Chekhov and that Tolstoy was moved to tears by the end of the reading. Other later passages of rare power include the personal crises that were faced by the protagonists of The Death of Ivan Ilyich, and of Master and Man, where the main character in the former or the reader in the latter are made aware of the foolishness of the protagonists' lives.

Tolstoy had a profound influence on the development of Christian anarchist thought. The Tolstoyans were a small Christian anarchist group formed by Tolstoy's companion, Vladimir Chertkov (1854–1936), to spread Tolstoy's religious teachings. Philosopher Peter Kropotkin wrote of Tolstoy in the article on anarchism in the 1911 Encyclopædia Britannica:

Without naming himself an anarchist, Leo Tolstoy, like his predecessors in the popular religious movements of the 15th and 16th centuries, Chojecki, Denk and many others, took the anarchist position as regards the state and property rights, deducing his conclusions from the general spirit of the teachings of Jesus and from the necessary dictates of reason. With all the might of his talent, Tolstoy made (especially in The Kingdom of God Is Within You) a powerful criticism of the church, the state and law altogether, and especially of the present property laws. He describes the state as the domination of the wicked ones, supported by brutal force. Robbers, he says, are far less dangerous than a well-organized government. He makes a searching criticism of the prejudices which are current now concerning the benefits conferred upon men by the church, the state, and the existing distribution of property, and from the teachings of Jesus he deduces the rule of non-resistance and the absolute condemnation of all wars. His religious arguments are, however, so well combined with arguments borrowed from a dispassionate observation of the present evils, that the anarchist portions of his works appeal to the religious and the non-religious reader alike.

During the Boxer Rebellion in China, Tolstoy praised the Boxers. He was harshly critical of the atrocities committed by the Russians, Germans, Americans, Japanese, and other western troops. He accused them of engaging in slaughter when he heard about the lootings, rapes, and murders, in what he saw as Christian brutality. Tolstoy also named the two monarchs most responsible for the atrocities; Nicholas II of Russia and Wilhelm II of Germany. Tolstoy, a famous sinophile, also read the works of Chinese thinker and philosopher, Confucius. Tolstoy corresponded with the Chinese intellectual Gu Hongming and recommended that China remain an agrarian nation and warned against reform like what Japan implemented.

The Eight-Nation Alliance intervention in the Boxer Rebellion was denounced by Tolstoy as were the Philippine–American War and the Second Boer War between the British Empire and the two independent Boer republics. The words "terrible for its injustice and cruelty" were used to describe the Czarist intervention in China by Tolstoy. Confucius's works were studied by Tolstoy. The attack on China in the Boxer Rebellion was railed against by Tolstoy. The war against China was criticized by Leonid Andreev and Gorkey. To the Chinese people, an epistle, was written by Tolstoy as part of the criticism of the war by intellectuals in Russia. The activities of Russia in China by Nicholas II were described in an open letter where they were slammed and denounced by Leo Tolstoy in 1902. Tolstoy corresponded with Gu Hongming and they both opposed the Hundred Day's Reform by Kang Youwei and agreed that the reform movement was perilous. Tolstoys' ideology on non violence shaped the anarchist thought of the Society for the Study of Socialism in China. Lao Zi and Confucius's teachings were studied by Tolstoy. Chinese Wisdom was a text written by Tolstoy. The Boxer Rebellion stirred Tolstoy's interest in Chinese philosophy. The Boxer and Boxer wars were denounced by Tolstoy.

In hundreds of essays over the last 20 years of his life, Tolstoy reiterated the anarchist critique of the state and recommended books by Kropotkin and Proudhon to his readers, whilst rejecting anarchism's espousal of violent revolutionary means. In the 1900 essay, "On Anarchy", he wrote; "The Anarchists are right in everything; in the negation of the existing order, and in the assertion that, without Authority, there could not be worse violence than that of Authority under existing conditions. They are mistaken only in thinking that Anarchy can be instituted by a revolution. But it will be instituted only by there being more and more people who do not require the protection of governmental power ... There can be only one permanent revolution—a moral one: the regeneration of the inner man." Despite his misgivings about anarchist violence, Tolstoy took risks to circulate the prohibited publications of anarchist thinkers in Russia, and corrected the proofs of Kropotkin's "Words of a Rebel", illegally published in St Petersburg in 1906.

Tolstoy was enthused by the economic thinking of Henry George, incorporating it approvingly into later works such as Resurrection (1899), the book that played a major factor in his excommunication.

In 1908, Tolstoy wrote A Letter to a Hindu outlining his belief in non-violence as a means for India to gain independence from British colonial rule. In 1909, a copy of the letter was read by Gandhi, who was working as a lawyer in South Africa at the time and just becoming an activist. Tolstoy's letter was significant for Gandhi, who wrote Tolstoy seeking proof that he was the real author, leading to further correspondence between them.

Reading Tolstoy's The Kingdom of God Is Within You also convinced Gandhi to avoid violence and espouse nonviolent resistance, a debt Gandhi acknowledged in his autobiography, calling Tolstoy "the greatest apostle of non-violence that the present age has produced". The correspondence between Tolstoy and Gandhi would only last a year, from October 1909 until Tolstoy's death in November 1910, but led Gandhi to give the name Tolstoy Colony to his second ashram in South Africa. Besides nonviolent resistance, the two men shared a common belief in the merits of vegetarianism, the subject of several of Tolstoy's essays.

Tolstoy also became a major supporter of the Esperanto movement. Tolstoy was impressed by the pacifist beliefs of the Doukhobors and brought their persecution to the attention of the international community, after they burned their weapons in peaceful protest in 1895. He aided the Doukhobors in migrating to Canada. In 1904, during the Russo-Japanese War, Tolstoy condemned the war and wrote to the Japanese Buddhist priest Soyen Shaku in a failed attempt to make a joint pacifist statement.

Towards the end of his life, Tolstoy become more and more occupied with the economic theory and social philosophy of Georgism. He spoke of great admiration of Henry George, stating once that "People do not argue with the teaching of George; they simply do not know it. And it is impossible to do otherwise with his teaching, for he who becomes acquainted with it cannot but agree." He also wrote a preface to George's Social Problems. Tolstoy and George both rejected private property in land (the most important source of income of the passive Russian aristocracy that Tolstoy so heavily criticized) whilst simultaneously both rejecting a centrally planned socialist economy. Some assume that this development in Tolstoy's thinking was a move away from his anarchist views, since Georgism requires a central administration to collect land rent and spend it on infrastructure. However, anarchist versions of Georgism have also been proposed since. Tolstoy's 1899 novel Resurrection explores his thoughts on Georgism in more detail and hints that Tolstoy indeed had such a view. It suggests the possibility of small communities with some form of local governance to manage the collective land rents for common goods; whilst still heavily criticising institutions of the state such as the justice system.

Death

Tolstoy died in 1910, at the age of 82. Just prior to his death, his health had been a concern of his family, who were actively engaged in his care on a daily basis. During his last few days, he had spoken and written about dying. Renouncing his aristocratic lifestyle, he had finally gathered the nerve to separate from his wife, and left home in the middle of winter, in the dead of night. His secretive departure was an apparent attempt to escape unannounced from Sophia's jealous tirades. She was outspokenly opposed to many of his teachings, and in recent years had grown envious of the attention which it seemed to her Tolstoy lavished upon his Tolstoyan "disciples".

Tolstoy died of pneumonia at Astapovo train station, after a day's rail journey south. The station master took Tolstoy to his apartment, and his personal doctors were called to the scene. He was given injections of morphine and camphor.

The police tried to limit access to his funeral procession, but thousands of peasants lined the streets. Still, some were heard to say that, other than knowing that "some nobleman had died", they knew little else about Tolstoy.

According to some sources, Tolstoy spent the last hours of his life preaching love, nonviolence, and Georgism to his fellow passengers on the train. (Source: Wikipedia)